THE LONG EXILE

THE LONG EXILE

GEORGES SIMENON

Translated from the French by Eileen Ellenbogen

A HELEN AND KURT WOLFF BOOK
HARCOURT BRACE JOVANOVICH, PUBLISHERS
SAN DIEGO   NEW YORK   LONDON

Copyright © 1936 by Editions Gallimard
English translation copyright © 1983 by Georges Simenon

Library of Congress Cataloging in Publication Data

Simenon, Georges, 1903–
The long exile.

Translation of: Long cours.
"A Helen and Kurt Wolff book."
I. Title.
PQ2637.I53L6513   1982   843'.912   81-48019
ISBN 0-15-152997-3

Printed in the United States of America

First edition

B C D E

PART ONE

1

THE LIGHTS OF A CAR TRAVELING IN THE OPPOSITE DIRECTION briefly illuminated the milestone, and Joseph Mittel, leaning forward, just had to time to read: FORGES-LES-EAUX 2 KILOMETERS.

This was not much help, since he had no idea where along the route between Paris and Dieppe this town was situated.

He sat down again on the empty barrel, grasping an iron stanchion with his right hand, which felt icy as it brushed against the wet tarpaulin roof. They were traveling fast. It was a small light van. In front sat the driver, a tall boy with a broken nose, and Charlotte beside him, but Mittel could not see them from where he was.

Facing backward, all he could see was the gleaming road, on which, every now and then they skidded dangerously. Now that it was dark, the asphalt seemed more glassy than ever, to the point where it looked like a canal, with trees on either side.

They had passed through Pontoise, then Gournay, and finally Forges-les-Eaux. Mittel could see the milestones from the rear, indicating the distance from Paris. They would pass through a town or a village, and it was not until they had covered a few more kilometers that he would find out its name.

He had forgotten to bring his watch, which meant, in effect, that he would probably never see it again! And all the clothes he had with him were his gray suit, the oldest and flimsiest he owned, and a thin gabardine raincoat.

How could he have known what would happen when he had set out from home that morning? In Paris, although it was November, the weather had been mild. Now he felt stiff—partly because of the draft in the back of the van, and partly because he was cramped and uncomfortable. The van was piled high with packages, and he dared not move hand or foot, for fear of dislodging something breakable.

From time to time, the two in front exchanged a few words. Mittel could hear most of what they said, except when the tarpaulin flapped in the wind.

"Are you and he lovers?" was the driver's first question.

"For the past two years," Charlotte had replied.

Then, a little later: "Do you know Dieppe?"

"I've been there!"

And after they had passed Pontoise: "He's done something silly, I suppose, like sticking his hand in the till? He looks very young. . . ."

"He's twenty-two, same as me. We were both born in the same week."

Every time Mittel heard Charlotte's voice, he felt the same sense of dismay. How could she take it all so calmly?

At one point, in response to a murmured suggestion from the driver, she even managed a laugh, that strangely vulgar laugh of hers. The driver had said, "Do you feel like going out tonight? Look here, if he'd rather stay in, how about the two of us going dancing? I know a little dance hall, down by the port. . . ."

Charlotte was still laughing, so the driver went on: "You can't say I haven't been good to you. I've given you both a lift all this way, and no questions asked. For all I know, I may have let myself in for a load of trouble. The least you can do is to be nice to me in return."

"I'll come dancing with you," she promised. "I'll meet you on the Place des Grèves."

"How come you know where it is?"

A car sped by so close that it almost hit them. Someone's voice could be heard swearing in the dark, and the tarpaulin roof was battered by another heavy cloudburst.

"I'll have to let you off at the top of the cliff, before we reach town, to make sure my boss doesn't spot you."

And Mittel, still clinging to the stanchion, felt more and more sickened by the stench of herring, which arose from even the remotest corners of the van.

"Lend me your scarf. I might run into someone who knows me, and I don't want to be recognized."

They were at the top of the cliff, where the van driver had left them. The steep road into the town was lit on either side by gas lamps, and a lighthouse beam swept the sky. Somewhere in the distance, they heard the whistle of a train.

Charlotte was wearing a black serge skirt suit, which was even less effective in keeping out the cold than her companion's outfit. She was also wearing a black hat and black shoes, so that virtually all he could see of her was her face, and her flesh-colored stockings, which were spattered with mud.

"No! Don't take my arm!"

She was walking rapidly, resolutely, and Mittel could not bring himself to look at her.

"You promised the driver . . ." he began.

"You can bet you life I won't be there! He never stopped stroking my knee the whole way. . . . Turn right here. I'd rather keep clear of the main streets. . . ."

They had reached town. Without hesitation, Charlotte threaded her way through a maze of quiet, dimly lighted back streets, from where they caught an occasional glimpse of the illuminated window displays on the Grand Rue. Joseph Mittel followed her, looking worried every time a human figure emerged from the shadows. Automatically, whenever this happened, he gripped Charlotte by the arm.

"I told you not to do that."

All the same, she, too, was on edge. Her forehead was creased in an anxious frown. When they reached the docks, she pulled up the scarf still farther, until only her eyes and the bridge of her nose could be seen.

"It's high tide," she announced. "We're in luck."

He knew nothing about such matters. He caught a glimpse of

the dark waterfront, where there was light only on a single quay. Puzzled, he moved closer.

Four trawlers, which had just put into port, were docked opposite the fishmarket. And then, suddenly, they were in the midst of uproar, milling crowds, obstructions of every sort, unfamiliar sounds and smells, patches of darkness and light.

"This way!"

Charlotte threaded a path among the rows of flat barrows that had just been wheeled onto the quay by women—fishwives, as they were called—who would later load them with fish for the market.

Everything was dripping wet. Some of the fishwives were wearing their aprons over their heads. Thick electric cables trailed in the mud, and here and there glaring light bulbs were being hung above the decks of the trawlers, where seamen were hauling up baskets of herring from the holds.

Some fifty meters from here was another world, empty, dark, silent. The town was over on the other side of the railroad tracks.

"What are you looking for?"

Charlotte was slinking from barrow to barrow. Now she suddenly gripped Mittel by the arm and whispered, "Come on! Hurry! She's here."

"Who?"

"Mother . . . My sister is sure to be with her: they always work as a team."

They went straight ahead, not toward town, but toward the Faubourg du Pollet, which was built into the side of the cliff. They crossed an iron bridge, and came to a halt in a little square. Some features of this square Mittel was never to forget: the huge ironworks, the butcher shop that had a gable with a recess in which stood a blue-and-white figure of the Virgin.

"Wait here for me."

His hands and face were wet. Water had seeped through the shoulder seams of his raincoat. He longed to lean against a wall while Charlotte, almost running, disappeared down a little street on a slope beside the butcher shop.

6

Impasse des Grèves. A lane barely a meter and a half wide. Here and there, steps, and water streaming between the cobblestones. Through a lighted window, Charlotte could see an old man mending his pipe with a length of wire. The other houses were deserted: the men were with the herring fleet, and almost all the women were out working in the fishmarket.

Four houses . . . five . . . a standpipe with a brass faucet on the left. Charlotte slid her hand under the pipe and groped for a gap between two cobbles, searching for the key that, in years past, her parents had always hidden there.

And still did!

She glanced around. No one had seen her. The sixth house, her home, with its door painted blue, its heavy lock, and the smell of fish which so nauseated Mittel.

"Anyone at home?" she called out, just to be on the safe side, and then opened the door onto a dark interior.

Wisps of smoke from a dying wood fire lingered in corners. Her groping hand touched cups on the table. Feeling her way, she went into the next room.

Here was her parents' bed, with its quilt of red ticking and its feather mattresses. Her hand groped between the two for the wallet.

Something stirred. As Charlotte slipped the wallet into the pocket of her jacket, she could hear a whimpering sound.

It came from her sisters' bedroom. She might have slipped away, but she opened the door; she could just make out a hump in the bed.

"Is that you, Jeanne?"

"Who's there?"

"Shh! It's me, Lolotte! Don't make a sound. Are you ill?"

"I've got a sore throat."

She was just eight. Charlotte came up to the warm bed, bent over it, and touched the child's burning cheek.

"Shh! You're not to tell anyone I've been here—ever!"

"I was frightened. Are there a lot of boats?"

7

"Four."

"So they won't come home for a long time! I'm thirsty, I'm so thirsty!"

Charlotte got some water and gave her little sister a drink. The child was in the bed that had once been hers.

"I have to go now."

"Can't I have some light?"

"No! Good-bye, Jeannot."

"Lotte!"

"Shh!"

"Come on!"

Mittel had the feeling that she had changed somehow. Out in the dark street, she shoved the wallet into his hand.

"Look and see how much there is. Go on, over there, under the gas lamp."

There were other things besides money in the wallet. Mittel found a trawlerman's registration papers, a receipt from a savings bank, a copy of a birth certificate, and two thousand-franc notes.

Charlotte had been waiting a few steps away. She came to join him.

"Well?"

"Two thousand."

"They must have just paid the rent," she sighed. "Oh, well."

By now they had been drifting along for hours, surrounded by confusion, darkness, and damp, and through all this time Mittel kept wondering where they were going.

Earlier that day, he had stopped in at the little bookshop on the Rue Montmartre, a popular meeting-place for a small clique of freethinkers, as he did every day, knowing that Charlotte would be there. He found the shop empty of customers. The expression on the face of Bauer, the owner, boded no good.

"Go into the back room. Hurry!"

In the back room he found Charlotte, with fat Madame Bauer, who was peeling potatoes.

"How much money do you have on you?"

"I don't know . . . about two hundred francs."

"And at your place?"

"Nothing."

Charlotte, very tense, clenched her teeth with rage.

"And Bauer has just settled his account with Hachette! He's only got eighty francs left!"

"I don't understand. What's all the fuss about?"

Whereupon she looked away from him and said curtly, "I've just killed a man. Do you understand? I've got to make a run for it. And here you all are with scarcely a penny between you!"

Bauer had fixed them up through the good offices of his express-delivery van driver, who tanked up every afternoon in a bar on the Rue Montmartre. It was not yet dark at that point, though the sky was overcast, and it was raining heavily. The taxis in the streets sent up showers of spray. The evening-paper boys were already shouting the headlines. Madame Bauer, almost in tears, kissed Charlotte. The other members of the little coterie were absent, having seen the two-volume edition of the works of Karl Marx in the front of the window, a warning signal meaning "Danger. Keep out."

And Mittel had sat on his barrel while the driver, as Charlotte herself admitted, had stroked his passenger's knee and exchanged a few words with her from time to time.

"Now we've got to head for the dock where the freighters berth."

She led the way, as before. They followed the deserted water-front, Charlotte striding rapidly ahead.

"You haven't explained yet . . ." he said.

"Later. It's a long shot, but we may be able to get aboard a ship leaving with the tide."

To their left, in the liquid dark, the somber buildings of the oil refinery. Opposite, a moored ship.

"Greek!" declared Charlotte. "No point in trying."

She walked on. He knew nothing about the sea, never having even seen it except in Nice, when he had had his photograph taken outdoors on the Promenade des Anglais. He stumbled over a coil of rope.

"Careful!" she warned.

Or, a little later, "Watch out! It's slippery."

Another dock. A ship moored to the quay. A group of men.

"Stay here!" she ordered.

He could hear her distinctly:

"Excuse me, gentlemen. Is this ship leaving on the next tide?"

"In an hour or two, madame."

"Where is it bound for?"

"Panama and South America."

"Is the captain on board?"

"You're more likely to find him at the Grand Ridin."

"Hear that, Jef? Do you think anyone could recognize me, looking like this?"

Her misshapen hat brim flopped over her eyes, and she was muffled up to the nostrils in her scarf.

"I don't think so."

"Then it would be better if I came with you."

More than a kilometer of muddy docks to cross, and then they were back in the milling throng around the trawlers that were still unloading. There were herrings everywhere, smooth and slimy, on barrows, in baskets, and on the ground, gutted herrings, glutinous herrings underfoot.

He would have liked to give her hand a little secret squeeze, but she had already pushed open the door of the garishly lighted café and sat down at a corner table. It was she who ordered:

"Two coffees laced with rum."

And here, too, the smell of fish. Oilskins sequined with herring scales. Then, in marked contrast, the smell of rum and pipe tobacco.

"Six hundred baskets," announced someone nearby.

"We'd have got even more if the cable . . ."

It was hot inside, and suddenly Mittel felt the blood rush to his head. But Charlotte kept peering intently at the faces around her, then pointed to a colossus wearing a blue seaman's jersey, a pea jacket, and a peaked cap with no badge, who was talking to one of the town residents.

"That must be him! Wait till he goes out."

They waited a quarter of an hour and drank three more coffees with rum; Mittel was beginning to feel very drowsy when, at last, the two men got up and made for the door.

A sign from Charlotte. He, too, got to his feet. The two men were in the doorway, about to go their separate ways.

"Excuse me, sir. . . ."

Although she had coached him in what to say, there was an appreciable pause before he could utter a word. Then, suddenly, his hands clenched in agitation and distress, it all came pouring out. The captain was considerably taller than Mittel, and at least twice as broad. He leaned over. All around them was shouting and jostling, and they had to duck out of the way of the barrows, which the fishwives were pushing along at a run.

What the hell! He had no choice but to tell the whole story.

"She killed a man, understand? But, of course, you couldn't possibly understand."

The man listened, one eye half closed, a cigarette, extinguished by the rain, dangling between his lips.

"One moment," he said.

He went across to the window of the café, where a gap in the curtains offered a good view of the interior. He stood for a long time watching Charlotte.

"Is she your mistress?"

"Yes. That is to say . . ."

"Are you the jealous type?"

"You don't know us. We're intellectuals, concerned with ideas, and for us physical love . . ."

The captain shrugged.

"You want to come, too, naturally?"

"I . . ."

It was still raining. They could see the green and red lights at the harbor mouth, and the lighthouse up there, whose beam from

11

time to time illuminated the Chapel of Notre-Dame de Bon-Secours on top of the cliff.

"Wait here for me."

He had to wait for ten minutes, while the captain sat inside the café, next to Charlotte, with his arm lying along the back of the bench behind her. At last they came out together. They seemed on the best of terms.

"You go on ahead, all right? You know the way."

And to Mittel: "You come with me. I take it you at least have the necessary papers?"

"I have."

"You're not afraid of hard work, I trust?"

"I'll gladly do any job I'm given."

"That remains to be seen."

He did not sound convinced.

"I have worked carting vegetables at Les Halles, you know."

The captain was not listening. He walked ahead rapidly, opened the door of a little hut beside the bridge—the harbormaster's office—and called out to someone inside, "The pilot in half an hour! Michel will be coming to guide us through."

"Bon voyage, Mopps!"

He was off again. Another quay. The maritime registration office.

"Already?" exclaimed the clerk, seated at a black desk.

"Is the roster ready?"

"It just needs signing."

"Hold on. There's one more name to add, a stoker."

"Is he an enlisted seaman?"

"Not yet. You, what's your name?"

"Joseph Mittel."

"Address?"

"32b Avenue Hoche, Paris. Perhaps I should explain . . ."

"What?"

"How I came to be living on the Avenue Hoche."

"I don't give a damn!"

The office was dingy and filled with smoke. When the roster had been taken away for signature, Captain Mopps occupied himself by reading the notices on the wall.

"Another wreck!" he growled.

His hair and eyes were gray, and his nose slightly crooked.

"Here it is. Bon voyage, Captain."

Mittel followed him out, and was on the point of accompanying him into a nearby bistro when the captain stopped him: "Wait for me here."

He ordered a glass of whisky at the bar, but, leaving it untouched, went straight to the telephone booth, and was in there almost ten minutes.

"Off we go!"

Mittel felt that he no longer had any identity, any will of his own. He could only obey.

"How old is the girl?"

"Twenty-two, the same as me."

"I don't give a damn about you. How long have you been together?"

"Two years."

"And before that?"

"She was a good girl."

That made the captain laugh. They went back the way they had come, crossing the same bridges, going past the oil refinery. A figure loomed out of the shadows: Charlotte. She came forward, looking confident.

"It's all settled, darling. Just let me have a word with those gentlemen up there. You, Mittel—that is your name, isn't it—you can come aboard with me."

There was a rope ladder hanging over the side of the ship. At least ten times Mittel felt himself slipping, and was uneasily aware of the gap, almost a meter wide, between ship and shore. Three men stood waiting on the dimly lighted deck, three shadowy outlines, three pallid faces in the slanting rain.

"All set? Where's the customs inspector?"

"In your cabin, with the first officer."

The captain leaned over and whispered to one of the ghostly figures, "Understood?"

"Understood, Captain."

And the man slid nimbly down the ladder and walked across the quay to where they had left Charlotte.

Captain Mopps looked Mittel up and down and seemed to hesitate.

"Take this one to the seaman's quarters. And have him kitted out with coveralls and oilskins."

From then on it all seemed like a dream—or, rather, a nightmare. Mittel had not a moment to himself in which to regain his identity, to reflect, to get his bearings.

He had never before set foot on a ship. He was made to stumble across decks littered with obstructions: ropes, bollards, scraps of metal of every sort, then, right at the front, in the bows, he was taken through a low door into an overheated room with ten men in it, which smelled even more strongly of rum and fish than the rest of the ship.

Some of the men were already bedded down in tiered bunks, like rows of pigeonholes; others were eating or writing letters at a table.

"The new stoker!" announced his guide.

A little round stove, glowing white-hot, stood in the middle of the quarters. Nearby, a half-naked black man was cutting off a corn on his foot with a penknife.

The metal plates of the ship clanged all over, as if they were being struck with hammers.

"I'll have a set of coveralls assigned to you, and, if there are any to spare, a pair of sea boots. Till then, make yourself at home."

And there were all the men watching him in silence. He was a new recruit! They were sizing him up, resolved to wait and see.

And in the meantime, what had become of Charlotte? What was the meaning of all this noise, all this banging? A grating sound, louder than the rest, set everything in the quarters shuddering and rattling. It was the anchor being raised.

Someone came to the door and shouted, "Jules! Louis! On deck, at the double!"

The quarters were like barracks, only dirtier and more dilapidated.

"Take your boots off. Your feet must be soaking."

"I'm used to it," said Mittel, with a bitter smile.

Where was Charlotte? Why were they being separated?

Someone brought him a set of coveralls, which were too wide and too long. He wanted to keep on his gray pullover underneath.

"Don't worry, you'll be warm enough, I promise you!"

So he had to strip to the waist, and reveal to all his skinny frame and prominent ribs. A man who was eating at the table spat a piece of sausage skin onto the floor.

"Is this your first time at sea?"

"Yes."

No one said anything, but the men exchanged glances.

"Never been to the tropics, either?"

"No. I've spent pretty much the whole of my life in Paris."

He was offered a drink.

"What's your name?"

"Mittel . . . Joseph Mittel."

"All right, Mittel. We'll have to see about getting you a mug and a messtin. Well, well! We must be under way."

The blast of a siren, shouts, a muffled noise presumably coming from the propeller.

"Where are we bound for?"

"South America."

"Nonstop, in a little ship like this?"

"Little? Five thousand tons!"

The light was painful to the eyes, streaming, as it did, from a powerful bulb enclosed in a wire cage. A man came down the ladder and took off his oilskins.

"There's a girl up there," he announced.

15

"You're joking!"

"I am not! The captain kept her hidden in his cabin while they got that drunken customs man off the ship."

"What's she like?"

"No great shakes, in my opinion."

"May I go up on deck?" Mittel asked humbly.

"If you don't mind getting soaked!"

He was naked under his blue coveralls. They showed him the way, and he found himself suddenly engulfed in darkness, cold, and rain, just as the ship, swinging slowly away from side, was gliding out to sea between the wooden piers.

The town lay behind them magically bathed in light, serene and alluring, as towns appear only when seen from the sea. He felt a sudden yearning to stroll along those rectangular boulevards, surrounded by houses with lighted windows, every one of which seemed a welcoming shelter.

They were sailing close to shore, and the cliffs rose steeply on their right, with a lighthouse and a chapel at the top.

One could already feel the swell rolling in from the open sea, as it suddenly lifted the stern of the ship and sent the bows plunging downward. Mittel, dazzled, was taking it all in when suddenly his eye was caught by the pulsating heart of the ship, the center of all its activity, the small, white, dimly lighted cubicle, high above the deck, where two men could be seen in shadowy outline.

Using a megaphone, they were shouting orders above the noise of the wind and rain, and, in response, other dim figures sprang into action on the deck, ropes slid about, hawsers tautened, and the grinding of a winch suddenly ceased.

The jetties receded. The lights melted into one another.

The last link with land seemed broken when suddenly Mittel saw, bobbing close beside the ship, a little boat, scarcely bigger than a dinghy, looming clearly, right up to its mast, out of the fog.

It puzzled him. He was a total novice. A mile farther on, the freighter stopped, and the little boat, with some difficulty, drew alongside, whereupon a man, having just come down from the bridge, climbed over the rail and slid down a rope ladder.

Mittel, suddenly enlightened, said to himself, "The pilot!"

Another blast from the siren. Seen through a curtain of rain, the lights seemed far away. Mittel hung back like a schoolboy outside the principal's office.

The deck was swarming with seamen, bulky figures in oilskins and sou'westers. The ship heaved twice, three times, and then began gathering speed. Mittel had to grope for something to hold on to. He staggered like a drunk toward the beckoning lights above.

An iron companionway. He groped his way up it, terrified of being flung overboard. He felt for the door handle. A voice called out, "Come in."

And suddenly, in his sodden coveralls, with his hair plastered to his head, he found himself in an oasis of peace and silence. A seaman was standing at the helm. Captain Mopps, also on his feet, growled a casual order every now and then.

"A little to port . . . Good . . . Steady as she goes . . ."

A sea chart was spread out, illuminated by a yellowish electric lamp, and in a wicker chair sat Charlotte, dressed in navy-blue wool trousers and a close-fitting knitted jersey, with a bottle of champagne on a little table beside her.

"Ah! There you are," said the captain.

"I hope I'm not intruding. I just wanted to know . . ."

"Tomorrow, my boy! Tonight there's work to be done. Right, Charlotte? You should be in bed. Go get into some dry clothes. Have a hot drink. A little more to port . . . Good!"

Charlotte remained motionless as Mopps opened the door, shook the tips of Mittel's fingers, and pushed him out into the night.

"I'll explain it all to you later," he called out, by way of dismissal.

2

HE HAD BEEN LENT A YELLOW SUIT OF OILSKINS, A SOU'WESTER, and a pair of red rubber sea boots, for he was unable to sleep, still less to spend the night in the overheated quarters, where he felt seasick.

For the past half hour, he had been searching for someplace on deck where he could settle down, lean back against this metal plate or that, but it was the same all over: cold, damp metal, hard objects which he was forever bumping into in the dark, and ropes which constantly tripped him up.

At first Mittel had thought that there was no one stirring anywhere, except up in the captain's cabin, from which emanated a mellow light. But now he could see here and there, looming out of the darkness, the figure of a man, motionless and stiff in his oilskins, his face impassive.

"What's that?" he asked one of the men, pointing to a powerful searchlight very close to the ship, directed toward the sea.

"Herrings."

Trawlers, like the four he had seen unloading their catch in Dieppe! There were ten of them nearby, and others could be seen farther out to sea.

"How far have we come?" he asked another of the men.

He realized at once that this was a meaningless question, for the man merely shrugged. Far from what? The coast? No, since the Ailly lighthouse was still in view.

But he himself was far away, far away from everything. He no longer even felt the cold. From time to time he licked his lips and tasted salt. Was it still raining, or was this sea spray on his face?

He looked at the light above him, picturing the captain standing at the wheel, with Charlotte sitting beside him. Then he searched hastily for something to lean on, for he had not yet found his sea legs.

He was only now beginning to realize how far they had traveled. From the moment he had set foot in Bauer's bookshop—which must have been shortly after three in the afternoon—till now, he had, to all intents and purposes, had no control over events. He had not even stopped to consider their possible consequences, but had simply plowed ahead, because it was necessary, because he had no choice.

And now here he was, dressed in clothes that did not belong to him, on a cold ship which was slippery underfoot, with treacherous obstructions and sickening smells everywhere. He remembered suddenly that, this very evening, he had planned to attend a private showing of an avant-garde film. What would they make of his absence? Had they already heard the news?

Another trawler, a patch of light on the deck, shadowy figures milling around . . .

He bent down and saw that the light was coming from a skylight, very close by, and found himself gazing into a strange, hitherto unsuspected world, deep in the bowels of the ship. It was a maze of huge machines, all in motion, with three men in charge, quietly going about their business, as in a factory. One of them, who was holding an oilcan, looked up and glanced for a second at Mittel, whose face must have been barely visible to him in the pale glimmer of the skylight.

A bell clanged, and Mittel was conscious of some change in the rhythm of the ship. It took him a few minutes to realize that the engines had stopped. The freighter was pitching more noticeably in the heavy swell. The captain opened the door of the wheelhouse, cupped his hands in his mouth, and shouted, "Chopard!"

A shadowy figure ran past Mittel.

Mittel turned to another dark figure beside him: "What's going on?"

"I've no idea!"

For almost an hour, the freighter remained stationary. Men hurried back and forth between the bridge and the foredeck. Mittel got the impression that someone was signaling with a lantern, but no other vessel was in sight anywhere.

Voices could be heard swearing. The bell clanged again, and this time the ship turned around, as if intending to return to Dieppe. Almost immediately a lighthouse sprang into view, then, a quarter of an hour later, lights could be seen strung out along the coast like a necklace, signaling the presence of a town, and, to their right, a reddish patch of hazy light hung in the sky above the port of Le Havre.

Charlotte, seated on a cushion on the floor in the wheelhouse, had fallen asleep, a meter away from the man at the helm, who turned his head once in a while to look her up and down. Mopps, in a furious temper, had tossed down the remains of the bottle of champagne. He had barked out his orders to Chopard, the bo'sun, who had a swollen neck.

"Get ready to launch a boat. If the current isn't too strong, we may be able to avoid getting soaked. Or we could drop anchor a mile to the north of the jetty downstream."

He shrugged and, awaiting developments, proceeded to pass the time by tapping on the glass with his forefinger and looking down at the small female bundle asleep on the floor.

One after another, the seamen had emerged from their quarters. They could be seen leaning over the rails, lighting a pipe or a cigarette, their eyes fixed on the lights, which were now closer.

"Is it Dieppe?" Mittel asked someone.

Not until later did he realize that it was the black man to whom he had spoken.

"Fécamp."

"Are we going to put in there?"

"Only the captain can tell you that."

They stopped engines again, less than a mile from the piers at the harbor entrance. They could see the red and green lights. There was a grinding of winches. A boat was lowered, with a four-man crew, and the captain slithered down the rope ladder and took hold of the tiller, as four oars dipped into the water simultaneously.

It had stopped raining. For a moment, Mittel thought he was going to be sick. Then, stumbling on a coil of rope, he sank down onto it, and eventually fell asleep.

"Row to the stone steps," ordered Mopps.

Within seconds, the seamen had shipped their oars at the bottom of some steps covered with a green slime that had been left by the receding tide.

Above their heads, on the edge of the quay, a man in a cloak was waiting, silent and motionless. Mopps went slowly up the steps, shaking his head.

"We've cracked a bearing," he grumbled. "All we can do is wake Mestré and get a new one from him."

The man he was addressing, a customs officer, merely shook his head in reply.

"I'll go call him from Louis's place."

It was just across the street, the only bistro still open at this late hour. Behind its frosted-glass windows, moving shadows could be seen. Mopps went in and took in the six customers at a glance. They were all fishermen except one, who was a telegrapher. Louis was playing *belote*, but he interrupted the game to come shake Mopps by the hand; he looked somewhat anxious.

"Haven't they left yet?" growled Mopps.

"Of course! At eight o'clock, as arranged. What will you have?"

"Makes no difference."

Mopps was frowning, his lips compressed in annoyance. He was deep in thought, seeking a solution to the problem.

"Are you quite sure the *Philibert* started out at eight?"

"Absolutely certain! I took the call myself when you phoned from Dieppe."

"But I've searched the whole area."

"I can guess what's happened. I warned them. . . ."

"Warned them of what?"

"For the past week, the engineer has been complaining that the engine needs greasing. If they've cracked a cylinder . . ."

Mopps swallowed the whisky that was poured for him, and went out without so much as saying good night. He rejoined the customs officer on the edge of the quay.

"I called him. . . . He doesn't have any bearings in stock."

"What are you going to do?"

"Don't know."

He went down the steps and jumped into the boat.

"Back to the ship!"

Mittel did not witness their return. By the time he awoke, much later, the freighter was already under way, and he was bewildered to find that the lighthouses were no longer where they had been.

Mopps had pulled Charlotte to her feet and shoved her into the cabin, ordering her curtly to go to bed.

"But . . . what about you?"

"Go to bed!"

Then he had kicked the door shut.

"What do I do now?" the helmsman asked from time to time.

"Keep going!"

They were moving in circles, like a merry-go-round. Ten men were on watch, peering seaward intently. It was five o'clock in the morning before one of them at last announced, "Here she comes!"

Nothing could be seen, but they had heard three discreet little siren blasts. Soon a white light loomed out of the darkness, then the port and starboard lights of a vessel.

"Stop engines," came the telegraphic signal.

Then Mopps's voice, "Man the winches below."

Mittel was jostled in the rush. Within ten minutes, a little sailing boat, a fishing smack with an auxiliary motor, could be discerned quietly closing in on the freighter. Almost another quarter of an hour went by before the two boats were made fast to each other and a man climbed on board. He was wearing fisherman's gear: rubber thigh boots and a rubber apron around

22

his waist. In spite of the cold, sweat was streaming down his forehead, and he sighed as he shook hands with Mopps.

"Three hours wasted repairing the damage!" he grumbled. "I was in such a state, I was on the point of ditching my engineer in the drink! You must have been worried stiff!"

"I put in at Fécamp."

"What did they tell you?"

"There was some talk of a cracked cylinder."

The winches were already in motion, lifting immensely heavy crates from the hold of the sailing boat. Mittel had a close view of one as it swung onto the deck, and he was able to read the markings: ICE MANUFACTURERS, FÉCAMP. But the crates did not contain ice: if they had, they would have been damp. He counted up to fifty crates, then, since there seemed no end to the loading process, lost interest and stopped.

More than ever, he was struck by the inhumanity of life at sea. It was, for instance, only by a miracle that these present maneuvers could be accomplished without mishap. It would have been all too easy for a man to become entangled in a steel hawser, or to be crushed under a crate, or bashed by a swinging hook. The fishing smack, at the mercy of the heavy swell, was alternately sucked away from the iron hull of the freighter and flung violently against it. Yet in spite of all this, the seamen quickly scrambled up the rope ladder to the deck, encumbered though they were by sea boots, stiff oilskins, and gloves made from the inner tubes of old tires.

Charlotte came out on deck for a few minutes. Looking half asleep, she tottered unsteadily out of the cabin, her hands folded across her chest as a protection against the cold. She looked around blindly, dimly aware of seamen hurrying about their business, but, feeling too weary to attempt to understand what was afoot, she soon went back to bed.

When the transfer was completed, bottles were exchanged between the freighter and the fishing smack. Mittel found that he, too, was holding a bottle. He had no idea what it contained, but he did as the others did, and took a swig from it.

"On our way!"

And that was that. Mittel, his head swimming, his chest aching, his stomach chilled, returned to his quarters, slumped onto the first bunk he saw, wrapped himself in a blanket that smelled of tar, and fell asleep. Before long, his cheeks were burning and his eyes smarting from the heat of the little stove, which someone had filled to the very brim.

Mittel was wakened by the smell of coffee, followed by the clinking of tin mugs. When he half-opened his eyes, he could see three or four men climbing down the ladder, their eyes gleaming white in faces blackened with coal dust. Some of the bunks were still occupied by sleeping men.

"What time is it?" he asked, climbing down from his bunk.

"Ten o'clock. You're on the midday shift."

"May I help myself to some coffee?"

He felt he had to ask permission. He had yet to learn how to behave. On top of the stove stood an enormous blue enamel coffeepot. But after the first mouthful Mittel almost got sick, and scrambled up the ladder onto the deck.

There he stood motionless, confused by his overpowering feelings. He was at sea. There was nothing particularly remarkable in that, and yet it was like nothing he had ever imagined.

A white sky, so dazzlingly white that it made him blink. Then water, all around the black bows of the ship—gray water, stretching to infinity, flecked here and there, as far as the eye could see, with tiny white crests.

They were gliding along slowly, forever followed by a long wake, above which hovered a few sea gulls.

Mittel looked up at the bridge and saw the captain in his glass-walled wheelhouse, with Charlotte beside him, quietly talking to him.

Was the bridge off limits for Mittel? Never mind! At all costs, he must go up there. Charlotte greeted him with a cool "Good morning."

She was wearing the same navy-blue trousers and jersey as the

24

night before, but now she had her hair tied up in a black scarf, which lent her a faintly exotic air.

"Good morning, Monsieur Mittelhauser!" said the captain, but whether seriously or in jest, it was impossible to tell.

He was unshaven. His shirt was unbuttoned, revealing his hairy chest, and he was wearing felt-soled bedroom slippers.

Through the open door, Mittel could see into the cabin. It looked a mess, with the bed unmade, Charlotte's dress thrown down carelessly, dirty water in the washbasin, a comb, a toothbrush.

"Did you tell him?" asked Mittel.

But lying on the table was the *Journal du Havre* that Mopps had picked up in Louis's bistro in Fécamp.

GENTLEMEN OF INDEPENDENT MEANS LIVING ON THE BOULE-
VARD BEAUMARCHAIS MURDERED BY YOUNG WOMAN ANARCHIST.

Mittel read the news item, which ran over onto page 3, as Charlotte joined him and read over his shoulder.

"They haven't wasted any time," she remarked with perfect composure. "It must have been the concierge. I was hoping she hadn't spotted me."

Monsieur Hubert Martin, aged fifty-four, formerly a commission agent in Les Halles, lived with his wife on the Boulevard Beaumarchais.

No photograph yet. It was too soon, but the Paris papers would probably already have one.

In the absence of Madame Martin, a former maid-of-all-work visited her ex-employer this afternoon.

Mopps looked from one to the other, his expression inscrutable. Charlotte had reddish-gold hair, or, rather, hair that was reddish at the roots and blonde near the end.

She had a round face, such as normally went with a plump figure. She had fairly regular features, and a reasonably fresh complexion, her only distinguishing mark being a scar on the left side of the neck. It looked as though she had had an operation for the removal of her thyroid gland.

Her figure, too, was rounded, its curves accentuated by the

seaman's outfit she was wearing. She was smoking a cigarette, half-closing her eyes every time she blew out the smoke.

A neighbor who was giving a violin lesson at the time thought she might have heard a shot, but had not been paying much attention. . . .

She well remembered the violin lesson, which consisted of six notes, repeated over and over, and the teacher's voice, audible but muffled through the party wall: "Keep your elbow down . . . your elbow. And the bow must be horizontal. . . ."

By a fortunate coincidence, an employee of the gas company called a few minutes later. . . .

So that was how they managed to get on to it so quickly! Otherwise the body would not have been discovered before seven in the evening, when Madame Martin was due to return home after giving a hand to her sister, who owned a butcher shop in the twelfth arrondissement.

The concierge at once drew attention to the visit of the maid-of-all-work. This young woman was well known as an active member of a group of anarchists and freethinkers.

Mopps, never taking his eyes off the young couple, was filing his nails. Mittel's eyes were red from having a restless night and sleeping too close to the stove. It was also possible that he had caught a cold during the night. He had a small head and a scraggy neck, with a prominent Adam's apple and eyes that never lost their feverish appearance. He wore his brown hair very long, and it did not look well with his blue coveralls.

It was learned that the former maid had been Monsieur Martin's mistress, and remained so even after she left his service. The commission agent had in fact set her up in lodgings on the Rue Montmartre. . . .

"What will they think of next?" exclaimed Charlotte furiously.

By the time the police arrived the bird had flown, but she was traced as far as a specialized bookshop in the neighborhood, where she joined up with her lover, a young man named Joseph Mittel, in whose company she made her escape. . . .

"Bauer didn't give us away," she murmured. "Read on!"

And she pointed to the words:

Robbery with assault . . .

"Did you believe that?" she asked the captain, in a hard voice. The captain looked up.

"What?"

"That it was robbery with assault? Well, if you want the truth, just listen to me. When I first arrived in Paris, I went to work for the Martins as a cook-housemaid, on the Boulevard Beaumarchais. The kitchen was a sort of closet without light or air, barely a meter wide. Which did not deter the boss from making a beeline for it, the moment his wife was out of the house."

Mittel averted his eyes.

"You can guess what followed, I'm sure. I didn't have the guts to refuse. I was an ignorant fool. But then I started reading. I began moving in freethinking circles. It didn't take me long to learn the ways of the world, and when I did, I told Martin straight that having a mistress for the price of a maid, and being waited on hand and foot in the bargain, was too much of a good thing. . . ."

From one moment to the next, she had reverted to her fish-market accent.

"I insisted he pay me a thousand francs a month, and I took a room on the Rue Montmartre, near the Librairie des Temps Futurs. And that's where I got to know Jef. . . . This is all about two years ago."

Only now did she notice the presence of the helmsman, standing impassively with both hands resting on the wheel. Oh, well, that meant one more in her audience! She went on:

"I must point out that as soon as I had left his service, Martin lost all interest in me. He hired another servantgirl, and I have no doubt that he treated her in exactly the same way. I had no choice, if I wanted to be sure of my thousand francs, but to threaten to tell the whole story to his wife. He came to see me once a month—hardly ever more often than that—to bring me the money, and toward the end he didn't even attempt to kiss me."

Mopps scratched his head, looking skeptically amused.

"Don't you believe me?" she asked him, in that hard voice.

"Of course, of course!"

"What are you grinning at, then?"

"I'm not grinning, I assure you. So this poor fellow, Martin . . ."

"Oh, so you think he's to be pitied?"

"I wouldn't go as far as that. But after all, the poor fellow is dead."

Mittel averted his eyes to gaze out at the gray-and-white expanse of ocean, against which the freighter stood out in sharp outline.

"So he's dead! Well, listen to me, and I'll tell you why. Naturally, you don't believe in the Cause—you don't believe in anything. Well, that's your business. But we do, our little band of brothers and sisters scattered over the world. We work for the Cause, and to do that, we need money. Propaganda leaflets cost money. Our newspaper, *Liberté*, costs five thousand francs a month to produce. Well, three days ago, at the regular Tuesday meeting, when everyone was wondering where on earth we were going to find the money to pay the printer, I stood up. I asked how much we owed. Three thousand? And what if I myself should be able to lay my hands on sufficient funds to keep the paper going for a year?"

Mittel turned to the captain with a little nod, as if to say, "That's true!"

"For two whole days, I kept a watch on the apartment on the Boulevard Beaumarchais, waiting for an opportunity to catch Martin alone at home. Yesterday I saw my chance, and I seized it. It was the maid's day out, and Madame Martin had gone out. I put my proposition to him: that if he gave me a large sum there and then—say, thirty thousand francs—I would never trouble him again. Does that sound like robbery to you?

"Well, say something! Was I getting so much as a penny out of it for myself? I've always been in the habit of carrying a revolver in my bag. I threatened Martin, just to scare him, because he was being stubborn. . . ."

"And then, of course, you had to pull the trigger!" concluded Mopps, unimpressed.

Deeply offended, she gave him a dirty look.

"And as a result, not only have we got a hundred cases of contraband machine guns aboard, but also a murderess wanted by the police!"

He winked at the helmsman, and, picking up his already filled pipe from the table, lit it.

"As for you," he went on, addressing Mittel, "it seems to me that your situation is even more complicated."

For the newspaper had devoted a banner headline and several paragraphs to the young man:

Joseph Mittel, who accompanied Charlotte Godebieu in her escape, is a well-known figure in extremist circles. He is, in fact, none other than the son of the notorious Mittelhauser, a member of the one-time Bonnot gang, although not arrested as such, because the authorities were unable to obtain sufficient evidence.

During the period in question, Mittelhauser was living with a young woman, known to her friends as Bébé, who is at present employed as a proofreader in a firm of printers working for the stock exchange.

This woman was the mother of Mittelhauser's son, now Joseph Mittel, the lover of Charlotte Godebieu.

The end of Mittelhauser's story is well known to everyone. During the war, he was arrested for passing state secrets to the enemy, and died in prison, having opened the veins in his wrists with the handle of a spoon which he had sharpened on the edge of his plate over several days.

Mittel, in response to an inquiring look from the captain, replied curtly, "It's all true."

He had been just two years old at the time, so he had never known his father, who was regarded by some as a scoundrel and by others as a martyr.

His mother, who had lived for years with a Russian lover, had sent the little boy away to boarding school. After that he had been passed from hand to hand, but always in the same milieu, comprising those who had known his father in the old days and shared his ideals or activities.

Some had grown rich over the years. They included a member of Parliament, a government minister, and the editor of a weekly paper.

"Well, well! If it isn't young Mittel!"

In their eyes he had always remained a child. They would ask him to their homes for dinner. They were always at pains to help him find a job. An opening was found for him in one office, and then another, until finally he ended up working for a film company, where he had been learning the techniques of montage.

Since rent was the most expensive item in his budget, free lodgings had been found for him in an apartment building on the Avenue Hoche. The manager, needless to say, was an old friend of his father's. But the accommodation was a maid's bedroom on the third floor, overlooking the courtyard, and to get to it he had to use the service stairs.

The captain had by now gone into his cabin and was sitting on the bed, pulling on a pair of thick woolen stockings.

"What's done is done," they heard him say, sighing. "Look here, Charlotte, I don't mind your washing your hair in my basin, but you might at least take the trouble to empty it."

She did so, with very bad grace.

"As for you, young man, as I said yesterday, something will have to be done about you. You don't have the experience to work as a deck hand, still less to be of use in the engine room. So, things being as they are, I have put you down on the roster as a stoker. It's not as tough as they say. Once we reach the tropics, if you find you can't stand the heat we'll find something else for you to do."

He sounded fretful. As he talked, he bent down to lace up his shoes, then looked up sideways at the young man and asked bluntly, "Ever had TB?"

"I did have a spot on the lungs when I was a boy. I spent two years in a sanatorium."

"If I can fix you up with a passport, and if they're willing to have you in Panama, you should be able to make out pretty well. The climate isn't too bad. . . ."

Naked to the waist, he fetched a clean shirt, then put it on and got into his jacket. He looked from one to the other of the young couple.

"At noon, you will go on shift with the others. Watch out for the black man, who'll pick your pocket as soon as look at you. As for the bo'sun, I daresay he'll make it his business to give you a crack on the jaw one of these days, but he's not such a bad sort, really. . . ."

The first officer had come silently into the wheelhouse and was bending over the charts. He was a tall young man, thin and melancholy. He ignored Charlotte and Mittel.

"Everything OK?" he asked, shaking the captain's hand.

"In three or four days, we'll have the heat to contend with."

Mittel did not know whether to stay or to go. As Mopps was speaking, Charlotte went into the cabin, leaving the door ajar. Suddenly Mopps appeared to remember that Mittel was still there.

"Go in and have a word with her," he said. And, with a shrug, he himself shut the door on the pair of them.

"Did he lay a hand on you?"

Charlotte was bending over the swinging washbasin, brushing her teeth.

"This morning," she replied, her mouth spattered with foaming toothpaste. "He was very sweet. He came and woke me with a cup of hot coffee."

A pall settled on Mittel. He stood in the middle of this cabin with its masculine smell but where, at the same time, a woman's hairpin had been left lying on the pillow, next to the flesh-colored stockings spattered with mud.

"What are you going to do?"

She turned to look at him in astonishment.

"What do you expect me to do? At Panama, we'll leave the ship and after that we'll have to see."

"It's almost time for my shift. Will you come and see me now and then?"

"He won't let me. Apparently, if the crew were to get a good look at me, there would be an outbreak of jealousy and squabbling."

Mittel snickered.

"Oh, don't get me wrong, it doesn't mean a thing! He just took me because I happened to be there. I doubt if it even gave him much pleasure. He has more important things on his mind."

"The machine guns!"

"He doesn't put on any airs, that's for sure. He told me frankly that he was a scoundrel, but said it was better than being a fool. . . . I think he's taken a liking to you."

"Really!"

"Don't be like that, Jef! You've always said that it was stupid to be jealous, and that going to bed with someone meant nothing in itself. Here! Pass me my slip. . . ."

She was naked to the waist, and her breasts were pallid in the harsh light streaming in through the porthole. He looked at her without desire, merely with resentment.

"Is my suit dry?"

He tested it and handed her the skirt. Since she did not have a spare pair of stockings, she put the ones she had in the washbasin, to soak.

"Why did you kill Martin?"

She gave a start.

"I told you why just now! Don't you believe me?"

"Was there no other reason?"

"How can you, of all people, speak to me like that? Answer me! How can you?"

"I don't know . . ."

"What don't you know?"

"Nothing!"

"Because, if there's anything on your mind, you owe it to me to speak up. Why are you looking at me like that?"

What did she mean? Like what? There she stood in her black skirt, her breasts thinly veiled by her crumpled pink slip, with bare legs and feet, and black shoes, washing her stockings between her knuckles in the soapy water.

"Are you beginning to have regrets?" she asked.

"What about?"

"About coming with me."

"No, of course not, Lotte! You know very well that's not true."

"What is it, then?"

"I don't know. I'm all confused."

The door opened. The captain stood in the doorway, looked from one to the other, and said grumpily, "Oh, all right."

Behind him, the first officer was adjusting his sextant.

"I can't help it, young man, if you like these domestic dramas. It's time now for you to join your shift."

He looked around the cramped little cabin with a frown, and then turned to the first officer.

"We must have a cot somewhere around, Voisier. Find it, and have it brought up here."

And finally, to Charlotte:

"Hurry up! Lunch is served at twelve sharp!"

"See you later," murmured Mittel timidly, coming out of the cabin and stepping out onto the iron companionway that led to the deck.

The handrail was icy, the treads slippery. He shrank from this brutal heap of metal, which bruised his clumsy body at every turn.

"You and I are on the same shift," called out the black man, who was crunching a herring and spitting the bones overboard.

3

"SEE THIS PRESSURE GAUGE?"

Mittel, who was rather short, climbed onto a mound of coal.

"If you ever let the pressure go above fourteen, the boiler will blow up, and so will we! If you let it get below twelve, just wait and see what the chief will have to say about that!"

After three days of this, Mittel was beginning to get his bearings, but his first shift had been sheer hell.

There were two boilers in the ship, each with two furnaces.

Mittel and the black, who was from Guadeloupe and was known to everyone as Napo, worked as a team on one furnace. The other team worked on the starboard side, and were barely visible over the top of the mound of coal, in the yellow-and-black light. That was the only way to describe it, so thick was the coal dust in the yellow glow of the wire-caged light bulb.

And the noise—the unceasing throbbing of the engines, and the roaring of the furnace every time the doors were opened.

"The furnaces must always be filled with coal to a level of fifteen centimeters above the grate," he had been told.

And then, every six hours, the clinker had to be broken up with a great iron hook. Every morning at ten, the ash pan had to be emptied. The water had to be watched the whole time. Every two hours, the three taps attached to the gauge had to be turned on.

What if he should forget something? What if he should make a mistake? Napo, at his side, seemed to have no anxieties on this score. On the other hand, Jolet, the chief stoker, who had given

Mittel the instructions, seemed constantly distressed.

"If ever, when you come on shift, you smell something like rotten eggs, it means that the boiler is on fire, and you must sound the alarm immediately."

"Does it often catch fire?"

"I've seen it happen three times, on other ships."

It was at this point that Mittel realized that they were in the very bowels of the ship, and calculated that, by the normal route, it would take ten minutes to reach the deck. But there was an iron ladder—the very thought of it made him dizzy—inside the funnel, through which, very high above, could be seen a small, pale disc of light. Droplets of water would occasionally drip down from up there. Would he ever find the courage to climb that ladder?

As for physical fatigue, he felt none during his first shift, so bewildered was he by the pressure gauges, the taps, the air cocks, and the instructions and warnings issued by Jolet. At four o'clock, like all the others on the shift, he climbed onto the deck; then, seeing that it was already dark, he went and collapsed on his bunk without even bothering to wash his face.

"Is it true you're an anarchist?"

He stared in bewilderment at the man who had spoken with his mouth full: a deck hand, still wearing his rubber sea boots.

"Who told you that?"

"It's in the paper. Have you ever thrown a bomb?"

He felt that he would never be able to make them understand. Besides, he was too weary.

"Never," he said with a yawn, snuggling down in his bunk.

"What's the point, then?"

Naturally! As far as they were concerned, the only reason to be an anarchist was to throw bombs!

Napo yanked him out of his bunk at five minutes before eight in the evening, and he spent the next two hours shoveling coal into the boiler.

It seemed to him that he had just fallen asleep when Napo woke him again. It was two in the morning.

It was a quiet night. A pale glimmer of light issued from the captain's cabin. The calm sea murmured faintly.

"Tomorrow, you will only do two shifts. We do three shifts every other day, because we're short-handed."

He soon acquired the habit of dropping off to sleep anywhere, any time, of getting out of bed like a sleepwalker, slithering down the ladders leading to the stokehold, opening the furnace door with the iron hook, breaking up the clinker, and throwing in a couple of shovelfuls of coal, like an automaton, before coming fully awake and rolling his first cigarette.

From morning till night, from night till morning, Mittel had a foul taste in his mouth and a permanent headache, but he never complained.

He had no time to think anyway, at least for the first three days. Between shifts, he either slept or stood all alone, leaning over the rail, staring at the gray expanse of sea, which was now less wild. There were no longer any sea gulls following in the wake of the freighter.

For the following three weeks, life on board continued unchanged. Mittel observed that Captain Mopps, perched up there on the bridge, seldom left his quarters. For days at a stretch, he never took off his carpet slippers, never set foot on deck, and took his meals alone in his cabin—or, rather, alone with Charlotte, who was now his constant companion.

As for the two other officers and the chief engineer, they had their own quarters on the poop deck, and Mittel scarcely ever set eyes on them, though he occasionally saw their Annamese cook emptying buckets of scraps and peelings over the side of the ship.

The man who was really in charge of the crew was the bo'sun, a kind of marine liaison officer between the bridge and the men. He was small, dark, and cantankerous, and forever poking his nose into everyone's business. For the first two days, he pretended to be unaware of Mittel's existence, then, one evening, happening to run into him on deck, he stopped in his tracks and stood facing him. Slowly he raised his hand and grasped Mittel's chin between two fingers.

"A word of advice, wonder boy! If you don't want trouble, keep well out of my way."

"But . . ."

"That's all! I have just one more thing to say. We sailed together in the same ship for two years, Godebieu and I. Do you understand?"

Then, roughly, he shoved Mittel against the rail and walked away without a backward glance.

Mittel just stood there, stunned. He tried to imagine what would have happened if he had found himself face to face with Charlotte's father. And yet he was in no way to blame! She had already been a militant anarchist when they first met, whereas he was generally regarded as being halfhearted, at best.

And here was the bo'sun, the man upon whom his fate depended, revealing himself as a close friend of old Godebieu!

They don't understand, he thought, but they'll find out in the end that I am not what they take me for.

He even went as far as to borrow books from the chief stoker, Jolet. For Jolet, as soon as he was off duty, made a habit of retiring to a quiet corner of their quarters to study, reading aloud to himself under his breath, repeating the same formulas over and over, with an air of melancholy determination. He was about twenty-five, and anxious to qualify as an engineer. He was married, and already the father of three children.

"It's the mathematics that I find so difficult," he explained.

And, on their third night, watching the sun set over a sea suddenly so calm that there was not a ripple in sight, Mittel, for some inexplicable reason, felt close to tears. He was sitting on a hatch, next to a seaman who was carving a model of a schooner out of a piece of wood. The portholes of the captain's cabin were open. Leaning on the ledge, as it were—looking reassuringly like someone leaning out of an ordinary window—Charlotte was smoking a cigarette; she caught sight of Mittel and waved to him.

The weather was still cool, but every now and then there were faint little puffs of warm air. Ahead of the freighter, an Italian steamer, bound for New York, cut across its bows.

They must by now be sailing close to Portugal, and in three days they would reach the Azores.

Turning abruptly to the seaman who was carving wood, Mittel asked, "Do we have a radio on board?"

"I should hope so!"

Come to think of it, he could see the antenna. He sat brooding for a while.

"Which one is the radio operator?"

"The skinny officer, the one wearing tortoiseshell glasses."

Mittel had never set eyes on him. Probably things would change when they reached warmer latitudes, and the crew would begin to emerge from their various cubbyholes! Already, those who were not on duty were taking advantage of the pleasant evenings by coming out in ones and twos for a stroll on deck. From up there on the bridge, Mopps was watching Mittel, who on this occasion had cleaned himself up and changed into a fresh pair of coveralls.

"Come on up," the captain called after a while.

Mittel was by now so familiar with the chain of command on the ship that he looked around, to make sure it was not someone else being summoned. Someone had lent him an old cap, and he took it off as he went into the cabin.

"Shut the door! Let me look at you."

Puffing smoke into his face, Mopps scrutinized him attentively.

"Not finding things too rough?"

"I'm getting used to it."

"So I've heard. Aren't you going to kiss Charlotte?"

No! Even in Paris they had not been in the habit of kissing when they met. Theirs was not a passionate relationship, and, more often than not, they spent their time together discussing politics or philosophy.

"I'm bored, Jef!" she sighed. "The captain is very kind, but there isn't even a book. . . ."

She was still wearing seaman's trousers and jersey. She had not changed. Mittel noted that she was wearing lipstick, a bit too much of it. Well, she never had learned how to use makeup properly.

"I smoke all day long, I sleep, I stare at the sea. . . ."

"A glass of brandy?"

"No, thank you. I don't drink. It makes me cough."

It was Charlotte who clinked glasses with Mopps, as the sun began sinking below the horizon, and a shoal of porpoises did somersaults barely a hundred meters from the ship.

"Excuse my asking, Captain, but you have a ship's radio; has there been any news?"

"The *Philibert*, the ship that transferred the cargo to us at sea outside Fécamp, broke down again just as she was going through the harbor gates. She crashed into the jetty. It is such an old ship that the bows were crushed in and three men were drowned."

Out of respect, Mittel paused for an instant before asking, "And about Charlotte?"

"Nothing . . . From now on, reception will just get worse until we reach the West Indies."

Then, when he was least expecting it, the captain, watching Mittel's expression intently, asked, "Do you have the strength to keep going?"

"What do you mean?"

"Stoking the boiler and all that."

"Yes."

"Let's go for a little walk."

"And what about me?" said the girl.

"You stay where you are."

He led Mittel out on deck, toward the stern, where there was no one around.

"Do you intend to stand by that girl?" he asked point-blank, resting his hand on his companion's shoulder. "You can speak freely to me. Understand? I won't repeat anything you say."

"Of course I do."

"Why?"

Mittel started, so shaken was he by the question.

Indeed, why had he fled with Charlotte, and what had prompted him to declare just now that he would stand by her?

"Come on now, man to man! I've spent every minute of the past three days with her, sizing her up. Well, between you and me, she's no better than a trollop."

He seemed to be expecting Mittel to protest at this, but the young man said nothing.

"I don't deny that she's fun to be with, but, then, so is a pet cat. First of all, she's totally devoid of feeling. She gives herself because she has no choice, or because there may be something in it for her. She thinks of nothing but making herself appear interesting, and when she saw that I wasn't impressed by her free-thinking notions, she dropped the subject. Is it true that one of her terrorist friends killed himself because of her?"

"I don't know."

"Which means it's not true! Everything she says is a pack of lies. She makes up all sorts of tales, to build up her image. Is it true she volunteered to assassinate a European dictator?"

"I don't think so."

"You see! She spends all her time in bed, smoking and thinking up fresh lies. Did you burst into tears the first time she darned your socks?"

At this Mittel hung his head. It was true! But how could the captain be expected to understand? Mittel had never experienced an orderly existence. He had been passed on from hand to hand, living mostly in squalor, denied the security of continuous care. And there, suddenly one morning, was Charlotte. While he was still asleep, she had darned his socks, and there she was, soaking them in the sink and mending a tear in his jacket.

"She told you that!" he stammered.

"And the rest! Your mother refused to let you go see her, because of the Russian she was living with? Is that right?"

"It's a lie," he said angrily. "She asked me to keep away—because she was jealous of everything, even of the past. All the same, I used to go and see her at the printer's."

"Keep your shirt on! I'm saying all this with an eye toward the future. When we get to Panama, she'll make out all right, you can be sure of that. And so will you, if you're prepared to go your own way. But if you stick with her . . ."

He slapped Mittel heartily on the back.

"Do you understand what I'm trying to say?"

"I understand."

"I just wanted to be sure. Oh, yes, one other thing: as of tomorrow, you will only be doing two shifts. Twelve hours at the furnaces every other day is too much for you."

"I assure you I'm quite capable . . ."

"Off you go now! It's too cold for you out on deck in those clothes."

It was almost dark, and there was a nip in the air. Charlotte was probably looking out through the porthole. Sick at heart, Mittel walked across the deck and climbed down into his quarters, where he grabbed his messtin and went to the hatch, to get it filled with stew from the kitchen.

Sometimes there was a spare seat at the table, sometimes not, depending on how many men were on watch. This time there was no room for him, so he sat on the bench, with his messtin on his knees. The stew stank of rancid lard. His hands, in spite of much scrubbing, smelled of soot, and, having just come in from the fresh air, he was nauseated by the ever-present mustiness of the place.

He had a meal break of half an hour. At eight o'clock he would be back in the bowels of the ship with Napo, Jolet, and the fourth member of their team, whose name he did not know.

He had eaten only two or three spoonfuls of stew when he heard heavy footsteps approaching. A shadow fell across the doorway and a man came in. He stood among them, looking around, scrutinizing each face in turn, then came toward Mittel, who rose to his feet automatically.

It was the bo'sun, Chopard, Charlotte's father's friend.

Everyone fell silent, sensing that something was about to happen. Mittel himself was suddenly overcome by an uncontrollable physical weakness. He was terrified. His whole body was shivering with fear, and yet he could not have escaped to save his life.

The bo'sun took two steps forward, then another.

"I warned you, didn't I?"

Warned him of what? What was going on?

"Take this, you stinking trash!"

And as he spat out these words, the bo'sun drove his fist hard into Mittel's face.

Mittel swayed, tipping over his messtin. The hot stew poured out over his coveralls. Chopard stood watching him, as if to give him time to respond.

Mittel put both hands up to his nose, then looked at them to see if there was any blood. Dimly, he saw a sea of faces turned toward him, and then at last the bo'sun retreated and began climbing the companionway with slow, deliberate steps, gratified at having accomplished his mission.

There was a profound silence following his departure, then the sounds of spoons clinking against messtins. Someone asked, "What's he got against you?"

In a daze, Mittel stammered, "I don't know."

He was trying to puzzle it out. He sensed confusedly that the bo'sun's attack was somehow related to his conversation with the captain. But what could he have said to cause offense?

He had not even committed himself to abandoning Charlotte. He had not uttered a word against her!

"You'd better bathe it in cold water."

They went on with their meal, unmoved, still watching him.

"It'll hurt like hell in the stokehold!"

The incident occurred ten minutes before the end of the shift. Mittel's face and upper lip were much swollen. Napo, who could see that he was feverish, kept glancing at him furtively, and twice insisted on taking over the stoking of Mittel's furnace.

42

Why, on that night of all nights, there in the bowels of the ship, with his temples throbbing, should Mittel suddenly think of Mrs. White? The memory welled up out of his unconscious, like a delicious whiff of perfume. Instantly he concentrated his whole mind on recalling every detail of that extraordinary adventure.

A short while ago, the captain had referred to his emotional response to seeing that Charlotte had mended his socks. His only other experience of love had been with Mrs. White. No two women could have been more unalike!

It had been a Sunday, three or four in the afternoon. The weather had been glorious. He had spent the day indoors, in his little servant's room on the third floor of the apartment building on the Avenue Hoche. He had been standing at the window, watching the servantgirls leaving one by one for their afternoon off. He could see the Bois de Boulogne and the Champs-Élysées crowded with people who were strolling about, the family groups gazing at the window displays in the smart shops, the crowded café terraces, the concierges sunning themselves on the front steps.

Mittel was doing nothing at all. He could not have explained why he had not gone out like everyone else. He was simply basking in his own idleness. Then, suddenly, his eye was caught by a figure moving around in the kitchen next to him. It was a young woman whom he had never seen before. She was wearing a white silk suit, a close-fitting white cap, and gloves. She was dressed to go out.

The windows were open. The unknown woman and Mittel were barely six meters apart, and Mittel watched her as she went to the stove and nervously turned the knobs.

She could see him, too. At first, she ignored him, then suddenly, as if at the end of her tether, she called out, in English, "Please!"

She beckoned to him. Her expression betrayed frustration, almost anguish. He could see that she was feeling utterly lost in an alien environment.

"Come here, please. Can't you smell it, too?"

There was a distinct smell of gas, no doubt about it.

"Everybody has gone out. I've turned the jets on and off, but it makes no difference. What should I do?"

Mittel, in his turn, fiddled with the jets to no avail. Then he had an inspiration. He searched for the mains, and turned off the master jet.

The kitchen was luxurious, the walls decorated with copper pans.

"Do you think the danger's over?"

"We'll know in a minute or two," he said. "If the smell doesn't clear, we'll send for the repairman."

And this was how they became acquainted, as they awaited developments. The gas escaped through the window. The fetid smell gradually cleared. The young woman kept looking at Mittel with an odd little smile, and he suddenly realized that he was wearing no jacket, and that his shirt was unbuttoned to reveal his boyish throat.

He coughed.

"It's the gas," she said. "You need a drink."

She must have seldom had occasion to set foot in the kitchen. In the same way as she had turned the gas jets on and off, she opened various cupboards only to find them empty.

"Come with me. There's some whisky in my dressing room."

"Watch out!" whispered Napo, shaking him.

He was almost asleep. He gave a start, opened the door of his furnace, and caught a glimpse of the bo'sun, who had come in to take a look around, probably in the hope of catching him in some misdemeanor.

He swayed on his feet, his forehead burning as never before. He clung even more resolutely to the recollection of that feminine apartment, back there on the Avenue Hoche, of the woman herself, offering him cigarettes from a gold box studded with jewels. It was like being in fairyland, with precious ornaments all around.

She joined him in a glass of whisky, watching him with tenderness tinged with irony, observing his long bohemian haircut, his feverish eyes, his tall, gawky figure.

"What about a cocktail . . . ? Yes, I insist. I was at a loss for something to do today."

As she spoke, she turned on the phonograph and picked up a cocktail shaker.

Madame White—or, rather, Mrs. White, as she called herself. Her husband lived in America. She, however, spent six months of the year in Paris.

None of that seemed real any longer, here, as he stood next to the boilers, up to his ankles in coal, a shovel in his hand!

And yet he had been her lover, if only for a single hour of a single day. He himself could never understand how it had come about. It was only by an effort of will, now, that he could persuade himself that that apartment had really existed, with its gold box studded with diamonds and emeralds, its black marble bathroom. . . .

And she above all, barely twenty-five years old, ensconced amid all her priceless treasures with that candid smile!

She, who had kissed him greedily, passionately, calling him, in English, her baby . . .

"What is it?" he shouted, pressing his hand to his forehead.

"Lie down on the floor! Lie down! Quick!"

He was bewildered. Something had fallen on his head, and he could hear a strange noise, a shrill, continuous whistle, while the air grew hotter and more suffocating.

Obedient to Napo's command, he had stretched out on a bed of coal. He opened one eye and saw steam squirting out of a burst water gauge.

Jolet came running, too. The black man was turning off one faucet, and he hastily turned off another. Both were splashed with boiling steam.

"You there, get me a replacement."

The whistling ceased. Mittel realized that he was unhurt, apart from a wound on his forehead which caused him no pain.

"What's happening? Is it my fault?"

Guilt overcame all other emotions, for he realized that he had allowed his mind to wander from his duties.

"Of course not! Here, take this!"

All four of them were galvanized into action.

"Give me a wrench. . . . It seems to be holding all right."

Jolet kept his head, working with care and precision.

After five minutes, the new gauge was securely in place and Jolet was testing it.

"This often happens," he explained. "If there's a flaw in the glass, it takes no more than a slight draft to blow it. Let's have a look at your forehead. A little lower down and you'd have lost an eye . . . When we go off duty, I'll give you some ointment."

At that very moment, up above, the bell was sounding the change of shift. It was all over. Not so much: a moment of panic, a crisis, four men rushing to deal with a faulty piece of machinery.

All Mittel could think of was that he had nearly lost an eye. He wondered whether he would find the courage, next day, to return to his post, so overcome with weakness did he feel.

"That's how it is with boilers," explained Jolet as they crossed the deck. "Once, in Amsterdam, I remember seeing a tugboat blow up in the harbor. And, believe it or not, they found half the body of one of the men on a rooftop more than sixty meters away. We're lucky that our boilers aren't too old. They installed replacements right after the war."

"I've a headache," sighed Mittel, leaning over the side.

"I wouldn't stay here if I were you, if you want to keep out of trouble. Strictly speaking, we stokers are forbidden even to walk across the deck."

The only light burning in the quarters, where some ten men were asleep, was an oil lamp. Several of the men stirred, without opening their eyes. Jolet opened his kit bag, which he used as a pillow, and got out a can filled with brown ointment.

"Rub this on your forehead. . . . Try to get some sleep. We'll manage somehow on the morning shift."

46

Mittel dreamed about Mrs. White. She was turning jets on and off. He kept following her around, endeavoring to stop the hissing and the spurts of steam that poured into the kitchen.

"Come on, have a cocktail, just a small one," she was saying, laughing at the same time.

Suddenly there was no more steam. He could see a pink silk pillow, pink silk sheets, lace edging. . . .

"What a baby it is!"

The "baby" was himself.

"Charlotte has no feelings," the captain had said. That could not be said of Mrs. White!

"Pull yourself together! . . . You're wanted up there."

He had to make a supreme effort to concentrate his wandering wits. At last he managed to scramble to his feet in the gray light of the quarters, where half-naked men were getting washed.

"Who wants me?"

"The captain."

"What time is it?"

"Seven o'clock."

Mechanically, he combed his hair and gulped down a mouthful of coffee from someone else's mug.

He was almost knocked flat by the wall of sunlight which hit him as he reached the top of the companionway. He had never seen such brilliant, concentrated sunshine. Even the sea seemed incandescent, barely distinguishable from the sky.

There were small creatures leaping out of the water. He could scarcely believe that he was seeing flying fish so early in the voyage.

He almost bumped into the bo'sun, who, standing on a hatch, was supervising the setting up of awnings above the deck.

There was no one in the wheelhouse except the first officer, who said curtly, "Knock on the captain's door."

He knocked, and a voice called out, "Come in."

Mopps, wearing nothing but a pair of trousers, was sitting on the edge of his bed, his hair tousled. Charlotte was still tucked into her cot.

"Jef! she cried. "They've traced us!"

"Who?"

"The police. Someone must have given us away. . . ."

"Take it easy!" growled Mopps, getting to his feet. "What's that on your forehead?"

"I was injured by a splinter from a burst water gauge."

"I see. You heard what Charlotte said? We've just heard news of you over the radio. The police tracked you down as far as Dieppe. And then, since they could find no trace of you in any hotel or rooming house, or at the railroad station, or any car-rental firm, it didn't take them long to work out that you must have left by sea."

"So?"

"So only two ships sailed on that particular night, ours and a banana boat that plies between Dieppe and Las Palmas once a month. The banana boat reported that it had no passengers on board."

Charlotte was staring fixedly ahead; Mopps crossed to the washbasin.

"What are you going to do?" Mittel asked, shattered.

The captain shrugged, spread toothpaste on his toothbrush, and then, wheeling around, said, "What are *you* going to do, you mean."

"Yes, what are we going to do?"

Charlotte sat up in bed, revealing the top half of a salmon-pink slip that just concealed her breasts.

"Order some coffee," she sighed, a foul taste in her mouth.

"There's the bell, near the door," said Mopps, and added, "Nothing can be done at San Domingo. You'll just have to stay on board. Panama is even more of a problem. It's possible that the French government has already applied for your extradition. It's a common-law crime, and . . ."

"It's a political crime!" protested Charlotte.

"Whatever you say. No need to lose your temper. Call it what you like, it won't stop them from clapping you into jail the minute you set foot in Panama."

48

"I'll hire lawyers to defend me!"

"Don't be a fool! Let's get serious for a moment. Beyond Panama, there are islands that are almost uninhabited. . . ."

Practically beside herself, Charlotte forgot her scanty attire and leapt out of bed, then began striding restlessly up and down the cabin.

"Filthy skunks! Rotten swine! Let's face it! What you're planning is to ditch me on a desert island! Isn't that what you want? And you have the nerve to call yourselves men!"

Tears welled up in her eyes. Suddenly she burst into sobs and flung herself down on the bed.

"Skunks, that's what you are! Always on hand when you see a chance of taking advantage of a woman, but when it comes to shouldering responsibility . . ."

Mopps wiped his lips. The Annamese came in with the tray of coffee.

"Leave one cup here, and take the others to the wheelhouse," ordered the captain. He was losing patience with Charlotte, her tantrums, curses, and tears.

"Come with me," he said to Mittel, who seemed rooted to the spot, unable to decide what to do.

On his way out, the captain picked up his jacket.

4

"WHO OWNS THIS SHIP?" ASKED MITTEL IDLY.

Lying on his back, he could see, above his head, the sunlit awning and part of the funnel, the part encircled by a red line. Through a gap in the awning, a little patch of blue sky was visible.

"Chopard isn't around, is he?" asked Jolet before answering his question.

He, too, was stretched out, lying on top of one of the hatches, facing into the light breeze. He raised himself up on his elbows. He was naked to the waist. It was a hot day, the sun so fiery that at times the air seemed to shimmer.

"I'll tell you all I know," murmured Jolet.

Other seamen were spread out on deck—all those, in fact, who were not on duty. Some, stark naked, could be heard shrieking and laughing as they sluiced down their comrades with the fire-hose, on the foredeck. Napo just stared straight ahead, as though he could already see the purple mountains of his island home.

Mittel, for his part, kept glancing up at the bridge, but there was no sign either of Mopps or of Charlotte.

"This is only my third crossing with him," murmured the chief stoker, "but some of the crew have been with him for ten years or more. Take the bo'sun, for instance. He and Mopps were together when Mopps was trading in illicit liquor during Prohibition."

"Oh, so he was a bootlegger?"

Mittel, entranced by the somnolent atmosphere, sounded remote, even a little bemused.

"Over the years he must have owned twenty ships, perhaps even as many as thirty. He would buy one in Amsterdam, Le Havre, or somewhere in Germany, sail in her, and almost always make the return passage on a different ship. In those days he sailed in the Pacific, plying between Canada and the United States. Eventually he was caught, and did a spell in prison with the bo'sun."

Mittel was well satisfied with this information. It tied in neatly with the impression he had formed of Mopps. Yes! Such a man would think nothing of serving some time in prison, of trading in one ship for another, perhaps even of sinking a ship deliberately?

"He was married at one time."

"What?"

"To a little American girl, just a kid really, in San Francisco. He bought her a house in Florida, and she had her own car and chauffeur, and Chinese servants. I don't know exactly what went wrong, but there was a divorce, and she sued him for maintenance, and won. He still has to pay her alimony."

Mittel marveled at this superman, who had been through so much, and who was now loafing in his slippers in his untidy cabin.

"Is he still a rich man?"

"He's been a millionaire in his day. His ambition was to settle on land, so he bought an export company in Le Havre. Within four years he had lost everything, and so he went back to sea."

"Does he own this ship?"

"The ships are never registered in his name. This one belongs, nominally, to a man in Dieppe, an insurance broker. He doesn't have a penny of his own, but he's useful to the captain as a front man. I've met him. Our last voyage involved a fraudulent deal over a cargo of iodine, and that meant squaring things with the customs people."

Mittel turned his head a little and made out the shadowy figure of the first officer on the bridge. This man looked so composed, so honest, that Mittel asked, "Are the officers involved as well?"

"There are thousands of merchant seamen on the dole," retorted Jolet.

"And if they're caught?"

"They don't have to know everything."

Somehow the wife abandoned by Mopps in San Francisco merged, in Mittel's mind, with his own American friend, Mrs. White of the Avenue Hoche.

He would have liked to have further talks with the captain, to become his friend, but that was not possible on board ship. The crew numbered twenty-seven in all: he had counted them. The men were separated into little groups according to their function; the officers kept to their own quarters, the deck hands were almost inseparable, as were the engineers and stokers.

The deck hands were Bretons; when they spoke at all, which was seldom, it was to one another, in their own language. One of them was carving a little sailing ship, complete with masts and rigging. Another was an expert cobbler and repaired the men's sea boots for the price of a plug of chewing tobacco.

As for the chief engineer, the father of five or six children, he could be seen regularly, three times a day, pacing the deck with long strides for the sake of his health. He counted his steps, taking deep breaths, and then disappeared into his cabin, which adjoined the engine room, and remained there behind closed doors at all other times.

"He gets paid more than two thousand two hundred francs a month," Jolet had told Mittel admiringly.

Mittel was puzzled. Most of the people he knew in Paris earned a lot more than that, with fewer qualifications and, above all, in much less arduous and dangerous jobs.

"Look! Here comes your wife."

Jolet was incapable of malice or sarcasm. He could not keep his eyes off Charlotte, who had unearthed a pair of white linen trousers from somewhere—probably from the signals officer—and a striped cotton jersey.

Stepping onto the deck, she approached the resting men and called, "Jef!"

"Coming."

He got to his feet with a sigh, and followed her to the stern of the ship, where there was no one around, but also no shelter from the sun. The water was as blue as an advertisement for laundry detergent. The wake, in contrast, was dazzlingly white, and here and there could be seen a tiny crest melting like ice cream.

"What were you and Mopps talking about?"

Twice she had seen Mittel and the captain chatting on deck. It had made her uneasy. Her expression was hard, her lips compressed. Her features seemed to have coarsened.

"I don't remember exactly. He wondered what we were planning to do."

"What does he suggest?"

Mittel was embarrassed. Mopps's advice to Mittel consisted mainly in urging him to abandon his companion to her fate. She suspected that this was the case, and she went on defiantly:

"He's trying to persuade you to give me the heave, isn't he?"

"More or less."

"And what about him? Has he told you what plans he has for me?"

"If he can't manage somehow to smuggle you illegally into Panama, all he can do is to try somewhere else."

"I know, on a desert island. Did you agree to that?"

Mittel looked at her uneasily, for it seemed to him that they had suddenly become enemies. His reaction to this was not at all what he would have expected. For one thing, he felt no desire to put his arms around her. Indeed, he wondered how it was possible that they remained lovers for so long. He felt he was seeing her for the first time, with her bulging forehead, her prominent cheekbones, and the freckles under her eyes.

At the same time, he was thinking about Monsieur Martin, and recalling, with a blush, how often he had stood waiting outside Charlotte's apartment for the lease-holder to come out, before going in.

This was not ancient history, but barely three weeks earlier. Yet he could no longer believe that it had really happened. Once, when he was considering attending a conference in Germany and taking Charlotte with him, he had gone so far as to declare, "I think we'd better get married. It's only a formality, of course, but it would make it easier for us to get passports."

And then there was Bauer, that disturbing, dim little man, with his pink-cheeked wife, prowling for hours in the quaint little bookshop on the Rue Montmartre!

Librairie des Temps Futurs . . . He gazed at the sea, at his comrades stretched out on the foredeck hatches, and he no longer recognized himself, or his companion.

"Suppose he really can't smuggle you ashore in Panama?" he murmured.

"That's no problem. I'll simply arrange to have the ship impounded. I'll inform the authorities about all that stuff in the hold. I know how to use my head, and don't you forget it! Ah! Here he comes."

And there, indeed, was Mopps, approaching them with a teasing smile on his lips.

"Straightening everything out, are we?" he asked, laying his hand affectionately on Mittel's shoulder. "I have news for you, my young friends. We will not be putting into port in the West Indies. We have ample stocks of coal, and, four days from now, we will have reached the entrance to the Panama Canal."

"What about me?" demanded Charlotte, looking him straight in the eye.

"You, I'm afraid, are going to be very warm. I've just had a word with the chief engineer. He's going to unscrew one of the panels, and you will remain sandwiched between two sheets of metal for forty-eight hours at the minimum."

She said nothing. She must have been terrified, for she was breathing deeply and her lips were pressed together more tightly than ever.

"If they have had prior notice from the French authorities,

they will search the ship from stem to stern, but I can promise you they won't find you."

The bo'sun was hovering nearby, looking as hostile as ever. Mittel's memory of the blow this man had dealt him was still so fresh that he could not take his eyes off him.

"Go take a walk up there on the bridge," said Mopps to Charlotte. "You heard what I said. Off with you!"

"More plotting, I suppose?"

"That's right. And deciding the manner of your death. Off you go, for heaven's sake!"

His eyes were twinkling. He looked first at the bo'sun, then at Mittel.

"Come over here, Chopard."

Had the fracas in the seamen's quarters been reported to him? Had he been told that the bo'sun was constantly hovering near the young man, as if to catch him in some petty misdemeanor?

"Do you hold it against him?" the captain asked Mittel, when the bo'sun had come closer, his tousled red hair glinting in the sun.

"I can't figure it out," Mittel hastened to reply. "I haven't done anything. I would have welcomed the chance of explaining to Monsieur . . ."

"Monsieur!" guffawed Mopps. "That's rich! He calls you Monsieur, do you hear that, Chopard? And you haven't even the grace to thank him! Now see here, you two, you'll just have to make up."

"Godebieu is my friend," growled the bo'sun stubbornly.

"So what?"

"This is the miserable wretch, him and his ideas, who turned the girl's head. I know the Godebieus, don't I? You won't find a more respectable family in the whole of Dieppe. There are three other daughters, and I wish you could see them, at the crack of dawn in the fishmarket, working themselves to the bone, harder even than the men."

Mopps, in a jovial mood, was looking with some amusement from one to the other.

"And what do you have to say, Mittel?"

Mittel answered gravely, deeply unhappy at being misunderstood. "When I first met Charlotte, she had already given up her job."

"Do you hear that, Chopard? She had already left her job."

"And who turned her into an anarchist? And what is an anarchist, anyway? Someone who kills a respectable citizen for his money? Is that it? Well?"

His temper was rising. If the captain hadn't been present, he would have attacked Mittel again.

"Explain yourself, Mittel. You're apparently an anarchist."

"You wouldn't understand."

"Chopard won't understand, but I will."

"It was my father who was the anarchist, at a time when a lot of others were, too, people who have since become respected public figures."

"And you?"

"Me? They seemed to think of me as their personal property. I told you you wouldn't be able to understand. Every job I had was found for me by my father's old friends. I couldn't turn my back on them. . . ."

It was impossible to explain. He knew what he wanted to say but could not find the right words, especially in this place, with the sea all around, and the snowy wake left by the black freighter.

He was no anarchist, but he was the son of an anarchist, and this made him a kind of aristocrat among aristocrats. He was forced to attend all their meetings as an example to the younger generation.

"The son of Mittelhauser, a martyr to our cause."

There was no escape for him! Everywhere, in Germany, Hungary, Barcelona, London, and even America, there were anarchist groups, cells, only waiting to grab him and do him honor.

"The son of the French martyr . . ."

For an instant, he had a mental glimpse of Mrs. White, the cocktails on the low table, the silk sheets on her bed. . . .

"Even his name isn't French," mumbled Chopard stubbornly. "I myself sweated out the war in the mines under the Boches, so that even now . . ."

"What is your nationality?" interrupted Mopps, doing his best to keep a straight face.

"French."

"And your father's?"

"French likewise. With some Rumanian blood."

No one knew for sure. There was a lot of talk about forged identity papers. Some people claimed that Mittelhauser had not been his real name.

"Do you hear that, bo'sun? The Rumanians were our allies."

"What will they do to the girl?" the bo'sun retorted, still resolutely hostile. "Is it true, what she told the signals officer?"

"What did she tell him?"

"That she escaped from Paris without a sou, by cadging a lift on an express truck, and then robbed her old folks of all their savings?"

Mittel bowed his head.

"I didn't know where she was going," he sighed.

He would have done anything, just then, to gain the good opinion of this stubborn man who had struck him and who was still watching him on the sly. Up to now, he had felt himself to be something of an outsider on the ship. Except for Jolet and the black man, the crew scarcely addressed a word to him, looking upon him as an oddity. If anyone did speak to him, it was to say: "Well, well! if it isn't our friend the anarchist!"

Was he to be saddled with that name for the rest of his life?

"Do you have any complaints about my work?" he said abruptly, looking beseechingly at the bo'sun.

"No, he's pulling his weight," the bo'sun replied indirectly, addressing the captain.

"I do my very best. . . . When the gauge burst, I wasn't to blame. Everyone admits that. . . ."

"Well then, Chopard? Why not admit that he's a decent little bugger? I can't say as much for Charlotte up there."

"She is Godebieu's daughter. . . ."

"She certainly doesn't do your friend much credit! Come on now, shake hands with the fellow."

The seaman, after a moment's further hesitation, at last held out his hand, and there was something about this moment so precious, so unexpected, with the sun so brilliant, the sea so beautiful, and Mopps's expression so full of kindness, that Mittel had to avert his head to hide the tears that glittered in his eyes.

"Shall I tell you what you ought to do now? They can manage without him in the stokehold, but you have only five deck hands. Take the kid in your charge."

"And what if he falls overboard?"

"Then, by God, your pal Godebieu will have had his revenge! Now, leave us alone for a moment. I have something more to say to him."

"You'd have died of suffocation down there," explained the captain when they were alone. "Up here, at least, there's a breath of air. Tomorrow we'll be in the Caribbean, and after that, the Panama Canal."

"I don't know how to thank you!"

"Spare me that, for heaven's sake! Don't forget, I stole your girl, the very first day. And the absurd thing is that now I'd be sorry to lose her. She's pure poison. She has a hateful disposition. She's as self-centered as a cat. And yet I've become used to having her around the place, seeing her sprawling on the bed at all hours of the day, looking a real mess, with smudges of makeup all over her face. If she could get her claws into me, she wouldn't hesitate. . . ."

The black man, standing some way off, gazed admiringly at his comrade, upon whom the captain was bestowing so much attention. Jolet had opened his math textbook. As things stood,

Mittel would now be leaving their team to join the clannish Bretons.

"I can't resist getting her hackles up by threatening her with a desert island. She has the idea I mean to ditch her all alone on an uninhabited rock. We'll do our best to get her as far as Guayaquil. After that . . ."

"Is Guayaquil where we'll be unloading the guns?" Mittel ventured to ask, so confidential was the atmosphere between them at that moment.

"Everyone on board knows that. There's a revolution brewing in Ecuador. All they need is our machine guns to ensure that within three days the republic will have a new president."

He almost seemed to be talking to himself, squinting against the sun and babbling on cheerfully as if he would never stop.

"Have you been coughing much lately?"

"No. No more than in Paris. Somewhat less, in fact."

"Did your father have tuberculosis?"

"No, my mother. My father could bend an iron bar with his bare bands."

"Was Charlotte unfaithful to you in Paris?"

It was obvious that he was not talking at random in returning to this subject. Mittel was taken aback.

"I don't know. I've never given it a thought. Martin used to visit her once a month, naturally."

His thoughts reverted to those times, that nightmare.

"I'm sure she was unfaithful," the captain persisted.

"Do you think so?"

"As far as she's concerned, it doesn't mean a thing. If the signals officer took an interest in her . . ."

A stern expression crossed his face, and Mittel was astonished to find himself suspecting the captain of being jealous.

"I've had experience with her kind once before."

"The American girl?"

"I see you've heard the whole story. She even managed to con me into employing her lover as a chauffeur. Come on now, off you go! Don't forget that, from now on, you'll be working under Chopard."

He gave Mittel a friendly pat on the back and walked away slowly, apparently deep in thought.

Mittel went across to join Jolet and the black. Neither of them asked any questions. The sun was sinking. Napo's glowing skin gave off an acrid smell. Someone pointed out a shark in the sea, and several of the men ran to the rail to see it, but it disappeared as suddenly as it had come.

Two days before they reached Panama, the hatch covers were removed, the winches were set in motion, and those at work in the holds could be seen from above, looking like tiny manikins.

The captain himself was down there, threading his way among the crates and casks, followed by the bo'sun, alert to carry out his orders. The object was to rearrange the crates of weapons in such a way as to divert attention from them, so that the Canal authorities would not ask to have them opened.

It was very hot. Most of the deck hands had stripped to their shorts, then ceaselessly wiped their brows on the backs of their forearms.

The intermittent grinding of the winches eclipsed all other sounds. As the iron hook was lowered, it caught and slipped through the ropes securing each of the crates, which one by one were then raised, swinging above the seamen's heads so that they had to stretch up as best they could to guide them.

"Batten the hatches!"

It was dark by the time this order was given. Soon, toward dawn, Mittel was to have another new experience, as the lights of the Panama Canal hove into view. Some men on deck were washing their clothes. One, inside their quarters, was ironing his things, and this caused great annoyance by adding to the already infernal heat.

Of course, by now most of the men had taken to sleeping on deck, wrapped in a blanket, with an empty sack as a pillow.

"You're due on watch up there at midnight," announced the bo'sun to Mittel.

The crew was under strength, for reasons of economy. It was said that Mopps did not have the wherewithal to pay for his coal in Colón, and that he couldn't give the crew anything until they reached Guayaquil, where he would be paid for the cargo of machine guns.

When Mittel went up to the bridge, on the stroke of midnight, it was his second night at the helm. He found on duty not Mopps but the first officer, who ordered:

"Steer west-southwest!"

It was easy. All he had to do was to keep his eyes on the luminous compass and turn the wheel sufficiently to keep the needle steady.

He could not imagine a more peaceful haven than this little cabin, with the officer puffing at his pipe and the sky thickly sprinkled with stars. The throbbing of the engines was barely audible. The open portholes admitted a breeze that was almost cool. Mopps—and Charlotte, too, no doubt—must be asleep in the adjoining cabin, the door to which had been left open, with a curtain drawn across which billowed out at every puff of wind.

The time passed quickly. When, once in a while, the ship lurched slightly, the officer gave a hand signal and Mittel realized that he had allowed the freighter to list to port or starboard: toward the end of his watch, he could no longer see the figures on the compass.

At three o'clock, sounds could be heard in the captain's cabin. Then a light was switched on. Mopps, in his pajamas, came out to scan the horizon; he marked one star among all the other stars.

"That's the lighthouse on the south bank," he said.

"It's been visible for the past ten minutes. Another eighteen miles to go, I'd say."

Mopps went back into his cabin and got dressed, making a great clatter. Then Charlotte could be heard murmuring, "What's going on?"

"Panama! And if you want my advice, you'll get up and stretch your legs and get a breath of fresh air, before we shut you up in your bolthole."

"Are you sure it's safe?"

"Idiot!"

"And what if it's a trap?"

"What would be the point of that?"

"To get rid of me."

She got up. Wrapped in one of the captain's dressing gowns, she came into the wheelhouse, not recognizing Mittel, who appeared to her merely as a blurred, anonymous figure at the helm.

"Oh, it's you," she said to the officer. "What time will we be there?"

"In an hour the pilot will come aboard."

"Where are we?"

He pointed to the lighthouse, which looked to her like one star among many. She was barefooted, and her hair was in disarray.

"The captain thinks they won't find me. What do you say?"

"It's a pretty safe bet."

"You don't think I'll suffocate?"

"The chief engineer has done all that's necessary."

When Mopps reappeared, he was wearing white ducks and a white shirt, with collar and tie, and his gray hair was smoothed down with lotion. His shoes creaked at every step, and he reeked of eau de cologne.

"Aren't you going to get washed?" he asked Charlotte.

"What's the use? They say it stinks in there."

"No more than the prisons in Panama. Ring for the steward."

She did so, then stammered, "I don't know why I'm so scared."

"You'll have all the time in the world to be scared when you're in there."

And to the Annamese, when he appeared in answer to the bell: "Is the hamper ready? Bring it here, and let me have a look at it."

The hamper contained ham, biscuits, two bottles of wine, several bottles of water, oranges, and chocolate.

"Would you like bacon as well, Charlotte?"

"It's gone bad."

"Do you want to keep my dressing gown?"

"Yes."

Another vessel was gliding silently alongside the freighter. There was barely five hundred meters' distance between them.

"A German oil tanker," said Mopps. "If they don't need to take on coal, they'll go through the Canal ahead of us."

He paid no attention to Mittel. Inside the cabin, Charlotte stirred restlessly, moved things around, paced to and fro.

"Come on! The pilot will be arriving any minute now. You can already see the lights on both sides of the Canal."

She came back onto the bridge, carrying her handbag, and glanced around anxiously. At last she recognized Mittel, who was standing motionless at the helm.

"Have you been to see it?"

"Get a move on!" interrupted Mopps. "Don't forget the hamper."

Her terror was palpable. The deserted deck was pitch-black. Mopps opened the door of the wheelhouse onto a sea of darkness.

"Jef! Listen! Promise me . . ."

She did not know what to say, or perhaps she lacked the courage to say it. She went up to him.

"You won't leave me locked up in there, will you?" she whispered. "I'm scared! If you'd just come and listen once in a while, to make sure I'm breathing . . ."

She was not weeping. Her face was drawn and twisted, and her eyes couldn't keep still.

"Well?" Mopps was growing impatient.

"I'm coming. You do understand, don't you, Jef? I don't trust him. He's a brute."

And all this while, Mittel's hands remained steady on the wheel. He was far from unmoved by Charlotte's emotional outburst. He felt that ahead of them, and especially ahead of her, lay some fearful, unknown fate. And everything was topsy-turvy, without rhyme or reason.

Charlotte was not even dressed. "I'm taking my shoes," she said. She was carrying them in her hands. Then she dropped her bag, and the captain bent to pick it up.

"Jef! You do understand?"

It was sad, but he had no desire to kiss her. Not to mention that it would have been absurdly inappropriate! From the seamen's quarters the deck hands were coming out one by one, dazed with sleep. They looked at the horizon, calculating the distance between the freighter and the lighthouse, and lumbered to their posts.

"Hurry up! You're stepping on the hem."

The dressing gown was too long for her, but Charlotte managed to descend the ladder without mishap, then walked across the deck and disappeared down a companionway to the engine room.

A quarter of an hour went by before Mopps returned. They could now hear a throbbing sound, which must be the engine of the still-invisible pilot boat. The bo'sun himself relieved Mittel at the helm, but the young man remained on the bridge, waiting for news.

At last Mopps arrived and, wiping his oil-stained hands on the curtain across his cabin door, announced, "All done! For a moment, I thought she was going to back out."

"Will there be enough air?" asked the first officer.

"The chief engineer will make sure there is. For one thing, she won't be able to move much. There were barely ten centimeters to spare! At the last minute, she burst into tears and buried her face in my shoulder. . . ."

Mittel, with a lump in his throat, crept away without a sound. He had the feeling that something very terrible had just happened, and they must all take their share of responsibility, almost like members of a firing squad.

Suddenly he missed Charlotte. He didn't even know where she was. It was the chief engineer, the man who had fathered five or six children, who had prepared the hiding place for her between two sheets of metal, and now she was screwed in, unable to escape from that narrow space.

Was it close to the boiler? He could remember the red-hot steel panels, and the sickening smell of oil.

And here he was, pacing the deck. The throbbing of the pilot boat's engines was very near now, though the boat was still invisible. Some of the seamen were leaning over the rail, already calling out to those on board the other vessel.

A rosy glow appeared in the eastern sky. It was beginning to be possible to identify the shapes of things in the gray dawn light.

"Hello there!"

The boat was right up against the freighter, and still Mittel had not seen any sign of it. A man leapt on board and made his way unhesitatingly to the bridge.

The radio was chattering. The freighter slowed down, then came to a dead stop. Thus it remained for a quarter of an hour, until the sun had risen above the horizon.

Then two—no, three—launches could be seen approaching the freighter. Groups of men stood in the bows, blacks in khaki uniforms.

At the far end of the bay were a few factory chimneys, some cranes, and ships, ten, fifteen, twenty ships, lined up along the quays. There were also many smaller boats, launches and tugs.

Pelicans clumsily circled the deck and dived into the water every time the cook threw scraps overboard.

"Police!" whispered a man standing near Mittel.

The first launch to hail them was a dazzling sight, all mahogany and brass, flying the United States flag. A number of stern-looking men climbed the ladder and marched in silence toward the bridge.

The customs and quarantine launches, the latter flying a yellow flag, waited alongside.

Mopps had put on a white uniform jacket and a new cap with a badge on its front. He could be seen going to and fro on the bridge, talking to his visitors.

The radio signal sounded. The ship began to move forward slowly. The sun swallowed up everything in sight. They were moving in a veil of light, through which everything else visible seemed to lack substance.

The chief engineer walked across the deck with a preoccupied air, as always. Mittel instinctively started to move toward him, but checked himself in time.

He was haunted by the thought of Charlotte. She had been taken from the cabin before the sun was up. He could see her in his mind with her bag, her hamper of provisions, her shoes dangling from her fingers.

He had not slept a wink the whole night; he stayed on deck, his eyes devouring everything in sight, all of which trembled like a mirage in the glare of the sun.

5

THEY WERE NOT EVEN IN PORT. THEY WERE NOWHERE, FOR HOW could one give a name to the mountain of coal that formed an island at the end of the bay?

They had brushed against the unloading platforms and the docks; they had had a close view of the passengers on the two cruise liners putting in at Panama; they had even caught a glimpse of a street, where there were little horse-drawn carriages with white, fringed canopies.

But they had not put into port. The medical officer had been the first to leave, taking his launch to the German oil tanker, where he would go through the same formalities. The American police had left a man on board, as usual, as had the customs service. And everyone had had a glass of whisky before leaving, with Mopps chatting to them in a pure Yankee accent all the while.

They were now moored under a floating crane that overflowed with lumps of coal, and the shore could be reached only by rowing straight across the bay.

Boussus, the chief engineer, was on deck, waiting to supervise the filling of the coal bunkers. While Mopps drank with the port officials, the first officer, Voisier, stood beside him, taking no part in their exchanges, and not drinking, but merely handing over the appropriate papers as they were required.

At first the captain's eyes had twinkled. Everything seemed to be going splendidly. The customs officers had not asked to check the cargo. The Canal police suspected nothing. As for the Panamanian police force, it was represented by a small half-caste who had been content merely to put the ship's roster into his briefcase and stand guard on the deck.

But now Mopps was frowning, as he scanned through his binoculars the fishing smacks and motor launches plying the bay.

"You're quite sure the signal to the French Line was sent?"

"It was sent two days ago."

"And the order for coal was given?"

The odd thing was that there seemed to be no one manning the crane, which should have been ready for loading, and no one standing on the mound of coal, either.

And there was no sign of the representative of the French Line, who, as ship's broker, should have been the first to arrive.

Until he turned up, there was nothing to do but wait. Only he could attend to all the formalities, such as ordering the delivery of the coal, signing for it as guarantor of payment, obtaining permission from the authorities to pass through the Canal, and settling the dues, which amounted to nearly eighty thousand francs. It was also his responsibility to arrange for a tanker to supply fresh water, provisions, and cans of oil.

The sun was mounting in the sky, and those on deck were weighed down by the stifling heat, which was different from anything they had so far experienced. Here there was not the slightest breeze, not the faintest stirring of the massive canopy of heat and light which seemed to close in upon them if they so much as moved hand or foot.

Mittel, on the foredeck, stood watching the bustle of the harbor in the distance; then he glanced up at the wheelhouse, where Mopps was fuming with impatience.

"Look, Voisier, something must be up. I would have preferred to stay on board, but I think I'd better go see what's going on. I know I can rely on you to look after things here."

The chief engineer was pacing the deck, waiting for the signal to start coaling. Everyone was waiting. The men, their arms dangling, gazed at the mound of coal.

"Hey! Boussus!"

Boussus climbed up to the bridge and knocked on the glass

door, for he would not dream of indulging in familiarity, but always saluted, spoke in a manner appropriate to a subordinate, and kept his composure.

"You'll keep an eye on you-know-what?"

"I will."

"I'm going ashore. It looks as if the French Line has forgotten us."

Normally they would have expected, on arrival, to find some twenty blacks on the floating crane, ready to coal the freighter.

"Lower a boat!" Mopps shouted from the bridge. "I'll need three men!"

Mittel longed to volunteer to be one of those three, which would have given him the opportunity to see the harbor and the town of Colón. But he could not bring himself to do it. He felt impelled to stay where he was, close to Charlotte in her prison between two metal plates.

With the captain gone, the sense of time passing in wasteful idleness grew stronger. They stood about in groups, eying the crane, the coal, the gaping bunkers.

Fortunately for them, the monotony was relieved by the arrival of a boat manned by blacks and half-castes, and filled with goods for sale—American cigarettes, cigars, alligator belts, writing paper, and the like.

The men were invited on board, and the ensuing bargaining provided an agreeable diversion.

The three seamen who had rowed the captain ashore remained in the boat, having no landing permits. Mopps leapt onto the jetty, shouldering aside the hordes of taxi drivers accosting him, and, his briefcase under his arm, strode hurriedly across the couple of hundred meters separating him from the huge office building of the French Line, where, in the dim interior, he could see employees working in their shirt sleeves.

"Is Gérard here?"

"In his office."

The door, inscribed GENERAL MANAGER in English, stood open.

A slight, pale young man, writing at his desk, looked up as the captain came in, and said, "Have a seat." He then proceeded to finish the letter he was writing.

The walls were covered with sailing schedules, maps, and tables of exchange rates. The French Line represented the South American interests, not only of small-scale shipowners, but also of the major French shipping lines.

"Didn't you get my signal?"

"I did."

The young man, distant but correct, held out his cigarette case, offered his lighter, and looked at Mopps with unwavering composure.

"What's wrong then? Not a soul on board! The cranes unmanned!"

The young man took a file from a drawer, opened it, and handed Mopps a document.

"Read this."

It was a telegram from Paris:

WITHHOLD ALL ASSISTANCE.

At this Mopps's manner changed dramatically. Before, he had been affable, but now his expression suddenly hardened, and his lips twisted in a menacing smile.

"What does it mean? Did you cable Paris for instructions?"

"Here's our cable."

With the same casual air, he handed it over.

THE CROIX-DE-VIE, AS PREDICTED, SEEKING PERMISSION TO REFUEL. AWAIT INSTRUCTIONS. FRENCH LINE COLÓN.

So it was war. For a moment that morning, Mopps had felt a twinge of anxiety that everything was proceeding just a little too smoothly. He had had a premonition of trouble ahead. But what trouble?

Crossing his legs, leaning back in his chair, his face wreathed in tobacco smoke, he asked disingenuously, "You've never felt obliged to cable for instructions before. How many times, as a matter of interest, have I sailed through the Canal? Twelve? Thirteen?"

"Something like that. I could look it up in the records."

"And what's troubling you on this occasion?"

"I'd rather not say."

"I take it the decision is final?"

"You've read the cable from Paris. My function here is simply to carry out orders."

Mopps looked at him expressionlessly, though the situation could scarcely have been worse: unless someone was prepared to act as his guarantor, he could not refuel, for he was in no position to pay the thousands of francs required to settle the fuel bill.

Nor was there any possible way of passing through the Canal.

In other words, he could neither advance nor retreat!

"I'm obliged to you. I presume your British, German, and Italian colleagues are of the same mind?"

"I have no reason to think otherwise."

"See you later, then."

With no outward sign of ill-humor, he rose, shook hands with the agent, and, tucking his briefcase under his arm, went out of the colonnaded building.

He hailed a horse-drawn carriage whose driver, a local man, had been on the lookout for custom, and had himself driven into Colón, stopping outside a small hotel near the market place. His shirt was already soaked. With a sense of relief, he went into the cool, spacious café, waved to the bartender, a half-caste, and made for a table at the back. He held out his hand and said gruffly, "Hello, Jules!"

"Hello."

They might have parted only the night before. Jules was the owner of the hotel and café, a fat, flabby man with close-cropped hair and a stomach that seemed to be resting on his lap.

"What will you have?"

"My usual . . . a Pernod."

Here they served genuine, prewar Pernod, with a lump of sugar in a perforated spoon balanced on the glass.

"I've just come from the French Line. . . ."

"And?" said Jules, wasting no words.

"You knew?"

"I suspected there might be a snag or two."

"Because . . . ?" asked Mopps, in English.

"Haven't you read the papers? The revolution has already broken out in Ecuador."

"What?"

"Yes. Understand? They couldn't wait for your sewing machines. So . . ."

"I see."

They both fell silent. Mopps drank his Pernod, staring ahead with narrowed eyes.

"And the other business?" he asked, at last.

"The girl?"

"So you know about that, too?"

"We got the French papers yesterday."

"Has the government started extradition proceedings?"

"It's easy enough to find out. It won't take five minutes."

"Let's go, then."

Mopps emptied his glass. Jules slipped on an alpaca jacket but did not change out of his slippers, for he suffered from flat feet and blisters.

"If anyone wants me, I'm at the police station," he told the bartender.

They crossed two streets, then went into a compound of buildings that had whitewashed walls and corridors crammed with blacks and South American Indians. Jules, who seemed to know his way around as if it were his own home, shook hands with various officials, addressing them in Spanish, and had no hesitation about entering the office of the chief of police without bothering to knock.

"Hello, Enrico! Allow me to introduce a friend of mine. Incidentally, I wonder if you'd mind telling me something. Did you get anything from France in the last delivery of mail?"

The Panamanian opened a drawer and produced a bundle of

72

documents, to which a photograph was pinned. There was no need for long explanations. The two men had understood each other from the start.

"Is that her?" Jules asked the captain.

Mopps made no reply, merely blinked. The photograph, the mug-shot variety, showing the subject facing the camera and in profile, was certainly of Charlotte, with a description below that included a scar on the left cheek.

"Is she to be extradited?"

"Not yet. The request has been made. It will take two or three days to complete the necessary formalities."

"And in the meantime?"

"The girl is to be kept under surveillance if she sets foot on Panamanian soil."

Jules nudged Mopps in the ribs. There were handshakes all around. The police chief, seeing them to the door, murmured, "She isn't planning to come ashore, is she?"

"I don't think so."

"It would be better if she didn't."

"I agree with you."

It had all gone very smoothly, with no unnecessary questions asked. As the two men left the building, Mopps pulled off his tie, stuffed it in his pocket, and unbuttoned his shirt collar, for it was noon by now, and there was no shade anywhere in the streets.

"Well, that's one problem settled, anyway."

"Yes," sighed the captain.

"What do you intend to do?"

"I've somehow got to lay my hands on a hundred fifty thousand francs, at the least."

They were standing on the sidewalk. Black girls walked by, their hips swaying. The smell of foodstuffs was so penetrating that one became aware of it four blocks away from the market square.

"Is the cargo paid for?"

"Of course!"

"What is it worth?"

73

"A million and a half. But there's two hundred thousand owing in bribes."

"I'll take you to see Hakim."

"The one who owns the store?"

It took them barely three minutes to get to the modern store, with three floors of merchandise and fifty salesgirls, which was a magnet for all the tourists from the cruise liners, who poured in, wearing white pith helmets and cotton or tussah-silk suits and dresses.

"Is Hakim up in his office?"

Hakim, deeply tanned, a young man with greasy hair, offered them Turkish coffee and cigarettes.

"What's up, Jules?"

"You know Captain Mopps. Of course you do, you've seen him at my place. . . . Agree to his terms and you'll make a hundred thousand francs for yourself in ten days."

From time to time they were interrupted by a sales clerk seeking guidance, or a telephone call for Hakim. Mopps explained the situation as succinctly as possible:

"I'll pay you a hundred thousand francs in interest on the hundred fifty thousand I need for the coal and Canal dues."

They discussed the proposition for ten minutes, without once raising their voices. The hundred thousand francs' interest became a hundred fifty thousand, and, by way of guarantee, Mopps had to sign a bill, just as if he were buying goods on credit in the store.

"My brother will go with you," added the Levantine in conclusion. "We're going to stop at the bank."

"It's closed."

"Not to me. Mademoiselle, be good enough to telephone the bank and ask them to have ten thousand dollars ready for me."

And all three of them went out together, Mopps with his brief-case still under his arm and his tie in his pocket.

Half the crew were asleep on deck, under the shade of the awnings, and the other half were loitering gloomily when the boat drew alongside and Mopps leapt onto the deck. He looked around for the chief engineer and called out to him, "Refueling will begin in ten minutes."

It was half past two. Mopps had not wasted his time. He had gone from office to office, including that of the Canal authorities, securing all the necessary authorizations and paying all the costs.

"Departure time, four A.M. The water tanker is on its way. The stores will be here by four."

Mittel, who was standing a little way off, gazed at him in admiration.

Next the captain called for Voisier, and the first officer emerged from his quarters, buttoning his jacket.

"Departure time, four A.M. We're first in line."

From then on, everything went according to plan. A heavy launch approached the mound of coal and disgorged a gang of half-naked blacks. Some of these went to man the crane and others climbed on board by means of rope ladders.

Noise and bustle broke out suddenly. Winches were set in motion, amid much shouting. The water tanker drew up alongside the freighter, and more blacks came on board, adding to the general uproar, the rumbling of machinery, the banging and clanging of metal.

It was as if someone had waved a magic wand and brought everything to life. Meanwhile Mopps, his briefcase still under his arm, went up to the policeman on guard, stuck an enormous cigar between his lips, and spoke to him in Spanish.

He even found time to pause for a moment, in passing, to reassure Mittel: "Everything's fine! I'll tell you all about it later."

Then, for the next three hours, he was nowhere to be seen. He must have been asleep up there behind the closed door of his cabin, while a whole community was at work on the preparations for departure, filling the coal bunkers, the ballast holds, and the stores.

There was an endless stream of rowboats and launches, loaded with entire carcasses of sheep and sides of beef, rigid in their muslin wrappings, and quantities of fruit and vegetables. The

Annamese cook hurried back and forth with drinks for the suppliers, who were then paid off by Voisier.

The chief engineer concentrated all his attention on the supplies of water, oil, and coal, but every hour, on the hour, he vanished briefly, and Mittel, though he lacked the courage to accompany him, guessed that he had gone to press his ear against the panel, and perhaps even murmur a word of encouragement to Charlotte.

The heat was becoming more and more unbearable. Most of the stevedores were naked but for skimpy loincloths knotted around their hips.

A boatload of women arrived, blacks and half-castes. A heated argument ensued, but the bo'sun finally allowed them aboard, and bargains were struck under the very eyes of the impassive Panamanian police officer, who had lunched in the officers' mess and drunk his fair share of French wine.

A quarter of an hour later, one of the black women stormed on deck raging like a Fury. She grabbed Voisier by the arm, complaining that Napo had cheated her of the dollar he had promised her.

There was nothing for Mittel to do. The ship had been taken over by the natives. He felt drowsy and he had a severe headache, but he would not for the world have missed the colorful spectacle being enacted, even though, toward the end, he felt so dizzy he could scarcely stand.

From time to time, the deep note of a ship's siren could be heard. In the distance, cruise liners, their decks crammed with passengers, headed for the open sea.

Fifteen aircraft ceaselessly buzzed overhead, patrolling the port and the Canal, and the sun blazed in a cloudless sky. There was not so much as a wisp of cloud to be seen, and the only shadows were those of the occasional pelican, gliding above the black iron plates of the ship.

"Can you hear her moving?"

It was five o'clock. The captain had sent for Boussus, to inquire after Charlotte.

"She starts moaning every time she hears anyone approach," he replied.

"Are you sure she's getting enough air?"

"Certain."

Mopps got up, sprinkled his chest with cold water, gargled, and began getting dressed. He called out to the Annamese, "Put some champagne on ice. Twenty bottles."

Stripped to the waist, he went out onto the bridge and called to Mittel, who was still leaning over the rail, "Come up here a moment!"

And when the young man joined him, he said, "Shut the door. I've seen the police about Charlotte. Needless to say, there won't be any trouble. The government of Panama have received a request for her extradition, with a mug shot and all the rest of it. . . ."

"Are they going to arrest her?"

"Nothing of the sort! In this country, it's always possible to make an arrangement. The warrant hasn't yet been signed. At the very worst, if she were to go on shore, the authorities would keep a discreet eye on her."

He paused, apparently unable to decide between two courses of action.

"As for you, there's nothing to stop you from entering the country. There's no mention of you in the extradition documents."

And he watched Mittel out of the corner of his eye.

"How does the idea appeal to you?"

"I'd rather stay with the ship."

"Are you afraid?"

"No!"

It was such an emphatic no that Mittel himself flushed as he stammered, "I'd rather remain with you."

"Very good. And what about her? What shall we do with her?"

One could never tell, with Mopps, whether he was being serious or teasing, especially when, as at present, his manner was so friendly and his expression so innocent.

"I don't know."

"Shall we leave her here? With Jules to look after her, she has little to fear. His place is not much better than a bistro, but I imagine he has more influence than the French consul. Do you understand?"

"Yes . . . no . . ."

He felt lost. He did not understand. He wondered what the captain was getting at.

"Shall we keep her?"

"That would be the best thing, wouldn't it?"

"Very well, we'll keep her. I'm expecting a few friends shortly. When I mentioned your name to Jules, he told me he'd met several friends of your father's in jail. . . . It's thirty years now since he broke out."

Too many words, too many unfamiliar sights, too much sun, too much heat! Mittel's head was in a whirl. He tried to listen but could make nothing of what was being said.

"We'll introduce them to Charlotte. . . ."

"But what about the police?"

"The police will drink with us. Go and clean yourself up. You're invited as well."

And he went back into his cabin to finish dressing.

"Take this to the police officer," said the captain to his steward, handing him a bottle of champagne.

Then, waiting for nightfall, they had drunk glass after glass. Hakim was there, with his brother, whom everyone called Fredo. The brother was much younger than Hakim: he looked about the same age as Mittel, and seemed rather shy, with his girlish face, his over-supple body, and huge brown eyes.

Jules, who had already removed his jacket, was accompanied by two other Frenchmen, whose way of life proclaimed itself unmistakably. They were underworld characters, in spite of their good manners and sparse conversation. Mopps had known them for years.

They had all arrived in Hakim's private launch, which was

now moored to the ship, manned by its two black seamen, who had been liberally supplied with beer.

Introductions had been minimal. No one had taken the slightest notice of Mittel, apart from Jules, who had remarked to him, "An odd fellow, your father. If he hadn't taken his own way out, he'd probably be here with me now."

They had gathered in the officers' mess, which was more spacious than the captain's cabin. Voisier was present, and also the two junior officers, Thiberghem, a tall, fair-haired youth from Dunkerque, the other, Berton, a more lively character from Paris.

"Have you seen Le Borgne at all, since we were together in San Francisco?"

"Only once, in Hamburg."

"How's he making out?"

"He's working as an interpreter in a hotel."

After Le Borgne, some other name was mentioned. The conversation was fragmentary, referring mainly to old acquaintances whose lives seemed to have progressed along widely different lines.

"What about your ex-wife?"

"She never stops slapping summonses on me, via every lawyer in the United States, because I'm behind on her alimony."

"I did warn you, didn't I? The trouble with you is that you're too softhearted."

At this Mittel looked up, his eyes turned toward Mopps. He had been much struck by the term "softhearted," which, inappropriate though it might appear on the surface, seemed to him not far from the truth.

"When are we going to see the girl?"

"One more glass, and we'll all go together and fetch her. But I'd better warn you, she won't be looking her best."

Mittel noticed, not for the first time, that the officers, in particular Voisier and Thiberghem, were far from comfortable in this company. They scarcely uttered a word, and drank as little as they possibly could without causing offense. Voisier was the first to leave, muttering something about having things to see to. Thiberghem retired to his cabin, which adjoined the officers' mess, and was not seen again that night. Only Berton, the Parisian, remained, his ears wide open and his eyes already sparkling with drink.

"Let's go! You first, Mittel."

The atmosphere was distinctly festive, almost as if they were taking part in a student prank. They marched across the deck in single file; then Mittel went through the skylight and climbed down the iron ladder. At the bottom, he hesitated, not quite sure where the girl was hidden.

At the end of one of the passages, he found the chief engineer, looking grave.

"Where are you going?"

Then Boussus caught sight of the rest of the party and froze.

"Hand over your prisoner," said Mopps, who had drunk a good deal.

Hakim still looked smart, as he smoked through a gold cigarette holder.

"The police officer is still up there. . . ."

"The police officer is drunk! Blind drunk! Don't waste any more time."

Mittel listened intently. He could hear no sound, and he had never experienced such misery as during the three minutes it took to unscrew the six bolts.

"Give us some light."

They were jammed up against one another in the narrow passage. Hakim's brother was wearing cologne. Jules was sweating, and hitching his trousers up over his stomach every few seconds.

"Remove the panel."

Mopps was holding the lantern close to the open space which was now revealed. The first thing they saw was a naked leg and a strip of dressing gown. Then, at last, a face cautiously peering out, a pair of eyes screwed up against the light.

A cry . . .

Charlotte, at the sight of so many people, imagined that they had come to arrest her, and she responded with a strident appeal, squeezing herself into the farthest corner of her hiding place, knocking over and breaking bottles as she did so.

"There's nothing to be afraid of. It's only us. . . ."

Eventually they had to drag her out, so resolutely did she shrink back. When a sliver of glass stabbed her in the calf, she did not even notice. Nor did she seem aware that she was virtually naked.

"What's going on? What's going on?" she stammered, putting her hands over her eyes.

"It's us. We've come to take you out of there. Say hello to these gentlemen, who are old friends of mine."

"What friends?"

Jules scooped her up under his arm, carried her, struggling, out of the narrow passage, and laid her on the deck next to the skylight.

"Oh, so you're here, too!" exclaimed Charlotte as she noticed Mittel for the first time.

She seemed on the point of throwing a tantrum but must have thought better of it. She screwed up her eyes, slowly becoming used to the light, and then the gathering darkness.

"Where are we?"

"Outside Colón. There's champagne waiting for us."

"What about the police?"

Ironically enough, just at that moment they went past the police officer, with his bottle of champagne beside him. He saluted obsequiously.

"There's your police officer. Did you see him?"

"I can't walk another step."

"Pick her up again, won't you, Jules?"

He dragged, rather than carried, her. Everyone was laughing, senselessly. The seamen on deck gazed wide-eyed at this extraordinary procession. Finally, it disappeared into the officers' mess. Five glasses of champagne were proffered to the young woman.

"Drink up, now! And cover yourself up a bit, if you can."

Everyone had seen her. Charlotte drank, put her hand to her forehead, and, looking from one to another of the men, slowly covered herself with her dressing gown.

"They're really not going to arrest me?"

"I swear it."

"Is it true, Jef?"

"It's true," he replied uncomfortably.

Another glass, and another. Eager hands pressed them upon her. She emptied them greedily, till she was shivering from head to foot.

"I'm bruised all over," she cried suddenly.

"Lie down here."

There was a leather-upholstered bench all along one wall, on which they laid Charlotte down. Hakim remarked to the captain, "She's a scream!"

Just at that moment, Mittel caught sight of Mopps's face and was struck by his worried expression. Mopps looked as though he failed to see the joke, and was beginning to regret having invited these people, and even . . .

Mittel was almost sure that he was experiencing a pang of jealousy, especially when Hakim's brother, Fredo, sat down on the edge of the bench and began stroking Charlotte's forehead, murmuring, "Get some rest now. . . . We've got the whole night ahead of us."

From a remote corner of the officers' mess, the third officer watched these proceedings like an adolescent gate-crasher.

"More champagne, Tao!" yelled Mopps, addressing the Annamese, who had, in fact, already arrived with more bottles. "Turn on the fans."

By now they weren't bothering to pop the corks, just breaking the necks of the bottles on the edge of the table.

"To Charlotte, and to the Panamanian police! Open a can of something, Tao! *Foie gras*, anything you can lay your hands on. And whisky for anyone who wants it. And let's not forget our friend the policeman. . . . Come to think of it, why shouldn't we ask him in to have a drink with us?"

He was talking very loudly, and yet he was not drunk. Mittel could sense this, for he was watching him closely, wondering what might be troubling Mopps so much that he was desperate to chase it from his mind.

6

"YOU GO AND GET DRESSED," SAID THE CAPTAIN SHARPLY TO Charlotte.

He was sitting on the other side of the officers' mess, next to Jules, who was smoking a cigar. The Annamese moved around silently, replacing the empty bottles with full ones. Already one glass had been broken.

"By the way, is Electrika still at the Atlantic?"

"She's gone to Mexico with a Yankee, who wants to marry her."

Like an inquisitive child, Mittel was drinking it all in. For him, everything that was said formed a kaleidoscopic pattern of brilliant color and light. He had not had even a distant glimpse of the town. He was not familiar with the broad, brightly lighted avenue, where every building included a bar, where from every door and window came the sound of music, shouting, and laughter, mingled with whiffs of alcohol; or with the sidewalks illumined by flickering neon advertisements in red, mauve, and yellow, where groups of seamen, mostly Americans in their white caps, pushed and jostled.

Moulin Rouge, Tropic, Atlantic . . . Dimly lighted saloons . . . Black jazz bands . . . And women at every table, Cubans like Electrika, Mexicans, anemic English girls, and timid teen-agers from the United States.

"And the little blonde?" asked Mopps. "You know the one I mean?"

"Tania? She's still here."

Mittel suddenly heard some noise on deck and went outside.

In the darkness, he saw a crowd of seamen making for the gangway, for a launch that waited below. They were the crew members who had shore leave for the night. Among them was the bo'sun, wearing a tight, over-starched white suit. They all looked as if they had been scrubbed with pumice stone, and were in high spirits over the prospects awaiting them.

When the gangway was removed and the engines of the launch began to throb, Mittel felt a pang of envy. Over there was the town, only a few minutes away. The clamor of its night life could be heard clearly, and he could imagine the cheerful bustle of its streets. But he would not see any of it!

Couldn't he have obtained shore leave like the others? Yes and no. The captain had invited him, Charlotte, and his friends to join his party, and he had not felt able to refuse.

Come to think of it, this was always the way with him. There was always something to prevent him from doing as he wished. He was forever compromising, forever putting himself in a false position!

The others were seamen, and they went ashore to have a good time, as seamen do. In the officers' mess, Mopps and his friends were likewise enjoying themselves. But what of Mittel himself? Where, precisely, did he stand?

He had never in his life known where he stood! He had had nothing in common with the aggressive freethinkers who haunted the bookshop on the Rue Montmartre, any more than he had had with his father's old friends, now rich and respectable members of the community. Even in Mrs. White's living room he had felt out of place.

After several glasses of champagne, he was growing maudlin over his misfortunes as he gazed nostalgically at the wake of the launch, which was speeding toward the town.

"You gave me a fright!" whispered a voice nearby. It was Charlotte; coming down from the bridge, she had almost collided with him.

"What are you doing all alone out here?"

"I don't know. . . . I feel depressed."

He did not feel at ease anywhere, not in the officers' mess, not here on deck. He scarcely glanced at Charlotte, though she was wearing her black suit, had done her hair neatly, applied powder and lipstick with care.

"Who are all those people?" she asked.

"One is the manager of a big store in Colón; then there's his brother, who will be coming with us. The others are French. Jules, the fat one, owns a hotel."

"Aren't you coming back in?"

"Yes . . ."

He wasn't sure. He would have preferred to brood on his misfortunes a little longer, but he needed a sympathetic ear, and Charlotte was eager to get back to the noise and the light.

Everyone cheered when she made her entrance, and she was indeed a striking figure in this setting, wearing her close-fitting suit, her face pale, her lips bright scarlet, every inch a Parisienne.

"Here's to you!" she cried, gulping down a glass of champagne.

"Come here," said Mopps gruffly.

She went over and sat on his knee, like a child, as he automatically stroked the back of her neck while carrying on a conversation with Jules.

Some two thousand seamen, passengers from ten cruise liners, Germans from Hamburg, British, Italian, and Japanese tourists, were strolling along the broad avenue, going from bar to bar, from cabaret to cabaret, attracted by the neon signs and the framed photographs of girls on the outside.

Taxi drivers, beggars, guides, peanut vendors, and women selling flowers were looking for custom everywhere, and would persist until daybreak.

In the officers' mess, where countless empty bottles were scattered around, Mittel endeavored, at intervals, to bring his surroundings into focus.

"I think I must be slightly tipsy," he confided to Fredo.

"All the same, I know what I'm talking about! Do you understand me? I understand *you* perfectly."

For, during the past quarter of an hour, they had been exchanging confidences.

"You listen to me, and you'll see how well I understand. You're a Syrian. Well, then, a Syrian has a lot in common with the son of an anarchist. What are we? Neither fish nor fowl! The French, the British, and the Americans regard you as an alien, but the natives don't regard you as one of themselves, either."

"You're absolutely right. If we were poor, life would be impossible. But we have money!"

"Yes, you have money," agreed Mittel with conviction, "whereas I have nothing. So there you are. I'm like a Syrian without money. . . . I can't be all that drunk, since I know what I'm talking about."

"Shut up, you two over there," shouted Mopps. "We can't hear ourselves talk."

Across the room, the rest of the party were quizzing Charlotte about the murder. She, too, had been drinking, but the wine had made her boastful, not tearful.

"I said to them, 'You shall have the thirty thousand francs you need to keep the paper going for a year!' "

"Why only for a year?" asked fat Jules, slurring his words.

"Be quiet. Let her speak. . . ."

"I knew the risk I was taking. But someone had to make the sacrifice."

"Why?" persisted the hotel proprietor.

"Why? For the Cause! For our ideals! I went to the Boulevard Beaumarchais. For two whole days I kept watch in the cold and the rain, wearing nothing but the clothes I have on now."

Mittel, overhearing, frowned and wiped his brow.

"I knew that I was capable of pulling the trigger. . . . I was ready to sacrifice my life."

She was still sitting on Mopps's knee, and he absently stroked her neck, his eyes elsewhere.

"Who's going to pour the drinks?" he barked.

"Someone was giving a violin lesson in the apartment next door. . . ."

She never omitted this detail, well aware that it enhanced the dramatic effect. Mittel wished he could shut her up.

"Is she the captain's mistress?" asked young Fredo in a whisper.

He nodded.

"Aren't you jealous?"

"You couldn't possibly understand. . . . I don't know the answer myself."

"And Mopps?"

"What about Mopps?"

"Is he jealous? Supposing, for instance, I were to proposition her?"

Mittel, staring down at the floor, reflected on this question.

"Obviously," he growled.

"Do you think I'd have a chance?"

Fredo could have as many women as he could possibly want in Colón, but there was only one woman on board this ship, and already she had succeeded in mesmerizing him.

"I think I shot him through the heart, but I didn't have the courage to look. Luckily, the violin was still playing. If it had stopped, I would have killed myself, rather than be caught. . . ."

Mopps sighed and took a gulp of whisky straight from the bottle.

"Here, why don't you have a drink, too . . . ? And then perhaps we might switch to a more cheerful subject."

With disdain she replied, "When do you men ever think about anything but having a good time!"

"True enough. Who's going to get some more bottles from the fridge?"

The atmosphere was so thick in the officers' mess that the light appeared dimmed, as if seen through frosted glass. Berton, the third officer, was almost asleep on his feet, but he was determined to stay, to keep watching and listening, as Jules, sodden with drink as he was, solemnly went on with his anecdotes.

It was about two in the morning, possibly later. In any event, the launch had returned with the seamen, and the bo'sun had changed from his starched white suit into his working clothes.

The deck was full of shadowy, whispering figures. Women had been smuggled aboard for those who had not gone ashore, and a good deal of pairing off had already taken place. Meanwhile, in the fo'c's'le, a party of half-castes and seamen were playing cards by the light of their cigarettes.

Waves slapping against the sides of the ship . . . klaxons sounding in the distance . . . the rumbling of aircraft, whose lights could be seen crossing the sky.

"Why are you looking at me like that?" Charlotte asked Fredo, who was now sitting very close to her.

"Because I've never met a woman like you."

She laughed, showing her pointed teeth. Girlish dimples appeared in her cheeks.

"What's so special about me?"

"Everything! In Panama, there aren't any interesting women."

"Is that what I am?"

Mopps was watching them from across the room as he listened to Jules describing a swordfish-spearing expedition he had undertaken with an English lord.

Mittel was all alone. No one was paying any attention to him, and he mumbled to himself in an undertone, "That's what I am, just like a Syrian . . . a Syrian without a penny to his name!"

It had become an obsession with him.

What had he made of his life? A man like Mopps could command a ship, smuggle contraband, talk to the Canal authorities in English, squeeze a hundred fifty thousand francs out of Hakim, converse in Spanish with the natives. What could Mopps *not* do? He was at ease in all circumstances. He was utterly self-

89

confident, so much so that, on the very first day Charlotte had come aboard, he had taken her without fuss, simply because he knew he could.

Mittel, on the contrary, had known her for three months before plucking up the courage just to mention love.

Yes, what was he? Even Napo was a competent stoker, spoke three languages, and could knock a man flat with a single blow of his fist.

"I'd be glad to," Charlotte said, rising to her feet.

Mittel followed her with his eyes. Fredo had suggested taking a turn on deck, and they had gone out together. Mittel's eyes met Mopps's. The captain's were somber.

Someone knocked at the door. It was the bo'sun, dressed in blue overalls, and smelling of liquor.

"It's three o'clock," he announced. "Should I give the order to raise anchor? They're already stirring in the pilot's office—I can see lights on in there. They'll be here in half an hour."

"Very good. Wake Voisier."

Five minutes later, Voisier emerged from his cabin. It was obvious that he had been asleep. He made his way across the officers' mess, averting his eyes from the appalling disorder all around him.

"See that I am called when the pilot arrives!" Mopps shouted after him, lighting his pipe.

Everyone was weary. The ship was alive with unfamiliar sounds. Mittel's legs felt leaden, and he lacked the will to get to his feet.

"Not now . . ." murmured Charlotte in the dark, leaning over the rail, shoulder to shoulder with Fredo.

"Why not?"

"Because!"

She felt the presence of someone behind her, but she did not move as the Syrian persisted:

"If I were to beg you . . ."

"Charlotte!"

It was Mopps's voice, hoarse and ill-humored.

"It's time to go back to your bolthole."

"But . . . you told me it would be unnecessary . . . that the police . . ."

"It can't be helped!"

"Why? It's frightening to be shut up in there. Unless there's some very good reason . . ."

"The reason is that I've changed my mind."

Mittel, sensing something amiss, came out of the officers' mess to find out what it was.

"Go and change into something more suitable. I want you ready in five minutes."

Fredo thought it wiser to say nothing.

Chopard passed by within hailing distance.

"By the way, what's happened to the police officer? No one has seen him for hours."

"He's just been found slumped behind a capstan. He's been sick."

Mopps looked around him, apparently uncertain what to do next, then climbed the ladder and went to join Charlotte in his cabin.

"I think he's jealous," Fredo whispered in Mittel's ear.

They could hear the murmur of voices, and then suddenly more muffled sounds, as if a fight was going on up there. A few seconds later, Charlotte reappeared, in the dressing gown that was too long and too wide for her, and made for the officers' mess.

"Where are you going?"

"To say good-bye"

"Don't bother!"

And Mopps, shoving her toward the hatchway, roared at the top of his voice, "Boussus! Hey there, Boussus!"

Mopps was still pushing Charlotte toward the narrow passageway, toward the unscrewed metal panel, when Boussus appeared. Mittel and Fredo exchanged looks but said nothing.

When Mopps returned, his expression gave nothing away. He listened intently, heard the distant throbbing of an engine, and went across to the rail, to await the pilot.

No one could have guessed that he had spent the whole night drinking. Opening the door of the officers' mess, he announced curtly, "Time's up!"

Handshakes were exchanged. They had nothing more to say to one another. Hakim's launch was still there, now visible in the milky light of early dawn. The two brothers embraced and drew aside for a moment, whispering.

"Bon voyage!"

"Good luck!"

Other ships were gradually beginning to loom out of the darkness, their funnels ringed with white, red, and blue. Drowsy seamen were stumbling to their posts.

"See you!"

Mittel also exchanged handshakes, but the party was over. The ship had become a ship again, under the command of Captain Mopps. Ignoring the departing guests, Mopps went up to the bridge, where the Annamese was waiting for him with coffee, and began shouting orders.

From Hakim's launch, handkerchiefs could still be seen waving. Mopps did not even notice.

"Did you go ashore?" Mittel asked Jolet, who was off duty, and lying stretched out on the deck. The ship was in the lock, being towed by a motor barge that was operated by the Canal men.

"No. Did you?"

"No, I didn't, either."

The stoker added, without rancor, "I didn't go because I can't afford to. It's no fun if you can't go into the cafés and shops, and buy from the street vendors. I've been on this route five times now, and I've only taken shore leave once—and that was in the morning, when everything is shut."

"Where do you live in France?"

"In Bénouville, near Fécamp, right on top of the cliff. My eldest, a girl, has just started school. My wife gathers crabs at low tide, and some days she makes as much as twelve francs!"

They were glistening with sweat. Everyone was out on deck, for indoors the heat was intolerable. The metal plates were scorching underfoot. Since early morning, they had seen nothing but jungle on either side of the Canal, and an occasional flat clearing that had mown grass, army tents in neat rows behind barbed wire, and American soldiers drilling.

When they had passed through the locks, a new pilot took over and guided them through a vast lake, where, here and there, a tree could be seen growing out of the water. Someone even claimed to have seen a crocodile, but no one believed him.

Mittel had dozed off two or three times but had never lost his awareness of the sounds aboard ship, or of the glaring light and infernal heat of the sky overhead.

Was he merely suffering from a hangover? In any case, he was experiencing a degree of unease that was like a presentiment. He was in the grip of fear. He could not tell why, but whenever he attempted to work out the time it would take him to get back to France if he should ever decide to do so, he found himself trembling all over.

The jungle was gray, impenetrable, hostile, and the air was filled with the buzzing of winged insects. It felt as if the whole earth were sizzling in the heat of the sun, as if nature had a life of its own, independent of man, and generated so much more power that Mittel had to close his eyes to shut it out.

"Do you like hot countries?"

"I don't mind them," replied Jolet, still lying on the deck.

A little way off, Napo was regaling his buddies with tales of his amorous adventures in the town.

The fact was that, once they had passed through the Canal, they would be in a different world. Mittel could visualize the map distinctly. He had a clear picture of that immense wall of land, the American continent, which divided the world in half, from north to south.

The Panama Canal was just a little manmade fissure in the middle, creating two separate continents, one on their right, the other on their left. In two hours, they would be in the Pacific Ocean!

But to return home . . .

That was the thought that terrified him. He had a presentiment that it would be incredibly difficult, if not impossible, ever to return.

Mopps remained at his post on the bridge, next to the pilot in his gray felt cap, smoking and looking straight ahead.

What did he intend to do with Charlotte? Maybe he himself did not know. The bo'sun had slung a hammock on deck for Fredo, and the young Syrian had been lying there since dawn. Two or three times, someone had brought him lemons.

And what if they should find Charlotte dead? In this heat, conditions must be unbearable in there, between two sheets of metal. Mopps had been in a filthy temper when he dragged Charlotte back to her hiding place.

"Are you asleep?"

"No . . . Are you?"

All the same, he did fall asleep eventually, his body rocked by the throbbing of the engines, which made the hatches vibrate.

They did not stop at Panama, which stood guard over the Pacific terminal of the Canal. For the next two days, there was a dead calm, though the sea was gray. The sky was gray, too, but with a powerful glare, which was intensely trying on the eyes.

Charlotte was ill. It was from Fredo that Mittel heard the news, for the captain never appeared on deck, but remained up there on the bridge, looking anxious and speaking to no one.

When Mopps was in this frame of mind, Chopard, taking his cue from him, became equally taciturn. He never addressed a word to Mittel, who was given virtually nothing to do on deck. To keep the deck hands occupied, he made them clean the rust off the bulwarks. This they did by chipping it off with a hammer and chisel, and then, after rubbing down the metal, painting it with a coat of red lead.

The noise was deafening. It was no longer possible even to think. They hammered away for hours at a stretch, then turned the fire hose on one another and lay down to rest in the shade.

"Mopps says it's nothing to worry about, but she's refusing all food."

Fredo, who was bored, was always hovering around Mittel and liked to stop for a chat.

"We're putting in at Buenaventura," he announced that same evening.

"Where's that?"

"It's a little seaport in Colombia. We'll be there by tomorrow morning."

"Why aren't we going to Guayaquil?"

"There are contradictory reports from the various radio stations. Bogotá claims that Gomez, the new dictator of Ecuador, has been assassinated. But the broadcasts from Lima report that Gomez has won control all along the line. They'll have the latest news at Buenaventura."

It was somewhere on their left. There was no sign of land yet, but it was not far off, twenty miles at most according to Jolet, who had spent years at sea.

"I'm sure Mopps has a grudge against me," Fredo confided to Mittel, not for the first time. He, too, seemed uneasy.

"On account of Charlotte?"

"Yes. He overheard me making up to her. He's never said a word about it, but I can see he's avoiding me. Whenever I go up there, he's always busy. . . ."

Everyone was on edge. It was probably the weather! The brilliant Caribbean sunshine was no more to be seen. Now there was only an ever-present, lowering, gloomy yellow disc. The air was humid. It was difficult to breathe. Jolet forecast that there would be rain within the next two days.

Not a wave could be seen, yet the freighter swayed gently, rocked by the undertow of the flat, gleaming black water, flecked with metallic glints.

Fredo was thinking about the future.

"I have a half share in this venture of my brother's. If it succeeds, I'll make five thousand dollars. I'll take a holiday, a couple of months in New York, or possibly even in France. I've been to Paris twice."

Jolet's forecast proved to be accurate. Those sleeping on deck had to move, for it began to rain. A light shower at first, but by morning it had swollen to a flood. No wind, not even a breeze. The heavy drops kept plummeting, and the awnings above the deck were very soon weighed down with water, which slopped noisily over the sides.

Even so, Mittel could not bring himself to sleep indoors. He awoke feeling damp under a sodden blanket, and saw, on either side, low-lying land covered with pale vegetation.

They had entered the mouth of a river. A launch, presumably the pilot's, followed slowly in their wake, and they had already reduced speed.

Never had Mittel seen a more desolate landscape. It was as if he were looking into an old, discolored, junk-shop mirror. Everything was distorted by the rain, but there was still not a breath of cool air.

A small motorboat was at anchor in the middle of the river, carrying three men on deck. What was it doing there? How long had it been there? What was it waiting for?

Jolet was in the stokehold. Fredo was nowhere to be seen. The chief engineer was taking his regular constitutional, oblivious of his surroundings.

As for the town, Mittel had caught a glimpse of it at a bend in the river. A quay built on piles . . . wooden mooring posts . . . farther inland, a concrete pile, a hotel presumably . . . railroad tracks on a stretch of waste land . . . finally, about a kilometer away, a little cluster of blackened, crooked wooden houses, tightly packed together.

"There's Buenaventura," announced Fredo, who, having just got up, was dressed in cream silk pajamas. "I was here before once, on an American plane."

To avoid paying harbor dues they did not put into port, but, like the little motorboat, dropped anchor in midstream, where there was also a stationary Norwegian ship.

Here the rainy season was well advanced. They could smell the yellow mud washed away by the floods, in which floated quantities of greenery, tree trunks, and even whole trees with their roots in the air.

Apart from the concrete hotel and the few wooden houses, there was no sign of human habitation in this low-lying, damp country, surrounded by jungle so dense that it seemed to cover the entire earth, and crisscrossed with turbulent rivers.

"That's Mopps calling me! Now we'll know."

The cabin door was open. Charlotte lay in her bed, her eyes open, but she did not even glance at Fredo as he came in.

"Hurry up and get dressed," said the captain to the Syrian. "The pilot couldn't tell me much, but some people from Guayaquil arrived at the hotel last night."

There was no work for the deck hands to do. They watched Mopps and Fredo climb down into a waiting launch and head for the quay.

When they got there, they could not even find a path, and had to pick their way between the rails and sleepers to reach the station, which was still in the process of construction. There stood waiting the only train of the day, bound for Cali, no more than three cars, which were already crowded with blacks and Indians.

The hotel foyer was vast. A few people wandered around, as if it were a railroad station and they were waiting for a train. On the right was a bar, tarnished by the humidity, with a slot machine on it. Mopps absent-mindedly inserted a coin.

"I want to see the manager," he said to the bartender.

He was dressed in white, as usual, but unshaven, and his espadrilles were soaked through.

"You're new, aren't you?" he remarked to the plump little South American who soon appeared.

"I took over the hotel last year from my brother-in-law."

"That's all right with me. You have some people from Guayaquil staying here, I believe?"

"We get more every day, but most of them are on their way to Cali and Bogotá. Today there's a plane due in at eleven, and there are sure to be more coming on that."

"What exactly is happening there?"

"Haven't you heard?"

"If I had, I wouldn't bother to ask."

"Gomez has been assassinated."

If Mopps was disturbed by this news, he did not show it. He put a half-peso into the machine and turned the handle. There was a click, and the machine disgorged two tokens, worth a peso each.

"Are you sure?"

"His brother came through here yesterday. They were out to get him as well."

"Get me a cigar."

He chose the biggest one and bit the end off, while continuing to feed coins into the slot machine, and winning.

"Is there still much fighting?"

"It's all over. Once Gomez was dead . . ."

The hotel proprietor looked more closely at Mopps's cap badge, then went across to the bay window overlooking the river and looked at the freighter at anchor, with its sodden French flag drooping at the stern.

"So it's you," he murmured admiringly.

"What do you mean?"

"Gomez was too impatient to wait for you. I suspect he was badly advised. There are rumors that his brother double-crossed him. They started too soon, believing they could capture the arsenal and arm themselves that way."

Scratching his head, the man went behind the counter and fetched a bottle of whisky and three glasses.

"What are you going to do now?" he asked.

"Give me some more half-pesos."

Mopps puffed slowly at his cigar, feeding the slot machine and turning the handle. If four discs of the same color turned up, it was possible to win as much as twenty pesos. He had already won five, six, and twelve pesos in succession, but he had failed to win the twenty, and, his eyes glazed, he stubbornly persisted in trying again.

"Give me some more change!"

"What are we going to do with the weapons?" ventured Fredo, irritated by his apparent indifference.

"Just one short!" thundered Mopps. "I had three black discs. You were saying?"

"What are we going to do with . . ."

"How the hell should I know?"

And he stayed there until midday, playing the slot machine, winning sixty pesos and ending up losing thirty of them, while Fredo, who was at a loss what to do, played billiards by himself, and the ship, anchored in midstream, was awash with rain.

7

THEY STAYED LIKE THAT FOR TWO WEEKS, AND DURING ALL THAT time Mittel heard not a single word of complaint or criticism regarding the captain. Nor did the crew appear in any way discouraged.

And yet from the very first it was evident that they were in for a long period of waiting. On the morning of the second day, Boussus went to see the captain and suggested that, to save fuel, the boilers should be turned off. Mopps merely stared gloomily at him, then murmured, with a shrug, "Do whatever you think best."

No one asked him to explain himself. They watched him go ashore, and hours later they saw him return, and when he went into his cabin without giving any orders, they knew that this was not to be the day.

The oddest thing was that they regarded him with the indulgence generally accorded an invalid. They took pains to avoid annoying him, even tried to anticipate his wishes.

Chopard had taken it upon himself to make an important decision. Instead of allowing the men to idle aimlessly on shore, he contrived, in spite of the rain, which was still pouring down, to organize a complete overhaul of the ship: scraping the hull, scrubbing the decks, renewing the paint work, and so on.

The freighter remained at anchor in midstream, swinging around with every tide, sometimes from the force of the current, sometimes from the confluence of the river and the ocean swell.

The water grew daily muddier under a milky sky. The men had tried wearing rubber sea boots, but they could not stand them for very long, because of the heat. The only alternative was to go barefoot.

News was scarce.

"Gomez has been killed, and they no longer want our weapons in Guayaquil."

What of the future? What did Mopps intend to do? What were he and Fredo planning, and what did Fredo have in mind when, on the fifth day, he boarded an American aircraft for Panama?

Charlotte had accompanied the captain ashore only once, and returned sickened by what she had seen. She spent most of her time in bed, complaining endlessly and becoming daily more neurotic and irritable.

Yes, what was Mopps going to do? They waited. They watched his every move, endeavoring to read the signs.

"One of these days, when we're least expecting it, he'll pull himself together," said Jolet, who had been given the job of unscaling the boilers. "One day soon, he'll be giving us our orders."

But what orders? It was precisely because the men could see no satisfactory outcome to his predicament that they were indulgent of Mopps's defeatist mood.

The captain would spend entire mornings in the hotel, feeding half-pesos into the slot machine and drinking whisky. Sometimes the proprietor would bring him people who had just arrived from Guayaquil, but he would not even look up.

What difference could it make to him, now that the revolution had failed, resulting in horrific reprisals, with severed heads left lying to rot? All these rumors buzzed around his ears like bluebottles, and he concentrated more than ever on turning the handle of the slot machine.

The stark fact was that he could not land his machine guns in Ecuador, and consequently there was no hope of payment. By now, the whole of South America was aware of the nature of his cargo. Was Peru in a position to buy arms?

He had cabled to that country, and also to Chile. Fredo had flown to Bogotá, but all to no avail.

What was to be gained by setting sail and using up the small stock of coal remaining in the bunkers? Hakim, in Panama, was furious. And on top of everything else, the rain never let up. Their clothes now clung to them like lukewarm compresses.

Mopps withdrew into himself, and no one could tell what he was thinking. Not once did he make the effort to go as far as the wooden town, a mere five hundred meters away. He plied regularly between the ship and the hotel. He fed pesos into the slot machine and glanced languidly at the people who disembarked from ships to catch the train to Cali next morning.

The Colombian government had dispatched four civil guards to keep watch in shifts on the wharf, to prevent the weapons from being brought ashore. As if he would want to unload machine guns that nobody wanted to buy!

He had no money to go back through the Panama Canal. He was a wanted man, and every harbormaster in France knew it. Did he have as much as a week's supply of coal? Barely . . .

All this time, Chopard, first-class petty officer that he was, supervised the repainting of the ship, raging over every speck of rust or dust overlooked, ensuring that all paint brushes were spotlessly clean and all paint was properly thinned.

To add to their troubles, the paint would not dry! Everyone was spattered with it. Water streamed down the companionways, and some days the curtain of rain was so dense that even the trees on the banks were invisible.

One of the Bretons had taken up fishing. He had caught two large fish, which looked like tuna, but within an hour they smelled so foul that no one dared eat them.

In the evenings, the men went ashore in little groups, like soldiers setting out from their barracks. They did not patronize the hotel, where the prices were too high. But in the little wooden town itself there was a long bar, and behind it shelves on which hundreds of bottles were displayed. There were two black bartenders. The seamen leaned on the bar and drank till bedtime, ignoring the few scruffy prostitutes who were always hanging around.

They never said to themselves, "There's no way out of this mess."

Or "Only a miracle can save us."

No, they were all of one mind: "Give Mopps a chance to think, and he'll find a way out!"

He had suffered a severe blow. They could feel that he was shattered, and going around in circles like a wounded bear. He was drinking twice as much as he normally did, but showed no outward sign of it, though sometimes he had to keep a very tight rein on himself to conceal his drunkenness.

"What, are you still here?" he would say to Charlotte, who was always in bed before he got back.

Roughly he pulled back the covers, looked thoughtfully down at the naked girl, then sighed and covered her up again. Charlotte was terrified.

"Do the police know I'm here?" she asked one morning.

"What do you think?"

"So what would they do, if I set foot on land again?"

"Nothing at all. France has requested your extradition from four or five countries, but fate has decreed that she forget Colombia. That's how it always is!"

For three days, he neglected to shave. As for Voisier, he was scarcely ever seen. He remained holed up in his cabin or in the officers' mess, filling a notebook with small, cramped writing. This was his diary, which he had been keeping for years.

This time, he confided to his diary, *I think we shall have to get ourselves repatriated as paupers. Mopps has gambled and lost. Eventually, he will be forced to abandon his ship, but God alone knows where.*

In any case, the *Croix-de-Vie*, with or without its illicit cargo, would not be able to show itself in any French seaport. The deception had been uncovered.

What a rain of harsh blows fate had dealt them! If only Gomez had not started his revolution too soon, everything would have been different. The machine guns would have been sold, Gomez would undoubtedly have been ruling the country, Mopps would have got rich from the sale of the machine guns, and Hakim would have been happy. . . .

One morning, as he was climbing over the rail to reach the motorboat, Mopps came face to face with Mittel, who looked wan, with dark circles under his eyes, and who, like all the others, was dreadfully pale. Mopps stopped in his tracks.

"How are you holding up?" he asked, frowning.

It was such a small thing, yet it was at that moment that Mittel first became aware of the captain's affection for him. Mopps regarded him as one would a delicate child, a child inescapably destined for misfortune.

"Chopard isn't too hard on you?"

Then, in a lower tone, almost confidentially: "Be patient. It'll only be two or three more days. . . ."

What was he mulling over in his mind? The map of South America must be forever in his thoughts. His ship had no more than a week's supply of coal in its bunkers. Doubtless, Mopps was endlessly steering the ship from north to south, from east to west, only to be defeated by the same obstacles—coasts, ports, customs, and police.

He was imprisoned in this river, under a canopy of rain. So, dragging his feet, he slouched into the hotel bar, and the river remained with him, for it was still there, visible from the windows, with the freighter in midstream tugging at its anchor, the flag drooping from its stern.

"Give me some change!"

He was hypnotized by the slot machine, so much so that he worked the handle like an automaton. A Frenchman, a sales representative in toiletries who covered the whole of South America, thought it only civil to introduce himself.

"It's such a pleasure to meet a fellow countryman. What will you drink, Captain?"

"Nothing."

"Have you come straight from France? Are you intending to return there in the near future?"

"Maybe."

"It's a shame you hit the rainy season. The rest of the year, the weather is quite tolerable. You can take it from me, because I've been coming to South America for the past twenty-two years."

Mopps turned his back on him.

"Go get Dominico!" he called out suddenly to the bartender. "Tell him to come and see me at once."

The freighter had now been at anchor outside the port for ten days. Dominico had come aboard on the second day. He visited every ship soon after it arrived, for he dealt in such essentials as oil, coal, kerosene, and stores, as well as exporting coffee and cocoa and importing machinery. His offices were in the hotel itself, and occupied the whole of the top floor. In addition, he owned half the wooden houses in town.

On at least twenty occasions, he had come into the bar and taken a seat close to Mopps, as if he were expecting some approach from the captain. And now, all of a sudden, the captain had sent for him—and then, having done so, turned back to the salesman, looking as if butter wouldn't melt in his mouth.

"Sorry—I had something on my mind."

"Would you care for a drink?"

"Thanks, a double whisky. I'll pour the drinks myself; I've sent the bartender upstairs with a message for my friend Dominico."

"You have to watch out when you're dealing with him, I warn you. I've known him a long time."

"So have I."

"He started out selling ice cream in the street, in Bogotá."

"Cheers!"

Dominico came bustling in ahead of the bartender.

"I had a message that you wanted to speak to me," he said in French, with a strong foreign accent.

"That's right, you old so-and-so," retorted Mopps, in impeccable Spanish. "What will you have to drink?"

"I never drink between meals."

Mopps emptied his glass and, completely forgetting to say good-bye to the cosmetics salesman, led the Colombian into a corner near the misted window. If one of the crew had come in at that moment, he would have been stunned, then would have returned to the ship immediately to announce, "We're leaving! Any time now!"

For the captain had resumed his normal hard expression, with just a hint of an ironic smile twitching the corners of his lips. He spoke in an undertone. Dominico replied almost in a whisper. The proprietor of the hotel came in two or three times to watch, for even he sensed that something momentous was afoot.

Three hours later, the two men, wrapped in a haze of smoke, were still talking, forgetful that it was long past lunchtime.

On board, Charlotte, wearing slippers, was combing her hair and giving her face a cat's lick, like a little child. She looked about languidly for somewhere to rest her weary body.

The sky was a deeper gray than in midwinter in Dieppe, and there was not a soul aboard who would not have chosen to suffer freezing hands rather than having to breathe this stifling air and endure perpetually clammy skin. Even their sweat had a more acrid smell than usual. The cabins smelled of mold. When Charlotte took off her shoes at night, she always found them covered with a thin layer of white. Voisier, scribbling away in his beloved diary, had to wipe his hands every five minutes. The paper was limp.

Everyone sighed. It was noon, precisely. A small cargo boat with accommodations for passengers, belonging to the Grace Line, which had arrived that morning, was already preparing to leave, with fifty passengers on board.

They would be in Panama in two days, and in New York in less than two weeks. There was talk in the newspapers of a cold spell in the city, charcoal braziers burning in the streets, of the provision of aid for the unemployed, of a toll of sudden deaths. . . .

Mopps had not returned, but no one had an inkling that things had changed.

They sat down to their meal without appetite. They were already sick to death of the eggplant that was served at every meal, and even sicker of having the same tasteless meat. Jolet, who had written to his wife that morning, was peering through the mist as if he believed that the headland of Bénouville lay concealed behind it.

"The captain!" announced the first officer.

Water was trickling down from the canvas awnings, but getting soaked was preferable to sweating below decks. Mopps had just come down the steps and was shaking hands with Dominico, who lost no time in returning to the shelter of the hotel.

From the ship, they could see every detail of what was happening ashore. Mopps, his hands in his pockets, was strolling across the railroad track, stepping over the rails, weaving in and out between the rusty, deserted rolling stock, and finally striding across the quay, to await the arrival of the launch.

"He looks agitated," remarked Jolet, in surprise.

For they could see him gesticulating and could guess what he was saying to the crew of the boat:

"Why can't you ever get here on time?"

Only another three hundred meters to cover. The boat was driven off course by the current, but finally arrived at the foot of the ladder.

"Send for Boussus!"

They exchanged glances. Mopps had given the order crisply and was now looking around with a severe expression.

"Chopard! Kindly have all those paint cans removed!"

"What did I tell you?" exulted Jolet, almost before Mopps had turned his back.

"Do you really think so?"

"We're leaving, I'm sure! He's sent for the chief engineer. Next thing, we'll be starting up the boilers."

His eyes were moist. Suddenly he began eating with enjoyment.

Boussus remained up with the captain for a full ten minutes, and when he returned, it was indeed to issue orders.

"The boilers are to be started up tonight. The coal barges will be arriving at three."

"Coal!"

Jolet's expression was triumphant.

"He's done it!"

It was as if Boussus had won a personal victory. If coal was to be delivered, that meant that all was well, for you could not get coal without paying for it. And with the bunkers full of coal, they could travel great distances, perhaps even as far as Europe!

An hour later, a telegram was delivered on board. It was from Fredo.

ARRIVING BY AIR WEDNESDAY.

This very day! Mopps shrugged. Alone with Charlotte, over a meal, he never took his eyes off her, kept watching her with piercing intensity.

"What's the matter?" she asked. "Is there anything so special about the way I look?"

"There is something."

"Since when?"

"Since I first saw you."

"I want to know what's going on."

"What's going on is that I said, 'Go to hell!' "

"Who to?"

"To myself."

"I hate mysteries."

"Too bad!"

He did not yet feel ready to explain himself. At two o'clock, he went on deck to supervise personally the loading of the coal, which was beginning to arrive in the barges. Dominico was there as well, in black oilskins, checking the figures that his clerk was entering in a ledger.

"Mittel!"

The young man trembled as he went up to Mopps, who seized him by the shoulders and shoved him, not into his cabin, but into the deserted officers' mess.

"You and I are going to have to part."

Mittel was so shattered that he could not speak.

"It's hard to explain. Besides, you may already understand. You've seen what I've been like ever since we got here."

He filled his pipe and sat on the edge of the table.

"Stop looking at me like that, or I won't say another word! I was at the end of my tether. I . . . ."

He interrupted himself, and went on in a different tone of voice. "You know the expression 'going native'? It happens a lot in the colonies, and it means shacking up with a local girl. At first it doesn't seem to mean very much. One thinks of her as a sort of entertaining household pet. Then, gradually, one discovers that she has become indispensable. One's whole way of life is changed. One begins to shave less regularly, one no longer goes out at night, for fear of running into old friends. After a few months, one is eating nothing but native food. . . . And then, one day, one finds oneself longing to father a child. . . . Eventually one becomes practically unrecognizable as a white. I've known some to take to wearing only a loincloth. There are several not far from here, by the river."

Mittel was trying to fathom the relevance of all this.

"Well, in the last few weeks, I myself have been, in a kind of way, going native. I've been hanging around up there in bedroom slippers, trailing in Charlotte's wake, surrounded by her smell, her scruffy clothes, her personal odds and ends. . . . What's the matter with you?"

"Nothing."

He was simply bowled over, though he could not have explained why.

"I fully realized that I had to pull myself together. Especially since I don't for a moment mean to suggest I'm in love with her. Actually, if anything, I think I hate her! I've been driven to raising my hand to her, more than once. Sometimes a whole day goes by without my speaking a word to her. Do you understand?"

"No."

And yet he did, in a way, understand. There had been times when seeing Charlotte half dressed up there had reminded him of her room in Paris, and a lump had risen in his throat. And there had been times when he, too, had almost hated her.

"Well, now it's over."

And Mopps, drawing a deep breath, clamped his pipe between his teeth.

"I'm putting her ashore, and, under the circumstances, I'll have to leave you behind as well. There's nothing to be afraid of. I've fixed up everything. Tomorrow you will both be given forged passports in the name of Monsieur and Madame Gentil. The police will look the other way. . . ."

Mittel was so moved he could not speak.

"I need to be my old self, you know? I've gambled and lost. . . . Now what I need is a hair of the dog that bit me."

"What are you going to do?" Mittel asked, finding his voice at last.

Mopps shrugged.

"Will you go back to France?"

"That's out of the question."

"Do you have any money?" ventured the young man.

"Not a cent. Hakim is on his way here. I've asked him to extend my credit, but I'm sure he'll say no. I can't say I blame him, because, things being as they are, we'll never find a buyer for our machine guns."

He opened the door, as if to make sure that no one was eavesdropping, and closed it again.

"You're the one person I can speak the truth to. . . . When we're three or four miles out of here, in a couple of days, we'll ditch the guns in the sea, at a predetermined location, where the water is barely two meters deep at low tide. Are you beginning to understand?"

"No."

"Dominico has agreed to buy the weapons at a bargain price. He's arranging for a fishing boat—that square-rigged ketch over there, see?—to pick up the loot. It's worth every penny of one and a half million. . . . And d'you know what that swine is paying me? A few tons of coal, worth barely thirty thousand francs, and forty-eight thousand francs' worth of coffee. He is ruining me. One of these days, when I've managed to get my head above water again, I'll come back here and see how the two of you are managing."

It did not occur to Mittel to ask how he could make a living in this alien country, but Mopps had taken care of that, too.

"Dominico will put you on his payroll. You have a choice, either to stay in Buenaventura and work as a clerk, or to go upriver, three or four days' journey from here, and work in a small gold mine he owns."

Mittel was struggling to hold back his tears, and the captain averted his eyes.

"I can't leave Charlotte here all alone . . . and yet I don't want to drag her along with me, either."

"I understand."

"I'll be back, you'll see!"

It was obvious that he was being sincere, that he really hoped to be able to return.

"Come on. We'll go talk to her. I haven't told her anything yet."

Going out on deck, they met Fredo, who had just arrived.

"I was looking for you," he began. "My brother . . ."

"Won't give me any more money."

"How did you guess? What I can't make out is how you managed to get all that coal delivered."

"I'll explain, all in good time. Go and wait for me in the hotel. At the moment I've got other things to attend to."

———

Charlotte, who was washing clothes in the basin, looked up as the two men came in and realized at once that something important was afoot.

"What's going on?"

"You're going ashore tomorrow with Mittel."

"And the police?"

This was her obsession. It was a trap, she was sure, suspecting them of God knows what treachery.

"You will be given a valid passport. I've found a job for Jef."

"Is that true, Jef?"

"Perfectly true. The captain has done his utmost to help."

"Why couldn't he drop us off somewhere a bit more civilized?"

Mopps winked at Mittel. What could he say? Charlotte looked from one to the other of the two men before her with equal mistrust. Perhaps even with equal hatred? And yet both were ready to exert themselves to the limit for her!

Mittel almost quivered with happiness at the thought of living with her again, and Mopps, who sensed this, could barely suppress a twinge of jealousy.

"You'll sleep here as usual tonight. . . . No, on second thought, it would be better if you both spent the night in the hotel."

"Where's my passport?"

"It's being delivered this evening."

Still she was not wholly reassured.

"How are we going to earn a living?"

"I've told you already: Mittel has been promised a job."

But she persisted, and the two men had to smile.

"What kind of job?"

"President of the republic!" retorted the captain on his way out. "Come on, Mittel. I want to introduce you to Dominico."

"Well, should I get dressed or not?"

"You do that, and pack your things, too."

"So long, Jolet. I . . . I'm extremely grateful to you for being so kind to me. You, too, Napo. I'd never have been able to manage without you."

All around them was rain, coal, bustle.

"Are you staying on here?"

Mittel nodded. He couldn't speak. The river banks were pale-gray shadows in the fog. Only the concrete hotel stood out plainly, because it was four stories high.

"So long."

He shook hands with both men and looked around for Chopard.

"Good-bye, Monsieur Chopard."

And Chopard, who was also peering at the river bank, growled, "A smart pair, aren't you?"

"What do you mean?"

"All those tricks you two have been up to . . . If Godebieu had been here . . . Oh, well, the best of luck anyway."

Further handshakes, but more perfunctory ones. The launch was waiting. Charlotte, in black, was a depressing sight. She walked across the deck, ignoring everyone, and sat down on the wet seat in the launch.

"Row!"

Yellow fog, railroad tracks, derelict rolling stock to be avoided. They were taken up to the third floor of the hotel, to a room with twin beds hung with heavy mosquito nets.

Mopps had stayed downstairs, but he was not playing with the slot machine. He was arguing somewhat vehemently with Fredo.

"Well, if you insist, you can come with us. You'll be able to pay yourself out of what we get for the coffee, if we ever manage to sell it."

"I'd better cable my brother first."

"You do that!"

At eight o'clock the freighter raised anchor, but it did not at once make for the open sea. Rocked gently by the current, it was moored alongside the quay, where electric floodlights were being rigged up.

The dock gates were opened, and some fifty blacks and Indians began loading the coffee while groups of women and children, unprotected from the rain, stood watching expressionlessly. Perhaps this was their idea of entertainment?

"I'll look after them as if they were my own children," Dominico had promised when the captain introduced the young couple to him in the bar of the hotel.

He was a fat man with tiny hands and feet, dressed in a tussah-silk suit. All he cared about was the salvage operation to be carried out by the fishing boat. Ten times he went across to the quay, getting soaked each time, and on his return whispered in Mopps's ear. Mopps, looking far from happy, was sitting in the bar with Mittel and Charlotte, drinking.

"Do you have any money?" asked the captain.

Charlotte replied, "Nearly two thousand francs."

She did not notice Mittel flushing at the memory of the little alleyway in Dieppe, the darkened house, the money stolen from under her parents' mattress while her little sister sobbed with fear in her bed.

Mopps took some dollar bills from his wallet.

"You can pay me back when we meet again. I don't know what your decision will be, but if I were in your shoes, I'd go upriver."

The look he gave Mittel was charged with meaning. It was because of Charlotte that Mopps advised him to get as far away from the town as possible.

"What will I do with myself?" she asked.

"Housework, cooking . . ." He added, with an odd touch of irony, "Why not have a baby?"

"Thanks a lot!"

The hotel was almost empty. Nobody ever stayed there, except when a ship came in. The rest of the time the lobby was deserted, and there were not five people eating in the huge dining room. The half-caste waiters were wearing grubby shirts, and dinner jackets shiny with age. Their manner was familiar, and as they came and went, they looked Charlotte straight in the eye and smiled.

A short blast on the siren summoned Mopps aboard.

"When we meet again . . ." he repeated.

Then, patting the girl lightly on the cheek, "So long, Charlotte, my little imp of mischief . . . You're a strange bird, and that's a fact!"

For a moment he hesitated, then put his arms around Mittel and said, "So long, my boy. Chin up!"

And he was gone. The young people were alone in the bar, except for the waiters clearing away the glasses. There was nothing to do but go up to bed.

"I don't have any underwear, shoes, anything," remarked Charlotte as she took off her stockings.

Mittel lay in bed, crying soundlessly, until, at last, he fell asleep. Almost immediately, however, he sat up again, awakened by two blasts on the siren.

Day was breaking. He ran to the window and, braving the gusting rain, opened it.

The freighter, emitting a plume of black smoke, was steaming slowly toward the estuary. In the distance, two or three black, shadowy figures could be seen on deck. Chopard, most likely, whose job it was to be there, and one of the Bretons. But perhaps Jolet was also there, peering at the bank, hoping to catch a glimpse of Mittel?

A kilometer away, a small fishing boat was drifting with the current.

"What are you doing?" Charlotte asked drowsily.

"Nothing. They're leaving."

"Has Fredo gone with them?"

"I think so, yes."

She turned on her side and mumbled, "Get back to bed. Shut the window."

A jet of steam from the funnel, then a few seconds later the final blast from the siren.

The freighter's farewell!

There was no one in sight anywhere, not on the railroad tracks or on the patches of waste land.

Gently Mittel closed the window and, after a moment's hesitation, got back between sheets that were damp with his sweat.

PART TWO

8

CHARLOTTE WAS READING OVER MITTEL'S SHOULDER, BUT SHE WAS a faster reader than he was, or perhaps she skipped a sentence here and there. At any rate, periodically she would wander off until he had turned the page.

My dear Joseph.

I have received your letter giving me your new address. As you requested, I have addressed the envelope to Monsieur Gentil. I am glad to hear that you and Charlotte are both in good health, and I lost no time in passing on your news to our friends. The day after your departure, poor B . . .

In earlier and more troubled times, Mittel's mother had acquired the habit of referring to her friends by their initials only. In this instance, the man in question was Bauer, the bookseller on the Rue Montmartre.

. . . was taken to police headquarters and kept there for two days. Fortunately for him, Marthe (Bauer's wife) *is known to be of good character. It was she who came to the printer's to tell me what had happened, and to assure me that there was no need to worry. She's always smiling, such a cheerful soul that one would never guess that she has breast cancer.*

Mittel was also tempted to skip a sentence here and there.

I have seen D (an old friend of his father's, who was now editor of a weekly paper). *He says that Charlotte would be in deep trouble if she were caught, especially on account of the money she stole from her parents before she left. And while we're on this subject, some of the newspapers here say it was you who led her astray, and always refer to you by the name I need not mention. Little do they know!*

That "little do they know" was so typical of Bébé—even now she was known to all her friends by that nickname—who was hopelessly gullible, and who, like Madame Bauer, always looked on the bright side.

Did I tell you that the government has fallen yet again, and that last week there were riots in the streets? As I was leaving the printer's, I just missed being hit on the head by a club. We're expecting an announcement this evening about the formation of a new government.

So you see, everything goes on very much as usual here, and there really isn't anything of interest to tell you. If you are making a lot of money, don't forget your old mother. I've been longing for a fur coat ever since I don't know when, and T won't even allow me to bring it up.

Take care of yourself. My love to you and Charlotte.

It was signed "Bébé." They had always been friends, rather than mother and son, and Bébé, endlessly plotting sedition at secret meetings all over the place, and forever on the move from some attic to some furnished room, had never really got used to the idea of this child of hers, born of a chance encounter. Mittel could picture her at the printer's writing her letter with the linotype machines chattering away and a pile of damp proofs waiting to be corrected.

He turned to Charlotte, who shrugged.

"A lot of money!" she said snickering. "How do you like that?"

They both felt let down, Mittel especially. For three months he had been looking forward to receiving this letter, and had hoped for great things from it. Of course, he had no one to blame but himself. What, to be honest, was there to hope for? What he had really dreamed of was a letter bringing vividly to life the atmosphere and familiar smells of France, of Paris, of the neighborhood of the Rue Montmartre, where so much of his life had been spent. He would have liked news of all his former friends and acquaintances, of their reactions to his flight, and their feelings about his present position and future prospects.

He would have liked . . .

And yet his mother had said all there was to say, in simple language, stating all the facts without trimmings.

My love to you and Charlotte.

As if they were away on vacation in the Vosges or in Normandy! Political crisis! Demonstrations on the Place de la Bourse!

He unbuttoned his khaki shirt at the neck and stretched out his legs, in their coarse leather boots.

"Haven't you been to see Plumier yet?"

"His door was still locked this morning."

Needless to say, it was raining. For the entire three months that they had been living in the Chaco, there had not been three days when it had not rained for several hours at least. They had reached the point where they were disconcerted when they could no longer hear the pattering of raindrops on the corrugated iron roof.

Their wooden shack was raised on piles, and the few steps down from its front door led to a mire dotted with puddles, leaving them no choice but to step precariously across improvised walkways of planks, or to paddle through the water.

Mittel was dressed like everyone else who lived in the Colombian jungle, in boots, khaki shorts, and a shirt unbuttoned to the waist. Charlotte made her own dresses out of light cotton and wore nothing underneath.

They had both lost weight, and had dark circles under their eyes. Their movements had become more languid. In order to survive, they had to reduce the pace of living, and to be wary of unnecessary exertion, or they would end up bathed in sweat.

Facing the bungalow a few palm trees grew, and beyond, mangroves along the marshy riverbanks. Fifty meters away, almost hidden from view, was another bungalow, with a plaque on the door reading ANGLO-COLOMBIAN MINING COMPANY.

This was the office! It was also where Plumier, the Belgian geologist in charge of operations, slept, on a makeshift cot.

The natives lived in a separate compound, a hundred meters

farther away, in mud huts roofed with palm trees. Most of them were blacks, descendants of former slaves, but there were a few American Indians of almost unmixed descent.

The mining area, which extended over roughly a kilometer, was dotted with "excavations," where the sand was dug and sluiced to extract gold dust.

And that, for them, was where life came to a full stop. Mittel had never ventured farther afield, nor had Charlotte, for they both knew that beyond this point there was nothing but swamp stretching to infinity, clumps of mangrove with twisted roots, and occasionally an *esteros*, a sort of narrow canal among the many tributaries of the river.

Thirty or forty kilometers farther on, one might possibly come upon another mining area, supporting one or two whites and fifty or sixty natives.

As for visiting Buenaventura, the nearest town, it was such a long and painful journey that Charlotte shuddered at the very thought.

"Are you sure there's no other way of getting there?" she had asked repeatedly.

There was no other way. Far inland, on a clear day, one could dimly see the foothills of the Andes, but between them and the mountains was nothing but swamps ever more densely hemmed in by undergrowth, and in many places impenetrable.

And, on the seaward side, more swamps and mangroves, interspersed here and there with sandbanks.

They had traveled from Buenaventura with three canoes, loaded with all the equipment and stores provided by Dominico, for he was general manager of the mine, which belonged to an English company.

"On the spot you will find a white man, a geologist, who has been there for the past two years. I suspect he's beginning to go out of his mind. You'll have to acquaint yourself with the nature of the work, and see what needs to be done. Once a month, Moïse will call on you to collect the gold. He will weigh it in your presence and give you a receipt for it. He will also be responsible for bringing your mail and provisions."

The three canoes had sailed down the river to the sea, and Charlotte had spent the first five days in constant dread of some catastrophe. Indeed, the narrow craft, stabilized only by a long bamboo pole at each end, drifting onward a few hundred meters from shore, had been violently tossed by the heavy swell of the coastal currents.

From time to time they came to a cross-canal in the swamps, an *esteros* leading into a forest of mangroves, and for a few hours they glided through calm, if muddy, waters.

At least fifty times they had seen crocodiles floating on the water, and the natives had gestured to Mittel, warning him not to shoot.

They slept in the canoe itself, tormented by mosquitoes and listening to the sounds, the cracklings, in the fetid air of the jungle. Sometimes they managed to sleep, sometimes not, and when, at the end of ten days, the two wooden huts with corrugated iron roofs came into view, it seemed to them, for a brief instant, that they had arrived in paradise.

"Ah! So here you are, come to spy on me!" Plumier had exclaimed as Mittel came into the bungalow.

He was a man of barely thirty, but his eyes glittered feverishly, and he was alarmingly thin.

"Dominico sent me to . . ."

"To spy on me, I know, and if necessary to finish me off, if I prove too much of a nuisance!"

"I swear to you . . ."

"I know what I know! Have you at least brought me any anti-ascorbic-acid syrup? And my rat traps? And my sanitary buckets?"

"No, I . . ."

The office was a miserable hovel, and Mittel saw lying on the wooden floor two dead rats whose heads had been crushed by the heel of a boot.

"You see! I've been waiting three months—three months—since I warned them that if they didn't send me the things I needed, I'd soon be dead."

The instant he became agitated, sweat began streaming down his forehead and cheeks, and his eyes glared more fixedly.

"So they didn't show you my letters? Have you brought any syrup for your own use?"

"I was advised to do so, yes. I have six bottles. I could let you have . . ."

"Thanks a lot. And the traps?"

"I didn't know . . ."

"Where did you used to live?"

"In France."

The geologist snickered, gathered the papers scattered all over his desk, and declaimed:

"Make yourself at home here. All *I* ask is to be spared any contact with your esteemed self. Do just what you like. I have only one word of warning for you: Beware! I am on my guard! Furthermore, if anything untoward should befall me, there are people in Buenaventura who know the whole story. I trust that this is the last time I shall have occasion to speak to you."

That was three months earlier. Mittel had spent the first few days roaming around the mining area on his own. It had not taken long to learn the ropes.

The digging and sluicing was done by some sixty blacks and half-castes, some naked, some wearing a pair of old trousers, most of them barefoot.

His work consisted in choosing the right location—bends in the river enclosing alluvial deposits. The soil was loaded into a long, sloping wooden trough, open at both ends. Water was poured onto it at one end, gradually washing away the soil, until there was nothing left in the bottom of the trough but the gold, which not only was heavier, but also was held back by the roughness of the wood.

Before long, Mittel began talking to the work force in halting Spanish, with the aid of a dictionary that he had brought with him.

But until Moïse's next visit, he could do nothing officially. Whenever he went into the office, which was also Plumier's bedroom, the geologist either stalked out or began sluicing himself with buckets of water. As he had threatened, he spoke not a word, but mumbled to himself unintelligibly, snickering and gesticulating all the while.

Moïse turned out to be a genial old man who arrived with three Indians in a canoe. He adopted a pleasantly teasing manner toward Charlotte.

"How is he?" Moïse asked, pointing to the office.

"He refuses to speak to us."

That day Plumier went and hid deep in the jungle to avoid Moïse. The old man took advantage of his absence to instruct Mittel in how to keep records, pay wages, and distinguish between gold-bearing and barren soil. About Plumier he advised, "Ignore him. There's nothing we can do about it. He absolutely refuses to return to Buenaventura. The only way to get rid of him would be to take him back by force."

"How long has he been mad?"

"He's not altogether mad, but after living alone so long, he's got a lot of strange notions in his head. He believes the company has it in for him because he keeps writing unfavorable reports. According to him the desposits aren't worth the labor, and he claims that he's being used as a scapegoat for heaven knows what malpractice. . . ."

Mittel frowned. Moïse introduced him to the men and instructed them to take their orders from him. Next day he left, carrying a little bag of gold dust. He also undertook to mail the young couple's letters to France. And this was how Mittel was able to inform his mother of his new address, and tell her to write to him under the pseudonym of Gentil.

Moïse was paying his third visit. The company owned other claims besides this one, and the old man, who forty years before had panned for gold on his own account, regularly visited them all in his canoe, accompanied by his three Indians.

Leaving Mittel to read his mail, he had wandered off to the office to check the books.

Charlotte had relit the stove, for in honor of Moïse she always cooked a proper meal of almost European quality, and even set the table with a cloth.

Mittel got up to go join the old man, and had reached out his hand for his pith helmet when Charlotte, wiping her wet hands, suddenly said, "Jef!"

"What is it?"

"Don't go yet. There's something I've got to talk to you about, now that Moïse is here."

He was amazed to see that she seemed grave, even emotional.

"I've been meaning to tell you for a long time. . . . Don't look at me like that. . . . I'm pregnant, Jef!"

He gave a start, for this was the last thing he had expected.

"What? You! You're . . ."

It had never entered his head that Charlotte might have a child.

"Are you sure?"

"I couldn't be more sure. I'm in my third month."

He did not know what to think. He put his helmet on the table and gazed at the floor.

"A child . . ."

Suddenly, he jerked up his head.

"Whose is it?"

For it was just three months since they had reached Colombia, and he had not forgotten Mopps, from whom they had had no word in all that time.

"Listen, I can't swear to it, because I'm not absolutely sure, but you remember that first day in Buenaventura?"

He had often thought of it. He could even remember that it was a Sunday.

After the freighter had sailed away, he had tried to go back to sleep but had not been able to. Feeling totally abandoned, he had got up without making a sound and crept into Charlotte's bed, simply seeking company in his loneliness.

"What is the matter with you?" she had mumbled, only half awake.

He was weeping with pity for himself, for her. Why, he wondered, had he allowed Mopps to . . .

It was strange how they had come together again, their former love for each other reawakened in both of them. It was five in the afternoon before they had got up and went downstairs, where Dominico had surveyed them with a knowing leer.

They had never, from that day to this, referred to the episode. They had enough to do facing the troubles that beset them from day to day. Every evening Charlotte, in her nightgown, held up the electric lamp—the *foco*, as it was known locally—while Mittel waged war on the rats. Sometimes they managed to kill ten, sometimes as many as fifteen, and yet no sooner had they gone back to bed than the scratching, chittering, and squealing resumed, first behind every wall and then on the floor, like a party of guests arriving for a ball.

Now Mittel understood why Plumier's bungalow was full of dead rats. He understood the need for traps. Indeed, Moïse had just brought them some.

But there remained the fleas and the spiders.

They had also had to cope with illness, with no medical aid available. First they had encountered dysentery, and for days they had both felt utterly drained, like a couple of collapsed bladders, and had been scarcely able to walk as far as the door of their bungalow.

"If other people have coped, so can we," Mittel declared repeatedly.

127

They had a supply of medicines, quinine and anti-ascorbic acid, which they took at regular intervals. They also carefully watched their diet.

They had no time to think of other things. They lived in close proximity, united as never before, and not once did they have the leisure to talk about themselves.

And then there was Plumier, who terrified them. He never moved unless he had an enormous Colt revolver tucked in his belt. From the moment he first set eyes on Charlotte, he had taken to roaming around outside the bungalow when Mittel was away. Sometimes he even ventured inside, and stood gazing at the young woman and snickering, while fiddling with some object he had picked up. Then, suddenly, he would leave, slamming the door violently behind him.

"Do you think it could be ours?" stammered Mittel, unable to overcome his emotion.

A child of his own! He wiped his forehead with the back of his hand. He felt unable to keep still.

"Three whole months . . ."

"I felt I ought to talk to you about it, because I'm sure there are arrangements that have to be made."

Still unable to take it in, he looked closely at Charlotte. She had lost weight and there was a new air of seriousness about her. He murmured, "You're going to have a child."

But it did not occur to him to take her in his arms. Since that Sunday three months ago in their hotel room, they had not been living as man and wife. Even before, when they had been together for two years, they had been friends more than lovers, and the closest they came to any expression of affection was when, just before going to sleep, they addressed each other by pet names:

"Good night, Jef."

"Good night, Lotte."

Suddenly he exclaimed, "I must have a word with Moïse about it!"

He rushed out into the rain, splashing through puddles, and she had to call him back, because he had forgotten his helmet. They scarcely ever got a glimpse of the sun. The sky was always dark and lowering, and yet the solar rays were so intense that it was dangerous to go out of doors bareheaded.

Once Charlotte had gone out without her helmet and had spent the next two days in bed, suffering from appalling headaches and dizziness.

"Listen, Moïse . . ."

"Shh. Three plus seven plus four equals fourteen . . . carry one . . . eight plus nine plus . . ."

There was no sign of Plumier, and the bungalow was a mess, with the cot unmade and a dirty shirt lying on the floor. Most of the time, the Belgian kept the door locked against the native boy who was supposed to be his servant, because he mistrusted him, as he did everyone else, and he always cooked his own food.

"What do you want?" Moïse spoke with a foreign accent, German or Alsatian, but Mittel had always felt too shy to ask him where he came from originally.

"Charlotte is expecting a child."

"When?"

"In . . . let me think . . . six months from now."

The old man found it hard to keep from bursting out laughing.

"I see! Well, you've got plenty of time to think about it, my dear boy!"

"But don't you see, there are all sorts of arrangements to be made. Wouldn't it be advisable for her to see a doctor, for instance? And when the time comes we'll have to travel to Buenaventura."

"Easy does it! Don't jump the gun! Who's to say whether things will ever reach that stage?"

"What do you mean?"

"Here in the tropics, there's always the risk of a miscarriage. We'll talk it over again in two or three months, if necessary. And another thing: I've known women to manage very well without a doctor. The natives are amazingly skillful in such matters."

Mittel's eyes flashed with anger.

"Come now, there's nothing to get excited about. You're still new to these parts. You look at things as if you were still in Europe, and besides, you're very young. I know what I'm talking about. I've fathered seven children, and three of them were delivered by no other midwife than myself. I'm sure you'll manage just as well."

"I don't agree."

"Let's leave the subject for the moment. Oh, and by the way, how are things with our friend Plumier? This time I haven't forgotten to bring him his anti-ascorbic acid. Mind you, in my day we didn't go in for all these fancy medicines, and I'm still here, and none the worse for it. . . . Here's the bottle. Tell him what's in it when you give it to him. As for the traps, there just wasn't room for them in the canoe."

They were both soaking wet. It was always so here: everyone was streaming with a mixture of rain and sweat.

"What's troubling you?"

"I'm thinking about the baby."

"A baby who may never be born! Incidentally, Fredo is back in Colón, but he didn't travel in Mopp's ship. Mopps dropped him off in some little backwater in Mexico, and hasn't been heard of since."

Mopps, Napo, Jolet, Chopard, the stokehold, the boiler, the seamen's quarters, the bridge looming above, the captain's cabin with the two beds in it . . .

All that was already so remote that Mittel found it difficult to believe that it had ever really existed. He had been abruptly transported to another world, and now the only reality was this muddy bog drenched in rain, where there was a community of some hundred souls engaged in extracting from the soil the gold that Moïse came to collect every month.

And as far as Moïse was concerned, Charlotte and the child she was expecting did not exist! With a few brief words he had swept them out of his mind.

"Have you heard that they have found platinum on the Timbiqui site? We ought to be prospecting for it here as well. If Plumier was fit for anything, I'd have a chat with him about it, and, who knows, we might come across a seam. . . . The river, the terrain, and the nature of the soil are all very similar."

"Tell me honestly—you're experienced in these matters—are there no precautionary measures we should be taking, such as sending for essential medical supplies?"

"So we're back to that again! No, of course not. I know! Let me have a talk with the girl myself."

Mittel chose not to be present at this meeting. He was sure that Moïse was not one to mince words. When Jef went back to join them in the bungalow, he found Charlotte looking stricken.

"What did I tell you? She's got the courage of a lion, that girl. One of my wives, my third or fourth, I can't quite remember, I've had seven in all, counting only the legal ones—as I was saying, one of my wives kept right on working up to the very last minute. . . . I was out at the time, and when I got back that evening, the baby was born. He'd done it all by himself, like the manly little fellow he was."

Charlotte was so pale that Mittel feared she would faint.

"What are you giving us for dinner? I hope you noticed that I brought you an ample supply of provisions. Fifty cans of beef, and fifty of sardines. That's in case I find I can't manage to get here next month."

"Aren't you planning on coming?"

"Well, the thing is, one of my sons is getting married in Guayaquil. If Dominico has any feelings at all, he'll have to give me leave to go to the wedding, especially since the bride is from one of the best families in the district."

"That means two months without . . ."

Without seeing a soul! Without any kind of contact with the outside world! Moïse might not be the most desirable of companions, but that did not alter the fact that they looked forward eagerly to his visits and took comfort in his company.

Mittel couldn't help having a new attitude toward Charlotte. He would have liked to make sure she got plenty of rest, to look after all her needs, to feed her on expensive and tempting delicacies.

"I've made a stew of bacon and haricot beans," she said, lifting the cover of a casserole.

But the smell that filled the kitchen made her stomach heave.

"I've brought two bottles of whisky as well," announced the old man. "No matter if you don't drink it yourselves. I'm here, aren't I? Come to think of it, I wouldn't say no to a glass."

It was not a day like any other. Mittel did not go to work at the excavation. After lunch he and Moïse strolled over there together, but merely for the walk. They knew that Plumier must be skulking behind some clump of trees, but the geologist was careful to keep out of sight.

"In my time," observed Moïse, pointing to the blacks, "the work force was mainly freed slaves. Just think, all of them were brought over from Africa in chains! Now there are some who can't even find work. I can remember when, if they wanted to earn a living, they had to hack their way into the jungle, to find the bark to extract quinine from. As for the Indians, we used to call them the *arrieros*. They were employed as bearers. Traveling across the country, one was carried in a litter from village to village, changing bearers at every stop, the way the stagecoaches used to change horses."

There were very few Indians left. They formed less than ten percent of the work force. The rest were blacks or half-castes.

Mittel gazed up at the dim gray mountains, which looked like a cloud bank. Beyond were more mountains, with rivers and valleys between. A vast continent, crossed here and there by mountain ranges, sparsely populated with little communities, whites from Europe, and the black descendants of slaves from Africa.

And it was here, in one of these tiny communities, that he, who had lived in Paris such a short time ago, was going to become a father!

We're expecting an announcement this evening about the formation of a new government, his mother had said in her letter.

Tonight meaning approximately four weeks ago! Even time moved at a different pace here.

Moïse always brought his own hammock with him and hooked it up in a corner of the bungalow, which consisted of a single room with a built-in cupboard for provisions.

The rat hunt took place as usual, but on this occasion they killed only three. Charlotte had already gone to bed. Now Moïse could be heard puffing as he hitched himself up into his hammock, then tossing and turning, trying to make himself comfortable

"Good night, you two."

Nothing by way of light but the pale circle of the *foco*, which Mittel switched off as soon as he got into bed.

As a rule, on account of the heat, he lay as far away from his companion as possible, but tonight he groped in the dark for her body, and gently, silently, almost without touching her, he slid his arm under her head.

Charlotte did not move. He could feel her hair against his cheek, the dampness of the back of her neck, her arms folded on her chest.

The rain had stopped, as sometimes happened at this time of night. He could hear nothing but the water still dripping off the sloping roof and, from time to time, coming from the river, the sound of a tree hitting some obstacle as it was borne away on the current.

Then furtive footsteps. Another thing he had had to become accustomed to. The blacks could never bring themselves to retire for the night like other people. Like cats, or wild animals, they would get up in the middle of the night and wander off, God knows where. Some went fishing. But the rest?

"Pay no attention," Moïse had urged on his first visit. "They're all alike. You find the same thing in Africa."

And he had added, with a laugh, "They're like tom cats on the prowl, mostly."

They made almost no sound, which was all the more disturbing since it was impossible to tell whether they were coming or going.

A rat pattering into the middle of the room . . . There was a sound of scratching.

Charlotte remained motionless, and, almost without thinking, Mittel drew her closer and pressed his cheek against hers.

He could think of nothing to say to her. He felt great pity for her. He believed that there was a chance she might die, and if that were to happen, what would her life have amounted to?

Gently he lifted one hand and did something he had never done before: he stroked her forehead. He had not closed his eyes. He could see nothing, but he lay there wide-eyed, staring into the dark.

He felt hot, but not uncomfortable. He lay still, thinking. . . .

"You're suffocating me!" she sighed, moving out of his reach.

And what were her thoughts as she lay there? In any case, after shaking Mittel off, she felt for his hand and gave the tips of his fingers a furtive little squeeze.

It was so brief, and she resumed her normal position so quickly, that Mittel wondered. Had she done it out of kindness, so as not to hurt his feelings, or was it her way of expressing what he himself felt, that this day had been different from other days?

Then he thought of Mopps.

A quarter of an hour later, feeling keyed up, he groped for the lamp, got out of bed, and knocked the rat across the bungalow with his boots.

9

ANOTHER TWO MONTHS PASSED. PLUMIER REMAINED FAITHFUL TO his oath never to address a word to Mittel, even though he had to go into the young couple's bungalow almost every day to collect his share of the provisions. He never knocked, but always strode in, carrying an enamel saucepan. Then, taking his time, he would go to the larder and pick out what he needed. Often, instead of leaving at once he would linger there, as if it were his own home, sometimes even glancing through a pile of papers on the table, lifting the cover off a saucepan, or examining Charlotte closely from head to foot. Particularly now that she was pregnant: he seemed to derive some amusement from the young woman's changing shape.

Mittel had leaned from Moïse a little more about his disquieting colleague. Plumier came originally from a little village near Liège. His parents had owned a farm there, and he had been educated in a Jesuit college.

At twenty-five, having completed his education, he had applied for jobs in the Belgian Congo, but, nothing suitable being available at the time, he had taken a position at the Cockerill Works. He remained with the firm for three years, until, one day, he came across an advertisement in the Help Wanted column of a technical journal:

Geologist with first-class qualifications required for senior post with gold-mining company. Surety must be provided.

His parents had paid out a hundred thousand francs, which, supposedly, was invested in the company.

It was a grave emergency that finally persuaded him to break his vow of silence.

Moïse must have gone to attend his son's wedding in Guayaquil, as he had said he would, for he failed to pay his regular visit at the end of the month. A further two weeks went by, and then suddenly Charlotte began showing signs of extreme debility. Yet this was one of the few periods of the year when they sometimes enjoyed several consecutive days without rain. The sky was brighter. The sunlight, shining through the mangroves, made elaborate shadow patterns on the ground.

For the first three days, Charlotte wandered listlessly around the bungalow, but on the fourth day she was unable to get up and had a temperature of 104°. Mittel did not leave her side all that day, and late that afternoon he grew even more alarmed, when she became delirious.

Plumier chose this moment to arrive, as usual without bothering to knock. He went to the cupboard to fill his saucepan with rice, then crossed to the bed, opened the young woman's mouth, and peered down her throat.

Mittel lacked the courage to protest. The intruder's expression was blank, his manner phlegmatic. Putting his saucepan down on the floor, he pulled back the sheet and, without embarrassment, hitched Charlotte's nightgown up as far as her stomach, which was covered in little red patches that temporarily disappeared when pressed with a finger.

Mittel was completely bewildered.

"What is it?" he asked.

"Typhoid."

And, picking up his saucepan, Plumier walked out of the bungalow, leaving Charlotte's stomach still exposed. For a moment or two, Mittel was so stricken by this revelation that he sat frozen in place. Then, suddenly, he sprang to his feet and dashed into the geologist's bungalow, to find him calmly preparing his meal.

"I think it's essential for us to get away from here," he panted. "We'll go to Buenaventura, where at least there is a doctor available. But meanwhile, I beg you, tell me what to do."

"What do you mean?"

"How I can set about getting there."

"There's no means of *getting there*, as you put it," retorted Plumier sententiously.

The sun was setting, and its slanting purplish-red rays streamed into the office. The Belgian had lit a kerosene stove and was busy stirring his bubbling rice.

"Why not in canoes?" murmured Mittel, who felt that there was no time to be lost.

"It's true, we have two canoes, but no men capable of getting you as far as Buenaventura in them."

"I don't understand. There's the work force. . . ."

"They're a feeble bunch, and not one of them has ever made the trip. They'd never be able to find their way through the *esteros*."

Mittel's eyes widened as he recalled the first thing that had struck him on arrival here: it had surprised him that the Indians who had brought them had gone back to the town instead of remaining with them.

"Do you understand now?" said Plumier, with gloomy satisfaction. "Neither you nor I will ever get out of this place, that's what I mean! Take a good look around you. This landscape is the last you will ever see, as long as you live!"

"It's not possible. . . ."

"And why not? If there was even a ten-to-one chance of escaping, do you imagine that I would still be here?"

He snickered, turned off the stove, and sat down to his meal at the end of the table.

"I tell you we're prisoners here, all three of us, even if you are one of *them* . . ."

Mittel did not know what to make of this. There were times, it seemed to him, when Plumier behaved like a perfectly rational man, and others when his colleague's gestures and grimaces scared him out of his wits.

"What's to prevent me from selecting six natives and just leaving?"

"They'd refuse to go with you."

"We'll see about that!"

The day's work came to an end. The men were back in the village, squatting outside their huts. Mittel looked around him for those he knew best. But when he spoke of returning by canoe to Buenaventura, they shook their heads.

"But why not?"

"Señor Moïse has forbidden it."

Mittel's temper rose, he tried to insist, but the blacks remained impassive and went on shaking their heads. Mittel returned to Plumier's bungalow, his eyes hard, his expression fierce.

"It's true!" he exclaimed.

"You don't say."

"They won't take me. The fact is that they won't take orders from anyone but Moïse!"

"Well, I told you, didn't I?"

"But why should they want to keep us prisoners here?"

"I've already explained. They don't want it to come out that the mine produces only a few thousand pesos' worth of gold per month. The project was launched with a fanfare of publicity. They have persuaded thousands of dupes to invest in it, and will persuade thousands more. That's why none of my letters that refer to the mine ever get through, not even those to my mother. Yours are opened and censored as well." He laughed wildly. "They told you I was mad, didn't they? Well, I could name someone else who very soon will be."

After a long silence, Mittel asked, "Are you sure it's typhoid?"

"Do you see that medical textbook above my bed? Take it and read it, but be sure to return it when you're done with it."

Charlotte lay very still, except when, from time to time, she stretched out her hand as if to grasp some nonexistent object, or, at other times, pressed her hand against her left side and whimpered.

It was growing dark. Mittel had already read the chapter on

typhoid fever ten times at least. His eyes glazed, he reverted ceaselessly to the concluding paragraph:

Typhoid in pregnant women is likely to produce abortion or premature birth. Roughly ten percent of mothers die in childbirth. The fetus is in most cases born dead. In rare cases, usually in the eighth month of pregnancy, the child may be born alive and survive.

Charlotte was thirsty. He was forever bringing her something to drink, wondering whether this was the right thing to do. The trouble with Plumier's book was that, although it described the symptoms of diseases, it had nothing to say on the subject of treatment.

After about three weeks, the temperature goes down.

But what should he be doing for her during those first three weeks? Should he still be giving her quinine?

And the rats still came, in spite of the *foco*. They were frightened of nothing! Mittel had not even thought about eating.

Surely the best thing was to get the patient to sweat? He had covered her up to the chin, and she lay there for an hour, her skin dry, her face flushed. She felt stifled and tried to throw off the covers.

Then Mittel heard furtive footsteps. A passing native, perhaps? But when the door opened, it was Plumier. With assumed indifference, he went up to the bed, took Charlotte's pulse, and once more opened her mouth to look at her tongue.

"There's something I think we might try. Would you agree to it?"

"What do you have in mind?"

"That you and I should carry her to the river between us, give her a good soaking, and then wrap her in heated blankets. If we get her to sweat, she'll at least have a chance."

"Do you think so?"

"When my sister had the same thing, during the war, my parents sent for the best-known doctor in Brussels, and that was how he saved her life. The question is, as far as your wife is concerned, whether she wouldn't be better off dead."

"What do you mean?"

"Nothing. The way things stand now . . ."

Mittel could not make up his mind. It was Plumier who stripped the covers off the invalid and put his hands under her arms to lift her.

"You hold her feet. Leave the *foco* where it is; otherwise we'll be tormented by mosquitoes."

Through the tree trunks, they could see the fires from the native village, and a few shadowy, crouching figures. The two men braced themselves, then sank their feet into the sandy riverbank.

"We'll have to dip her under just once, to keep a grip on her."

There was no moon. Indeed, it was so dark that they could barely see the pallid form they were carrying.

"One, two . . . go!"

And Plumier, holding down the girl, who had suddenly started struggling under water, barked, "Go and get the blankets ready!"

When Charlotte reappeared in the bungalow, lit only by the *foco*, Mittel was forced to avert his eyes. Water was still dripping from her face. She was drooling, and the wet hair clinging to her skull made her head look very small.

"Good night!" said Plumier.

"What am I supposed to do now?"

"Wait. If you wait long enough, we'll all be dead."

And he went out, snickering.

In pregnant women . . . said the medical textbook.

Mittel sat down on a stool. An hour later, just as he was about to doze off, he seemed to see beads of perspiration forming on Charlotte's forehead.

He could keep awake no longer. At first, after switching off the lamp, he lay down on the floor, but later, in the dark, he roused himself and stretched out on the bed, beside the body, burning with fever, of his woman.

By the third day he had read the whole book, paying special

140

attention to the chapters on childbirth. He scarcely ever set foot outside the bungalow. Plumier did not show up for two days, and Mittel had no idea why. Then, one morning, Plumier came in, with the sarcastic greeting:

"Not dead yet?"

Was he thoroughly mad, or only intermittently, with intervals of lucidity, as when he recommended immersing Charlotte in the river?

At any rate, the treatment had made her sweat, and her temperature had dropped to 102°. But the delirium persisted, as did the pain in her side.

Mittel had also read the chapter on appendicitis. He was bewildered. There were so many possible causes; how could he tell which was the relevant one?

"Two babies died this morning in the village!" announced the Belgian cheerfully.

"What of?"

"Typhoid, of course! I can't think of a better solution to our problems than a raging epidemic that would put an end to all of us, followed by a great flood to wash away all the bodies and shacks. Then nature would reclaim her territory, leaving no trace of its former occupants, not even our friends the rats."

Then, after a pause for thought, "When I think that you came here to spy on me, and it was I who . . ."

Mercifully, the visit did not last long. Plumier walked out, setting his battered khaki helmet back on his head. Mittel and Charlotte were alone together once more. The outer world had receded. Now there was no Chaco, no mangroves, no river, no mine.

There was only a man and a woman. Mittel nursed Charlotte. He gave her liquids to drink. He swept the bungalow as best he could, and stayed on his stool by her bed.

It was very hot. He went around all day in pajamas and bare feet. Since he had given up shaving, he had the beginnings of a beard.

His mind was sluggish. He was still too distressed to feel fear or resentment, but his thoughts took on the color of the dingy floorboards, of the bedclothes, of the wooden box in which they were imprisoned.

If Charlotte were to die . . .

He wondered whether there was a single happy event for her to recall in her last moment. If one were to draw up a balance sheet, what would her twenty-two years of life amount to?

She had spent her childhood in Dieppe, on that steep little overcrowded street, a bare-bottomed infant with a runny nose. She had not stayed at the local public school long enough even to complete her elementary education. Instead, she had worked on the quayside, helping her mother to load herrings onto a barrow, when she was not at home looking after her younger sisters.

Paris . . . the apartment on the Boulevard Beaumarchais, the kitchen where Monsieur Martin used to seek her out . . .

Her fate was already sealed! No sooner had she grown disenchanted with her status in the little circle of freethinkers . . .

The truck from Paris to Dieppe . . . Mopps . . .

Had any of it been worth the effort? And suppose, he, too, were to die?

It was pitiful! He thought of Mrs. White, and others like her. Happy and successful people, like famous artists and statesmen, who might die before they were fifty, but not before they had lived life to the full.

Then he thought about the child. Who could tell? It might be born alive. No, according to the medical textbook, it would take a miracle. Charlotte herself had a ten percent chance of not pulling through.

And Plumier, who was not yet thirty! Twice Mittel reread his mother's letter, and then, for no good reason that he could figure, tore it up.

On the tenth day, looking much thinner, and still wearing his pajamas, which were now very crumpled, Mittel was sweeping the floor when he heard a voice behind him:

"What are you doing?"

For a second he could not believe his ears, then he turned around, gaping, and tore over to Charlotte's bedside, to find her watching him, her eyes clear and alert. She was no longer delirious. She was simply trying to understand what was going on. He felt so elated that he hugged her, until she whimpered, "You're hurting me."

"Listen, Charlotte! . . . You're out of danger!"

An expression of bewilderment filled her eyes, which had never left his face.

"It wasn't typhoid you had, I'm sure of that now! Otherwise your temperature would still be high. . . . Do you want to know what I think? I think it was a viral infection. . . ."

He felt triumphant. He burst out laughing. He was tempted to go get his medical textbook, and point out the relevant passages indicating the differences between the two diseases.

"You don't understand yet—how could you? Let me explain. If you had typhoid, the child would be dead. Whereas now . . ."

There were tears clinging to his eyelashes. He kissed Charlotte on both cheeks. Her skin still felt hot and feverish. And the young woman sighed wearily.

"Move back a bit. . . . Give me room to breathe."

"Whatever you say . . . I'll tell you the whole story later."

"I'm thirsty."

"Here, drink this. Plumier is going to have the shock of his life!"

For it was Mittel, and no one else, who had wrought this miracle. Now, with hope beginning to dawn, he wondered how he had managed to survive the last ten days in this temperature. He longed to fling open all the doors and windows, to talk to someone, anyone at all, to see men bustling around and laughing among themselves.

"In your case there was a ninety-percent chance of recovery, but there was no hope for the child."

Still utterly bewildered, she frowned, then closed her eyes. A few seconds later she was fast asleep. But what did it matter now? He was the one who had been right! He had refused to accept the possibility of Charlotte's dying before she had had any real chance to live!

The same was true of him. But they were both alive; all three of them were alive!

He was so overwhelmed that he could not wait to tell Plumier. He ran across to the office and found the geologist asleep, but shook him awake.

"It wasn't that!" he cried.

"Wasn't what?"

"Typhoid. A few minutes ago, she opened her eyes and spoke to me perfectly coherently, knowing exactly what she was saying. According to the book, it must have been a viral infection. . . . I've read the book from end to end—I know it by heart. Only another week or so . . ."

Plumier turned over, grumbling to himself.

"Is that all it means to you?"

"Why should it mean anything to me?"

"I thought . . ."

"I don't give a damn. I hate spies!"

"But I've already told you that . . ."

"Leave me alone, I want to get some sleep! I can't throw you out, since this is the office of the company, but I appeal to you to respect my privacy."

Undoubtedly, there was an element of exhibitionism in his makeup. At times he seemed to work at being obnoxious.

"And by the way, don't, on any account, forget to return my medical textbook," he shouted after Mittel's retreating back. "Since she got away with it this time!"

The next day, Charlotte was completely lucid. But she was still so weak that she could not hold a glass of water up to her lips. When she uncovered her body, Mittel was forced to avert his eyes: she was so painfully thin that it was terrifying to behold.

Was it possible, in spite of everything, that she could give birth to a healthy baby? She was nothing but skin and bones. She had the body of a starving child. When he touched her, she felt like a limp rag.

"Tomorrow I'll start catching up on my paperwork in here, because it won't be long now before Moïse's next visit. I'm completely out of touch with the digging. . . . Do you understand? I don't even bother to get dressed any more."

"You've grown a beard," she observed. Her voice sounded like a little girl's.

"Oh, yes . . ."

He laughed. His beard! His hair! He suspected he must look a little like Alfred de Musset, and he went to study himself in the little mirror on the wall.

"Take my word for it, I haven't had much time to think about such things. I've neglected a lot of other things, too, though I can't tell you everything, all at once. But listen! Just imagine a country where French is spoken, a real country, with towns and roads, trolley cars, houses built of stone and brick. . . ."

"Give me a drink!"

"Of course . . . Suppose we should find ourselves in such a country. I could take any old job, as a bank teller, say, or a bookkeeper. . . . I couldn't hope to earn more than a bare living, but we might manage to get a three-room apartment. And you'd pick me up at the office, bringing the little one with you. . . ."

Presumably, she could not understand what he was talking about, for she listened in blank silence, staring at the ceiling, and occasionally wincing with pain.

"In Paris, any such notion would have seemed laughable. But I've been brooding on it for ten days. I believe that now I could even work in a factory. After all, I managed well enough on board ship, didn't I? In spite of the fact that stoking is one of the most arduous of unskilled jobs."

"I actually think I'm hungry, Jef!"

"The book doesn't say whether it's safe for you to eat. I'll tell you what: I'll give you a little condensed milk, diluted with water."

He prepared it for her. It was still daylight, and the shuttered window admitted a few slanting rays of sunshine.

"When Moïse gets here, I'll put it to him straight."

"What?"

"I'll ask him whether or not we are being held prisoners here. . . . But I'd forgotten, you don't know anything about all that. When you fell ill, I wanted to take you back to Buenaventura, but Plumier swore it couldn't be done."

"So you're on speaking terms at last?"

"He even helped me take care of you. He's a queer fish. I instructed the blacks to take us back, but they refused. . . . They have orders from Moïse."

He had resolved not to cause Charlotte any anxiety, but now that he considered her cured, he could not help voicing his apprehensions.

"You'll see. I'll explain it all to you in detail. Plumier's theory is sound. It stands to reason that if the company is being fraudulently run, the last thing they'd want would be for us to return to civilization. According to Plumier, even our letters are censored."

He was ashamed of himself for having said so much when he saw that she could scarcely keep her eyes open. This time she had nightmares, muttering incoherently in her sleep and then suddenly letting out a piercing shriek.

He was still sharing her bed, unconcerned about the risk of infection, and he had not bothered, throughout her illness, to take even the most elementary precautions.

The next day it began raining again, with a vengeance. There was thunder and lightning as well, and a tree caught fire barely a hundred meters from the house. Perhaps it was the storm that had distressed Charlotte. While he was giving her a drink, she suddenly gripped him by the hand.

"You know, Jef, I've been thinking a great deal, too. I really believe the child is yours. . . . I'm sure of it! I feel it!"

"Of course."

"You had your doubts, didn't you? And it's been making you

146

unhappy. I'm very fond of you, you know! No one else would have looked after me the way you have."

"Shh! Don't talk such nonsense."

It made him feel ill at ease. He was almost afraid of anything approaching an endearment, because it would raise awkward questions about exactly what Charlotte meant to him, questions to which he did not know the answer. For instance, he was chary of using the word "love." In the sense in which he understood the word, he had never loved anyone.

If he had loved her, would he have retained his objectivity, or would he have been blind to all her faults?

He had abandoned her to Mopps without a struggle, and had it been the captain's wish, he might even have left Charlotte in Panama and stayed with the freighter.

More than once he had despised her. At other times he had come close to hating her.

But all that was over now. There was something new to bind them together, as well as these past ten days spent incarcerated in an atmosphere of fever and death.

Above all, there was her approaching childbirth, not to mention other ineffable factors, their solitude, their union in the face of hostile men and a hostile environment.

"I had the strangest dreams, Jef! I can't quite remember all of them now, but I know that I was weeping endlessly, I couldn't stop. And all the time, you were beside me."

He stared, and ran to the window.

"Moïse is here," he announced.

And he hastened to straighten the room.

"Get me a damp cloth and a comb."

She was too weak to comb her own hair, so he did it for her, as well as he could.

"Kiss me!" she begged.

Moïse was kicking the mud off his shoes against the steps.

"Anything wrong?" he asked, as he came in.

"My wife has been very ill. She's had a viral infection, but she's better now."

"I have just come from seeing my son married to the prettiest girl in South America. They've gone to Europe for six months."

Mittel and Charlotte exchanged furtive glances.

"What's the matter with you?" asked Moïse, whose sharp eyes never missed a thing. "You haven't even offered me a drink."

Mittel went to the cupboard, got out the bottle of whisky which was kept there especially for the old man's use, and poured a full glass: Moïse always drank it straight.

"There's something I've got to ask you, Monsieur Moïse. Why have we been left stranded here, with no one capable of paddling the canoes?"

"Good Lord! Don't you know why?"

"I'm almost afraid to know."

"Well, it's simple enough. The crop in these parts isn't cocoa, or coffee, or even rubber—it's gold, and in the future it may be platinum as well. What if it should occur to someone to make off with the loot?"

"Is that really the reason?"

"That's all there is to it."

"And what if one should find oneself needing to go into town to fetch a doctor, as a matter of life or death?"

"What would be the use? In a desperate case, such as you picture, it would be too late anyway."

"Another thing. Last time you were here, I mentioned Charlotte's forthcoming childbirth. Did you pass my request along to Dominico? Will he allow us to return to Buenaventura for two months?"

"There's no hurry."

"I demand an answer now."

"I daresay. . . . I suppose so. . . ."

"But it's not definite?"

Mittel spoke harshly, for the first time in his life. His beard, which he had decided to keep, had also wrought a change in him. Charlotte stared at him in amazement.

"Nothing is certain in this life."

"One last question. Is it true that our letters are censored?"

"What letters?"

Mittel was losing patience.

"Come on, Monsieur Moïse, don't play innocent. You know very well what I'm talking about."

"What I can see very clearly is that you have allowed yourself to be bamboozled by the maunderings of a madman. I trust, madame, that you are more levelheaded. And what's more, I have brought a letter addressed to you, and you can see for yourself that it hasn't been opened."

The envelope and writing paper were of the kind that could be bought at any little general store. The writing was ragged, the letter full of spelling mistakes.

My dear sister,

I am writing to tell you that I am well, and I hope you are the same.

It was from Marie, one of Charlotte's sisters, who was just sixteen. All her family's letters opened with that sentence.

I have only just learned your address, but Papa doesn't want us to write to you, and has even told the little ones that you are dead.

For two weeks after you passed through Dieppe, everyone was talking about you in the fishmarket, where I work with Mama. There were plenty of herrings, but the shoals were in very low water, and Papa's boat was put out of commission three weeks before the end of the season.

Mama hardly cried at all, but she never stops drinking. Papa beat her the day before yesterday.

Charlotte dropped the letter on the bed and listened to what the two men were saying.

"It's plain enough, surely. Did you or did you not sign a three-year contract?"

"Possibly. But I wasn't paying attention," retorted Mittel.

"Be that as it may, you did sign it. You are therefore under an obligation to honor it. You can't expect the company to turn everything upside down just because you've taken it into your heads to have a child."

He poured himself another drink.

"Come on now. Let's not have an argument. I can certainly understand your anxiety. I've brought you a whole case of oranges, which will do your invalid a world of good. . . ."

Mittel remained silent and mistrustful. He, too, was exhausted, and for the first time Charlotte saw him swallow a mouthful of whisky, which brought on a fit of coughing.

"Let's go take a look at the excavation."

"If you wish."

Charlotte was left alone with her sister's letter, which she slowly reread.

Lucie has a job in a café on the waterfront, but she spends all her earnings on dresses and silk stockings. There's nothing left over for anyone else. Papa lets her do exactly as she pleases. I had a boyfriend who had a summer job, but we had a fight at the movies, and . . .

Charlotte looked up and saw Plumier's face glued to the windowpane.

10

"TELL ME HONESTLY, JEF, DO I SEEM LIKE A SELFISH MONSTER TO you?"

"What on earth makes you think that?"

"I don't know. I was thinking about Mopps. . . . He always claimed I was a monster.

She spent her days reclining in a hammock, for she was not yet strong enough to be up and about. She spoke in a thin, quavering voice.

"For instance, do you think I have it in me to look after you the way you have looked after me?"

"I suppose so," he replied, without conviction.

His mind was on other things. During her convalescence, Charlotte had talked a great deal about herself and their relationship. This was not altogether surprising, since she spent hours and hours every day with no company but her own thoughts.

"Well, if you want to know what I think, I'm almost sure I have. I'll never be able to persuade anyone that I'm telling the truth, and yet it *is* the truth that I did what I did in Paris only for the sake of the Cause, as a means of getting the money we needed to produce our paper. . . ."

He was busy getting dressed and not really listening to her. During those two weeks when the two of them had been shut up alone together in the bungalow, he too might have been tempted to look into his own heart and hers. Now that she was out of danger, he longed to escape from that stifling intimacy, and was somewhat irritated by Charlotte's attempts to restore it.

"If we hadn't had to leave France, would you have married me?"

"Why not?"

"Because you weren't in love with me, nor I with you. I regarded you as a friend. Even now, I sometimes wonder . . ."

"Excuse me, I have to go to the work site."

He kissed her on the forehead, brought her a jug of lemonade and put it down beside her, and reached unthinkingly for his pith helmet. His mind also had been returning persistently to a little clutch of problems, but not the same ones that she was preoccupied with.

"I'll have a word with Dominico." Moïse had made this vague promise before he left.

He had been referring to Charlotte's delivery, and the subsequent urgency of their return to Buenaventura. But he had spoken without conviction, almost as if he did not believe what he was saying.

Days had gone by since then, and Mittel wondered at times whether he was not beginning to succumb to the same illness as Plumier. That it was a genuine illness, Mittel had at last come to appreciate.

At this very moment, for instance, as he left the bungalow, he found that it was no longer raining, though it had poured all the previous night. The river was silvery-gray, the color of mercury. Water dripped from the mangroves. As he looked around at the water, the sky, the skeletal trees, Mittel was overcome with queasiness, or, rather, with anguish, a feeling sometimes experienced in a nightmare, when one longs to run away, but finds himself glued to the spot.

He longed to run away, to take flight, to escape, anything for a change of scene! On the front of Plumier's bungalow was the black-and-white plaque bearing the name of the company. He passed it at least ten times a day, and each time he glowered resentfully at it. Sometimes he was sorely tempted to wrench it off.

The mountains on the edge of the horizon, though they were

no more than gray shadows among the gray clouds, seemed to be bearing down on him, crushing him.

He must get away! It was an obsession with him. When he reached the work site, he glared malevolently at the never-changing faces of the blacks. One of them had a habit of greeting him open-mouthed, with the meaningless grin of a halfwit, and Mittel felt that if he had had a horsewhip in his hand at the time, he might have been capable of using it to vent his exasperation on the man.

By the time anyone reads these words, I shall be dead, and stripped of everything. Perhaps then my enemies, who never cease to spy on me from the shadows, will believe themselves safe, because they have got possession of this diary. They would do well to disabuse themselves. I am in full possession of my faculties, and I have taken steps to ensure that the jackals will one day get their just deserts. Copies of this diary, and the accusations contained herein, are concealed in a safe place. . . .

These were the introductory words of Plumier's diary, which, as an act of bravado, he always left open on his desk. Every morning Mittel found it open at a different page, and as he turned the pages, he observed that the writing kept growing larger and more irregular.

Plumier was in the habit of getting up in the middle of the night to write this diary. Sometimes he wrote in red ink, sometimes in green, sometimes in pencil.

I am eager to discover whether he will have the courage to murder me.

"He" was Mittel, of all people!

It is bound to come to that in the end, I'm sure, for the company is beginning to lose patience. To them, I represent a constant threat. . . .

The atmosphere was stifling. Mittel tried not to think about it, but the sight of a tree, a half-caste at his work, the distant bungalows, all added substance to his obsession.

Plumier had begun once again to resort to his tactics of mute aggression. He visited the work site, but paid no attention to the men or the work in progress. He came as a mere spectator, to satisfy his curiosity. From time to time he would snicker or rub a few grains of gold dust between his fingers, pursing his lips contemptuously.

Sometimes he would stand face to face with Mittel, peering closely at him, like a doctor looking for symptoms. Then he would shake his head, as if to say, "I don't like the looks of him today. He won't be able to take much more of this."

Lately Mittel had been finding it a fearsome effort to keep the books up to date, although it was a simple enough task. But what was the use? He had ceased to believe in it. It all seemed so futile, so pointless. Was it any longer possible to believe in the value of this work being carried out in a jungle clearing by a handful of blacks and Indians, with water pouring down on their heads and covering their feet to the ankles? And who cared about the gold, delivered first to Dominico's office in Buenaventura, and then to a huge stone building in England, where thousands of clerks busied themselves over it?

"We'll never escape from this place, not you, not me, not the girl, not the others!"

Plumier was so certain of this that he made no attempt to get away. He was resigned to his fate. Or, rather, he had found consolation in sinister plans for revenge. Recently his diary entries had consisted of repeated threats:

The jackals will get their money's worth. I can promise them an end worthy of them and their ignominy.

What did he mean? He was becoming more and more neurotic, and, more significantly, his complexion was growing more and more yellow. At times, while he was roaming around the work site, he would suddenly find himself obliged to lean against a tree, or he would sink to the ground.

"That's how I'll end up," thought Mittel as he watched him.

At times he longed to cry out, to wage war against the landscape, as if it were some sort of living monster that had him by the throat and was squeezing the breath out of his body.

"I won't put up with it! I'll go home to Europe! I'm too young!"

He wallowed in self-pity.

"Is it true or not that on board the freighter, Mopps was amazed at my energy and determination? I had never before worked with my hands, and yet I was able to keep my end up in the stokehold!"

He recalled this period of his life with pride. It was a source of comfort to him.

"I'm skinny and undersized. I have no muscular power to speak of, and yet here I am, still on my feet after nursing Charlotte night and day for two whole weeks! I took no preventive measures, and yet, in spite of everything, I have not caught her disease!"

Surely some reward was due to him for all he had encountered? Recently he had drawn up a balance sheet of Charlotte's life. Now he did the same for his own. Even at the age of thirteen, he had sighed over his lot, and spent long hours reading poems on the subject of death.

What did fate have in store for him now? Nothing at all! Humanity, in his eyes, was divided into distinct categories: peasants, manual workers, small shopkeepers, plutocrats, servicemen, and so on. And by categories he meant sealed enclaves, with their own social customs, established routines, rules, and manners.

He himself, by force of circumstances, was an outsider, excluded from all these enclaves. He was not even an anarchist, like his father. And besides, all that was a thing of the past, brought to an end by the Great War. The only reason he had never expressed this view to his associates, and instead had pretended to share their ideals, was that at least, in Bauer's bookshop and at the meetings of the group, he enjoyed the illusion that he was somebody.

The son of Mittelhauser! He was greeted with applause. The young treated him with respect, his elders with affection.

But what sort of world was that? What other benefits had he derived from it? When had the laws of chance ever operated in his favor? When had he ever enjoyed the experience of getting something for nothing? Once, just once! A woman had given herself to him freely and without exception, one sunny Sunday afternoon. . . .

At the thought that he might die here, as Plumier had predicted, he clenched his fists in rage, held them up defensively, as though someone were threatening him, and looked around him, his eyes blazing with fury.

And all this while, all Charlotte could think of was whether he considered her self-centered! What could it possibly matter, one way or the other?

No sooner was she on the way to recovery and renewed strength than he lost all interest in her, and could think of nothing but how to escape from this prison of a jungle. He would escape, he must, even if it meant paddling the canoe himself!

Sometimes, when he was alone, having brooded so long that he was bathed in sweat, his head throbbing, he even went so far as to resolve, should it become absolutely necessary, to leave Charlotte behind.

Yes, his panic had bitten as deep as that! Especially when he saw Plumier, and what life here had done to him. Especially when he read a passage from his colleague's diary:

The rats have been at it again, performing their danse macabre *in premature celebration of my death. . . . Will they dare to go as far as to devour my flesh? Needless to say, Moïse has neglected to supply the sanitary buckets I asked for. It did occur to me to steal one from the Mittels. . . . She didn't die after all, that girl! I'm almost glad of it. Observing their misery at least takes my mind off other things.*

For although they are not yet aware of it, they are already in torment, a torment that will last for weeks, months. Maybe we could agree to die all together—on the eve of Moïse's next visit, say. I can just see the old man's face when he finds three corpses to greet him!

No, Mittel resolved, he must at all costs force himself to think of other things! Otherwise he would end up in the same state as the Belgian. Of what possible benefit could it be to the company to leave them there to die? Besides, Moïse would be coming again soon. The situation could be clarified then. Mittel had put the question to him point-blank; it therefore followed that Moïse would be bringing Dominico's answer.

And, of course, he had only himself to blame. The Colombian had offered him a clerical job in Buenaventura.

To think that he had turned it down at the time, because Buenaventura had struck him as such a cheerless dump! He had thought then that nothing could be worse than the huge concrete building, that derelict railroad station, that river spattered with rain, that little huddle of wooden shacks in the distance!

He had been so thrilled with his new gear, the boots, the khaki trousers, the pith helmet. . . .

Well, the solution was simple enough. He would go to Buenaventura for Charlotte's delivery, and, once there, he would inform Dominico of his intention to stay in the town. Since he was under contract to the company for three years—though, having been ill with a fever at the time, he had not even read the contract before signing it—he would abide by its terms, in the meantime saving every penny he could.

What was there after that to stop him from earning a living in some other country, a civilized country, such as Canada or Australia?

It also crossed his mind occasionally that there was nothing to prevent *him* from returning to France. But he always thrust such thoughts aside, because there was Charlotte to be considered, not to mention the child.

All the same, some time in the future, when he had saved enough money, there would be no harm in going home, just for a few weeks, to visit his mother.

It was crazy, being marooned in this place, when there were people living in Paris this very minute, traveling from one part of town to another on the platform of a bus, going into bars and cafés, ordering a beer or an apéritif, or sitting peacefully reading the papers!

Even the poorest of the poor could claim the right to enjoy clean streets, shopwindows full of goods, the intermittent sound

157

of music. And the movie theaters, filling, emptying, filling again! All along the Seine were men with fishing rods, spending hour after peaceful hour there, solely for the pleasure of catching little fish which they had no desire to eat.

It all seemed like an impossible dream. One had only to hold up one's arm—like so—for a taxi to draw up, and drive one wherever one wished to go!

And to think of the taxi drivers, gathering in little bistros that smelled of savory stew and were staffed by young waitresses from the provinces.

There were moments when he shrank from returning to the bungalow, because there things were even worse. It was a hermetically sealed box. Charlotte's voice was painfully weak. Sometimes he wondered if she might be putting it on, to hold his interest; then he felt ashamed of his suspicion, and was overcome with a new wave of tenderness.

"We are just a couple of pathetic little people."

Oh, yes, she every bit as much as he! Even if she had committed murder, and not so much from devotion to the Cause as from bravado, because she wanted to prove that she was something better than a servant.

What they must avoid from now on, at all costs, was illness. He was so anxious on this score that, to keep up his strength, he ate twice as much as his appetite demanded.

And this was yet another cause for anxiety. The provisions brought by Moïse were barely adequate. Each morning, Plumier came in and went to the store cupboard. Mittel watched him as he went out, calculating how far he had depleted their stock of rice and, above all, their cans of meat. He craved canned meat above all else. At every meal, he opened a can and ate the entire contents, without crackers, while Charlotte could still manage no more than watered-down milk.

What would become of them if, for some reason or another, Moïse were to miss a visit? Next time he came, Mittel would bring up the subject. He would demand more abundant rations, enough to last them for three months at least.

158

All these preoccupations were wearing him out. They seemed to be constantly nibbling away at his brain. They never ceased; even at night, in his sleep, he tossed and turned uncomfortably, suddenly waking up from time to time in a state of terror.

The kid is beginning to lose his marbles.

Mittel came upon these words one morning, written in red ink in Plumier's diary, and their effect was to send him scurrying off to look at himself in the mirror. Why had Plumier written that? It was true that he was very thin, and his beard accentuated his emaciated appearance. But there were no signs of madness in his eyes.

"Have you noticed anything different about me?" he asked Charlotte, who for the first time had moved from one chair to another.

"No. Why do you ask?"

"No particular reason."

"You certainly haven't changed for the worse. Quite the contrary, I like you with a beard. Don't you remember, in Paris I suggested you grow one?"

Yes! One summer's day, when they were walking in the Tuileries and had almost reached the Place de la Concorde. As if he could forget it! He even remembered that there had been an exhibition of Flemish paintings in the Jeu de Paume. They would have liked to see it, but the admission fee was five francs, so all they could do was sit outside on a bench.

Why did she have to bring that up now, recalling Paris in the summertime, its streets almost empty, scarcely a taxi in sight, its buses full of foreigners, its concierges sitting on their doorsteps in the cool of the evening?

"What day is it?"

"I don't know."

"I told you to keep track of the days. After all, you've got nothing else to do."

He was just speaking the truth! Charlotte should not be allowed to revel in her idleness. Not wishing to have a native servant in the house, he had to do everything himself. Charlotte was frightened of the natives, and insisted on being locked in whenever she was left alone.

The natives were the least of Mittel's worries. He knew little or nothing about his workmen's way of life, except that their huts were overcrowded and dirty, that their food was insanitary, and that almost all the women were pregnant.

Once he had stopped for a moment, aware that a young girl was standing in his path, looking at him with big, gentle, smiling eyes.

The episode had lasted only a second or two; then he had shrugged and proceeded on his way. But somehow the girl seemed to have read his mind, for now, every time he saw her, she adopted a coquettish attitude, and there was a hint of mockery in her smile.

Plumier did occasionally visit one of the huts, in full daylight, with all eyes on him. He seemed to have a special preference for a matronly woman, who already had three or four children, and who sported a Spanish shawl he had given her.

"If Dominico won't agree to my terms, I'll paddle the canoe myself."

"Why shouldn't he agree?" Charlotte asked, puzzled.

He had repeatedly sworn that he would do everything in his power to spare her anxiety, but then suddenly he would find himself in the grip of a fit of unexpressed resentment. This was one of those occasions.

"Why? Because he doesn't want us spreading the story that the mine is one of the most unproductive in the company. The shareholders believe they're on to a good thing. How would they take the news?"

"He can't keep us here against our will."

"And what about Plumier?"

"Plumier is mad. His case is completely different."

"Do you really believe that? I'm not at all sure that he's as mad as he would like us to believe. When you were ill, he came in here and behaved perfectly rationally. . . . There was nothing of the madman about him then, I swear. One could almost say he was responsible for saving your life, by giving you that soaking in the river."

"Was I undressed?"

"Naturally."

"Oh!"

She looked embarrassed, recalling that long illness, during which Mittel had had to attend to her most intimate needs.

"I wasn't exactly the romantic ideal of a maiden in distress, was I?"

He shrugged impatiently. This was what it all boiled down to in the end, herself and her trivial preoccupations. What possible difference could it have made, what she had looked like?

"I suppose it's inevitable that you should bear me a grudge?"

"Why on earth should I?"

"For being . . . for having been such a burden to you . . ."

"Don't be ridiculous!"

"Jef, why have you turned against me all of a sudden?"

"Don't shout at me."

He pulled himself up short. If he had let himself go any further, God knows what he might have said, in his present unreasonable state of anxiety and frustration.

And the rain forever beating down on the corrugated iron roof. And, to crown it all, in the last couple of days a rat must have died somewhere where it could not be found, and filled the bungalow with a revolting stench. Every now and then Mittel would resume his search for its body, poking into corners with a stick, but all he could find were spiders with furry legs.

"Spiders at dawning . . ."

Oh, hell! That's all he needed, to become superstitious! And there was Plumier, forever spying on him, relishing his ever-growing panic.

For that was all it was, panic at the thought that they might never escape from this hell hole! He counted the days. His mind was now made up. Nothing could change it. As soon as Moïse arrived, he would leave. Let them try to stop him! He had a revolver. Dominico himself had provided it, as he provided everything—there was nothing that man did not sell, which was how he could take back with one hand the money he paid out with the other.

He had even provided cartridges for shooting crocodiles! Mittel could just see himself having fun, taking pot shots at crocodiles from the riverbank! Three hundred francs' worth of cartridges. If they were still usable in this damp climate, it would be a miracle.

But that was how things were. Not a ray of hope. Nothing to cling on to.

Never an instant of pleasure or relaxation. Even the crackers were covered with mold, which had to be scraped off before they could be eaten. A tiny scratch, where Mittel had nicked his finger while opening a can, had developed into a suppurating wound over the past two months, so that he had to keep his right forefinger permanently covered with a dirty dressing.

For three days, he was never without a glass of whisky, which he sipped from morning till night.

"You shouldn't drink so much," Charlotte kept saying with a mournful air.

"Of course I shouldn't! But if you were in my shoes . . ."

On the fourth day, he had had a violent coughing fit which left him gasping, and when he looked at his handkerchief, he found there was blood on it. At this he went back into the bungalow, took the two remaining bottles of liquor, and threw them into the river.

Plumier drank only *chicha*. He always had a glass of it on his desk, and the very sight of it made Mittel retch. He had seen the stuff being made. The old men of the native village spent hours on end chewing corn, and eventually spat it out into an earthenware pot. Water was added to this mixture of corn and saliva, and the whole mess was left to ferment.

Nothing disgusted Plumier! Quite the contrary. He deliberately left the corpses of the rats he had killed lying around everywhere. It was left to Mittel to carry them out of doors, having first brushed away thick clusters of purple flies.

What if Moïse were to say no?

This was becoming an obsession with Mittel, and the most dreadful thing about it was that he knew it. He forced his mind away from the thought, finding a little light relief in recalling his mother's artless request for a fur coat!

No wonder she was known as Bébé! At the age of fifty, shapeless and wrinkled, she still dressed like a teen-ager, and covered her face with cosmetics. She did it in all innocence, never dreaming that it made her look ridiculous. She wanted a fur coat. What could be more natural than to ask her son to give her one?

Why couldn't he have had a family like other people's? In company, he acted out the role assigned to him, sneering at middle-class domestic values and boasting of being the son of a man who had died in prison.

"Oh, shut up!" he shouted suddenly at Charlotte.

"What have I done wrong?"

"Your fingers. Stop fidgeting, for God's sake!"

She was simply tapping her fingers absent-mindedly on the arms of her chair.

"I'm sorry, I didn't realize . . ."

"Don't start looking at me like that. You, too!"

"What do you mean, me, too?"

"Nothing."

But he knew perfectly well what he meant. Whenever he showed any sign of bad temper, she responded with the same look he always got from Plumier, the look a doctor gives a patient. She was trying to figure him out, wondering whether he, too, was falling ill.

It infuriated him. The days passed more slowly, more oppressively than ever. In a way, it was more bearable when it was raining, because then, at least, there was an excuse for grumbling as he waded through the mud. But no such luck! Three or four days went by with no sign of rain. The sky hung so low that it seemed to touch the treetops, and the atmosphere was stifling. Their leather suitcases had started growing a crop of fungi—real fungi, inside the bungalow!

And the work force carried on as usual, in slow motion, resigned and indifferent. They were the scum of the earth, a mixture of disease-ridden tribes who had lost man's most primitive instinct, that of self-respect. They responded to orders, like animals, and, like children, raised an arm to protect their faces when the white master showed signs of anger. They were unsightly and, for the most part, sickly. Mittel had noticed at least ten of them who showed unmistakable symptoms of tuberculosis.

In the tropics! With the temperature never below a hundred degrees! Yet another aspect of the life here that disturbed and disgusted him. And then there was the old man suffering from elephantiasis, who seemed always to be crossing his path—deliberately to annoy him, perhaps. Mittel was almost beginning to believe that this was so.

Charlotte was starting to move around a little. She always had a meal ready for him, although she herself ate nothing but crackers dipped in condensed milk.

"There are only two cans left," she told him. "Plumier helps himself to one almost every day. I don't dare to say anything to him about it."

"I'll speak to him myself."

"What's the point? Moïse will be here the day after tomorrow."

"If he comes at all."

"What makes you say that?"

"I have my reasons."

That morning he had read in Plumier's diary:

The hour is approaching, and the days of the jackals are numbered. There are already signs in the sky and on the earth. The spy can sense them and is beginning to show signs of revolt, but he will not escape his destiny, any more than the others, including the unborn child that the woman is carrying.

Was the Belgian's condition deteriorating? There was no doubt, at any rate, that he was growing weaker. Why had he kept his *foco* alight all last night? Mittel had got out of bed three times, and each time had seen the light burning in the bungalow.

Plumier had slept until eleven, in spite of the presence of Mittel, who was seated at the desk, putting the accounts in order.

It is only a matter of hours now, I am sure, before they resort to action, not realizing that their very crime will be the instrument of my revenge.

These hallucinations of his were finally beginning to take their toll, making him doubt the evidence of his own senses. Plumier's pupils were fevered pinpoints, and he muttered incessantly to himself without uttering a single intelligible word.

"Syphilis," Moïse had declared.

Could it be true? Mittel pondered the problem miserably, striving to understand.

Another night passed, and another. All through those nights, the lamp illuminated the window of the madman's bungalow. What could he possibly be up to?

The hour is approaching, and the jackals are already beginning to feel the breath of doom in their faces.

Then at last, one morning, the sound of a prolonged blast on a whistle. Charlotte sprang to her feet. Mittel ran to the door, his eyes sparkling. It was Moïse's signal! He had arrived with two canoes, and was carried to dry land on the back of one of the Indians, so he would not have to wade through the river.

"Well?" Mittel shouted, by way of greeting.

Moïse looked him straight in the eye, screwed up his face, and grunted, "Where's your wife?"

"She's in the bungalow. I'll take you to her. What did Dominico say?"

"What do you think he said? He's not a monster. You'll be leaving in a day or two, as soon as your replacement gets here."

It was like being let out of prison. Mittel felt like dancing a jig. He yelled, "Lotte! Lotte! We're leaving!"

He had begun to believe that they would never get away. He had allowed himself to be brainwashed by a madman! For now there was no longer any doubt! Dominico had acceded to his request without any difficulty!

"Come along. Would you believe it, I haven't even got a drop of whisky to offer you!"

He was almost laughing. He was full of emotion. He was sincerely apologetic.

"Did you drink it yourself?"

"No, but I was beginning to drink too much. . . . I thought I'd better get rid of the temptation, so I threw the two bottles into the river."

Moïse shrugged and growled, "It's just as well I brought a fresh supply with me. You have got yourself into a state, haven't you? What about your wife?"

They could see Charlotte at the window.

"Has she been ill?"

"No, that's all over now. Come in. Charlotte, did you hear? We're leaving."

He would have liked to leave at once, fearful that something might occur to prevent their departure.

"How's Plumier?" asked Moïse, looking anxious.

"No better. Worse, if anything. He keeps a light on all night in his bungalow."

"I wonder how he managed it?"

"What do you mean?"

"How he was able to get that whole mass of incredible reports into the hands of the Colombian authorities and the French consul. They had no choice but to set up a commission of inquiry. Luckily for us, everyone knows that he has a persecution complex."

Suddenly Mittel grew thoughtful. So Plumier's boastful entries in his diary, asserting that his reports were in safe hands and that, by hook or by crook, he would get his revenge, were not wholly without foundation.

"What is utterly incomprehensible," grumbled Moïse, "is how he managed to get all those documents from here to Buenaventura. There isn't a single man in the work force who could have managed the journey. And, except for me, not a soul has been near this place in I don't know how long. But I intend to find out while I'm here. Do you know what I think? I think he must have

166

bribed one of my Indians! I can't figure out any other possible explanation!"

"Dominico . . ." began Mittel.

"Dominico doesn't give a damn, needless to say. He's one of the richest men in Colombia. He has only to say the word and the inquiry will be stopped. However . . ."

"What?"

"I don't know the whole story yet. In his letters, Plumier states that he is marked down to be murdered, and that his murderer is already on the way here. He as good as claims to know the precise date! *They want to get their hands on the documents in the strongbox,* he writes."

A small portable strongbox that Mittel knew well, since it was used for storing the gold dust and the workmen's wages.

"Have you seen him today?"

"I don't think he's up yet. Lately he's got into the habit of sleeping till lunchtime."

"We'll have to keep a careful eye on him. God knows what he's cooking up. . . ."

Moïse opened the window and shouted to the men who were carrying the provisions, "Let's have the bottles first!" Collapsing into a chair, he murmured, "Am I ever thirsty!"

11

IT WAS ALMOST AS THOUGH MITTEL HAD A PRESENTIMENT OF HOW important even the most insignificant incidents occurring within the next two days were to be, so sharply and in such minute detail was everything etched upon his inward eye, and later recalled.

The black worker's hut, for instance. It had been about half past four in the afternoon. Moïse and Mittel were strolling at a leisurely pace toward the work site, to take a look around. They had gone by way of the native village, and Mittel had noticed that the hut occupied by the woman whom Plumier visited from time to time was shut up and apparently deserted. . . . Moïse must have been in the know, because as they went past the hut, he had turned to wink at his companion.

A few minutes later, they had arrived at the work site. Moïse, catching sight of the black woman's husband, had called out to him mockingly, "So, you're about to become a father?"

The man responded with a foolish smile, gesturing to indicate that this was news to him.

"Well, you can take it from me, you are," Moïse had insisted.

Neither man could have foreseen, at this point, the hideous irony that this joking was to assume. The weather was dry for a change, but—what was still more unusual—a fairly strong wind was blowing up, and clouds scudded across the sky above the mangroves.

An hour later, Moïse and Mittel were once more walking through the village. Continuing their conversation, they paused outside the hut and noticed that it was still shut up. As usual, there were children playing in the dust outside. Women, squatting on the ground, were picking over grains of cereal, or chewing corn for *chicha*.

At this very instant Mittel was for the first time struck by the indifference with which, up till then, he had looked upon this haunting scene. The scene lacked any sort of character. It could not even be called picturesque or exotic. It was impoverished, ugly, and sordid. Everywhere the mindless, empty eyes of degenerate beings were fixed upon him. The huts were as squalid as the shacks on the derelict outskirts of Paris. Here, as there, the materials used were old crates, tarred paper, food cans . . .

"Well, well!" exclaimed Moïse.

Mittel turned around and saw the door of the hut opening. All that could be seen of Plumier was a patch of light in the darkness within. In contrast, however, the little native girl came out boldly, still wreathed in mocking smiles, obviously very proud of herself as the chosen companion of a white man. Her right hand was clenched, most likely on a silver coin, and as she passed, she grinned broadly at Mittel, showing all her teeth.

"Our resident Don Juan really is going too far," exclaimed Moïse ironically.

The husband, who had just returned from work, came to a halt on seeing the hut door closed, then drifted away to squat among a group of neighbors.

When all was said and done, what could any of this possibly matter to Mittel now? He was about to leave. He would never again see those mangroves with their twisted roots, or those hundred all-too-familiar faces.

Charlotte had changed into a clean dress and was setting the table with a cloth. The bottle of whisky held pride of place in the middle. Before sitting down at the table, Moïse went to the door to give instructions to one of his boatmen. There was nothing remarkable about that; he often did it.

They ate rice with red peppers, and since Moïse had brought onions, Charlotte had fried some with corned beef, thus filling the bungalow with a powerful smell of home cooking, reminiscent of so many concierges' lodges in Paris.

Mittel could remember it all, down to the most insignificant detail, such as the fact that one of the prongs of his fork had been bent. Moïse, who was in a foul temper, had been drinking so heavily that even his neck was red.

At about nine o'clock, he got up with a sigh and slung his hammock on the two hooks driven into the wall for the purpose. These hooks had been so placed that the hammock blocked the front door, thus preventing anyone from entering or leaving the bungalow without disturbing the sleeping man.

At this time of night, Moïse's eyes were always swollen: he consumed the better part of a bottle of whisky a day, and by nightfall he was fuddled, clumsy, and ill-humored.

He went outside for a moment and stopped beside a tree. Mittel had also taken advantage of this opportunity to go out, and had observed that there was no light showing in Plumier's bungalow.

This had not, at the time, struck him as significant. Quite the contrary, in fact: ever since he had learned that he was free to leave, he had lost all interest in what was around him, human or inanimate, and the glance he had directed at the neighboring bungalow was purely automatic.

"Good night, my dears."

Moïse, sighing, had scrambled into his hammock, then tossed and turned for a while before falling asleep. It was a few minutes to ten. Charlotte had fallen asleep as soon as her head touched the pillow. Mittel stretched out his hand and turned off the *foco*, making a careful mental note of its position: when he woke suddenly in the night, usually startled out of his sleep by a nightmare, he often had to grope around for a long time to find it.

But tonight he was not plagued by bad dreams. At one point he thought he could hear footsteps outside, but he paid no attention to them. Charlotte was still there, close beside him. He went back to sleep.

170

The next time he opened his eyes, it was daylight, and Moïse was already up, stripped to the waist and busy shaving, while Charlotte made coffee. The hammock had been taken down. The washbasin, full of soapy water, was on the table.

"Is it raining?" he asked.

"Not so far."

The wind had risen still further since the day before, making a steady whistling sound as it swept across the corrugated iron roof, and the trees were swaying against a gray sky.

The door of the other bungalow was shut. A black man went by. Then, suddenly, they could hear hurried footsteps coming from the river, from somewhere near the place where the canoes were beached. One of Moïse's boatmen came up the steps, pushed open the door, and stood there looking distraught, his eyes full of fear. Without even pausing to regain his breath, he tried to speak.

"What did you say?" snapped Moïse, one cheek covered with shaving soap, his razor still in his hand.

"The white man . . . there . . . there . . ."

They could not get another word out of him. Moïse wiped his face, seized his pith helmet, and went out dressed as he was, in nothing but a pair of trousers. Mittel, in his pajamas, followed.

"Your helmet!" Charlotte called after him.

He was still not properly awake. The black man, itching to run on ahead, kept looking back, impatient at his companions' slowness. They did not have far to go. A hundred meters from the bungalow was a wide bend in the river, forming an inland bay sealed off by a bank of mud, which disappeared under water whenever it rained. At first all they could see was a crouching black man, another of Moïse's crew; then they became aware of a figure stretched out on the ground.

It was Plumier! He was the only one who always dressed in white. He was lying face down, and his body had sunk several centimeters into the mud.

"God Almighty!" screamed Moïse.

He looked around him in a rage, as though everyone present were responsible for what had occurred. At the same time, he leapt at the crouching black man and snatched from his hands the revolver that the native was staring at in bewilderment.

"You damned fool! Where did you get that?"

The black pointed at the ground, to a place close to the hand of the dead man. Moïse's overriding feeling at that moment was one of fury.

Mittel gazed at the back of the dead man's neck and felt his stomach heave. It was ghastly. The skull was shattered, and scraps of brain were lying all around him, some as far as a meter away.

They could see Charlotte on the steps of the bungalow, craning her neck to try to make out what was going on.

"What are we going to do?" asked Mittel, automatically.

"Yes, what *are* we going to do? Speaking for myself, I'd give anything to have a policeman, any policeman, to act as an official witness."

"What for?"

"Because that would prove that this brute here had taken his own life!"

Mittel did not at first understand his drift. The words echoed meaninglessly in his head for several minutes. Then suddenly he frowned and turned to stare at his companion.

Now it was all coming back to him, all that Moïse had said about the official inquiry and the revelations contained in Plumier's letters. And now Mittel was finding it hard to escape the disturbing thought . . .

Had the Belgian really taken his own life?

"First of all, we'll leave him here, so that everyone can have a good look at him."

He gave orders to his men that the corpse must on no account be touched. He was about to take the revolver away with him when, changing his mind, he turned back and laid it on the ground close to the dead man's hand.

"He even took the precaution of shooting himself in the back of the head," he grumbled. "I wonder how the hell he managed it. He must have had to twist himself around like a contortionist, to shoot himself in the back of the neck like that. Damn and blast!"

A few moments later he was back in the bungalow, putting on his shirt and answering Charlotte's agitated questions.

"What's wrong? What's wrong is that that rotten bastard Plumier has shot himself, just to cause us trouble."

Mittel was so badly shaken that, after forcing down half a cup of coffee, he was violently sick.

"I forbid you to go near him," he said to Charlotte.

"Did he kill himself during the night?"

"Last night, or this morning . . . or early yesterday evening."

And Moïse, puffing and swearing, shoved his shirt tails into his trousers, drank his coffee laced with whisky, and stood staring out of the window, his eyes fixed, his vision as clouded as the sky above.

"He may have left a letter," suggested Mittel, who was taking advantage of the lull to get dressed.

"We'll go have a look. Are you ready?"

Moïse was still breathing heavily. This was a severe ordeal for him. It was easy to guess the painful thoughts that were passing through his mind.

When they reached the bungalow, the first thing they saw was that it was not just unlocked: the lock had been wrenched off. Mittel's eyes widened. His companion was no less shaken than he was.

"Open the door!"

The appalling sight that met their eyes checked them in their tracks. The whole place looked like a battlefield. The strongbox, lying on its side, was gaping open, and papers were strewn everywhere.

"It's not possible . . . not possible!" murmured Moïse to himself, with a deep sigh.

173

Yes, it was impossible to conceive that Plumier had been attacked, and that someone had ransacked the bungalow! What could they have been hoping to find?

"The gold . . ." said Mittel, when he had looked all around the room.

It had been there only the day before, a bag of it, weighing about a pound. The bag was no longer there. Nor was the diary, that notorious diary in which Plumier had made an entry every day!

Suddenly Moïse put both hands to his head and ran them through his hair. His features were contorted. He looked like a man striving desperately to regain his self-control.

"For Christ's sake, I'm not out of my mind! But I'm in such a turmoil that, if my hammock hadn't been slung across the door, so that you couldn't get past me, I really think I might have my suspicions even of you. . . . There isn't a single black or half-caste capable of causing all this havoc. . . ."

And between his teeth: "The filthy swine!"

"Who?"

"The Belgian. Who else? What other explanation can there be? Do you still not understand? He always swore he'd get us in the end. And you can take my word for it, he has! What is there left for me to say at this point? He took very good care to hold his hand until I got here. As for the documents, I bet you anything you like we won't find a single one. . . ."

"But I don't see what all this has to do with . . ."

"Don't you? It's as clear as day. He did everything he could think of to make it look as if he'd been robbed and murdered. Didn't he keep insisting that he was in possession of documents compromising the company? Well, those papers will never be found. It would therefore follow that he was murdered for his papers! You try and make anyone believe otherwise, and see how far you get. There isn't a living soul who would believe you!"

And what if it were true? Mittel averted his eyes, for fear that Moïse might read the uncertainty in them. The old man had slept in the bungalow, but who was to say that he had not got up during the night?

"No, it's not possible," he said, speaking his thoughts aloud.

"What's not possible?"

"Nothing . . . Who will be in charge of the inquest?"

"There won't be any inquest! Do you really imagine they'd go to all the trouble of sending a full complement of police officials and magistrates on a ten-day journey by canoe from Buenaventura? In this sort of case, people will believe what they want to believe, whatever seems to them most plausible."

He was rummaging among the scattered papers, none of which was of any value. The diary had simply vanished, as had the bag of gold.

"There's no doubt in my mind that, if we could drag the river, that's were we would find both things."

By now the entire village had congregated on the riverbank. The two men, heads bowed, each deep in his own thoughts, went to join the others. Mittel gave a start. There, beside the body and looking at it with indifference, was the girl they had seen the day before.

It all came back to him. The door of the hut, which had remained shut for hours. The young black woman emerging, looking very smug and clutching something in her fist.

At that moment, Plumier already knew. His mind was made up, for sure. Those hours spent with the two women represented a leavetaking. He had been bidding farewell to life!

The current was not too strong, so Moïse ordered his men to dive in search of the bag of gold dust. He had little hope of success, but he did what had to be done, in a plodding and half-hearted way.

Suddenly he looked like what he was, an old man, and the pouches under his drink-sodden eyes were darker and puffier than usual.

"There's nothing to do but bury him," he murmured to himself. "I don't see . . ."

What else, in fact, could he do? Notify the authorities in Buenaventura? A journey of ten days by canoe, each way.

"Come on now, get moving! Bury him!"

"Just like that? Without a coffin?"

He shrugged.

"What of it? The packing cases are all too small; we'd have to double him up."

He was not joking. One could sense that he had considered the possibility.

"No, this is the way to do it. We'd better have them dig the grave a little farther off, under that first clump of trees."

Mittel gave the necessary orders, and the blacks went off to the work site to fetch shovels. Every now and then they caught sight of Charlotte at the window of the bungalow.

As for the black women, they were all squatting a few steps from the body, chattering away among themselves until something happened. The kids were playing as if they were in their own village. It was left to Mittel to go fetch some sort of covering for the dead man's head. All he could find was a hand towel, the one that Moïse had used that very morning.

Moïse, in the meantime, was up to his knees in the river, supervising the diving operations, which had so far produced no results.

"This won't prevent us from leaving, will it?" asked Charlotte when at last Jef returned to the bungalow for a few minutes' rest.

His legs were so weak he could hardly stand. He had been on his feet the whole time back there, and in any case he had felt he had to get away, if only for a minute or two, from the sickening spectacle on the riverbank.

"I sincerely hope not," he replied.

He had firmly resolved to say nothing to Charlotte, but eventually he found he could not stop himself.

"Did you sleep soundly all through the night?"

"I think so, yes."

"You didn't hear anything?"

"What do you mean?"

"I'm not sure. Suppose, for instance, that Moïse had gone out . . ."

"Do you think he is capable of doing such a thing?"

"I've told you, I simply don't know. But I can't help wondering. Wondering and wondering, until my head's in a whirl."

The entire scene was visible from the bungalow window: the divers, the natives crowding around the corpse, the men digging a grave in the shade of a mangrove.

"No, surely he couldn't have done that. . . . What appalls me is that we should find ourselves mixed up in another death. . . ."

She started, and looked deep into his eyes.

"Jef!"

"I didn't say anything. . . . Please forgive me. . . . Of course, it's nothing but coincidence! But I can still see that girl yesterday, coming out of the hut. . . ."

"What hut?"

"You wouldn't understand. . . . So I'm trying to picture how he spent his last night. He was alone. He must have made his preparations with the greatest care. . . . Most likely he either threw his diary into the river or buried it with the bag of gold dust."

"Haven't they found the gold, either?"

"They're still looking. That's what the divers are doing."

And Plumier had managed to slink past the bungalow where three people were asleep! How he must have laughed! He had been obsessed with revenge, and now his moment had come.

"He wasn't thirty yet. . . ."

Whichever way he turned, he could see nothing that was not painful. The mountains, surmounting everything, formed a gray barrier between him and the horizon. For weeks on end he had gazed at them with loathing, and now his former terrors were reasserting themselves. Nothing on earth would persuade him to remain in this place. It was essential that he escape from its grip without delay. His anguish was so overwhelming that he walked across to to the river and asked Moïse, "When are we leaving?"

Moïse's bulging eyes were clouded. He shrugged.

"I'd like to recover the gold first. Otherwise Dominico will be furious."

"And what if it can't be found?"

"We'll leave as soon as the replacement arrives."

So it was true! There really was a replacement on the way! A man who would in turn be abandoned here, and left to the mercies of this stretch of jungle. Well, so much the worse for him! Mittel was beyond pity. As long as he could get away, let the others look after themselves.

"Isn't anything being done to mark the occasion?" he asked, pointing to the corpse, for the grave was now ready to receive it.

"What do you mean?"

"I don't know, a burial service . . . something. . . ."

It seemed to him indecent merely to bundle the corpse into the hole.

"Perhaps you would care to conduct a Mass?" retorted Moïse, tauntingly.

There was obvious nothing he could do. Nevertheless, he went to fetch Charlotte.

"Carry him to the grave," he ordered the blacks.

It took a considerable effort by three men to free the body from the mud. Moïse followed them, wearing his pith helmet and looking solemn.

"I hope you're not expecting me to sing the praises of that bastard," he grunted.

But no sooner had he said this than he felt ashamed, and, as the body was lowered into the grave, he automatically took off his helmet. Charlotte was dry-eyed, but her lips were trembling. As for the natives, they were pushing and shoving so much to get a look at the open grave that Mittel had to hold them back.

What else could they have done? There was not even a single ver. . . .

"Was he a believer?" he asked Moïse.

"How should I know?"

Moïse gave the signal, and the men began filling in the grave. "If only there had been a coffin!"

And now they were back on the familiar set: the two bungalows, the black-and-white plaque bearing the name of the company, the village behind the trees. . . .

Only the fat black woman was weeping, while her husband shoveled dirt into the grave. As for the girl, she was watching like any spectator at an outdoor entertainment.

"Time to go home now," Mittel said to Charlotte.

And in reply, she whispered, "When are we leaving?"

By nightfall, the bag of gold had still not been recovered. That afternoon Mittel had returned several times to the graveside, and it was he, brought up to despise all religious observances, who had taken the trouble to make a cross out of planks from an old chest, and to drive it into the ground. He made it with his own hands, as if to comfort himself with the discipline of craftsmanship. He even managed to root out a pot of tar, with which he wrote the name PLUMIER in crooked letters.

He had never known the Belgian's Christian name! What else was there to write on the cross? He would very much have liked to send Plumier's parents some memento of their son—personal effects, perhaps, or a last letter—but all he could find in the bungalow was a badly scorched cigarette holder and a photograph of a little girl, presumably the dead man's sister.

No address, nothing. He had ransacked the room before killing himself.

No one felt like eating any longer. Moïse washed down his food with pure alcohol. Charlotte had had to go back to bed, overwhelmed with weariness. But she did not sleep. She watched the two men warily, listened to their every word.

"Who is the replacement going to be?" Mittel asked, for the sake of something to say.

"An Italian who arrived in Buenaventura about a month ago. Before that, he lived in Equatorial Africa. When he disembarked, he had only three dollars in his pocket, and had traveled steerage from Panama because he couldn't afford a third-class cabin."

The blacks, too excited by the events of the day to retire to bed, sat around the fire, singing and drinking *chicha.* They accompanied themselves on a wooden drum, the rhythm of which penetrated far into the jungle, throbbed in one's ears, pounded in one's chest. At first one had a feeling of discomfort and unease. It was not until later that one realized that this was the effect of the merciless rhythm of the drum.

As soon as Moïse became aware of it, he sprang up, shouting, "I'm going out there to shut them up!"

Mittel went with him. They headed for the fire. Bodies were stretched out all around it. Moïse, kicking the recumbent natives indiscriminately, yelled, "No more music! Understand?"

They were all terrified into silence. Those who had been kicked were doubled up with pain.

Returning to the bungalow, the two men went past the company office, where last night Plumier had still been living.

"Only a madman could have gone to such lengths to pursue an obsession," remarked Moïse.

"Was he really mad?"

"I'll say he was! He should have been in a straitjacket! You surely don't believe all that rubbish about jackals and so on?"

"No."

But he answered so halfheartedly that Moïse himself started to feel terrified.

"Look, my boy, don't *you* do anything foolish now. . . . Aren't we in enough trouble as it is?"

"What do you mean?"

"I'm quite willing to take you both back to Buenaventura. Mind you, I shouldn't be doing it, but I feel sorry for your wife. In return, the least you can do when we get there is to help me out of this mess."

"What do I have to do?"

"There'll be a great many questions asked. In spite of everything, they'll have to make some sort of show of holding an inquiry. If you give any hint of wavering, it will be all over the papers, and God knows what that may lead to. . . ."

They were climbing the steps to the bungalow as they spoke.

"Is that you?" Charlotte mumbled, half asleep.

"It's us, yes. Go back to sleep."

"You do understand, don't you, old man? And just to be on the safe side, we'll work out in advance exactly what we're going to say when we get there. The main thing is to keep it simple. Look, what I mean is that, if we start babbling on about the ransacked strongbox, the scattered papers, and the lost diary, then people are bound to think there was something funny going on."

"You mean you won't mention those things?"

"I'll have to tell Dominico, naturally, but the commission of inquiry is a different matter altogether. It's none of their business."

Mittel, not for the first time, averted his eyes. Why all this secrecy? And the underlying threat? For Moïse had as good as threatened to leave him and Charlotte behind.

"Do you understand?"

"I understand."

No, he did not understand! Not yet, at any rate. He still felt deeply uneasy, tormented. He began undressing as Moïse slung his hammock and drank his nightcap of whisky.

Maybe he had not sneaked out during the night. . . . The more Mittel thought about it, the less likely it seemed that Moïse should have murdered Plumier.

But there was all that about "jackals."

Maybe the Belgian really had been mad, but had he been mad enough to invent such an elaborate structure of lies?

"The company has other fish to fry . . ." grumbled Moïse.

Ah, yes, the company! The company first, no matter what!

Plumier had died for the company, and Charlotte, too, had been on the brink of the grave, and had she died, the child she was carrying would have died with her. Now another man was coming, who . . .

"Dominico will see that you get your just reward. He's a very decent fellow."

"After the child is born, I'll have to live in Buenaventura," said Mittel, a note of shame in his voice.

Oh, to hell with it! So he was a coward. No one knew that better than he did. But the main thing was to get away from here, at all costs. He would have been willing to lie outright, to say whatever was required of him—even that he had witnessed Plumier's suicide—in order to escape from the jungle.

"Good night, my boy. I'm hoping we'll recover the gold tomorrow. If it's not in the river, then he must have buried it, and we'll have to search among the trees."

Charlotte was grumbling, because Mittel had inadvertently nudged her as he got into bed. She was already bathed in sweat. Somewhere behind the woodwork, a rat was scrabbling.

They found the gold! Moïse had not been mistaken. Mittel had the feeling that he was seldom mistaken. For all his grumbling, nagging, and stubbornness, Moïse forged ahead, allowing nothing to stand in his way. For all his assumed air of stupidity, the truth was that he knew precisely what he was doing, rather too much so, if anything. This, at any rate, was how he appeared to Mittel, and, for the time being at least, Mittel was prepared to dance to his tune, for fear that at the very last moment Moïse should decide to leave them behind.

He even went so far as to flatter him, to anticipate his wishes.

It was Mittel, for instance, who had suggested, "Perhaps it would be wiser not to mention that he was shot through the back of the neck?"

The old man gazed at him in admiration.

"Not bad! We'll need to discuss it further. . . ."

Mittel felt deeply ashamed, but he was at the end of his tether. It had started raining again. The depression in the mud made by Plumier's body was losing its shape and would soon disappear altogether. The bag of gold had been fished up at least twenty meters farther along, and Moïse had stowed it away in his hammock for safety. Work had been resumed at the mine, but the men seemed unsettled by recent events, and it was not until two days had passed that the rhythm of daily life returned more or less to normal.

In Charlotte's case, an extraordinary change had taken place, almost as if the recent tragedy had effected a complete cure. Only forty-eight hours earlier, she had still been in the early stages of convalescence, but now all that seemed to have been forgotten, and she was on her feet all day, busying herself around the house from morning till night. But from time to time she was stricken with the same terrors that haunted Mittel, and would ask repeatedly:

"Are you sure we'll be able to get away?"

"He promised we would."

Both were equally mistrustful. Moïse had become for them an all-powerful being, upon whom their very lives depended. Charlotte, like Jef, went out of her way to be friendly, and to anticipate his every wish.

On the third day, in the afternoon, as Mittel was returning from the work site, he caught sight of the old man entering the young black woman's hut. He felt strangely troubled.

Of course, when all was said and done, what did it amount to but that Moïse was a lecherous old man? Still, to pick on that particular girl! And at that particular moment!

He went into the bungalow feeling as if the world had turned upside down. Charlotte was folding her clothes into a chest that had just been brought in.

"Isn't he with you?"

They spoke of HIM, as if he were the only man on earth. He was the only one who counted. He alone filled all their thoughts, day in and day out.

"HE stopped in the village."

"Oh."

Without warning, Mittel suddenly spread out his arms on the table and, quite unable to explain it, even to himself, burst into tears, sobbed uncontrollably, like a child.

Day after day, those tears had been building up inside him, and now, at last, he was able to shed them.

12

LLUVIA . . . LLUEVE . . . EL VIENTO . . .

By now Mittel was more or less able to express himself in Spanish, but there were some words that he hated having to say. They were the first words he had heard on landing in Colombia, and ever since he had heard them endlessly repeated:

Rain . . . it's raining . . . the wind . . .

But why now? It was their fifth day in the canoes. The weather was fine. Mittel and Charlotte were dozing in the one they shared, and Moïse, in the other, was traveling alongside. Suddenly the old man shouted, *"Deme mi fusil!"* Hand me my rifle!

There followed a shot. Mittel turned and saw a crocodile thrashing around on the bank, less than thirty meters away.

A second shot followed, and the brute lay still, whereupon, yelling in triumph, one of the blacks leapt into the water.

Why? Why kill the poor beast? Why swim toward it? Every time he heard shooting, Mittel felt acutely disturbed. He watched the black intently while Moïse unloaded his gun.

The whole episode lasted no more than ten seconds. Abruptly the swimmer stopped, struggled in the water, went under, reappeared for an instant, his mouth gaping, and then vanished for good.

Whereupon Moise said, "There were two of them!"

Two crocodiles, one on the bank, the other in the river.

Mittel said nothing. As the days passed he spoke less and less, but underneath he was seething with incoherent thoughts and feelings.

He had been much shaken by the arrival of his replacement, whose name was Garcia. He was rather slight of build, and young. This did not deter him, however, from alighting briskly from his canoe and, after a good look around, seeming to take possession of the territory.

There had not been a moment's hesitation! He strode into the bungalow, shook hands with everyone, glanced at Charlotte's waistline, and remarked, "I see now why you have to leave."

He would certainly have been incapable of understanding that they might have other reasons for leaving. The accommodations did not raise a frown. Within an hour he had rearranged the furniture to suit himself, and stowed away all his possessions, which he had brought with him in two canoes.

"Do you get a lot of rats?"

The answer did not surprise him in the least. Quite the reverse, in fact, and he immediately set about finding the best places for his traps. When he had his first encounter with the natives, he casually booted a couple of them in the behind, by way of asserting his authority.

And now he was there, all alone, for months on end, perhaps for years, but there was little doubt in Mittel's mind that he would survive!

As Charlotte, come to think of it, had done. How was it that, in her condition and in that climate, with no proper care or medication, she had managed to recover completely from a serious disease?

There had been no aftereffects. Even now, when they were on the water twelve hours a day, sleeping in cramped tents on the riverbank at night, and eating skimpy and irregular meals, she was growing stronger every day.

"Pour soul," she murmured, referring to the black who died.

How different was Mittel's reaction! He felt sickened to the core of his being. But it was he who was misguided. He recalled, for instance, that on board the freighter, Jolet, a humane individual, had once coolly remarked, "On a long voyage, one has to be prepared for at least one serious accident, if not a death. A burst water gauge on a boiler, or, more commonly, a man who's loading or unloading cargo falling into the hold . . . a limb sliced off by a steel hawser . . . But some trips are worse than others. It's as if a curse hung over the ship. You can feel it the moment you set foot on board. . . ."

The one who never lost his head was Moïse. He was amazingly well organized, especially where drink was concerned.

First thing in the morning he poured a shot of whisky into his coffee, and at ten o'clock precisely, without even having to look at his watch, he drank his first glass of pure alcohol.

By lunchtime he was on his third, but, as yet, he showed no outward signs. He was at his best then, in high good humor and ready to behave as if he were among close friends.

At the end of the meal, he stretched out in his canoe and slept for a good two hours; the first thing he did on waking was to open the bottle.

It was only after this that the symptoms of drunkenness began gradually to show themselves—a swelling of the eyelids, a glazed expression, harshness toward the natives, a note of menace in his voice, and a surly manner.

After dinner he could barely stand, and staggered into his tent, where he lay groaning until he fell asleep, but he never had a trace of a hangover the following morning.

All this reminded Mittel a little of Mopps. Moïse talked with equal callousness of his experiences of births and deaths.

"I remember, I delivered one myself . . ." he began.

And this, with reference to his third or fourth wife!

Of his not inconsiderable succession of wives, some had died, others had divorced him, but he was perfectly indifferent to the fate of any of them.

"Maybe he's got the right idea," Mittel sometimes thought.

But then he would pull himself together and recoil from what seemed to him a philosophy of despair.

On the night following the death of the black, he felt even

more uneasy than usual, and Charlotte, lying beside him in their tent, sensed that he was unable to sleep.

"Have you got indigestion? Are you having trouble digesting something?" she whispered in the dark.

He was tempted to reply, with a hideous pun, that he was having trouble digesting the black. He would have preferred to keep his thoughts to himself, but eventually succumbed to an overwhelming urge to unburden himself.

"It almost seems as if we're being pursued by the Furies . . ." he murmured, emboldened by the darkness, which concealed the look in his eyes.

"What?"

Ever since Martin . . . Plumier shot himself. . . . The native, just now . . ."

"I don't see the connection."

"What if there is some connection? What if it's true that blood cries out for blood? No, you couldn't possibly understand. Go back to sleep."

And so she did, as peacefully as a child, in barely five minutes. She was not in the least disturbed by what he had said.

It was all nebulous, of course. And yet, why not? He himself was keenly aware of a possible connection between the death of Martin, in his apartment on the Boulevard Beaumarchais, and the dramatic turn that their lives had taken since.

Martin had set the wheels in motion. Plumier had been the next to go, and now the black, swimming triumphantly toward the crocodile carcass.

And yet, by some strange quirk of fate, it was Charlotte, the murderess of the produce agent, who seemed to be protected by a special immunity! In spite of being stricken down by one of the gravest of tropical diseases, she had completely recovered. Mittel was by this time almost certain that she would give birth painlessly, almost without effort. . . . And so it would continue, as long as she lived.

The river lapped against the bank at their feet. Moïse snored in his tent nearby. From time to time Mittel squashed a mosquito that had landed on his cheek, and Charlotte groaned in her sleep.

Mittel's first impression of Buenaventura had been that the little wooden shacks of which the town was built were fit only to house the lowest of the low, the kind of blacks and half-castes that could be seen wandering around the narrow, sloping streets.

But now, little by little, he was beginning to discover a new world, whose existence he had not even suspected. On the Pacific Coast, the season of heavy rain was past, and the sun shone every day—or, rather, it glared without sparkle, and was depressing, not cheering.

Dominico, who had a sallow complexion and probably suffered from some disorder of the liver, frequently winced with pain as he talked.

"Moïse has told me the whole story," he said when Mittel presented himself in his office on the fourth floor of the hotel. "It's a great nuisance, and has involved me in a lot of unnecessary expense. It's the last time I shall ever permit a woman to be sent out. In a little while we shall have to go and stop by the police station."

Although the distance was barely three hundred meters, they took Dominico's big American car, which spent most of the time parked in front of the hotel.

Police headquarters turned out to be a wooden structure, not very much larger or cleaner than the other buildings. On the ground floor, some four or five native policemen were loitering, half asleep. They did not stir as Dominico led the way upstairs, followed by Moïse, with Mittel bringing up the rear.

They came to a landing where, on an artist's stool, stood a miniature palm tree in a blue-and-yellow glazed earthenware pot. On a table dotted with little mats was a collection of fairground china and spun-glass knickknacks.

The visitors were received without ceremony, by a servant dressed only in trousers and a shirt unbuttoned to the waist.

Leaving them on the landing beside an open door that led to a kitchen, where a black woman could be seen washing dishes, he went off to announce them to the chief of police.

Heavy curtains, flowered carpets, embroidered runners, some framed photographs on the wall, and others on a piano: a typical lower-middle-class European living room in the style of the late 1890s, only shabbier and dirtier.

As in most of the houses in Colombia, the walls were mere partitions, which did not reach the ceiling. They could distinctly hear a man in the next room brushing his teeth, and padding back and forth in his bare feet.

"At your service, Dominico!"

The chief of police appeared. He had a glass eye, and was wearing crumpled pajamas. By way of breakfast, he lit his first cigarette of the day.

"Have a seat, gentlemen. My wife is in Lima, for the Exposition, so I'm sure you'll understand if things are a bit topsy-turvy at the moment."

"I came to see you about you-know-who . . . this young man, whose name is . . ."

He hesitated. Mittel whispered, "Gentil."

"Ah, yes, that's it, Gentil . . ."

At this the chief of police winked at Dominico, to show that he knew the true identity of the young Frenchman.

"He will be able to testify that Plumier really did commit suicide."

"That is so," said Mittel.

"Were you present when it occurred?"

"No, I wasn't actually there, but . . ."

"You couldn't claim to have been an eyewitness? From your point of view it makes no difference, but to the commission of inquiry. . ."

Was it really possible that the chief of police, of all people, was inviting him to perjure himself?

"Don't you agree, Dominico? Unless the two of them were

190

to testify that they heard the shot, as they might well have done . . ."

Dominico turned to Moïse and Mittel with a smile.

"I agree that that would be the best course. This business has caused enough fuss already. Boitel is even talking of demanding an exhumation."

At this point they dropped the subject, to talk about other things and gossip about people who were strangers to Mittel. It was not until half an hour later that they left the apartment.

"There, that's settled! When the judge calls you as a witness, you will say that you both heard the shot. . . . You'll see about finding somewhere for him to stay, Moïse, won't you?"

Dominico accompanied them as far as the wooden town, where Moïse knew everyone. Needless to say, their first port of call was the bar, where, having had a whisky, Moïse asked the black bartender, "Do you know of any modest rooms for rent?"

The black pondered, then went over and spoke to some people sitting in a corner, and came back with an address. By midday, the problem of lodgings had been settled.

At street level there was a grocery store, owned by some Italians. The floor above, a somewhat stuffier version of the chief of police's apartment, was occupied by an elderly Colombian woman and her daughter. The husband had died some months previously, and the two women were prepared to rent their largest bedroom to anyone willing to take it fully furnished, complete with the family portraits on the walls.

"We only rent to quiet, respectable people," said the old woman firmly. She looked miserable, and was given to complaining for hours on end about nothing in particular.

"I'll go get your wife and bring her back in the car," suggested Moïse.

And Mittel, having nothing else to do, spent the intervening time wandering through the streets, which resembled the streets of Italy, in that the whole of life seemed to be lived outdoors. Now, for the first time, he saw that blacks were far from being the only people living in the town. Here and there throughout were brass plates on the fronts of buildings, inscribed DOCTOR, LAWYER, or DENTIST.

As he was walking past the bar, which seemed to be the social center of the town, he had the feeling that someone had got up and was following him. He had walked barely a hundred meters toward the river when a man came up beside him and murmured in French, "Pretend you haven't seen me. . . . Take the first right turn. I've got to speak to you. . . ."

Turning right, Mittel found himself in a deserted street at the end of which were a few houses on stilts, rising out of the river itself. Here the stranger came up to rejoin him.

"You're a Frenchman, aren't you? So am I. I daresay you've already heard of me."

"What's your name?"

"Boitel, Julien Boitel. I felt I must warn you. . . . Those people have got their hooks into you, and they'll do their utmost to keep you from seeing."

It was a strange experience to hear French being spoken, with a hint of a Southern accent, here, in this place. The man who had accosted Mittel was young, neatly dressed in a tussah-silk shirt, and wearing expensive shoes. All the time he was speaking, he never stopped looking around him uneasily.

"You'll see in a moment why it's better that we should not be seen together. . . . But, to begin with, tell me the truth: Plumier didn't commit suicide, did he?"

Flabbergasted, Mittel could find nothing to say.

"But . . ."

"You can be frank with me! Let me explain at once who I am. It was to me that Plumier sent all his papers. I am the trusted friend, of whom he must have spoken to you. Although I am a stranger to you, I am aware that you know nothing of this country and its ways, and that's why I felt it my duty to warn you. They will do all they can to win you over to their side. Dominico and his gang—they're nothing but a lot of thieves and murderers!

Unfortunately, they are also the political paymasters, so their word is law."

Mittel could not deny that, this very morning, the chief of police had urged him to bear false witness.

"I am married to a Colombian girl. The mine where you were employed belonged to my wife's family. It would take too long to tell you how Dominico got his hands on it, but I'm determined to get proof that he had Plumier murdered. It wouldn't be the first time he's done such a thing. Tell me what really happened there. Moïse was on the spot, wasn't he?"

"Yes."

No sooner had he said this than he regretted it. His eyes blazing, Boitel exclaimed, "Of course! He's their right-hand man, the hit man, as they say in the United States. Where did he sleep?"

"In my bungalow."

"Did he go out that night?"

"I don't know."

Another blunder! He bit his tongue, but the impulse to speak the truth was stronger than he was.

"I'm certain he did! And I bet you he arranged for one of his underlings to find the body. Am I right?"

"Yes!"

"You see? Just as one of his men recovered the bag of gold . . ."

Mittel, appalled, wiped the sweat from his forehead. How was it possible that so much should already be known in Buenaventura?

"I also know about the accident on the way back. A black compelled by Moïse to jump into the river."

"No!"

This was going too far. Moïse had not ordered the native to dive into the river. Quite the contrary. Mittel would never forget the black's joyful shout when he saw that the crocodile was dead.

"The man dived in of his own accord!"

"How naïve you are! Listen to me. There's a great deal more I

193

have to tell you. We're both Frenchmen. We must stand up to them together. I know I'm a stranger to you, but you could ask the French consul about me, or ask anyone who is not a member of the gang. Look, you must have heard of the Villers d'Avon, one of the most respected families in the Du Berry region? Well, the Count de Villers d'Avon is here. He'll tell you whether you can trust me. . . ."

Mittel could not wait to get away, to have some time to think. Boitel struck him as sincere, but he was obviously overwrought, frighteningly so, and his speech and manner were feverish.

"Where do you live?"

"Over there, on the second street on the left. I've taken a room with an elderly widow and her daughter."

"I know them. It would be unwise for me to be seen there. You had better come to my place, tonight after dinner. You won't have any difficulty in finding the house. It's—let me think—it's the tenth one on the right from yours. Use the door knocker. Knock lightly several times. . . ."

He was still very tense, his expression haunted, his eyes never still.

"I'll show you Plumier's letters. You won't understand until you've read them."

Charlotte, assisted by Moïse, was unpacking and putting the room in order. Mittel decided to say nothing of his encounter with Boitel. All their luggage had already come. The old woman could be heard pacing up and down the landing, probably hoping to find out as much as she could about her new lodgers. She had been most insistent that no nails were to be hammered into the walls, and no cooking would be allowed.

"I have news for you," announced Moise. "The hearing is to take place tomorrow morning. The judge is an old friend of mine! As regards lunch, you have a choice: either the hotel, which is expensive, or the bar almost next door to you, which serves a passable meal. If you decide to have all your meals there, special terms can be arranged."

Sun, sun, sun! Mittel could not remember when he had last seen so much of it. That concrete cube over there—in other words, the hotel—looked ready to explode, and the railroad tracks were two blinding streaks of light.

There was a ship anchored at the quayside, but its flag was hidden by the station building. Most likely an American liner, such as appeared regularly once every two weeks.

"What do you make of our two landladies?" whispered Charlotte, having put her ear to the door to make sure they were not lurking outside.

"The old woman seems pretty gloomy."

"And the young one is none too clean in her habits! The whole place smells musty. I'd better keep a hold on myself, or I'll have all those curtains down, and take up the carpets, and scrub the house from top to bottom! Are we going out for a meal?"

"Yes. And afterward we'll go see the doctor. I've been asking around, and I'm told there's one practically next door, an American."

"What do we want a doctor for?"

"So that you can have a thorough checkup."

"If you insist."

As far as she was concerned, there was nothing to worry about. Even her pregnancy did not seem to trouble her in the least.

"Apparently Dominico was more impressed by you than he had expected. Moïse himself has just told me so. And what's more, he went on to say there's an excellent job lined up for you. You have only to say the word!"

The building they ate in was like a barn, with the bar occupying one entire side. There were three or four other whites also having a meal, each eating in silence at a separate table. The menu was always the same: fruit salad, fried fish, stewed mutton, and eggplant.

"It's a bigger town than I thought," remarked Charlotte. "When we saw it that first time, I took it for a village."

Mittel's attention was fixed on a man in his fifties, eating at the table farthest away from them. He had white hair and a white mustache, and was the only man wearing a starched collar, which was so high that he couldn't move his head.

He kept his red-rimmed eyes fixed on the tablecloth, and he was afflicted with a tremor of the hands.

"Do you know him?" asked Charlotte.

"No. I haven't met him yet."

But he was convinced that this was the Count de Villers d'Avon. What was he doing in Buenaventura? What was his secret vice? For he certainly had one. His stiff collar enabled him to hold his head high, and his suit was also starched, of course. All the same, one could sense that it was merely a front. Even the half-caste waiter treated him with embarrassing familiarity.

The doctor proved yet another disillusionment. Mittel's first impression was of a household exactly like that of the chief of police: the same staircase, the same landing, the same bell pull, and it might have been the same slovenly servant.

"Do you want to see the doctor?"

The half-caste grimaced, obviously displeased. Voices could be heard whispering in the next room. Then someone swore in English. When the doctor finally appeared, he was dressed only in trousers and a shirt, and his hair was mussed.

In this place, it seemed, people spent the whole morning asleep, and then went back to sleep for the afternoon!

"Are you from the ship?" he asked, looking them up and down with disfavor.

"No, we've just arrived from the Chaco. My wife has been very ill."

He scrutinized her from head to foot.

"She seems all right now."

"I'd appreciate it if you'd examine her," said Mittel. "As you can see, she is in an interesting condition. Out there in the jungle, she contracted typhoid fever. I looked after her myself as best I could. . . ."

"Just give me five minutes, will you?"

He went back to his bedroom, drank a glass of water, and kept them waiting a full quarter of an hour in a red-and-yellow living room where there was nothing to be seen that was not at least twenty years old. When he returned, his hair smelled of eau de cologne and he was wearing a clean shirt and a linen jacket.

"Will you undress, please."

He seemed to entertain some doubts as to the necessity for this visit. While Charlotte was taking off her dress and underclothes, he remarked to Mittel, "If you've just arrived from the Chaco, then you must know all the latest news. Is it true that a white man was murdered out there?"

"You must be referring to my colleague, who committed suicide."

"Oh, so he committed suitcide, did he?"

The American's expression spoke louder than words: If that's how you want it! Have it your own way!

Charlotte would have been visible to anyone looking in from the windows across the street, but the doctor did not seem concerned.

"Well, you look perfectly healthy to me. . . . Breathe in. . . ."

Mittel was convinced that the doctor's mind was elsewhere the entire time he was examining the young woman.

"Nothing wrong with her lungs. . . . Her heart is sound. . . . All she needs is to put on a little weight."

Never had she seemed to him so painfully thin as in the harsh light of that living room. On the other hand, she appeared completely at ease, wandering around naked in this room that bore no resemblance to a doctor's office, and where nakedness seemed totally out of place.

"About the other matter, Doctor. About the baby, I mean . . ."

"What about it?"

"Can you tell us anything definite? Is it possible to say . . ."

"What do you want me to say? When the time comes, the child will be born, alive or dead. Is it your first, madame?"

"Yes, it is."

"No previous miscarriages?"

She shook her head.

197

"In this climate European women often miscarry the first time. But as far as I can see, there's no danger of that in your case."

It was over. He had washed his hands of the matter.

"Do you recommend any special diet, Doctor?"

"As much as she can eat."

"What about the typhoid?"

"It's left its mark. But it's over now, right?"

It was just like the incident with the black! Human life counted for nothing. The child would be born, alive or dead. So what? The typhoid fever had cured itself. The doctor had better things to attend to, such as returning to his siesta, perhaps, or visiting his fellow countrymen on board the liner.

"Don't you think you ought to have an examination?" said Charlotte, putting on her clothes.

And, to the doctor: "I've found blood on his handkerchiefs from time to time. He was treated for tuberculosis when he was a boy."

The doctor, who was almost two meters tall, looked Mittel up and down, as if to say: If it is tuberculosis, what do you expect me to do? This country is rife with it! If he survives, he survives, but it's hardly realistic to suggest sending him to Switzerland. . . . Given that, what else can we do?

Always the same thing, that contempt for human life. Mittel had lived for years and years without realizing it. Perhaps his eyes would never have been opened if fate had not decreed that he find himself in a huge, sparsely populated continent, where human beings were scarce and were regarded in a totally different light.

"How much do I owe you, Doctor?"

The doctor looked embarrassed.

"I don't know what to say. . . . Are you well off?"

"I earn a living."

"Working for Dominico! I doubt if he pays you more than three hundred pesos a month."

"Two hundred."

"Then he's cheating you out of a hundred. Give me two pesos."

And that was that. For two whole weeks out in the jungle, in that bungalow filled with the stench of disease, Mittel had spent every second, day and night, in a fierce battle with death. How had he managed to survive that fearsome struggle? Now, for the first time, he asked himself how it had been possible.

He had saved Charlotte's life, perhaps even the child's life. He had, at long last, returned to a civilized town, such as he had come to believe he would never see again. He had consulted a highly qualified doctor. He had wanted to know. And the doctor had examined Charlotte's emaciated body with a look of boredom, perhaps even embarrassment.

"The child will be born, alive or dead."

What, then, was the use of all that talk about scientific advances? He was filled with revulsion. Outside in the street he was silent, and so deep in thought that he walked past their door. Charlotte, grabbing his arm, said, "Where are you going?"

"I don't know."

His tone of voice was so fierce that she burst out laughing.

"There's no need to lose your temper. What's the matter? Is it because the doctor couldn't say whether it would be a boy or a girl?"

Yes, she was actually laughing, she who, after all, was the one principally concerned. What better proof that it was he who had got it all wrong?

"You'd better go inside. . . . I'm going to the office. . . ."

But when he got to the hotel, he stopped by the deserted bar and gazed at the slot machine, suddenly reminded of Mopps. He could see him still, feeding coins into the machine, day after day, with his mind on other things.

"Give me some half-pesos," he said to the bartender.

What had been in Mopps's thoughts as he stubbornly persisted in defying the laws of chance? Mittel's own thoughts were confused. They were not so much thoughts as a state of mind, a vague sense of unease, or, more precisely, a feeling of belonging nowhere.

And here less than anywhere!

"What'll you have?"

He did not want anything alcoholic, and, to the amazement of the bartender, he ordered a lemonade. He lost as many pesos as he felt like, nostalgically recalling the freighter swaying at anchor on the river, its French flag drenched with rain. By the end of the voyage he had come to feel at home, and, for the first time in his life, had made friends, especially with Jolet and Napo.

What was he to say in the witness stand the next day? That he had heard the shot?

And this very evening, would he keep his appointment with Boitel? And what would he say to him?

Dominico came into the entranceway, accompanied by Moïse, who was always obsequious in the presence of the boss.

"I'll leave him to you," Dominico was saying.

Of whom were they speaking? They had not spotted Mittel, and he had little doubt that he himself was the subject of their discussion. At that moment, the passengers from the American cruise liner came pouring into the hotel, looking as if they had not a care in the world and were concerned only to send postcards and look for souvenirs of Colombia, which were mainly little ivory knickknacks and plastic replicas of canoes manned by Indians. There was also a shopwindow full of stuffed baby crocodiles, their skins polished and varnished, pretty little things not much more than thirty centimeters long.

Mittel had already lost twenty pesos in the slot machine.

13

HE HAD BEEN AMAZED TO FIND, ON RETURNING TO HIS ROOM FOR
the first time, that there was some mail waiting for him, a letter
placed by the old lady in a prominent position on a table.

The envelope was headed *Monsieur and Madame Gentil*, followed by their full address in Buenaventura, which Mittel himself had just learned that morning. The paper was blue and of the
finest quality, with a monogram engraved on the flap. Charlotte
stood looking over his shoulder on tiptoe as he read it.

He groaned in vexation. He had not been expecting anything
particularly sensational, but even so it annoyed him to read:

Sir, and honored compatriot,

*I beg to apologize for having omitted this morning to invite
Madame Gentil to accompany you to our informal little gathering
this evening. My wife looks forward eagerly to making her acquain-
tance, as do also the other members of her family.*

*In respectfully requesting you to act as my intermediary in this
matter,*

> *I remain,*
> *Yours most sincerely,*
> *Julien Boitel*

"Do you want to go?"

"Rather that than spend the evening alone in this place."

And so here they were! Out of respect for her condition, they
had settled Charlotte in the most comfortable armchair, to the
right of the piano, beside the pink marble mantelpiece.

Even before he had set eyes on it, Mittel had foreseen that
Boitel's home would be identical to those of the chief of police

and their landlady. He was beginning to think that, some time toward the end of the last century, a wholesale consignment of mahogany furniture, clocks, dark velvet upholstery material, endless rolls of fringing, and quantities of fake china must have been sent out to Buenaventura.

Here, however, there was a differene As in Boitel's letter, there was an effort to express social superiority. Boitel's mother-in-law, who was short and very fat, almost as round as a ball, wore an ornate black silk dress, and her daughter was dressed in lilac. There must not have been many rooms in the apartment, since a tray of tea and cakes had been set out beforehand in the living room.

"Please be good enough to overlook the shortcomings of our humble abode. Won't you sit down . . . ?"

And Charlotte, taking it all perfectly seriously, assumed a prim expression that was admirably suited to her surroundings.

"I trust you are keeping as well as can be expected in the circumstances, dear lady?"

"I'm in the best of health."

"My husband has told me of your arduous journey. It's beyond me how you could have had the courage to undertake it!"

A touch of the tarbrush was clearly visible in the features of Boitel's mother-in-law, as was the case with most South Americans. As for Boitel's wife, she was slim, gentle, almost languid in manner.

"Would you care for some refreshment?"

But the sudden opening of a door was sufficient to shatter this carefully contrived veneer of elegance. There stood revealed a bedroom, containing three beds side by side, in a state of chaos reminiscent of a campsite. Madame Boitel's father, a very frail old man, tottered into the living room, and the other Boitels looked at their guests apologetically.

"My father-in-law," said Boitel, "was one of his country's most distinguished representatives."

He was now totally senile and had to be helped into a chair in a corner. Two young girls also appeared, dark-haired and black-eyed, one wearing blue, the other pink. They curtsied, like convent pupils, and retired discreetly, to sit with their backs to the wall. These were Madame Boitel's sisters.

"What do you think of our country?" the older woman asked Charlotte.

And Charlotte, looking thoughtful, nodded her head. "It's very interesting. Except for the rain . . ."

But Boitel felt that they had wasted enough time in social chitchat, and was resolved to get down to brass tacks.

"Does Dominico know that we have become acquainted?"

"I don't think so."

"If he did, he wouldn't sleep a wink tonight. Take a look at this."

He handed Mittel a brief, badly printed Spanish news-sheet, *El Corriere*, displaying the headline:

ANOTHER ENGINEER MURDERED IN THE BAJO CHACO.

"Read it later, at your leisure. Do you smoke? This afternoon, I deposited a strongbox at the bank, containing all Plumier's papers. It seemed a wise precaution. Obviously that gang would not think twice about arranging a burglary, to get their hands on them."

The room was dimly lit with yellowish electric bulbs, like the trolley cars of former times. As a result, the faces of those present were framed with shadows, as were the lilac, blue, and pink dresses of the three young women.

Everyone was respectfully attentive to what Boitel was saying. They clearly regarded him as the head of the family.

"I'll tell you the whole story in detail, including the various steps Dominico took to make his millions. . . . Listen to this! My family, today, would have been one of the richest in Colombia, if he had not stripped us of everything. . . ."

At first Mittel could not make out why he felt ill at ease in this setting, and then the reason struck him: it was seeing Boitel, a Frenchman to his fingertips if ever there was one, in this overwhelmingly exotic environment, where even the smells were strange and unfamiliar. And Boitel was not only a Frenchman, but a typical example of a distinctive class of Frenchman. He was a petit-bourgeois down to the cut of his jacket, the knot of his tie, and his manner of speaking—the epitome of provincial France, but transported suddenly to the other side of the world, and surrounded by people who, if one looked at them closely, were like supernumerary actors in some exotic stage spectacle.

For the young women also, with their solemn faces and sorrowful eyes, clearly had Indian blood in their veins. Indeed, when Mittel looked at them through half-closed eyelids, he was for an instant reminded of the coarse features of his workmen in the jungle.

Even all those French knickknacks, transplanted and set out in a different fashion, seemed altered in character!

"We are expecting the Count to join us. I'm surprised he has not arrived yet. Dominico fleeced him of more than a hundred thousand pesos. Everything is grist to his mill, don't you see? There is not a single business transaction, maritime or commercial, in which he doesn't have a hand. He has suborned every judge and politician in the place, so he holds all the cards, and everything he touches turns to gold. You've seen the hotel. It was built by a Colombian from Bogotá some four years ago. It cost a fortune, because twice, while it was under contruction, the walls collapsed. A few months after the opening, the Colombian went bankrupt, and Dominico snapped it up."

Mittel was unable to work up any indignation over these revelations, or to regard Dominico with revulsion, especially since he scarcely knew him.

"What you must do tomorrow is tell the judge all you know, and then insist on submitting a signed statement, because otherwise they wouldn't hesitate to twist your words!"

A bell rang in the entrance, followed almost at once by the appearance of the man Mittel had seen in the bar. He kissed his hostess's hand, and those of the two girls, and bowed to Charlotte.

"Allow me to introduce the Count de Villers d'Avon, a close friend, who has been resident in Colombia for the past ten years.

I was just saying, Count, that our friend Gentil has it in his power to destroy Dominico's influence once and for all. When it is known that Plumier was murdered on his orders . . ."

"Listen . . ."

Mittel was growing more and more uneasy; he felt suffocated.

"Are you related to the Gentils of Bordeaux?" asked Villers, sinking into a chair.

"No, I don't think so."

"There was a Gentil at the École des Chartes whom I knew. A most intelligent young man. He's probably in the diplomatic service by now. . . . Boitel tells me that you have the most damaging evidence against Dominico."

"No, it's not true! I don't know anything, and . . ."

Boitel drew his chair closer, his agitation mounting.

"You don't deny that Plumier was murdered, do you?"

"It's impossible to be sure. He was showing unmistakable signs of mental derangement. To give you an example, except during the period of my wife's illness he never addressed a single word to me."

"That was because he suspected you of spying for Dominico. He may even have thought that you had been sent there to eliminate him. However, be that as it may, it is still the fact that Moïse was on the spot, and that you can't be sure he never went out of your bungalow that night. You told me so yourself! You admitted that you did not hear a sound, and that the following morning the body was discovered by one of Moïse's men. Isn't that so?"

"Well, that is . . ."

"Is it not also a fact that Plumier's bungalow was broken into and ransacked, and his safe forced and emptied?"

"Yes."

"Very good, that's all we need. You have only to repeat to the judge what you told me, and insist on having it taken down in writing to be signed by you, and Dominico will have a hard time refuting your accusations."

"Would anyone care for more tea?" interposed his wife.

Charlotte responded with a winning smile. The heat was stifling, and it wasn't just the heat. Mittel felt as if he were being physically choked. He no longer knew where he was. He could see only dimly, as through a fog, and the faces around him looked insubstantial, like those of creatures in a nightmare.

The Count, his eyes red-rimmed, was smoking a long cigar and nodding his head. His legs were crossed, and his hands lay flat on his knees. The old man in the corner might not have existed, so little did he seem any longer to form part of the family circle, while his wife turned toward Charlotte from time to time, making polite conversation.

They were most anxious to demonstrate to their French visitors that they had been well brought up, as well as having the advantage of a French son-in-law.

Mittel caught occasional snatches of the conversation:

"I take it you'll be going up into the hills to have your baby?"

And Charlotte, straight-faced: "I don't know yet. . . . It all depends on my husband's business commitments."

Was it possible that, only last night, they had slept in a tent on the riverbank? They had not even been given time to catch their breath!

"You must insist on having a competent interpreter. Your Spanish is not up to giving testimony on a matter of such vital importance. . . . I have a friend who would do the job admirably. I'll write down his name for you. You'll have to ask the judge to appoint him officially, but it's no more than you're entitled to. . . ."

And Boitel went out to fetch paper and pencil, all set to orchestrate the coming hearing.

"I assure you . . ." protested Mittel, more than once.

"I wish the French consul could have been with us this evening. He's a Jew from Bogotá, but he's an honest man. Unfortunately, he's away at present, touring the northern region—he is also an agent for several American companies that deal in agricultural machinery."

Time passed slowly in this close, twilit enclave. Eventually, the rest of the company fell silent, and Boitel held the floor.

"If you should lose your job, there are ten of us ready to find you another, preferably in the interior, where the climate is much more suitable for Madame Gentil."

Outside on the deserted street, they could find nothing to say to each other. Mittel's shirt was sticking to him. Gérard de Villers had stayed behind, probably to exchange views about him with Boitel. The two men had accompanied them to the door.

"I trust we shall be seeing a lot of each other in the future."

And then, abruptly, they were on the street. There was no sidewalk, only wooden houses on either side. Occasionally they stumbled on a black, asleep on the ground. A fine drizzle was falling, bluring the light from the only two street lamps in the town.

"What are you going to do?" asked Charlotte at last, with a weary sigh.

He had no idea. Obviously he had not heard the shot, nor could he be certain that Moïse had not gone out that night. But that didn't prove anything. It still remained more than probable that Plumier had committed suicide.

He slept badly, and was awakened very early by his landlady's footsteps as she crept around furtively, like a mouse. Wearing slippers and a little apron, with her hair tied up in a scarf, she was flicking a feather duster over the ornaments.

"What are we going to do about coffee?"

As soon as she heard voices, the old woman came in, bowing and scraping, to say that she would make the coffee herself, since she did not want them to use a stove of any kind in their room, because of the mess it made.

The coffee was so strong that they could not bring themselves to drink it.

"When will you be back?"

"I don't know."

He didn't have the slightest idea. Once again he was on the brink of a new life. Bleary-eyed, he made his way to the hotel, where he found Moïse waiting for him in the lobby. Together they went upstairs to Dominico's office suite, where two Colombian clerks were already at work. But the boss had not yet arrived.

An office very much like any other, with white wood furniture, filing cabinets, a telephone, and promotional calendars on the walls. The windows looked out on the river, where, this morning, there were no ships in sight.

They were left to cool their heels there until eleven o'clock. Moïse, making himself at home, passed the time in reading letters he found lying about and poking around inside drawers. He had dressed with greater care than usual, and was wearing a celluloid dicky with a tie attached.

At long last, the telephone rang. Moïse answered it, then announced, "It's time to go. The boss will meet us at the judge's."

Mittel had the feeling that Moïse was no longer concerned with putting pressure on him. They talked of this and that, in particular the quality of the food served in the bar, but there was no mention of Plumier.

"This is it."

Yet another wooden building, with posters on the walls, and Dominico's car parked outside. They wandered through a maze of corridors until they came to a door on which Moïse knocked.

Dominico was already there, sitting with his legs crossed and smoking a cigar, and the judge sent his clerk out to fetch some more chairs.

The judge was young, and exquisitely dressed. His manner in greeting his visitors was very much that of a man of the world. Smiling, he held out his cigarette case to each of them in turn. When they were all seated the judge motioned to the clerk, who sat down at the end of the table and waited.

"I trust you won't object, Monsieur Gentil—you are Monsieur Gentil, are you not?—to answering a few questions?"

He, too, laid stress upon the name Gentil, and Mittel could not help suspecting that this was a veiled threat. The fact was, he had not rehearsed his responses, and indeed had still not made up his mind. Even now he did not know what he was going to say. He tried to shut out the recollection of Boitel's flat, the old lady, the Count, the senile father, and the three young women in pink, blue, and lilac.

"You saw enough of Plumier, didn't you, to be able to tell us whether or not he showed any signs of mental derangement?"

"Yes."

"Would you describe his behavior as eccentric? Did he seem to you to be suffering from persecution mania?"

"Yes, he did."

Dominico was coolly filing his nails, as if unconcerned with what was going on.

"Did he ever take you into his confidence?"

"He never said a word to me—or, rather, not until my wife became seriously ill."

"All right. On the night of his death, Monsieur Moïse slept in your bungalow, where you also slept. Isn't that so?"

"Yes."

"Well, he didn't go out during the night, did he?"

"No," said Mittel.

Phew! That let him out, anyhow. It was the easiest way, and certainly the safest.

"I repeat, he didn't go out that night? When you heard the shot, was he still with you in the bungalow?"

"Yes."

"In other words, there isn't a shadow of doubt that Plumier took his own life. That's all I wanted to know. I'm much obliged to you. Would you care for a cigarette?"

"I don't smoke."

And that was all! The others seemed impatient for him to be gone.

Dominico remained behind, as did Moïse. They left him to find his way out by himself. Suddenly he felt disoriented, as if everyone had abandoned him. The street was bathed in sunlight, and buzzing with swarms of flies. He did not know whether he was expected to go to the office or not. Eventually, he decided to return to his lodgings, where he found Boitel sitting with Charlotte.

"Do forgive me. . . . It seemed to me the best way of finding out, so I took the liberty . . ."

Charlotte was wearing a grubby, crumpled dressing gown, as usual. She gave no thought to her appearance except when she was going out. At home she was extremely slovenly in her personal habits, not even bothering to wash or do her hair until just before leaving the house.

"Well? Did you tell them . . ?"

Suddenly, without warning, Mittel flew into a towering rage. In a voice that even he did not recognize as his own, he shouted, "What did you expect me to tell them?"

"But . . . I thought we had agreed last night . . ."

"And what right did you have to dictate to me what my evidence should be? I answered the questions put to me—no more, no less."

"What did he ask you?"

Boitel, flustered by this unexpected display of temper, had risen to his feet.

"I don't remember. And besides, I've always understood that anything said to an examining magistrate is confidential."

Charlotte, too, was gaping at him in astonishment.

"I've had just about enough of all this, and that's the truth! How can I possibly judge whether Plumier took his own life or not? What business is it of mine, anyway?"

"I thought . . ."

Boitel, momentarily at a loss for words, snatched up his hat.

"When I learned that you were a fellow countryman of mine, I thought, and so did my wife . . . I'm sorry . . . please forgive me, madame, for having bothered you at such an inconvenient time."

He moved toward the door. Out on the landing, he paused for a moment, then finally left.

"They get on my nerves," continued Mittel, when he and

Charlotte were alone once more. "I just don't know what they're going on about! And, anyway, what do I really know about them? What's at the bottom of all these intrigues?"

He was under no obligation to tell lies, was he? He had always believed Plumier to be mad. Not certifiable, no. Not mad all the time. In fact, there had been occasions when he had seemed in perfect command of all his faculties. . . .

Which did not mean he was incapable of taking his own life just to spite those whom he regarded as his enemies!

As for Moïse, there was little doubt that he would not hesitate to kill in cold blood. But surely Mittel would have heard him go out during the night?

Well, then? That, and nothing more, was what he had said in evidence. True, he had allowed them to note down that he had heard the shot. But what difference did that make, one way or the other?

And it was only now that it struck him that they had not even asked him to sign his statement!

"Let's go have lunch," he murmured.

"I'm not quite ready."

While she was getting dressed, he stood at the window, looking out at the squalid street, down the middle of which trickled a stinking stream of water.

He might have—naturally, if only he could have!—at least been a little less positive. He could have hinted at the doubts which, in spite of everything, still lingered in his mind.

And what then? What would have been the outcome?

"Do you think this dress is too dirty to wear?"

"Of course not," he replied, without looking at her.

He deliberately ate a huge meal, as if he were venting his spleen on the food. Gérard de Villers, coming into the bar for a drink, caught sight of them and came across the room to kiss Charlotte's hand. It was ridiculous.

He hasn't seen Boitel yet, said Jef to himself. If he had, he'd have spared himself the trouble.

The Count, who was a bit of a fool, could find nothing to say but "Not a bad day, is it? Not too hot . . . If you'll excuse me, I'll leave you to your meal."

He had not taken three steps before Mittel muttered between his teeth, "That man's an ass!"

Which was enough to send Charlotte into gales of laughter.

As things stood, though he could not be described as happy, he was at least not miserable. Days passed, weeks passed, in an unchanging routine.

In the offices on the fourth floor of the hotel, the Venetian blinds sliced the sunlight into thin lines, and the electric fans buzzed unceasingly in his ears.

The office was light, almost cheerful. One of the clerks was a half-caste of predominantly Negroid appearance, but since he was originally from Martinique, he felt he had the right to look down on the other blacks. The other clerk was a Colombian who, with his dreamy eyes and slight frame, reminded Mittel of Boitel's sisters-in-law.

There was plenty of work to keep them busy all day. The immense scale of Dominico's operations was becoming daily more apparent to Mittel, though Dominico himself took it all in stride. Far from flaunting himself as a tycoon, he never spent more than an hour or two a day in his office. The rest of the time he was at home, playing poker with friends, drinking liqueurs, and smoking cigars. Women seemed to play no part in his life. If he had a mistress, Mittel was unaware of it.

On the other hand, all the import and export business of Buenaventura passed through his hands, not to mention a third or more of the mercantile traffic of the whole of Colombia. Cables, in a variety of different codes, were dispatched to Europe, America, and Australia. Occasionally, Mittel would see cables addressed to French companies, on the Rue du Quatre Septembre or the Rue du Sentier, which he had often walked past, never dreaming that their tentacles extended halfway across the world.

Only Moïse was never in the office. He was constantly on the

212

move, traveling to Cali, Bogotá, and Medellín, and, at the end of each month, setting out again to tour the mines.

One day, Dominico, who usually seemed oblivious of the existence of his employees, stopped at Mittel's desk.

"When is it due? You know—the baby?"

"In about six weeks."

"I've been meaning to tell you, you could send your wife to Cali, where there's a very good clinic. Naturally you couldn't go with her, but I presume that wouldn't worry you."

"I'll think about it."

Charlotte had got hold of a few popular French novels, and she spent most of her days reading them, lying with her feet up on the green moquette couch.

They no longer saw anything of the Boitels. They had not heard a word from them since Dominico had sued *El Corriere* for libel and won his case.

How did they manage to support themselves? Mittel often wondered. The in-laws came from one of the most notable families in Colombia. In the days of the great *haciendas*, which had consisted of tens of thousands of acres, they had been among the richest landowners, but they had sold their holdings piecemeal to foreign companies, and to individual entrepreneurs like Dominico, for what seemed to them a high price.

What had become of the proceeds? Had they speculated with the money, and lost? Now, apparently, it was all gone. They lived frugally, keeping themselves to themselves, with Boitel as their self-appointed champion, to delve into the records of long-concluded transactions in the hope of unearthing evidence of irregularities.

The old man was carried out on to the veranda every day, where he sat slumped in an armchair, glum and motionless as a sick dog.

The women did their household shopping wearing hats and gloves. Boitel made frequent trips to Cali and Bogotá. Mittel, from his window, watched him board the train, never speaking to a soul.

As for Villers d'Avon, Mittel now knew the reason for *his* presence in Buenaventura. Having come to Colombia originally for a few weeks' vacation, he had fallen in love with a young Indian servantgirl and had lingered here to be with her, for months and then for years.

By now he was believed to have two or three children, but no one had ever seen their mother. For he was reputed to be as jealous in regard to her as on the first day he saw her, and kept her shut up in their house on the extreme edge of town.

When his brother traveled all the way from France for the express purpose of reclaiming him from this entanglement, Villers d'Avon's response was to marry his native mistress in a civil ceremony, followed by a wedding in church.

Mittel had taken him for a man of at least sixty, but had since been told that he was not yet forty-eight! He had surrendered his rights of primogeniture in return for a small monthly allowance.

He still bowed to Mittel and Charlotte whenever they met, but never spoke to them.

At one o'clock every day, they lunched at the bar, where they had their own napkins and napkin rings, as in a family boardinghouse.

Mittel spent the afternoon at the office, from three to seven, and sometimes did not get home till nine o'clock. Then there was dinner, followed by a short walk through the dark streets or, occasionally, by the river.

This way of life could not have been more different from their life in the jungle, or even that on board the freighter. Here they had nothing to look forward to, and had ceased even to count the passing days. Only the fast-approaching date for the baby kept them aware that months had gone by.

They were neither happy nor unhappy. Night followed day, and day night, and every day was the same. It was always hot; at certain times of day the sun shone, and at others it rained. There were the white linen suits, the office fans, the old landlady in slippers, pottering around with her feather duster, and still, whatever they might say, making coffee so strong that they had to dilute it with water.

Eventually they became almost like sleepwalkers. They had ceased to think, except for the occasional image that flashed through their minds, and their conversations were inconsequential.

"Still no word from Mopps . . ."

"Has it ever struck you that the baby's legal surname will be Gentil? Doesn't that seem strange to you?"

One thing that he no longer found strange was the transformation of Charlotte, who had recently taken it into her head to adopt the same style of dress as Boitel's wife and sisters-in-law, and who now never went out without gloves.

"What time is it in France now?"

"Half past midnight."

"And here it's the middle of the day! I can just picture the neon sign on the Rue Blanche and the Rue Pigalle, and the doormen, and the bellboys."

Certainly one could conjure up all this in one's mind, but it seemed like an illusion now, almost as if such things had never existed. It was too remote, both in time and in space. There was nothing to do but sigh and change the subject.

"I've taught the cook how to make a stew the way we like it. He'll give it a try tomorrow."

They had grown sick of mutton, which was served at every meal. But there was no point in complaining, since that was all there was.

No, not quite all: once a fortnight, when the Grace Line ship put in, they would go aboard for dinner in the Louis XVI dining room, where they were served by girls in yellow dresses, to the accompaniment of dance music played by a trio. They always chose a corner table, having nothing to do with the passengers, who, anyway, mostly preferred to go ashore and sample Colombian cooking.

On these occasions they drank wine, which was served without charge to Mittel because Dominico was the company agent, responsible for provisioning the ships. Sometimes they would be given a present of a piece of beef or a fish on ice, and the cook at the bar would prepare it for them the next day.

Mittel could not be described as cheerful, but he was a good deal more relaxed than he had been in the jungle. As time went on, he talked less and less, to the point where one day Charlotte, puzzled, asked, "Don't you have anything to say to me?"

"No."

"A penny for your thoughts!"

"I've given up thinking."

It was very nearly the truth. What was the use of thinking? What was there to think about? He had sent two hundred francs to his mother out of his first month's wages, and in her reply she had said that she was saving the money toward her fur coat. Once Bébé got an idea in her head, nothing would dislodge it!

Everybody is still talking about a war. Take my advice and stay where you are.

She had been ill, following an unusually severe winter.

Some friends of mine are trying to get me a job on a paper in Nice.

He read the words without taking them in. Her world no longer had any meaning for him. He tried to conjure up a picture of Nice, where he had once lived: the Promenade des Anglais, the crowds strolling in the sunshine.

To think that over there people exposed themselves to the sun for the fun of it!

"Not a word from Mopps!" he told Charlotte every time there was a delivery of mail.

This weighed on him. It left a sort of vacuum in his life.

There was a map of the world attached to the top of his desk. How he wished he could pinpoint on it the exact location of the *Croix-de-Vie*, with Jolet, Napo, the bo'sun, and the rest of the crew.

"When the time comes, will you go to Cali?"

They had been discussing it for the past six days. Charlotte

216

could not make up her mind. In Cali the climate was better, the doctors more reliable, but it involved a journey by train, a complete change in their routine, and she was as indolent as he was.

So that when the pains began unexpectedly, late one night, Mittel had no choice but to go fetch the American doctor who had examined her soon after their arrival.

The doctor was furious: "You might have given me some warning!" No doubt he had been drinking heavily that night. In any case, he gulped down three large tumblers of water and got dressed. He had mislaid his medical bag. They wasted half an hour searching for it before finally unearthing it from under his jacket in the waiting room.

"Are you sure it's urgent?" he asked for the umpteenth time, as he followed Mittel out into the street.

14

SHORTLY AFTER NOON, WHILE CHARLOTTE WAS TAKING A NAP, AND their room was in its usual chaos, a letter arrived. Frowning, Mittel looked at the stamp. He had been in the middle of washing his hands, which were covered in lather, so he did not touch the envelope but peered closely at the writing, trying to recall where he had seen it before. It was a bold hand, written with a broad nib, and each word began with a capital letter.

Overanxious as usual, he glanced toward the bed, where the reddish top of a baby's head could be seen, muffled in bedclothes. Then, at last, he tore open the envelope and read:

Well, sonny boy,

If you've got nothing better to do, you have my permission to come and join me in Tahiti. I'm assured you'll get by with your passport, and Charlotte as well. I have accepted an appointment as captain of a pleasure boat out here. If I should happen to be away when you arrive, make yourselves known at the Anglo-French Club. Apart from this, I have no news of interest.

Your old buddy,

Mopps

It was an odd coincidence. Mittel looked toward the bed, and then at the letter, perturbed by this invitation that came from so far away, out of the distant past.

At the sight of the words and the bold, widely spaced lettering, he felt almost as if Mopps were actually present there in the house, a participant in recent events.

"What's going on?" murmured Charlotte drowsily.

"I've got a letter from Mopps."

"What's he been up to?"

"I don't know. He says he's been appointed captain of a pleasure boat in Tahiti."

Still apparently half asleep, she asked wonderingly, "Do they have pleasure boats in Tahiti?"

And she promptly drowsed off again. Mittel went out onto the wooden balcony and leaned on the rail, so that his landlady could straighten the room. Receiving Mopps's letter had thrown his thoughts and feelings into confusion. The existence of the child became somehow confused with memories of life on the South Seas, and the sun-drenched street below seemed suddenly sad and empty.

And yet, oddly enough, at that very moment his self-esteem experienced a tiny boost. The youngest of Boitel's sisters-in-law, who must have been approaching her sixteenth birthday, a girl with huge dark eyes, was passing by on the opposite side of the road. Being a well-brought-up young lady, she did not loiter in the street. All the same, when she caught sight of Mittel on his balcony, she made a point of dropping one of her gloves and bending down to pick it up, as an excuse to linger near him.

She had blushed vividly on seeing him, as she invariably did, and as she walked on, she kept her eyes resolutely lowered.

He smiled. It was something of a joke, really. Then his thoughts strayed to other streets, just like this one, to the bar, the hotel, and, finally, the port.

Mopps was in Tahiti! He could not have put it into words, but he had the comforting feeling that here at last was a dream come true. Whenever Mittel looked back on the past, it was always the reassuring figure of Mopps that came to mind.

Now something that belonged, in a sense, to the future had come into their lives, in the form of a baby boy, though Mittel seldom looked at him—he was still so ugly.

"He's going to be hideous!" he had said to the doctor.

"Nonsense! All newborn babies look like that."

"Oh!"

All the same, he was not wholly impressed. Charlotte had

expressed the same revulsion. When they had first brought the baby to her, there had been no transports of joy, no hint of tenderness, just a sigh of disappointment.

"He's going to be terribly ugly!"

He was born with a lot of hair, a great deal too much, in fact; his skin was red and wrinkled, and he was pug-nosed.

Mittel had to keep an eye on her while she slept, to make sure she did not lie on the baby and crush him, or push him onto the floor, for she seemed unaware that she was no longer alone in the bed.

Mopps in Tahiti! A French colony! Presumably, then, the murder on the Boulevard Beaumarchais was forgotten, since Mopps believed it safe for Charlotte to go to Tahiti. Of course, she would be traveling under the name of Gentil and using a forged passport.

Mittel had just gone to fetch the passport from one of their suitcases when a thought struck him. He found the passport, and frowned as he turned over the pages. Their child would bear the surname Gentil! In other words, a name that did not exist, a name without any real past or present.

The more he reflected on this, the more troubled he became, and he was suddenly overwhelmed with deep pity for his son.

He himself had repudiated his father's name of Mittelhauser in favor of Mittel, so that he wouldn't be constantly reminded of his unhappy past.

And now here was his son bearing yet another name, a name chosen at random for a forged passport.

A passport that, up to this moment, Mittel had never bothered to examine. Now, for the first time, he learned that he had been born in the Jura, and that he was twenty-five years old. Neither of these statements was true; he had never even set foot in the Jura region!

The old landlady had gone off to cook her lunch, and the room seemed deserted, unnaturally deserted, with not a single caller to gaze admiringly at the baby and congratulate its mother.

At one o'clock came a minor diversion, a timid knock at the

door. It was one of Mittel's colleagues, delivering a small parcel from Dominico, which turned out to contain a silver rattle of the kind sold in the local bazaars.

"Is it a boy?"

"A boy, yes."

"The boss says you don't have to come to the office today."

One solitary day off! If he had been in Tahiti with Mopps, and maybe even the others, Jolet, Napo, the whole crew . . .

Charlotte was taking the whole thing in stride. She had given birth, according to the doctor, like a woman who had already had three or four children, and afterward, the minute she woke up, she complained that she was hungry.

As for the baby, she handled it with a mixture of curiosity and wariness.

"I've never understood how anyone can see any resemblance between a baby and its father or mother. Babies don't look like people at all! Is this the best Dominico could do by way of a present? Have you made up your mind yet what to call him?"

For they had not yet decided on a Christian name for the child. Charlotte would have liked Christian, but Mittel considered this too fancy.

"What about Henri?" he suggested.

"I have a brother named Henri, and he's a policeman."

"Charles?"

In the end they agreed on Charles, and that afternoon Mittel took his passport and went to the town hall, to register the child. He passed Boitel in the street on the way, but Boitel cut him dead.

Mittel wondered what Boitel did with himself all day. He was forever rushing hither and thither, like a man engaged in urgent business. He dispatched letters and cables all over the place in pursuit of his obsession with recovering some part of the lost fortune of his in-laws, who in the meantime were living in abject poverty.

Mittel did not go home immediately, though there was nothing to keep him from doing so. He was in no hurry to get back to

221

Charlotte and the baby. It was not that he felt disillusioned exactly, but his feelings were certainly not what he had imagined they would be.

There was no great surge of happiness. For hours on end he had assisted the doctor, giving him things to drink, in a state of exhaustion, his nerves stretched to breaking point. When he had first been shown the baby, he had scarcely dared to touch it, for fear of causing it some mortal injury.

As a salve to his conscience, he had endeavored to treat Charlotte affectionately, but she was unresponsive, obviously wondering what had come over him.

Wasn't it a fact that at the back of his mind there had always lurked the belief that this event would bind them to each other, that it would transform them into a genuine couple, a household, a family?

But nothing of the sort! Everything was exactly as it had been before. Charlotte shared his room but not his life, and although the newborn baby slept in her bed, she was scarcely aware of him.

Finally he did go home. He intended to draft a telegram to Mopps, telling him the news, but was deterred by the thought that it could cost nearly ten francs a word.

"Are you breastfeeding him already? The doctor said . . ."

"What does the doctor know about it? It's just like when he tried to prevent me from eating."

"Have you eaten?"

"I got the landlady to bring me a cup of *café au lait.*"

Hours and days went by in this way, meaninglessly and uneventfully. On one of his brief stops at Buenaventura, Moïse exclaimed, "What did I tell you? You were always fretting about the baby's birth. Don't you remember the state you used to get into, back there at the bungalow? Women of that sort, who look as if a puff of wind would blow them over, are always tougher than all the rest of us put together. You mark my words, she'll see us all into our graves. . . ."

Those last words made a deep impression on Mittel, and he was often to recall them afterward.

"Your successor is another one. . . . You two were constantly complaining about the loneliness, the rain, the climate, the rats, and heaven knows what else. Whereas, when I called on him, I found him blissfully happy. He's taken on that little black girl, you know the one I mean. . . . She keeps house for him. Needless to say, she is already pregnant, but one of these days he'll ditch her for another one. As for the rats, if the need arose, I don't doubt he'd make a meal of them. . . . That's what I call a real man!"

Obviously! Mittel envied him his stamina, but he himself couldn't help being cursed with imagination, which, in the end, inevitably leads to suffering.

He was still the same man today. Ever since the arrival of Mopps's letter, he had come to see the town and the river in a new light. He asked himself how he could possibly have gone on living here all these months without concentrating his thoughts on the possibility of escape.

Recently, without a word even to Charlotte, he had been making calculations, with the aid of the fare schedules of the various shipping companies. The cheapest second-class fare to Panama was six hundred francs a head. The French ship plying between Panama and Tahiti was still more expensive. Admittedly, the journey took two weeks, but two thousand francs a head . . . !

The total for the journey alone would come to seven thousand francs. Even if he could find the money, it would be a lengthy business. There was only one sailing a month from Buenaventura to Panama, and once there, if they should miss the French mail-boat they would have to wait another six weeks.

All this had the effect of making Mittel feel as if he were trapped in a barbed-wire enclosure.

He had also made other calculations. By reducing their expenditure even further, for instance, by having only one meal a day in the restaurant, in defiance of their landlady's instructions—

after all, what was to prevent them from smuggling in cold food!—they could save almost a hundred fifty francs a month, provided the baby remained in good health and spared them the cost of drugs and medical attention.

Seven thousand divided by a hundred fifty . . .

Forty-six months! Almost four years!

And in her last letter his mother had reopened the subject of moving to Nice, dropping a hint that if she was successful in obtaining the job she had applied for, she would need money for the journey, and somewhere to live when she got there.

Dominico paid no attention to him. As far as he was concerned, Mittel was by now merely a cog in the wheels of his enterprises. One day, as he was filing some documents, he discovered the whereabouts of the ill-fated machine guns that had traveled with him aboard the freighter from Fécamp to Buenaventura.

Salvaged from the river by the little cutter, they had been secretly stacked in the hold of an ancient barge, which lay rotting in the harbor. There they had remained for a long time, until they had been transported by mules to Peru, where Dominico had found a buyer—never mind that war was likely to break out between that country and Colombia at any time.

Poring over the checkered history of these machine guns, Mittel was astonished to discover that the Peruvians had paid for them not in money, but by the transfer of a credit they had with an export company in Le Havre. With the French currency thus obtained, Dominico had bought a consignment of perfume, which was due for delivery by the next freighter. And then, without warning, he found Boitel blocking his path. For the Colombian government had granted Boitel the sole right to manufacture perfumes and cosmetics. And all his present comings and goings were directed toward preventing Dominico's cargo of perfume from being admitted into the country.

The two men traveled separately to Bogotá, canvassing members of Parliament, ministers, and civil servants, each accusing the other of the gravest malpractices.

It was during this period that Charlotte, now up and about again, demanded the services of a nursemaid: "I can't be dancing attendance on the kid from morning till night."

She thought nothing, however, of leaving him to cry for an hour at a time, and she forbade Mittel to get up and comfort him in the night. "I don't want him to get into bad habits."

She was not at all Mittel's ideal of a mother. Although deft enough at washing the baby and changing his diapers, she was ready to abandon him to the care of the landlady whenever she felt like going out. She had made friends with two half-caste girls, their skin more white than brown, in a dry-goods shop. Both were very fat. They were forever giggling, and spent their afternoons drinking little glasses of liqueur and eating cakes in the room at the back of the shop.

Charlotte was spending more and more time with them, and, to Mittel's dismay, nowadays he often smelled alcohol on her breath.

"Don't forget you're still breastfeeding the baby."

"What of it? Are you suggesting I'm drunk? Haven't I got plenty of milk?"

She had enough milk to feed two babies, and she was proud of it. She had no hesitation about unbuttoning her bodice and breastfeeding the child in public.

"The Caléro girls have found me a nursemaid. I've arranged for her to start tomorrow."

Why not, after all? True, it would eat into their savings of a hundred fifty francs a month, but would those savings ever be of much use to them? Four years, just to scrape together the fare to Tahiti!

Mittel was putting on weight. Before he had always been painfully thin, with delicate, brittle bones. Now, as a result of living in such an oppressive climate, he had grown a layer of fat, which gave his face a bloated appearance and did not signify any improvement in his health.

Charlotte, as it happened, had also grown plumper, but in her case it was a change for the better.

"You ought to ask your precious Dominico for a raise. Just give me time to get my strength back, and I'll speak to him about it myself! I haven't got a single dress left that's fit to wear. The Caléros are quite willing to let me have things on credit, but so far I haven't ventured to . . . Would you mind if I bought myself a little silk or linen dress?"

Once every two weeks, a steamer put in at Buenaventura, alternately north- or southbound. There was also the occasional small freighter, following the coastline from Chile to Panama.

Tahiti was never out of Mittel's thoughts. *I have accepted an appointment as captain of a pleasure boat. . . .* Reading between the lines of the letter, brief though it was, Mittel sensed that the captain was in low spirits. It read almost like a cry for help.

Dear Captain,

On the very day your letter reached me, Charlotte gave birth to a child. It is a boy. We are living at present in Buenaventura, where I am employed as a clerk in Dominico's head office, since life in the jungle did not suit us. Unfortunately, I can't see my way to finding any means of joining you in Tahiti in the foreseeable future. In the meantime, Charlotte and I send you our warmest greetings.

Mittel had endeavored to estimate the date of conception of the child, but the doctor had not been helpful, responding evasively to his question as to whether the birth had been premature or not.

There was still room for doubt. Mittel thought about it often. But even in this matter, his feelings were not altogether what he would have expected.

He could not find it in his heart to feel even a twinge of jealousy! It was really very odd. Indeed, he found it disconcerting. He was infuriated by Charlotte's daily visits to the two Caléro girls, where she spent the entire afternoon drinking contraband Benedictine, but the possibility that Mopps might be the child's father, and that he would probably never know the truth, scarcely troubled him. If he had been forced to choose between the baby and Charlotte, he would have chosen the baby.

But not Charlotte! She had even talked, at times, of having someone else nurse him. She would watch him at play with the nursemaid, who was as black as ink, with complete indifference, while Mittel was stricken to the heart.

"What does it matter, as long as she's clean? I make a point of inspecting her hands at least twice a day."

What sort of life was Mopps leading in Tahiti? He tried to envisage the pleasure boat. It must be a little steamship plying between the islands.

But what had become of the freighter? And its crew?

I have accepted an appointment as . . .

In other words, his project had come to nothing, and he had been obliged to take whatever he could get. When Mopps had explained to Mittel the meaning of the expression "going native," he had been referring to life in Tahiti. Had he himself finally "gone native," shacking up with a Tahitian girl wearing a chaplet of white flowers?

The one crucial thing was to keep his head. From his experiences in the jungle, Mittel had learned the lesson that, confronted with the slightest genuine possibility of escape, he would succumb to a fever of impatience amounting to panic.

He forced himself to stay calm, and to look upon Buenaventura as his home, where he would live till his dying day. He had made progress in Spanish. He had worked hard at mastering the complexities of Dominico's business affairs, with so much success that there was even talk of sending him, as Dominico's representative, on a mission to Bogotá, a few days' change of scene which he would greatly appreciate.

As at the mine, his enemy was the river. He had only to look at it—and it flowed endlessly, day after day, beneath his window!—fixing his eyes on the point where it joined the sea, to be vividly reminded of the *Croix-de-Vie* gliding out of the harbor, one Sunday morning long ago, to disappear at last in the deep waters of the Pacific.

He always experienced the same sharp pang whenever he watched a ship going out to sea, and for several days afterward would be a prey to black depression, so much so that he now avoided going aboard the *Santa*'s—as the Grace Line cargo ships with passenger accommodations were all named—for the occasional meal.

These emotions filled him with such shame and even terror that he sometimes wondered whether he was going out of his mind. For these feelings were not new to him. He recalled that in Paris, when he was a boy, he would spend countless hours leaning on the parapet of the immense bridge that spanned the Gare du Nord, staring down at the hundreds of railroad tracks spread out below.

The trains were mainly of two kinds, the short expresses, with a few bluish coaches behind the engine, and the long Pullmans, the very sight of which caused him a genuine stab of pain in the chest.

And yet they were not bound for distant places, just for cities like Brussels, Antwerp, and Amsterdam.

But for him the very name of Amsterdam had a lyrical sound. Some days, when the lights were on in the coaches, he could see the passengers sitting down to dinner, each table with its own little pink-shaded lamp.

There were identical lamps in the dining rooms of the Grace Line ships.

Another of his dreams had been to visit the South, and he had gone to live in Nice, working first as a photographer and then as an employee in a real estate agency. Yet, in the end, he had taken flight.

His whole life had been a series of escapes, much to the disappointment of his father's old friends, who had put themselves out to find him a job. Always it had been because he had felt that this was not where his destiny lay, that he had to go elsewhere to find it.

And now he had come to believe that the place he had been seeking all his life was beyond the nearby stretch of sea, in Tahiti, with Mopps.

As each day passed this longing grew more intense, and he took to rechecking his calculations to make sure that he had made no mistakes.

Then he went further and began to consider other possible ways of procuring the seven thousand francs. There was always money in the safe, to which he now had the key, for he had been promoted to chief clerk.

But he would barely have time to board a ship before the theft was discovered. And ships were equipped with radios, which meant that he would be arrested as soon as he set foot on Panamanian soil.

More shameful even than this notion was the thought that he might have acted more adroitly in regard to the Plumier affair, on his arrival in Buenaventura. Suppose he had said, "Let's make a deal. I will give evidence according to your wishes, but in return you will provide me with the means of going with my wife to Tahiti. . . ."

They would not have demurred. He could see that now. The fact was, he had practically been holding them in the palm of his hand, and yet he had lied without hope of reward. He had lied from cowardice, because he could not face the prospect of being sent back into the jungle, recognizing Dominico's power and his own inability to fight back.

These thoughts nagged at him now, day after day. And at night, when he lay on the narrow green couch: he no longer shared Charlotte's bed, on account of the baby. He was never tired enough to fall asleep immediately. Always he would lie there uneasily recalling Boitel's apartment, and his parents-in-law, and the three girls dressed in blue, lilac, and pink, the cups of tea, the ungainly figure of Gérard de Villers, who was now an invalid whom nobody ever saw.

There was only one other memory from the past that recurred with equal persistence, but that was a happy moment which he positively strove to recall: the apartment on the Avenue Hoch, on that Sunday afternoon . . . the bright kitchen . . . the refrigerator . . . then the living room, the bedroom, the cocktails, and the sound of Mrs. White's laughter.

The one single moment of happiness unsought, unhoped-for, undreamed-of, that had come to him in his entire life!

On board the Grace Line ships, he had occasionally seen women who reminded him of her, and he would gaze at them in bemusement and wonder, as if they were freaks of nature.

For they were young, rich, and beautiful, and, so it seemed, totally insulated from all the miseries of humanity. They lived in a world filled with pleasure and luxury, free from worries of any sort, and they stared in amazement at the ordinary mortals swarming around them.

That was it! Mrs. White had been intrigued to discover a young man living alone and shunned by everyone, in a servant's attic bedroom in one of the most luxurious apartment buildings in Paris. Here, women of her sort expressed surprise when he came aboard on formal business: "Are you really French, and from Paris? How extraordinary!"

Once or twice, maybe, he could have repeated the adventure, for these women did not live according to the rules; they cared for nothing but the gratification of their own whims and fancies.

Once he had seen a photograph in a newspaper of a strikingly attractive woman who reminded him a little of Mrs. White, under which appeared the words:

One of America's best-known society women, who was found shot after a midnight orgy.

She had been only twenty-two years old! The incident had occurred in a sumptuous private house on Fifth Avenue, during a party attended by some ten guests, who could give no account of the incident, claiming that they had been too drunk at the time to notice anything.

Mittel returned home to find the black girl minding the baby. Nowadays Charlotte often got home very late.

"They've taught me lots of different card games," she would explain. "It's such fun! Today I won five pesos."

The apartment was dimly lit, and full of dingy furnishings of dubious cleanliness. The landlady, always in deep mourning, and her mournful daughter, who squinted, were even more depressing.

The daughter was suffering from unrequited love. Mittel could not imagine why, but the fact remained that she was forever lurking in wait for him, and when he appeared would blush and beg his pardon for being in the way.

He still had Mopps's letter in his pocket, but one night, deciding that there was no point any longer in brooding over such things, he tore it up. Indeed, it would have been better for him if he could have taught himself not to think at all.

Hadn't they had at last grown accustomed to the food? And the rainy season was over. The sun shone all day long. Of course, the heat was so intense in the middle of the day that to go out in it was almost to take one's life in one's hand.

Charles was two months old. Mittel found it hard to call him Charles before, because, for him, this tiny living thing had no name.

In the evenings he would sit close beside him, gazing at him, and wondering why things had turned out as they had. His idea of a family included a pretty cradle decorated with bows of ribbon, a tender, smiling young mother, a log fire crackling in the background.

Here there was only the whirr of the electric fan. They had not bought a cradle. Instead, the baby slept all day in a sort of canvas hammock, slung from the ceiling. The nursemaid never missed an opportunity, as soon as their backs were turned, of giving the hammock a hard shove, so that it swung violently from side to side. This worried Mittel, who had heard somewhere that it was harmful to the brain.

Since books of any interest were unobtainable, he had given up reading, apart from glancing at the local papers, where all the news was about coffee and cocoa, and the possible outbreak of revolution in neighboring Peru.

All for want of seven thousand francs or so! One day he wrote a letter to his father's closest friend, now editor of a weekly journal.

You may have my word that I shall pay you back at the rate of a hundred fifty francs a month. It's only a loan I'm asking for, I swear. . . .

He even went to the expense of sending the letter by air mail, so that he might get a reply within a month, or perhaps the money by cable even sooner.

He counted the days, wondering whether he had the dates wrong, and then, instead of a reply from his father's friend, he received one from his mother:

B telephoned me to say that he had heard from you. He was shocked to learn that at your age and in your position you had become a father. In his opinion, you have quite enough responsibilities as it is. In conclusion, he remarked that you seemed somewhat over-wrought, and that you seemed not to realize that life in Paris is a great deal harder than in the tropics.

Maybe he's right. There are scores of young people unable to find work. . . . I myself, being unable to go to Nice, have had to resign myself to living in an airless cage smelling of linotype, as a result of which I can't sleep at night for coughing. . . .

The situation in Europe is very tense, and . . .

He spent all that day alone and in tears—not of distress but of rage. The next day was marked by a brief flutter of animation in the life of Buenaventura. A white yacht, almost as big as the ships of the Grace Line, dropped anchor in the middle of the river, where it remained until noon, after which time it steamed into the harbor.

On this occasion Dominico himself elected to go aboard, for the owner was one of the richest men in the United States, and was widely known as the Clothing King.

Mittel was in what he called his aquarium, up on the fourth floor of the hotel, typing letters in Spanish and English.

Moïse, by coincidence, happened to be in Buenaventura, and he, too, went aboard. When he returned he announced, "They've come from the Galapagos, and they've put in here to take on a full load of fuel oil, because they're bound nonstop for Tahiti, and then on to Japan. . . ."

No one came ashore, except a few officers and seamen.

"They're as drunk as skunks," went on Moïse indulgently.

232

"They'd make you die laughing. . . . Three little old men . . . Winfeld, the owner, is a Polish Jew who made his fortune in Chicago. This is his very first cruise. . . . And instead of having lots of pretty girls aboard, he keeps company only with a couple more Jews of his own age, and they spend all their time in the saloon, swilling down bottles of champagne. . . . They took one look at the Galapagos and decided there was nothing to interest them there, so they gave orders not to drop anchor."

The whole town had gathered on the quayside to stare at the white yacht.

"They're leaving tomorrow on the morning tide. . . . Guess what Winfield said to the boss? 'If they were to drain the Pacific, they could track us to our journey's end by the champagne bottles on the ocean bed.' They sent all the way to Germany for a captain, a retired submarine officer, one of the world's greatest experts in diesel engines. They carry a crew of sixty. . . ."

Mittel turned his head aside. He was thinking of the boiler room, the seamen's quarters with the little stove in the middle, hours of rest and quiet on deck under tropical skies.

"What's the matter with you? You look half drunk."

When he got home, Charlotte also commented on his strange appearance.

He gave an odd little smile. No, he had not been drinking! But he made an announcement:

"I have to go out tonight. I'll explain later. . . ."

He was unable to swallow a single mouthful of food.

15

THROUGHOUT THAT NIGHT, FROM BEGINNING TO END, HE ABAN-
doned all self-respect.

As early as nine o'clock in the evening, anyone who had
recognized him roaming around the port would have been startled by his expression of mingled tension, anxiety, and self-
abasement. He wandered to and fro, never very far from the
yacht, peering at the seamen as they came ashore, sometimes
speaking to one of them.

"Won't the captain be coming ashore?"

These men, seeing him loom out of the darkness, mistook
him for a beggar and merely shrugged. Mittel counted fifteen,
twenty, twenty-two, going off like soldiers on leave. Some went
into the hotel, where they could be seen playing billiards or fiddling with the slot machine. Others, intrigued by the darkened
streets, made for the town in search of adventure.

But the captain remained on board, and Mittel lacked the courage to mount the gangway. One seaman, apparently a petty officer, passed by in company with several others, chatting in
German. And that was it. Now there was only silence, the dark
quay, the deck of the yacht faintly glimmering, and the drawn
curtains behind the portholes of the saloons.

There was nothing now to hope for, yet Mittel did not go
home right away; instead he spent a good quarter of an hour at
the bar of the hotel, saying not a word but listening to the seamen
talking among themselves, for these were the men who would be
leaving with the yacht the next day.

If only he had himself alone to consider!

A burly lout of a fellow asked him for a light, and did not even bother to say thank you. Two others, to pass the time, were engaged in a fierce boxing match in a distant corner.

Mittel slunk out, crept along the streets in the shadow of the houses, and went into the wooden bar, where another group of Americans were assembled. These were the ones who spoke German, and they must have had a great deal to drink already, for they were very rowdy. In their midst sat a man wearing a cap who had gold braid on his sleeves. He was fat, pink-cheeked, and bright-eyed, with a shaven head, and he was drinking little glasses of whisky chased by beer.

Imperceptibly, Mittel crept closer to him, and since he could not stand at the bar without a drink, he, too, ordered beer. No one paid the slightest attention to him. He felt their elbows digging into his ribs. The officer with the shaven head was complaining to the black bartender that his beer was flat, and demanding that a fresh case be opened. The bartender could not understand what he was saying, and Mittel, seizing his chance, came forward and offered his services as interpreter.

"*So!*" exclaimed the officer, overjoyed. "*Sprechen Sie deutsch?*"

"*Jawohl.*"

"*Wohnen Sie hier?*" he asked. "Do you live here?"

"*Ja,*" Mittel replied, glumly.

There were no conceivable depths of humiliation to which he would not have sunk. To please his companion, who was drinking steadily, he, too, drank little glasses of whisky with his beer, and paid for it with a searing pain in his chest.

And as the officer talked, he sat listening with an approving smile, which filled him with shame when he caught sight of his reflection in the mirror.

This man was the chief engineer. He talked with great pride of his engines, the finest, according to him, ever to be fitted on a yacht.

Enthusiastically, he described the yacht in great detail. She had cost a million and a half dollars, and although she had been completed two years ago, her owner had hitherto only sailed in her once, on a two-day trip off New York.

"He takes no interest in anything," complained the German. "He's never so much as set foot on deck. All he does is drink and gossip with his cronies. In Panama, they didn't even bother to take a look at the Canal. . . ."

And all this time he kept drinking. Mittel, whose head was swimming, decided to postpone his move a little longer.

"Who is in overall charge of the yacht?" he at last plucked up courage to ask.

And the officer, by now fairly drunk, hesitated for a moment before replying.

"Nominally, it's the captain. But I'm the one Winfeld really trusts. Most of the decisions rest with me."

"I don't suppose it would be possible for you to take a passenger or two aboard?"

"I could if I wanted to."

"Well, look, you're bound for Tahiti, aren't you? I have a wife and baby son, and I have friends out there. . . . Unfortunately, I can't afford . . ."

The black bartender was listening, but Mittel didn't care. All he could think of was that his whole family lay in the hands of this drunken man, and he clutched at the buttons of his jacket.

"Do you see what I'm getting at? I've worked at sea. . . . I'm an experienced stoker. . . ."

"We have no boilers on the yacht, only diesel engines."

"I'm willing to do anything, anything at all. . . . I have a friend in Tahiti, a merchant seaman, Captain Mopps. He must have some money saved. He'll pay whatever I owe you. . . ."

"I earn thirty thousand dollars a year. . . . Another drink, Sambo . . ."

Was he really listening? He was still drinking. Mittel clinked glasses with him, striving to interpret the expression in his blue eyes, which were beginning to water as he got drunk.

"A baby!" he grumbled.

236

"No one ever has to see him. My wife will be with him the whole time. All I ask is some little cubbyhole. . . ."

"Come and see me tomorrow morning."

"But you're leaving at ten."

"No, at noon. Come and see me. Ask for Vogel, Franz Vogel."

"Do you think you'll be able to fit us in? You do understand, don't you? If there's the slightest hope, we'll get ourselves packed and ready tonight."

"Come tomorrow morning."

"Will you really be able to help us?"

"Why else should I tell you to come aboard?"

Why indeed? Who could tell? Was he too drunk to know what he was saying, or wasn't he? Maybe it was just talk, a way to get rid of a nuisance?

"Hey, there, you fellows, it's time we got moving!"

Mittel could have wept, torn as he was between hope and fear that he was being taken for a ride. Vogel thumped him on the back, paid for all the drinks without even bothering to pick up his change, and repeated. "See you tomorrow morning!"

Charlotte was not asleep. It was four o'clock in the morning, and she was wondering what on earth could have happened to Mittel.

"Is that you?"

He stumbled up the stairs and had a hard time finding the doorknob. No sooner was he inside the room than he vomited up all the beer and whisky he had drunk.

"What have you been up to? Are you drunk?"

"Wait, I'll tell you all about it."

He felt very ill. Big drops of sweat trickled down his forehead.

"I'll tell you all about it, but first get me some water. . . ."

There was vomit everywhere, not only on his jacket.

"It's possible that we may be leaving tomorrow on the yacht."

"Have you spoken to the owner?"

"No, the chief engineer . . . I spent most of the night drinking with him."

Charlotte stared at him mistrustfully. She was not reassured to see him stretch out fully dressed on the couch.

"If I drop off to sleep, you've got to get me up by six o'clock in the morning. It's terribly important!"

He struggled hard to keep awake, but soon she could hear that he was asleep by his harsh, irregular breathing. It was she who lay awake, not because he had urged her to do so, but because she was by then unable to get back to sleep. At daybreak she got up, went over to him, and shook him.

"Have you forgotten what you told me last night? Your appointment . . ."

He sat up, his face drawn and haggard. The alcohol had left him drained and empty. He was as white as a sheet, with dark circles under his eyes, and his mouth hung open slackly.

"I know," he mumbled, lurching clumsily off the couch.

"Is it really true? Not just drunken talk?"

The cold water revived him a little. He dressed, shaved, and brushed his hair, drank another glass of water, went out into the deserted streets, and made for the port.

He no longer knew what to think. Uncertainly, he approached the yacht, where there was no sign of life. He had to wait a full half hour before a few barefoot seamen appeared and began scrubbing the deck. He called out to them, "Is Franz Vogel on board?"

They indicated in pantomime that he was still asleep. Mittel ardently hoped that he would wake in better shape than himself after a night of drinking.

It was such a little thing to ask of these people . . . only that they make up their minds whether it was to be yea or nay. . . .

And there he was compelled to stay, standing on the quayside, watching the town come gradually to life, until the hour passed when he should have arrived at his office. Probably his fellow employees could see him from the windows and were asking themselves what he was doing there.

So what? He no longer cared. He was indifferent to everything but the prospect of escape. His goal now was not even Tahiti, just to get aboard the yacht and escape from this place, no matter where to.

Dominico's car was parked outside the hotel. Mittel wondered with dread whether his employer intended to visit the yacht today.

"Isn't he up yet?" he asked one of the seamen from time to time, twisting his lips into a pitiful smile.

"Not yet."

And then, at long last, the chief engineer emerged through a hatchway, naked to the waist, with a towel around his neck, yawning and stretching and looking up at the sky with an ill-humored expression. This time Mittel rushed forward and went up the gangway.

"Ah, yes," sighed the German.

"You do remember me, don't you? I'm the one who . . ."

He was trembling. He would have given all he had for a favorable answer.

"We're so desperately unhappy here! In Tahiti we have friends. . . ."

"Not so fast! To begin with, are your papers in order?"

"I have them with me. . . . Here! This is our passport, in my name and my wife's, complete with the required photographs."

The chief engineer studied Charlotte's photograph for a long time with a slightly lewd expression, but Mittel forced himself to keep smiling.

"Are you certain you'll be allowed to land in Tahiti?"

"I'm sure of it. As you see, I have a French passport, and Tahiti is a French colony. . . . And besides, I have influential friends there."

He was lying, but in his present mood he would gladly have told worse lies than that.

"Good!"

The chief engineer returned his papers to him, but Mittel dared not assume that "good" meant "yes."

"Do you mean . . . ?"

"Hurry up and go get your wife. Didn't you tell me that there was a child as well? No matter . . . We leave at ten."

"You told me noon."

"Now I'm telling you ten."

It was already eight o'clock. Without waiting to thank him, Mittel ran all the way home. The next two hours were the most chaotic he had ever known. He could not rid himself of the fear that something might yet prevent him from leaving. He was driven by a sense of frenzied haste to get aboard, certain that, once he was there, no further mishap could befall him.

"We're leaving in ten minutes!" he called out to Charlotte. "There's not a moment to waste! We're off to Tahiti!"

"But . . ."

"We're got to be on board before ten. . . . Hurry!"

The black girl was cradling the baby stark naked in her arms.

"Two of my dresses are at the cleaner's."

"What difference does it make?"

He flung his belongings haphazardly into the suitcase and called for the landlady.

"We're leaving!" he cried. "We're going to Tahiti on that yacht lying in the harbor."

"You'll have to pay the full month's rent."

"Of course I will, that goes without saying."

What would Dominico have to say about it? he wondered. Had not Moïse been at pains to remind him, on one occasion, that he had signed a three-year contract? If it weren't for those office windows overlooking the harbor, Mittel could probably have slipped away unobserved.

No matter, provided he got away. He ran hither and thither, throwing into confusion all Charlotte's attempts to prepare for their departure in an orderly fashion.

"You owe the bar for four dinners."

"I'll pay on the way out. . . . Listen, I have to dash now, to have a word with the boss."

And dash he certainly did, so much so that he collided with Boitel. He apologized and was just about to tell him his news when he remembered that they were not on speaking terms.

His colleagues looked up as he came into the office.

"Is the boss here?"

And, having knocked at his door and gone in, Mittel began hurriedly, "Excuse me. . . . Listen, Monsieur Dominico, you have been very good to me, and I'm grateful, but an entirely unexpected opportunity of going to Tahiti has just come up. . . . On that yacht, yes . . . It's all arranged. I've come to beg you to let me go. . . ."

How could anyone be expected to understand his febrile excitement? Dominico must have thought that he was suffering from sunstroke. Why all this babbling and twitching, and waving his arms around in that absurd fashion?

It was hard to tell whether he was laughing or crying.

"You know that I've done my best to give satisfaction."

If it should come to that, he was prepared to lay it on the line, reminding Dominico of Plumier's death and the evidence he had given under pressure.

Which made it all the more astonishing when his employer replied simply, "How much is owing to you?"

"This month's salary . . . but I'm quite prepared to . . ."

Yes, he was prepared to go to the length of forgoing the money due to him! He couldn't think straight. His temples were throbbing. He felt that at any moment he would hear the yacht siren.

"Here are four hundred pesos. . . . I wish you both the best of luck out there, you and Madame Gentil."

He gave a most dignified performance, accepting the situation with complete composure. This was so unexpected that Mittel could not help thinking there must be a catch in it somewhere.

On the way back to his lodgings, he hired three natives to carry their luggage. The black girl took up the rear, with the baby in her arms. Charlotte put her arm through Mittel's, and everyone stared at them as they went past. They walked fast. It was already half past nine.

"Have you paid our bill at the bar?"

"I forgot, but it doesn't matter. . . . I *knew* last night that I was right."

Right to stick at it, to put up with anything, for the sake of getting away. It was to be hoped, at least, that the German was not stringing him along.

The little procession met with guffaws from the yacht's deck, which soon turned to gasps of astonishment. When they reached the foot of the gangway, they were stopped, and someone went off to fetch the chief engineer.

The German pointed right away to the little nursemaid, and muttered, scratching his head, "You didn't say anything about her."

"But she's not coming with us!" exclaimed Mittel. "Neither are these others."

For the porters were standing around on the deck, awaiting instructions.

"I'm glad to hear it. . . . I'll show you to your cabin."

He seemed somewhat out of sorts. He glanced once or twice at Charlotte, but did not seem particularly impressed. Their luggage was distinctly shabby, and Mittel and his wife themselves appeared anything but well dressed on the deck of a ship where even the seamen wore custom-made uniforms.

Unlike the freighter, this yacht had no iron ladders or companionways, but comfortable staircases. They passed through the seamen's mess, which was all freshly painted in gleaming white, and where plates bearing the remains of a breakfast of bacon and eggs had not yet been cleared off the tables.

"This way . . . I'll be obliged if you would get rid of the black girl."

His tone was so insistent that they were obliged to bid her good-bye there and then in the passageway. Mittel realized that he had forgotten to pay her and called her back, then found himself carrying the baby.

242

"I'm putting you in this little cabin here. I'll see that you're fixed up with a cot for the baby."

Whereupon the German, without further ado, left them alone. He did not seem exactly proud of what he had done, more resigned to the inevitable. His lack of enthusiasm had not escaped Mittel and Charlotte, and they dared not venture outside the cabin, for fear that he might change his mind.

On either side of the cabin were two-tiered bunks. They sat down on the lower ones, Mittel still holding the baby on his knees.

"What's the time?"

"Oh, Lord! Now that you mention it, I left my watch hanging on the hook by the bed!"

A solid silver watch!

'It didn't keep very good time anyway. We'll buy a new one in Tahiti."

"Did you get any money from Dominico?"

"Four hundred pesos. I bet you anything you like he's up there with the captain, settling the account for the oil."

Time passed, and still no sound could be heard to indicate that they were preparing to leave. At noon they could clearly hear the bells of the Catholic church ringing.

"What do you think is holding them up?"

They spoke in whispers. Charlotte had the baby at her breast, but was afraid to open the cases to get out some clean diapers.

"Once we're under way, we'll feel easier in our minds."

"Yes . . . Listen!"

But it was not the signal for departure. It was the luncheon gong, being sounded outside the corridors, followed by the arrival of a steward, who announced in English that a meal awaited them in the mess.

Mittel and his wife, dazzled and yet uneasy, entered the mess, where there were already at least thirty seamen seated at tables, eating. They were being waited on by stewards in white coats, as in a restaurant.

It was disconcerting. There was nothing to remind Mittel of

life aboard a freighter, as he had known it. Every corner of the yacht was as clean and elegantly equipped as the section of a cargo liner reserved for passengers.

Charlotte noticed that the cutlery was silver! The meal was plentiful, and rounded off with huge pastries, which Charlotte ate in abundance.

Contrary to what might have been expected, their presence created little stir. Of course, the men had turned to look at them when they came in and had exchanged a few remarks, but that was all, and now, as the men went out, picking their teeth, they merely glanced at the strangers.

They all had fresh complexions, with pink cheeks, as if they belonged to some athletic club.

When at last they heard the blast of the siren, Mittel gave a start. He turned to Charlotte, his face transfigured with joy, and could not resist squeezing her knee between his.

"We're leaving. . . ."

They were on their way! Through the porthole they watched the piles under the quay receding. It was so unexpected that Mittel could have shouted for joy.

"Charlotte!"

Suddenly, he was overcome with emotion. Never before had he felt so strongly that they were a close-knit family of three. It seemed to him self-evident as they finished their meal and returned to their cabin, where they found the baby crying. And there they remained, behind closed doors in their cozy quarters, a self-contained enclave in the midst of the bustling life of the yacht.

Somewhere, at the other end of the ship, Winfeld must be lunching with his two cronies. Did he have any inkling that he had other guests aboard, a man and woman with their infant son?

"Do you think he'll be angry when he finds out?"

"I don't know. It would be best for us to keep out of sight, until we hear from the chief engineer what is expected of us."

But no one came to tell them anything. They were simply ignored. It was not till about five o'clock, after thay had been at sea for some hours, that Frank Vogel opened the cabin door, and then, seeing that Charlotte was feeding the baby, apologized for intruding.

"Do please come in."

"There's no need. I just wanted to be sure you had everything you required."

And he left as abruptly as he had come.

This state of affairs persisted for two whole days, so that at times they had an uneasy feeling that they were living in a dream. On board the *Croix-de-Vie*, people had put themselves out for Mittel and Charlotte, and they had participated in the life of the ship. Here it was as if the word had been spread that they were to be left in peace; or perhaps the crew were somewhat shy, or wished to respect their privacy. Whenever they appeared on deck, the men, gathered in little groups, went on playing cards or doing exercises, and Mittel and Charlotte might be there in their little corner for two hours or more without having anyone address a word to them.

The only one who exchanged a few words with Mittel from time to time was the chief engineer, who was eager to show him around his precious engine room. But he was no longer the same man. On board he never touched whisky, and Mittel had the feeling that he was a stern disciplinarian with the crew. On one occasion Charlotte saw a seaman being carried across the deck unconscious, with bruises on his face. Since she happened to be alone at the time, and understood no German, Franz explained the scene to her in pantomime. First he raised an imaginary glass to his lips, then adopted the stance of a boxer, from which she concluded that the man had been beaten for drunkenness.

The weather changed with disconcerting suddenness. They were scarcely out of sight of the coast of South America when they were able to go on deck bareheaded, even when the sun was at its height.

Above all, it was the taste and smell and texture of the atmosphere that were different. Sometimes it reminded Mittel of sunny summer days in Europe, with the air so clear, and the sky and sea in ever-changing shades of blue. The nights were cool, a sensation that Mittel and Charlotte had not experienced for a very long time.

The yacht skimmed through the water at a steady twenty knots, more than double the speed of the freighter, and they would gladly have stood for hours watching the brilliant play of light on its glittering wake.

"Some time I must show you the gyroscopic compass and the sonar equipment. This is the only yacht equipped with such instruments. . . . The compass alone cost a million of your francs."

The one thing they were unable to discover was whether the owner was aware of their presence on board. Mittel dared not ask the German, for fear of vexing him: he judged the chief engineer to be somewhat arrogant.

For when all was said and done, what was it but arrogance that had prompted him to say yes? And then, the next day, he had had too much pride to admit that he had spoken recklessly in his cups the night before.

If this were so, he gave no sign of it and showed no trace of ill-feeling. They rarely saw him, but that was because his cabin was in the officers' living quarters, in a different part of the ship.

The officers had their own deck. They could be seen there, playing bridge, waited on by Chinese servants. Every morning, wearing undershirts and shorts, they indulged in sporting activities such as boxing and gymnastics, while the seamen, on their deck, were doing exactly the same.

As for the owner and his guests, in whose behalf all this money and energy were being expended, nothing was ever seen of them.

Their quarters consisted of vast saloons and staterooms, furnished with every comfort and refinement. For example, Franz mentioned that in every stateroom there was a lever that one had only to move left or right to obtain precisely the desired room temperature.

246

This high standard obtained in all things. Probably the bosses played bridge, too—while drinking champagne and receiving the latest news from all over the world by radiotelegraph.

"Do you see that, Charlotte?"

His eyes glittering, Mittel was gazing all around him. It was not the multimillionaire whom he envied, whose life style he admired, but all the others, down to the lowliest cabin boy. Their way of life was almost unknown to him, with everything around them clean and neat, down to the smallest detail, everything beautifully designed and made of the finest materials. And, within this setting, a life of ease, good health, and harmony.

As if to enhance the magic, even nature played its part, for here, in the middle of the Pacific, there was a dreamlike quality to the sea and the sky, and the very air they breathed seemed benign.

"I truly believe that, once we get there, our lives will finally be changed for the better."

"Assuming you're able to find a job."

"Of course I'll find one! You'll see! All we needed was to break out of the circle."

"What circle?"

"It's hard to explain. It was as if we were walled in on every side, and that's why I felt we had to get away at all costs. There were times when I was seized by a kind of madness, longing to bang my head against those walls until I split my skull. Now, by sheer chance, we have found our way out. It was a bit of luck that I had a strange sort of presentiment, the very first time I set eyes on the yacht. Otherwise I might never have found the courage to persist. In a way, I didn't want to, you know. . . . At least ten times, I almost gave up and went home. Standing there on the quayside in the dusk, I felt a bit like a streetwalker!"

"What an extraordinary notion!"

Naturally, it was impossible to make her understand. But he understood, all right, and as each day passed, he found himself able to breath more deeply, to fill his lungs with the fresh, clean air, and to indulge in the heavenly dream of becoming a different man in a new and better world.

Sometimes he found the waiting unbearable. He longed for the time when they would reach Tahiti and perhaps find Mopps waiting for them on the quay. Childlike, he imagined the pride with which he would step ashore from the magnificent yacht. He could see it all: his friend, unable to believe his eyes, stammering:

"What's this? It's you . . . and Charlotte . . . and a baby, too!"

Basking in the sun, lulled by the soft humming of the ship and the silky rustle of water against the bows, his mind was awhirl with these thoughts.

Sometimes he could almost believe that all those millions spent on the yacht had been for his benefit alone.

It would not have taken much to persuade him to pick a star in the sky and say, "That one is mine. You'll see, we're going to be happy."

Even the baby's looks were improving, and one day Mittel began timidly, "Don't you think the lower half of his face . . . ?"

"Well, go on."

"I don't say he looks like me . . . but do you remember my mother's mouth and chin?"

Once the miracle had occurred, why should he worry about anything else? For it was nothing less than a miracle that had brought them here.

Could a man like Bauer, for instance, in his little bookshop on the Rue Montmartre, have believed it possible that he, Mittel, along with Charlotte and their baby, could ever hope to find himself steaming across the Pacific in the most luxurious yacht in the world?

Mittel had come to regard Franz Vogel as a sort of guardian angel, and he had only to catch sight of him to be overwhelmed by a surge of gratitude.

"I think he's the best man in all the world. You didn't see him in Buenaventura. . . . When we reach Tahiti, I daresay he'll start drinking again. But the splendid thing about him is that he was prepared to keep a promise he'd made the previous night, when he was dead drunk. . . ."

Life was beautiful! Life was good! Even the American cooking was palatable, now that he could see things in a different light.

"I daresay we'll have a few laughs over it when we have a home of our own. All the same, I have noticed that my digestion has improved, and I'm sleeping a lot better."

"Don't you think you're laying it on a bit thick, Jef?"

And with a sigh and a laugh he said, "Oh, women! Women!"

How could they be expected to understand such things? They, who could always find just the right words to clip one's wings and bring one down to earth? But he did not want to be brought down to earth. He had been waiting too long for this soaring of the spirits, this great surge of hope. The day the chief engineer finally took him to see the gyroscopic compass, he praised it with almost lyrical fervor, in order to please his benefactor.

It was a complete mystery to him, but it was a thing of beauty. Everything was beautiful! And surely, in the end, happiness must come to everyone!

Some mornings, Charlotte would find him in the cabin, stripped to the waist, endeavoring to do the exercises he had learned from watching the seamen.

"You'll wear yourself out," she would say.

Always those discouraging words which brought one down to earth. And what if he did wear himself out? It was his choice, wasn't it? Why shouldn't he strive to turn himself at last into a man like other men, a man able to run and jump and use his fists?

He promised himself: "In Tahiti."

Surely at twenty-three it was not too late to change one's life, above all to strengthen this feeble body, of which he was growing more and more ashamed.

Charlotte would understand in time. As for the child, he would be brought up in clean, cheerful surroundings, with plenty of sun and fresh air, and would grow up as lithe as a young animal.

Mittel had made up his mind on that!

PART THREE

16

NEEDLESS TO SAY, THEIR ARRIVAL WAS NOT QUITE AS HE HAD IMAG-
ined it. And yet, compared with anything he had previously experienced, it was still magnificent.

His greatest disappointment, almost like that of a thwarted
child, was to be denied access to the deck when the yacht was
suddenly no longer in the open sea, but gliding through the calm
waters of the lagoon. The water was a limpid blue streaked with
green, shimmering here and there with red and gold highlights,
as if it were not real water, but a dreamlike symphony of color.

"I'll come fetch you when it's convenient for you to land," the
German had said, sounding a little embarrassed. "Until then, I'd
be obliged if you would stay in your cabin."

It was kind of him, for it strongly suggested that the chief
engineer had taken him aboard without consulting Winfeld. Unless . . . Mittel flushed. He had grown unduly sensitive to these
small humiliations. Now that they were putting into port, and
crowds were gathering on the quayside to admire the yacht, they
were altogether too shabby, he, Charlotte, and the baby in her
arms, to be seen in company with the crew in their smart
uniforms.

Even so, dazzled and enchanted, he gazed through the porthole
at the shore, and at the sight of a little spur of sand, a row of
coconut palms, a few scattered huts, and, as if floating on air, two
canoes rocking on the water, he gasped with pleasure.

This landscape, at least, was all he could have wished, and
exactly as described in the travel books he had read. Then, very
nearby, barely three meters from the porthole, another canoe

suddenly appeared, paddled by a handsome youth who was laughing so that all his gleaming white teeth could be seen, and shouting something to the seamen on deck.

More canoes . . . Girls in *paréos* . . .

"Do you see, Charlotte?"

"Yes," she replied, without enthusiasm. "I can't understand why your friend is keeping us hidden."

It was trivial, after all, but why did she have to say "your friend," as if she felt that the chief engineer had treated her poorly?

It was all this waiting that had made them so touchy. They had nothing to do but listen to the bustle around them. Instead of steaming to the quay (of course, Mittel did not even know whether there was a quay), the yacht dropped anchor in the middle of the bay, some hundred fifty meters from the shore.

In the sunlight, motorboats plied back and forth. A large crowd of people had gathered on deck. They could hear voices speaking the local language and, from time to time, the strains of a guitar. Mittel stood there with his nose pressed to the glass of the porthole, like a schoolboy kept in as punishment.

It was ten o'clock in the morning. Not until one, after all the bustle had died down, did Franz Vogel come to fetch them.

Charlotte didn't even blink, but Mittel was overwhelmed by the panorama that suddenly smote his eyes, his nostrils, his skin, his whole being. He wished it had not been necessary for him to cross the deck in the wake of the man who was carrying their luggage.

The spur of sand and the coconut palms were only a minute part of the landscape. Facing him, and very close, was a mountain two thousand meters high, a mass of brilliant green, and nearer still, almost within touching distance, was the town of Papeete, with red roofs surrounded by gardens, exotic, trees such as he had never seen before, a little church, and houses painted in vivid colors.

A young girl on a bicycle rode past along the quay, a sight he was to remember for the rest of his life.

But he was forced to keep on the move: to go down the gangway, and take the baby in his arms once they were in the launch.

The chief engineer did not go ashore with them. "You must excuse me, I still have work to do. . . . I hope to see you again in town."

One could hardly have found a more awkward spot for saying good-bye and expressing one's gratitude!

"Yes, this evening . . ."

The air shimmered in the sunshine. It was the hottest time of day, and the town was deserted. When they reached the quay— for there was a quay, with a customs shed—a very fat native in a tropical khaki uniform watched the newcomers disembark without bothering to approach them.

It was up to Mittel to take the initiative. He went up to the man, holding his passport open in his hand. The official, without even looking at it, nodded him through.

"Could you please direct me to the Anglo-French Club?"

"It's right at the end."

The fat, uniformed official pointed to the row of trees bordering the quay, which seemed to stretch to infinity.

Mittel carried the suitcases, and Charlotte the baby. Thus laden, they hurried as much as they could, anxious to make contact with Mopps as soon as possible, after this long time, or at least to find out whether he was still there. Now, having so much else to think about, they were scarcely conscious of their surroundings.

"Those were taxis," insisted Charlotte, referring to two cars that they had seen near the harbor, with native drivers asleep at the wheel.

"I wasn't sure. I didn't like to . . ."

"You aren't carrying the baby!"

"The cases are heavy, too."

A large, pale building: the post office; next to it the British consulate. Then a small, two-story hotel built of wood, where Chinese waiters could be seen scurrying among the tables.

And here it was, at long last! The club bungalow, which had been pointed out to them, was set in a beautiful garden and had a tennis court to its right. There was a car parked at the entrance, but the clubhouse itself seemed deserted.

All the doors were open, and the rooms empty, cool, and quiet.

The first room they came to was an undistinguished-looking bar, with two used glasses on the counter still smelling of Pernod. To their left was a small dining room, then a bathroom and a kitchen.

"Is anybody there?" Mittel called repeatedly, going from room to room.

After all, the car must belong to someone. Surely the whole place couldn't be deserted!

Charlotte found somewhere to sit, and was feeding the baby. Minutes passed, and then, at last, a door opened and a man appeared, rubbing his eyes. He was about fifty, dressed in a pair of dubious trousers and a shirt steeped in sweat.

The first thing he saw as he approached was Charlotte breast-feeding the baby, a sight that rocked him back on his heels.

"What's going on?" he asked in a working-class accent.

"We were hoping to find Captain Mopps here."

"Surely not at this hour!"

"Could you give us his address?"

"Look! That's his car out there."

"But where is he?"

"At this hour, he'll very likely be at Tita's place, having his siesta."

In spite of himself, Mittel glanced covertly at Charlotte, recalling the captain's cabin on board the freighter, but she did not notice.

Two hours had passed since their arrival. The man, a former soldier of the Foreign Legion whose name was Félix, had returned briefly to his room to comb his hair, and all three were now drinking together, while exchanging idle chatter.

"Here he's just known as the captain. For the past month he's been president of the club, and he treats it almost as his own home. Come to think of it, when you arrived his glass was still there on the counter."

"Doesn't he go to sea any more?"

"Occasionally. He'll be back here at four-thirty on the dot, you'll see. Then he'll go off to the American Bar near the harbor for a whisky. . . . And after that, he'll come back here."

In spite of the heat, the climate was much milder than in South America, and the scent of flowers drifted in from the garden through the wide-open windows.

"Are you planning to settle in Tahiti?"

"Possibly . . . Mopps wrote to tell me that . . ."

"Listen—that's him coming now!"

So here at last was the moment they had waited for. But this, too, was turning out differently from Mittel's hopes and expectations. Unable to hide his emotion, Mittel ran to the door to meet him. A hundred meters away, lumbering along the pavement, he saw the tall, bulky figure of a man whom he did not at first recognize.

In fact, for a brief second, an uneasy and distasteful thought entered his mind: "Surely it can't be Moïse!"

But it really was Mopps! Mopps, wearing a yellowing linen suit, an open-necked shirt, and, to crown it all, a huge cartwheel hat of woven coconut-palm leaves decorated with shells, as was the fashion in Tahiti. As he drew near, he called out, "Is it really you, my boy?"

And he slapped him on the back, looking toward the harbor as if searching for something.

"But how on earth did you get here? Where's Charlotte?"

"Yoo-hoo!" called out Charlotte, appearing at the window of the bungalow.

Mittel longed to give Mopps a big hug, and even perhaps to

burst into tears. He followed him indoors, snuffling, and explained, "We got permission to travel aboard the yacht."

The captain, having just caught sight of the baby in Charlotte's arms, halted abruptly on the threshold, and exclaimed with a groan, "Good God!"

For a few seconds he stood there, gazing at the two of them with knitted brows. Mittel could not bear to watch, for he had guessed what the other was thinking. Mopps was wondering, as he himself did, whether . . .

"Congratulations! You've done all right for yourselves, the pair of you. Bring us some champagne, Félix."

"Right away, Captain."

It took them several minutes to overcome the awkwardness of their reunion. Even Mopps seemed a little ill at ease, and Mittel was becoming more and more convinced that he had changed.

It was no accident that, a few moments ago, he had been reminded of Moïse. There was a resemblance between the two men, in that both were equally tall and broad. But in the old days Mopps had been firmer and tougher, whereas Moïse had been flabby, with weak features. But Mopps had put on weight since then. His body was no longer hard, trim, and powerful, and now there were deep pouches under his tired eyes.

"So you decided on impulse to come and try your luck here?"

If only one could be sure that he was at least pleased to see them! If so, it was at best modified rapture. He seemed to have forgotten that it was he who had invited them to come to Tahiti.

"Your very good health! And we mustn't forget to drink to the son and heir of the Mittels—or, rather, I should say, of the Gentils. . . . I'd forgotten for a moment. . . . Mind you, here it makes no difference one way or another. This is an earthly paradise. You won't find any nitpickers here. All you need to do is keep your own counsel. . . ."

Two or three times he went up to the baby and tickled it, and each time Mittel felt distinctly uncomfortable.

"You haven't changed much, Charlotte! No trouble with the delivery?"

"It all went very well."

"What happened to the *Croix-de-Vie?*" Mittel inquired at last, broaching what he hoped was a safer topic.

"It no longer exists!"

"What happened?"

"Listen! First of all, I sold it in Mexico. It had to be given a new identity, because it was blacklisted in every port. There it returned to life as the *Santa-Maria*, though, of course, the whole transaction was a fiction. . . . Incidentally, while we were in Vera Cruz, the black got married and stayed behind. Now he's a stoker on a tug there. His wife is enormous—at least a hundred ten kilos. . . ."

"What about the others?"

"Give me a chance! I heard that there was a demand in Tahiti for a steamer to ply between the islands. They used to have to make do with sailing ships. I arrived here with my freighter, and the deal was in the bag. The only conditions I made were that I should retain my command at a salary of sixty thousand francs a year."

"How come you're not on board?"

Mopps sighed and looked away.

"I passed it up this time, because I wasn't feeling too great. She'll be back in three or four days. . . ."

His discomfiture was plain to see.

"Come on, you're not drinking! Not to mention the fact that we can't just sit here. We've got to arrange somewhere for you to stay. I'll tell you what: for a start, I'll take you along to the Pacifique. That's that little hotel you must have seen near the quay. I won't pretend it's particularly comfortable, but the proprietor comes from Marseilles, and he does a marvelous *bouillabaisse*. After that, we'll see. . . . Félix! Put the luggage in my old jalopy."

Still this sense of frenzied haste. Mittel wished he could be given more time to dwell on his first impressions, to digest them, to try to understand. They were already inside the car. They drove a couple of hundred meters, to be confronted with new faces, a new environment.

"Hi, Marius! I've brought along a couple of young friends of mine. I want you to put them up for the time being. . . ."

And Marius, whose head was twisted to one side, shook hands with them and asked, puzzled, "How did you get here?"

They were going to be asked that question over and over in the days to come, since there was only one ship a month each way on the Panama-Australia route.

"They came in their own yacht, believe it or not."

They were taken up to a somewhat dreary room, furnished with an iron bed and a dressing table, with hooks on the wall for hanging their clothes. No mention was made of price, which worried Mittel more than a little.

"You, Charlotte, stay here and have a rest. As for you, young man, you're coming with me. I want to show you around the town, and then we'll have a chat."

Downstairs were two Tahitian girls in light dresses. Mopps patted them both on the cheek.

"They're good girls. . . . I'll introduce you later. . . . Everything is pleasant here, you'll see!"

And Mopps got back into his car, drove two or three hundred meters, and, within a few seconds, drew up in front of the American Bar.

It was crowded with seamen from the yacht, but Franz Vogel was nowhere to be seen. Some little while later, Mittel saw him drive past, in company with another officer and two native girls wearing chaplets of white flowers.

"What will you drink? Oh, of course, I'd forgotten, you don't drink hard liquor."

Mopps was drinking heavily, much more than in the old days.

He shook hands with various people, then rested his elbows on one end of the bar counter.

Outside, on the quay, were two large buildings, general stores selling all sorts of merchandise—shirts, phonographs, pith helmets, and sewing machines. Both stores were owned by British settlers.

Then, farther along, were the shops owned by the Chinese. In the relative cool of the evening, the whole town was coming to life, and the streets were crowded, mainly with bicycles ridden by natives in European dress.

"It won't take you more than a few days to become acclimated, and then you'll understand how things work here. But right now we have serious matters to consider. See here, I want you to tell me honestly: is Charlotte capable of cooking a decent meal?"

"It depends what you mean by . . ."

"Oh, I'm not talking about *haute cuisine*, just good, plain, wholesome food."

"I think so, yes."

It was true. In other ways she was useless around the house, but she was an excellent cook, which had never ceased to surprise Mittel.

"There you are, then! You've seen our club. Most of the members are officials of some sort, and we're all bachelors. Félix has had it. More often than not, he's laid up with malaria, which isn't surprising when you realize that he spent twenty-five years in Africa. If the two of you were willing, we could take you on as managers of the club."

Mittel considered this offer with a marked absence of enthusiasm, though he could not at first understand why.

"You'd be living in. You'd make a modest but adequate living, without too many worries. How does it strike you?"

"It would be one way of solving our problems."

"But you're not wild about it?"

"I don't know."

It was not what he would have chosen for himself, but he could not for the life of him think of a better alternative. He was still a stranger in the country, and had so far seen nothing of it but its bars.

"We're holding a committee meeting tomorrow, and I'll raise the matter then. I'm president of the club, and I may as well tell you that what I say goes. The same again, bartender!"

The seamen from the yacht had attracted a throng of local street vendors, selling shell necklaces and cheap knickknacks of every kind, carved oyster shells, palm-leaf hats like the one Mopps wore, *paréos*.

"What was life like out there? You know, I see a great change in you."

Mittel could scarcely tell him that the feeling was mutual!

"It was all right, although we went through same bad times. Charlotte contracted typhoid out in the jungle, at the back of beyond. The only other white man there committed suicide. . . ."

Another subject that he would have preferred to avoid.

"Why did he do it?"

"No reason. He was mad, and became obsessed with the delusion that someone was planning to kill him. After that, we went back to Buenaventura."

"Filthy dump, isn't it?"

"Yes."

He could not open his heart to this man, as he could have done to that other Mopps, the sea captain from Dieppe who swore like a trooper and who could be counted on as a tower of strength.

Not that Mittel needed anyone to lean on. He almost regretted not having to fend for himself. If he had had to, he felt, he would have viewed the country in a different, clearer, light, facing his responsibilities like a man.

But here was this new Mopps, proposing to turn him into a club servant!

"Don't go. . . We have no secrets here."

Two more white men had come into the bar and, sitting down

at a table with Mopps, had ordered whiskies. Mittel gathered that one of these men owned one of the big stores. He was an Englishman with graying hair, and he spoke no language but his own.

The other was the captain of the sailing ship that was visible at the far end of the quay.

They chattered away, but Mittel was not listening. He was too much absorbed in watching everything that was going on around him.

"Did you hear that, young man?"

"No, sorry," he said, coming out of his daydream.

"Your pal has had quite an adventure, it seems."

"Which pal?"

"Winfeld, the man who owns the yacht. Earlier today, he expressed a wish to see a fishing expedition in the lagoon. So they laid one on especially for his benefit, calling on all the best spearsmen on the island. . . . And you'll never guess how it turned out!"

"What happened?"

"He was in the launch, leaning over the side, when he lost his balance and fell overboard."

"Did he drown?"

"Not at all. The water was too shallow. He broke an arm on some coral. There are three doctors in Tahiti, and every one of them is on board the yacht, but the old gentleman has made up his mind to leave immediately for New York. . . . What a hoot!"

But Mittel did not even smile. Mopps, who had already drunk several whiskies, looked offended.

"You certainly have changed a hell of a lot. And there I was, telling my friends that you were the most delightful fellow on earth."

At that he turned back to his friends and continued his conversation with them in English. An hour later there were five men at the table. People were coming and going all the time. The main topic of conversation was a recent circular from the governor on the subject of coconuts, and Mittel, huddled in his corner, could not, try as he might, wipe the glum expression off his face.

"If you'd rather, you can go wait for me at the Pacifique. I was forgetting that you're a family man now!"

Mittel could have sworn that he detected a hint of bitterness in this remark.

"Thanks. I'll see you later, then."

"In Papeete one runs into one's friends a hundred times a day."

These were the first steps he had taken unaccompanied on the island. The sun was setting, and the lagoon was more red than blue. The yacht still lay at anchor out there, ghostly white in the setting sun. The chugging of motorboats could be heard as they came and went across the lagoon.

On the quayside, people stood in idle groups, men and girls, chatting and sauntering up and down in a leisurely way. From time to time a car shot past, with a European at the wheel.

Glancing at the post-office building, Mittel suddenly reflected that if he had not been set apart from other men, he would, as of right, have found some mail awaiting his arrival. But who was there to write to him? His mother, perhaps? With another request for money?

Inside the Pacifique, he found Charlotte already seated in the dining room, and he looked around anxiously for the baby. A local girl in a red dress, very pretty, slender and bronzed, was dandling him on her knees. She addressed Mittel without a trace of an accent: "Are you his daddy? You're a lucky man!"

Not in the least embarrassed, Charlotte explained, "This is Mopps's friend."

"Oh, I'm not the only one! Still, I'm the one he's living with at the moment. Is it right that you two left France on board his ship?"

"Yes."

"He told me all about it."

What had he told this native girl? Had he spoken of his relationship with Charlotte?

264

What distressed Mittel most was having to think of such things in this new environment, pleasanter and more reassuring than anything he had ever imagined possible.

"Would you care for a small Pernod?" asked Marius, who had just come into the room.

"No, thanks. I never touch hard liquor."

"You'll be the only who doesn't in this place. Oh, by the way, I've reserved that table in the corner for you. And I must apologize in advance for any noises you may hear at night. My young ladies come in any time between midnight and four in the morning, and sometimes they're not too steady on their feet. Anyway, I've put you in the room next to Céline. She's quieter than the

"Because she's always sulking," explained Tita.

"Shut up, you! You needn't think, just because you've been with Mopps for the past week . . ."

"Two weeks!"

"Two weeks, then. That means it will soon be over, and you'll be back here begging me to let you have a room!"

"What a horrid thing to say, Marius!"

A light breeze was blowing in from the sea, making the leaves quiver.

"What did Mopps have to say?" Charlotte asked when Marius had gone.

"He wants us to manage the club for him."

"What a marvelous idea!"

"He asked me if you could cook, and I said yes."

"What are you looking so glum for?"

"No reason."

"Are you jealous?"

He turned away his head. What a time to choose to ask him such a question! It was hardly the place, either.

"Is he jealous?" exclaimed Tita, in astonishment. "Here no one would think of being jealous. He'll soon get used to our ways, you'll see."

She was still playing with the baby, who by now had big china-blue eyes.

Mopps arrived, accompanied by two friends.

"We'll all have dinner together tonight," he announced. "It's the least we can do to celebrate your arrival. . . . Hello! So you're here, too, Tita."

"Why shouldn't I be?"

"And I see you've already made friends with our youngster."

Our youngster? Mittel pretended not to have heard, and rose to his feet.

"I have to go out for a little while," he announced. "I had no opportunity this morning of thanking the chief engineer, who gave us a berth on the yacht. I promised him . . ."

"Don't bother."

"What do you mean?"

"He was at this place on the point, having a good time, until a few minutes ago, when he was ordered back to the yacht," said Mopps. "He was dead drunk by then, but that doesn't alter the fact that the yacht is leaving in half an hour. Winfeld has got it into his head that the only place he can get proper medical attention is San Francisco, so he's abandoning the rest of the cruise and going home."

"Are you sure?"

"Absolutely certain," interposed one of Mopps's companions. "I signed the ship's papers myself."

And he was, in fact, dressed in uniform and wearing a cap with gold braid.

"Get to work, Marius! Let's have the best dinner you can produce, and plenty of it, and let's have some music. Send for Alexandre."

What with the heavy meal and the wine, albeit a moderate amount, Mittel felt as stupefied as if he had drunk quantities of whisky. Tita had joined them at the table and was sitting next to him. Céline walked past the table at one point, and she, too, was invited to join them, although she contributed nothing but barbed remarks.

"Do you remember Tuesday night, Mopps?"

"No!"

"Well, I do, and I will have a word or two to say to you about it later."

They were served by Chinese waiters. They ate *bouillabaisse* and drank French wine. Alexandre, who was a taxi driver by day and a bandleader at night, soon arrived, accompanied by his native musicians.

Mittel knew that among the guests was someone from the maritime registration bureau and an official from the governor's Secretariat, but several other men had joined their party, and he could no longer tell who was who. The normal night life of the Pacifique was getting under way. The regulars had their own reserved seats, and their own table napkins. Friends shouted to one another across the whole length of the room.

"Aren't you having dinner here? The *bouillabaisse* is terrific."

Mittel was introduced all around.

"A young newcomer and his wife . . . You couldn't find a nicer pair of kids!"

Charlotte was laughing. Mopps must be entertaining her with comic anecdotes. As for the baby, he was passed from hand to hand, for they did not want to risk leaving him alone upstairs. He ended up sitting on the lap of one of the Chinese waiters, who gazed at the child in fascination.

Too much wine, too much music, too much shouting, too much noise altogether, and too many people. No one could hear himself speak. One member of the party was drunk.

"Has the yacht left?"

"It has."

"They never even set foot on the island!"

A cruise costing millions, and nothing to show for it in the end but a broken arm! The others were vastly disappointed, but not Mittel.

"It was that quack who scared the hell out of him by telling him that coral wounds could turn nasty. . . ."

"It's true."

"Still, that's hardly a reason for breaking off the cruise and going back to America!"

"Do you come from Paris?" Tita asked Mittel.

"Yes, I was born there."

"Is it really as big as they say?"

Charlotte was in high spirits. All eyes were on her, filled with admiration and possibly lust—during the cruise she had almost regained her girlish figure. Mopps could not take his eyes off her.

"What do you say to going on to La Fayette?"

"But what about the baby?" she said. "Is it far?"

"About fifteen kilometers. Here nightclubs are restricted to the outskirts of town, so they're all some distance away."

"Out of the question," cut in Mittel. "We can't possibly leave the child."

It crossed his mind that perhaps they were hoping he would offer to stay with the child while they went out to have a good time.

"Never mind, another time . . . Tita, let's have a dance from you!"

She did not have to be asked twice. She took off her shoes and performed a native dance, to the accompaniment of chanting by the band.

"Charlotte!" barked Mittel, taking advantage of the comparative lull.

"What is it?"

"It's the baby's feeding time. We'd better go upstairs."

"Surely, just this once . . . ?"

"It's his time," he repeated firmly.

Mopps looked at him oddly. After another round of handshakes, they followed the Chinese servant upstairs, but they could hear the noise of the party below for an hour longer.

"Are you really jealous?"

"What of?"

"Of Mopps."

"Of course not . . . I just want to go to sleep."

17

"YOU DON'T HAVE TO WORRY ABOUT A THING," MOPPS KEPT SAYING soothingly.

And, true to his word, he achieved miracles. In the morning, except for the iron bedstead occupied by Félix, the bungalow was virtually empty; by noon it was fully furnished. Mittel did not have the least idea where all the furniture and utensils had come from. Mopps had everyone on the run, picking up one thing here, another there.

"Go and ask Brugnon if he has a large mirror to spare."

Félix promptly did so, and returned a quarter of an hour later with the mirror—presumably the property of the hospital, since Brugnon was its senior physician.

And it was the same with everything. Mopps's system, Mittel discovered, was to stop a youth or a man at random in the street and send him running messages.

"Go tell the harbormaster not to expect me before five."

And his orders would be promptly carried out.

"Well, young man, there's your home and your job all arranged. Are you satisfied?"

"Yes, everything is very nice."

What more could he ask for? He had pleasant accommodations at the club. A local servantgirl had been hired for them, and she was already helping Charlotte get the house in order. And the setting was enchanting. They did not even have to set foot outside to enjoy their view: the ever-changing waters of the lagoon glinting through the trees. Mittel, following the local custom, had bought himself a wide-brimmed straw hat, and had adopted the fashion of wearing shorts, favored by the British residents.

But what was he expected to do by way of work?

"Stop worrying!" Mopps never tired of repeating. "You'll see. . . ."

But that was just the trouble. Day after day went by, and still he did not see. Félix had been taken on by Marius, the proprietor of the Pacifique. Every morning Charlotte got up, put on her dressing gown and slippers, and proceeded to follow Maria, the servantgirl, from room to room, supervising her work.

"Jef," she would call out, as the floors were being swept, "call the butcher, will you, and order a kilo of cutlets."

He did her telephoning for her, played with the baby for a while, and then could not think what to do with himself.

"Jef, don't forget to mend the blind in the dining room!"

This, too, he did willingly; then, on the dot of ten o'clock, the familiar figure of Mopps would invariably appear in the doorway.

"Good morning, young man. Good morning, Charlotte, my sweet."

She was quite shameless in the presence of Mopps. She would go on with her housework, her dressing gown gaping, her hair hanging down her back, and Mopps, instead of stopping in the bar, would always follow her into the kitchen.

"Jef, look after things here, will you? I'm going to take a shower."

She would go into the bathroom, leaving the door ajar, and would carry on a conversation while scrubbing herself under the shower.

"Is the doctor coming to lunch?"

"He promised to do his best to get here today."

Mopps was thoroughly at home in the club. He poured his own drinks and made a note of them on his tab. For days at a stretch, life went on in this carefree manner, as if the world outside did not exist. And Charlotte continued as shameless as ever.

She would come out of the shower half naked and finish dressing in front of the captain, sometimes calling him to come help fasten her dress.

Mittel, preferring not to witness these scenes, would take his straw hat and go out, to wander aimlessly around the tennis court, picking up fallen leaves, coconuts, or broken branches off the ground. He had found a rusty old rake at the foot of the garden, and he used it to keep the paths tidy.

The bungalow was never out of his sight. Charlotte, when she had finished dressing, would take her place behind the bar, in an attitude that had already become habitual with her. Mopps, too, had his regular habits, and always sat in the corner between the bar counter and the wall.

There they would remain, drinking and chatting until noon, though Charlotte disappeared into the kitchen from time to time, to keep an eye on the cooking.

"Jef, go and chop some wood for me."

Jumping to it, he did as he was told, and chopped wood. The sky was clear, the air so pure that it lifted his spirits like wine, so that, at times, he felt like shouting for joy. From the far end of the garden the children could be heard coming out of school, and the bells of the Catholic church chimed in harmony with the twelve crisp strokes of the clock on the Protestant church.

"Jef, where's the wood?"

On his return to the bungalow, he would find more people drinking at the bar. Brugnon, the senior physician, who had lived in the colonies for forty years, was almost always there, along with an official of the governor's Secretariat and a lawyer who lived in the bungalow next door.

"What will you have? And you?"

They drank and chatted idly, with Charlotte always at her post, her elbows on the counter. She got into the habit of drinking two or three apéritifs in the morning, and still more in the evening, and the later it was, the shriller her laughter and the coarser her accent became. They would lead her on deliberately, and Mittel, sickened by the whole business, would leave the room.

He had never before felt any jealousy on her account; on board the freighter, her conduct had scarcely touched him.

What, then, had brought about this change? Was it that she had grown dearer to him? He did not know the answer himself, but the fact remained that he was growing even gloomier and more irritable, especially where Mopps was concerned. The captain pretended not to notice, and the affectionate paternalism of his manner never varied.

"You see, young man, all you have to do is drift with the tide!"

"I'd much rather be working."

"Well, isn't that charming!"

"What do you mean, charming?"

"That you should take such a tone with me. Perhaps, my dear sir, you have forgotten the circumstances of your unheralded arrival in Tahiti, with a woman and brat to boot. Overnight, our fine young gentleman is housed, fed, and provided with service, and now we find him complaining that the lady is too beautiful!"

"I'm sorry. . . ."

What was the use of trying to explain? Mopps was no longer the same man. Or perhaps it was just that, in former times, Mittel had looked at him through different eyes. No, that was not possible! He *had* changed. Witness the fact that he no longer even bothered to sail from island to island in his own ship.

It had been merely as a courtesy that he had taken Mittel aboard soon after his arrival.

"Do you remember the old days?" he had asked.

Mittel remembered them so well that his eyes filled with tears. He scanned the deck for friends, but found none. All the married men had left the ship and returned to France, including the bo'sun, Chopard, who had contracted a tropical fever in Mexico. One or two of the original crew were still there, but they were not among those Mittel had known.

He went down to the seamen's quarters, then farther down into the very bowels of the ship to see the boilers, and for a moment or two wondered whether he would not have been better off remaining a stoker.

272

"Do you want to sign on?"

"Why not?"

He would gladly have done so, but Mopps had been joking.

"You must be out of your mind. You stick to your comfortable billet, with your son. What's the use of wearing yourself out when you don't have to?"

That was also the doctor's advice, only he was considerably more discouraging. He was a strange character, who seemed to believe in nothing. He never showed the slightest emotion, or even any interest in anything.

"I'll show you over the hospital whenever you like. Among other things, I have a splendid collection of lunatics."

With equanimity he described hospital cases that made Mittel shudder, and recounted endless horrifying tales of life in the African bush, where he had lived for many years.

Jef was often sorely tempted to take him aside and ask him to examine him, saying, "Do you think I'll make it to old age?" For he often woke in the night in a cold sweat.

"So do I!" retorted Charlotte, when he mentioned it to her.

"No, you're wrong. You do perspire, but that's not the same thing as a cold sweat."

"Oh, really? What's the difference?"

He knew well enough what the difference was: he was almost certain that his lungs had never completely healed. Only the night before, while the apéritifs were being served, the subject of tuberculosis had arisen.

"Half the local population have the disease," Brugnon had asserted, matter-of-factly.

"How can that be, in this lovely climate?"

"That's just the point. It's totally wrong to suppose that tuberculosis is confined to cold climates."

If Mittel had dared to consult him about his own case, Brugnon would have been quite capable of blurting out, "You've got a year or two at most to live."

After all, what did it matter to him, one way or the other?

Mopps was still living with Tita, but he never brought her to

273

the club, and spoke of her as he might of a lap dog or a pet parrot. Charlotte was given to teasing him on the subject.

"You know, Captain, it looks to me as if you've 'gone native,' to use your own elegant phrase!"

On that occasion, he responded with a feeble pun:

"I'm not so much going native as joining the club."

It was certainly true that he was spending more and more time—indeed, most of the day—at the club. Occasionally, in the morning, he would even go to the market himself to buy the fish and vegetables, and would come back full of himself, followed by two native girls who carried the provisions.

"Hello, young man! And how's our baby today?"

Maybe it was intended as a joke, but it made Mittel flinch every time. Right from the first day he had found Mopps's attitude toward the child distasteful.

By now matters had come to such a pass that, when the captain was alone with Charlotte, Mittel would sometimes spy on them, listening at the window or creeping into the room without a sound.

Had she told Mopps about their day together in the hotel in Buenaventura? Had she told him that she was certain Mittel was the child's father?

Every day Mopps seemed to treat the subject more and more jocularly, skating around it or remarking to his friends, "He's a lovely kid, our baby, don't you think? When I say 'our' I mean that we're both responsible. Isn't that so, young man? Come to think of it, we ought to have tossed for him."

Tipsy the captain might be, but that did not prevent Mittel, who said nothing, from feeling sick at heart, especially when Charlotte joined in the laughter.

She was growing more beautiful all the time. Never had her complexion been so fresh, her eyes so bright, nor had she ever before sparkled with so much vivacity.

She was obviously in her element. The more people there were, the happier she was, and at night it was almost impossible to persuade her to go to bed.

"Don't forget, you're still feeding the baby. . . . You really shouldn't drink so much."

"The doctor says it makes no difference. You'll never guess what he told me when I asked him about it. His exact words were 'The sooner he gets used to alcohol, the better.' So there!"

No, nothing mattered to them, not even the possibility that the child's health might be impaired, like Mittel's. None of them had any moral sense whatever. One day, Mittel asked Mopps about the lawyer, Tuilier. His Christian name was Georges, which was Tioti in Polynesian, and that was what he was always called.

"Tioti? He's the most lovable scoundrel I know. He's got a wife still living somewhere in France. He was involved in some rather nasty legal malpractices and was disbarred, so he came out here to live."

"Anything very serious?"

"Enough to earn him two or three years in prison, I believe."

But this did not prevent him from pursuing his career as a lawyer here. He was nearly always the one to suggest, in the evening, that they all go on to La Fayette.

Mittel had never set foot in the place, but Charlotte somehow managed to wheedle him into letting her go. One evening, after dinner, the conversation turned to the subject of native dancing, and Tioti suggested, as usual, that they go on to La Fayette.

"Oh, yes, let's do it. I've been dying to go there!" exclaimed Charlotte. "Are you coming, Jef?"

But she knew very well that he wouldn't go, that he would never dream of leaving the baby alone with the native nursemaid.

"You really shouldn't," he whispered in her ear.

Whereupon Mopps exclaimed, "You would do well to keep your mouth shut. Do I make myself clear? You have no right to . . ."

He used a very coarse expression. Charlotte had already started changing her dress, in full view of the assembled company. Sometimes Mittel wondered whether she did it deliberately. She seemed to get a thrill out of displaying herself half naked and seeing the eyes of the watching men light up with lust.

Mittel was left alone. The episode had sickened him. He went to bed but could not sleep. The whole crowd had bundled into two cars, and probably, as usual, had picked up a few prostitutes on the way.

And yet he had everything he could wish for to make him happy. That was what was so infuriating. Every morning, the sight of the sunlit garden and canoes gliding across the lagoon filled him with the same ecstatic joy, and he listened intently to every sound and breathed in all the sweet familiar scents that wafted in on the breeze.

Which was why, incidentally, he had appointed to himself the task of caring for the garden. Out there he had the place to himself. He did his best to forget the bungalow. Naked to the waist, and wearing his broad-brimmed straw hat, he was happier than at any other time of the day, until a shrill voice shattered his peace:

"Jef!"

What madness had possessed her to go to La Fayette and come back tipsy at four o'clock in the morning, alone with Mopps in his car? She had been wearing *tiaré* flowers in her hair, and their scent lingered in the house until the following afternoon.

One thing he must acknowledge, in fairness to her: she was up at nine as usual the following morning, somewhat weary perhaps, but still ready to busy herself around the house.

"How did your evening go?"

"We thoroughly enjoyed ourselves. By the end, all the girls had joined us at our table. Tita went home with Tioti, and Mopps never said a word. Of course, he was very drunk by then. . . ."

"And you?"

"What about me?"

"What did you do?"

"Listen to me, Jef! You really are becoming impossible. Am I free to do as I like, or am I not?"

"No!"

She was astounded at this reply.

276

"And why not?"

"Because you have a baby now."

"So what?"

"Do you really not understand? Then you're more of a whore than I thought you were. . . ."

The word just slipped out. It was not in his nature to say such things—quite the contrary—but suddenly he had felt sick with revulsion. Now she stood facing him, her mouth set.

"What was that you said?"

"You heard."

"Listen, Jef. I've been very patient so far, but . . ."

She, too, felt the need to express her indignation; without warning she slapped his face. A peal of laughter resounded from the doorway.

"Bravo! You two are having things out, are you? I trust I haven't come at an inopportune moment?"

"Do you know what he's just called me? Say it again, Jef, if you dare."

"I said that, if one had a child to consider, one no longer had the right to . . ."

Mopps patted him on the shoulder with affectionate amusement.

"Take it easy, young man! Do you think moral indignation is quite your style?"

Rather than reply, Mittel chose to stalk out of the room and take refuge at the foot of the garden. It was not a question of moral indignation. It was his life, their life together, that he was fighting to protect.

For months on end, he and Charlotte had been swept along with the current of events. For months on end, Mittel had been unable to envisage any possibility of escape, and yet he had never given up the struggle. Out in the jungle, for instance, had the daily struggle for survival not been of almost heroic proportions? Surely, after all he had endured, he had at last earned the right to the life he had striven for?

There were three of them. Eventually he had grown fond of

Charlotte, perhaps because she owed him her life. Now they had a child and . . .

No! They had no right to destroy all he had built up. It was Mopps who was their evil genius, who had started the downward slide, dragging them along in his wake.

Not everyone in Papeete was tarred with the same brush. At the foot of the garden, some hundred meters away from the club, was another bungalow, the cleanest and best kept in the town, with its green door and brilliantly polished brass plate engraved with the name of the owner, a shipping-company agent.

Mittel often envied the tenor of life in that bungalow.

The agent's wife was young and pretty, and she, too, had a baby. Every morning he watched her as she bathed the baby near the open window.

Charlotte never bathed her own baby. That was left to the native girl, except when Mittel himself took over.

That other bungalow was bright and cheerful. No one there shuffled around in dressing gown and slippers until lunchtime, and there were no dirty glasses reeking of alcohol left lying on every table.

One morning Mittel had seen the couple at the market, surrounded by a throng of natives, and they had presented a picture he would never forget. Arm in arm, they had moved slowly from booth to booth, their heads bent together as they examined the multicolored fish and tropical fruit piled high.

By what right was he denied an orderly life like theirs? What had he done to deserve the squalor that always surrounded him?

Squalor was the only word for it! Try as he might, he always ended up in squalor, and now he was sick of it.

"What did Mopps have to say to you?"

"That he was disappointed in you."

"Is that all?"

"Isn't that enough? True, he blames it on the climate. It makes lots of people irritable, he says."

"Is that how you see it?"

"I have no idea, but one thing I will say. My life has been one long misery up to now. I've often had to go hungry. Now, thanks to Mopps, I've found peace at last, and I don't have to worry about what tomorrow will bring. Do you understand? It seems to me that you've picked the worst possible moment to throw your weight around, and to get all maudlin about things that didn't use to worry you."

"What do you mean?"

"You never showed any signs of jealousy during that time when I was sharing Mopps's cabin."

"My one thought then was to save us both from the consequences of your actions."

"All right, go on!"

"I beg your pardon! There's the child to think of. . . ."

"So?"

"There's a child to be considered, that's all!"

"You really are a fool. You can't even be sure the child is yours!"

No sooner were the words out of her mouth than she regretted them. He turned deathly pale, and for an instant she thought he was going to strike her.

"What's that you said?" he asked, his throat parched.

"Nothing . . . Anyway, you drove me to it."

"Whose child is he?"

"Stop badgering me!"

"I want a straight answer! Whose child is he?"

He grasped her wrists with surprising strength.

"I haven't the slightest idea. . . . Let go of me. . . . He's yours."

"Can you look me straight in the eye and swear you haven't said the same to Mopps?"

"What business is it of yours?"

"So you admit it! You told him he was the father, didn't you?"

"I know what I'm doing; you're the last person I could rely on to get us out of a mess."

He felt deeply ashamed, for himself, for her, and for the child. His sense of ignominy was beyond anything he could have imagined.

"You said that to Mopps!"

He had let go of her, but as he spoke, dry-eyed though he was, he was racked with sobs.

"So that's why Mopps is always here . . . because he believes . . . and naturally he's spread the news around as widely as possible."

"What's that to you?"

"Charlotte!"

He was reluctant to abandon all hope. He spoke her name in the tone of voice he had used to call out to her during her illness in Chaco, when he would wake up in the night fearing that she might be dead.

"Well?" she replied sullenly.

"Nothing . . . You've just done something very wicked. You've tainted everything I valued."

"What do you mean, 'tainted'? Who began all this, anyway? We're safe and comfortable here, and we could be happy, but you have to go and spoil everything by prowling around and looking at everyone who comes in here as if you didn't trust them. You surely don't imagine that people don't notice? What's the use of coming from a background like yours if you end up as narrow-minded as a suburban housewife?"

She stopped suddenly and glanced toward the door.

"Shh! Here comes Mopps."

Mopps again. The new, sickeningly flabby Mopps. The Mopps who spent his time dragging his gross body from bar to bar, drinking Pernod all morning and whisky all afternoon, until it was time to stagger home to bed.

"Hello, my pretties . . . Not quarreling again, I hope?"

"Of course not!"

"I must confess I'm getting a little tired of these scenes."

"It's all Jef's fault. He's so stupid."

"I know. I'm afraid he'll end up doing something he'll regret."

"Such as what?" growled the young man, his nerves stretched to breaking point.

"Who can tell? But you're on the wrong track! I gave you credit for more sense than that. I've always had a soft spot for you, too much so, perhaps. . . ."

It was true. Mittel felt a stab of emotion. But why in God's name had it all turned sour?

"Here we were, without a care in the world, and then you had to turn up with your hatchet face, your yellow complexion, and your prying eyes."

This also was true. Mittel flushed at being thus exposed.

"I . . ."

"You're nothing but a pain! I've said it before, and I'll say it again. There's only one cure for you. Find a lovely girl like Tita for yourself. She'll make you forget your troubles. Tita is at her place now—or, rather, at my place. Go see her. Tell her I sent you to give her my love, and don't forget to add that I say you're a fool."

He laughed and went over to the bar to pour himself a drink.

"Won't you have something with me?" he called to Mittel. "Just to show there's no hard feelings."

What precisely was he up to? Were he and Charlotte lovers again? Did he regard the child as his?

Mittel had to go for a walk, keenly aware that he was reaching the end of his tether. He walked all along the quay, right to the end of the lagoon, waving his arms around and talking to himself.

If Mopps considered himself the head of the household, what place was there for Mittel? What must people think of him?

And there was no way out that he could see! He toyed with one plan after another, only to reject them all as impracticable.

Join the crew of the freighter, and spend two months at a time sailing from island to island, as a stoker or a deck hand?

"Yes . . . I'll do it . . ." he said to himself.

And then what? That would mean giving up his son, leaving his upbringing to others. People would simply say, "The young fool has gone to sea. . . . That'll teach him a thing or two."

Life at the club would continue unchanged, with Charlotte behind the bar, and Mopps sitting facing her in his corner.

He was free to return to France, unlike Charlotte. He hadn't committed murder! And that was another thing he had forgotten. Charlotte was a murderess, and he was on the run because of the crime she had committed. . . .

There had been nothing to stop him from remaining in Paris and starting a new life. . . .

No, that wasn't true, he realized in a moment. Until he had set foot aboard the freighter, he had never really lived, he had been nothing but a kid. Little by little, life aboard had made a man of him.

What he might have done was to settle on the point, where there was a small colony of whites who had settled for the simple life, growing cocoa and bananas. He had seen them from time to time in town, dressed even more scantily than the natives. With Charlotte at his side, this is what he would have done. He had it in him, he felt sure, to clear a patch of land, to work from morning till night with his hands, even to spear fish for the pot, like the natives.

Instead of which, they were trapped inside the club, which was nothing more than a bistro—worse, a bistro patronized by people who had lost all hope, as Mopps himself had admitted.

For nothing escaped the captain's eagle eye. Heavy drinker that he was, dead drunk as he might sometimes be, he was aware of every action, every feeling, of those around him, and this, above all else, was what Mittel found so infuriating.

What, then, should he do? Take an office job? They would never let him go. They would never let Charlotte go: they had all come to depend on her too much.

Nowadays, Charlotte *was* the club. They had said as much to him. In Félix's day it was generally deserted, and there had been talk of closing it down. Now there were ten or a dozen regulars who came in several times a day, just for a quiet chat with Charlotte, who greeted everyone with the same smile, the same raucous laughter. She took her responsibilities very seriously. She knew that she was desirable to men, and she must have seen herself as a courtesan in a romantic novel.

He hated her, that was for sure! At least, he wanted to hate her, but he was incapable of leaving her.

"It's on account of the child," he kept repeating to himself. But was that the only reason? Wasn't he really caught in the same trap as all the others?

She was not a beauty. Motherhood had not spoiled her figure, but any little local girl was more desirable.

Where, then, did her attraction lie? She was not even intelligent, and she was spiteful and common, with the guttersnipe's instinct for mischief and antisocial behavior.

Lately she seemed to have developed an absolute passion for dropping bricks. For instance, he had heard her say to Tioti, "Everybody I meet here seems to have a criminal record."

Tioti had tried to laugh it off, but his laughter was hollow.

And to the doctor: "You must admit that twenty years in the tropics would drive anyone nuts!"

"Thank you, my dear. I, who have had forty years of it . . ."

"I wasn't thinking of you in particular. All the same, you could never settle back down to life in France now. And I must admit that, if I were ill, I wouldn't feel too happy about having you as my doctor."

They all roared with laughter: they found her quips delightful. And the more they laughed, the worse she behaved.

Mittel was now beginning to wonder whether he had been much more of a dupe than he had suspected. Who could tell? Maybe he was the laughingstock of the colony. Maybe Charlotte had received every one of these men with open arms.

Crimson in the face, bathed in sweat, he stood at the water's edge next to a native hut where a little girl stood eating a banana.

He had a headache. At that moment, he would have given anything for a kind word, a gesture of sympathy. Surely there must be a woman in the world willing to take a man in her arms and croon over him tenderly: "Hush, little one, don't think about it. . . . Remember, life is good, in spite of everything. . . . You'll see. . . ."

He had never experienced that kind of tenderness, not even from his mother, who had always had other things on her mind.

What were they talking about in the bar? For they were still there, he knew, drinking their second or third Pernod. And as always, Charlotte would be with them, her dressing gown gaping. . . .

At this time of day, in the interval between cooking lunch and dinner, it was Maria, the native girl, who took care of the baby. Charlotte had started weaning him. Mittel was against it, but the doctor had pronounced in Charlotte's favor. "You'll have so much less to worry about!" he had said sagely.

Never mind that the milk was no good, that it might harm the child!

He lay down on the sand, on the bank of the lagoon, right up against the first dying wavelet, and the little girl, intrigued, came and squatted beside him, gazing at him in perplexity as she munched her banana.

18

Before replying, Mopps, without bothering to make sure that they could not be seen, put his arms cozily around Charlotte and, holding her close, rested his cheek briefly against her hair. Although not without tenderness, his embrace had a somewhat mechanical quality. They were in the sunlit bar, near the counter. It was the coolest time of the morning, and Maria was sweeping the room next door, but this did not worry them in the least.

"Yes, Jef is out there somewhere," sighed the captain, while Charlotte straightened her dressing gown and began arranging the glasses on the shelves.

He pointed toward the section of town where the market was, and where Mittel had recently taken to roaming around.

"Have you noticed how changed he is?"

One of the peculiarities of their relationship was that whereas Mopps had addressed Charlotte by the familiar *tu* from the first day, she still, even now, called him "Captain" and used the more formal *vous*.

"We've all changed, old girl. Don't you realize that I myself am not the man I was?"

"I hadn't noticed," she said, to flatter him.

"Well, I know I have. You've changed, too, but in your case it's for the better."

"That's not what I meant. . . . Maria, I can smell something burning on the stove."

Rinsing glasses and looking out over Mopps's shoulder at the sunlit harbor beyond, she went on: "I'm beginning to be seriously worried about him. Did you know that he had meningitis when he was seventeen?"

"So what?"

"I don't know, but sometimes Jef reminds me of Plumier. . . . He has that same look in his eyes."

Mopps, who was filling his pipe, looked up at her briefly as she rattled on: "I'm not suggesting he's out of his mind. But I'd like to know how he strikes other people. For the past two weeks, he hasn't once lost his temper with me. He wanders around looking as if he were forever tossing over some pleasing idea. When he's not in the garden, he's out at the market. He's always on his own. . . . What are you looking at me like that for?"

"No reason. Go on," said Mopps, with a touch of irony.

"It's all right for you to make light of it! You don't spend your nights alone with him in this shack!"

"What about Maria?"

"Do you think she'd do anything to defend me? She'd be more likely to take his side. In fact, she already does!"

"What do you mean?"

"Just that, in the past few days, the beds have been changed around. Jef has moved his into the room that used to be Maria's. She's still sleeping there, actually, and at night they take the baby in with them."

"Didn't you protest?"

"I asked if he was going out of his mind, but he gave me such a look that I didn't dare put my foot down. When he's in that mood, there's something sinister about him, and that's why I'm beginning to feel really scared. You don't know Jef!"

"You think so?"

"He's always been different from other people. And what's more, he's always been a loner. When we were on board the ship, for instance, he never really fitted in with the crew, did he? No! And it's the same here. He doesn't fit in with the rest of us. It's more like he's against us. Well, it was just the same in Paris, all that time ago. He was on the fringe of the group, never a part of it; if he did join in, it was never for long. I've heard friends say

286

that his father was the same way, and that his mother is a little strange, too. You only have to read his letters. . . ."

"Come off it, Charlotte." She was startled by something odd in his tone of voice. "Does he pester you?"

"Of course not! What a stupid thing to say. You men are all alike. I confide in you about my worries, and your first reaction is to start getting ideas. Why do you think Jef has moved out of my bedroom?"

"Because he's afraid of finding me there, if you really want to know."

"He wasn't so particular on the ship. And why does he insist on having the baby with him? Not that I really care. At least now I get a decent night's sleep. But what I want to know is, what's going on in Jef's mind."

"He's probably wondering whether he's the child's father."

She flushed under Mopps's intent gaze.

"Don't think I'm not aware that you've said the same thing to both of us. Don't tell me you didn't swear to him that the child was his, just as you swore to me that it was mine. Damn it, Charlotte, you don't take me in."

He patted her on the shoulder. For some time he had been holding his pipe, already filled, and now at last he lit it.

"What do you expect to get out of all those lies of yours?"

"Nothing!"

"Come on, tell me. You know very well you'll have to in the end."

"It's no good talking to you. You've got it all twisted in your head."

"Don't worry about that, baby. Just say what you have to say."

"What I'd like is for the doctor to give him a thorough checkup. Then at least I'd know where I stood. And there's another thing. Suppose he was never really cured of his tuberculosis. The baby would be in danger of . . . ."

"I see what you mean. Give me a drink."

And Mopps turned, with a peculiar smile, to look at the native girl, who was still busy sweeping. So she was now sharing a room with Mittel and the baby!

Yet the captain was thoroughly convinced that Mittel was chaste, and had never so much as looked at the girl in that way.

"Don't you think it's a little strange, Lotte?"

"What?"

"That we should have come to this! When I realize I have finally retired . . ."

And so, in fact, he had. He had sold his ship and invested the money, and was living on the income.

"And here's Jef, jealous of an old has-been like me!"

"Not without justification, surely?" she retorted, with a coarse laugh.

As usual, she understood nothing, trivialized everything.

"Will you be staying while I take my shower?"

"Go take it anyway."

Every day she went through the same ritual: leaving the bathroom door open, she went on talking loudly as she took her shower and got dressed.

"Above all, don't forget to tell Brugnon about the meningitis. I don't know much about it myself, but I've been told . . ."

"That the brain is sometimes permanently affected," Mopps concluded with cynicism.

Living in slow motion, like someone recovering from a grave illness, was enough to make one cherish every minute of the day. And this was what Mittel was aiming for as he feasted his eyes on the marvelous sights that were all around.

He was familiar now with the way the lagoon changed color according to the time of day. He knew every fishing hut in the place, and often sat nearby and just looked at them. But he was especially at home in the market place, where he spent hours every morning, sitting on a stone bench.

In the old days, he used to sit that way in the Parc Monceau sometimes, watching the children at play around him.

Here, the square was surrounded by little Chinese shops, and

Mittel was beginning to feel that he knew all the shopkeepers, although they had never exchanged a word.

For instance, there was the fat Chinese on the corner, a youngish man, with a luxuriant mustache and a short upper lip revealing big teeth, who spent his whole day unfolding, measuring, and cutting lengths of silk and cotton.

At the back of the shop, his diminutive wife, who looked about sixteen, worked at her sewing machine, while a naked baby wriggled in a cot at her side.

There were four other children, all with the same huge eyes, who kept getting under the feet of the grownups but never incurred so much as a harsh word.

These people kept their shop open from five in the morning to seven in the evening. Even after they were closed, the lights remained on in the shop, and the whirr of the sewing machine could still be heard. They had come here from a distant country with a very different culture, but they were happy.

Next door was the butcher, also a Chinese, and next to him the Chinese carpenter, with his four apprentices.

Cars drove by with Britons and Americans inside. Outlandishly dressed tourists strolled around. It was not uncommon to see a white woman wearing a *paréo* incorrectly draped.

On the opposite corner was a garage owned by a local man. He was young, tall, and powerfully built, with the muscles of a wrestler. He, too, spent all day out of doors, chatting with customers and friends, mending tires, making telephone calls—for the telephone booth was simply a wooden roof on stilts. The cars were also left out in the open.

There were women squatting in the square all day, selling chaplets of *tiarés*, or baskets of oranges, lemons, and mangoes.

Mittel drank in the many and varied aspects of the scene as eagerly as Mopps drank whisky, and was affected in much the same way: his head would swim, his eyes become fixed and glazed.

He wished he could forget his personal problems, but this was not possible. When he returned to the bungalow, he hid his feelings behind a ghost of a smile, even if there was someone at the bar blatantly making up to Charlotte.

"We're out of firewood," she would say to him.

Meekly he would go out to chop some logs. He had never behaved more obediently, but at the same time he had never seemed more remote. He never opened his mouth until spoken to, and then replied as briefly as possible.

"Two new officials will be arriving on the next boat."

"Really?"

What possible interest could it have for him?

And Charlotte, coming into the bar in a white dress crackling with starch, and powdering her nose, looked around to be sure Jef was not there and whispered confidentially to Mopps, "Sometimes I feel really scared. Men like him can be capable of anything. At night I always lock my door, and yet sometimes I wake up in a panic, with a feeling that he's there in the room with me, and that he is about to . . . Shh!"

Mittel was walking across the garden, heading for the door at the rear of the bungalow, so as to avoid the bar.

"Did you see that?"

There was no disguising the fact that the scene had been rehearsed in advance. Dinner was over. Mittel, as usual, was about to retire to his bedroom. No one knew what he did in there—play with the child, perhaps, or go straight to sleep?

The doctor said suddenly, "Say, Mopps, is it all settled about tomorrow? You'll be stopping in at the hospital, as agreed?"

Mittel started, immediately sensing that something was afoot.

"About ten, if that suits you?"

"Why don't you come with him, Jef, old boy?"

He was on the point of saying no, then suddenly, without quite knowing why, he found himself saying yes. Perhaps it was because, although he felt he ought not to do it, some mysterious power was driving him to go.

"I'll pick you up on the way," said the captain.

Together, at ten o'clock the next morning, they went through the vaulted gateway of the Papeete Hospital. After they crossed a vast courtyard surrounded by buildings, they found Brugnon waiting for them in the entranceway. He was wearing a white coverall and carrying a thermometer.

"Go and wait for me in my office. . . . I'll be with you right away."

The office was undistinguished, dimly lit, and, like every other room in the town, filled with the racket of electric fans.

"You know, Jef . . ."

Mittel did not bat an eyelid.

"I'm going to give you a piece of good advice. You've neglected your health for far too long. Don't pass up this chance to ask Brugnon to give you a thorough checkup. When you meet him socially, you wouldn't think he added up to much, but the fact is that, professionally, he's as knowledgeable as any of the leading specialists in Paris."

Mittel was wearing that disturbing little ghostly smile of his, tinged with bitterness and irony.

As the doctor came in, Mopps hastened to say, "Our young friend here would not object to your looking him over. . . . He had a couple of serious illnesses as a boy. . . ."

"I had tuberculosis in one lung, and meningitis," stated Mittel coldly.

"Well, then, it might be a good thing . . ."

"Of course, of course! Just let me shut the door. . . . Meanwhile, Jef, you'd better get undressed."

He did so, coolly, as if in defiance of the two men and their plotting, and also of Charlotte, and of many others—indeed, the whole of mankind.

Mopps pretended to be absorbed in the few books on the shelves while, for almost half an hour, the doctor subjected Mittel to a thorough examination. It was very hot. All three men were sweating. From time to time, ash would fall from the tip of Brugnon's cigarette.

"Well, now, my dear boy," he said at last, with a sigh.

Mopps turned around, a book still in his hand.

"You certainly owe no gratitude to your parents. All you've inherited from them is a fine load of trouble! Is your father still alive?"

"No!" said Mittel sharply, buttoning up his damp shirt.

"And your mother?"

"Yes." He had to force himself to reply, and his eyes were glazed.

"Is she very stable, mentally?"

Mittel lowered his eyes, so that the others would not be able to read his expression. For now, suddenly, he sensed a trap. Hadn't Charlotte always insisted that Bébé was a bit touched? How, otherwise, would such a question have occurred to the doctor, in the middle of a physical examination?

"Perfectly!"

"Haven't you ever noticed anything odd about her behavior?"

"Never!"

"You don't smoke or drink, do you?"

"You know very well I don't."

"Well, that's in your favor, at any rate. Any form of overindulgence could have disastrous effects."

"Would you mind not beating around the bush? Just tell me straight out what's wrong with me. Oh, you can speak freely in front of Mopps, things being as they are."

"Were you ever pronounced cured of your lung trouble?"

"No . . . I walked out of the sanatorium because I couldn't stand another minute of it."

"That was a grave mistake. I'll take an X-ray, and then you'll be able to see for yourself."

"How long?"

"What you mean?"

"I'm asking you how long I've got to live."

"I can't possibly answer that. It depends . . ."

"A year?"

"Longer than that, I'd say."

"Two years?"

"Perhaps. There have been cases . . ."

Mittel's forehead was bathed in sweat, but his face remained expressionless.

"Thanks for all your trouble . . . I thought we were supposed to be shown around the hospital."

"As soon as you like."

The three men went out together, but Mopps loitered in the courtyard, chatting with a nurse, and by the time they had seen a couple of wards, he had disappeared.

"It doesn't matter. He'll come another time."

On a stone step sat four little native boys, not playing, just sitting. Mittel stopped dead at the sight of them. He could not take his eyes off them, for their skin was blue, almost sky-blue in color.

"What's wrong with them?" he asked.

"They're juvenile lepers. Nowadays we treat them with methylene blue, injected under the skin, In a few months they won't be contagious any longer."

Mittel, with a lump in his throat, turned away. Every bed in the maternity wards was occupied, and the sheets, dazzling white in the sunlight, made a kind of background to a symphony of wailing.

"As you see, everything is spotless. Here are the kitchens."

Two vast copper vats in a room filled with steam, and Chinese cooks milling around them. The doctor knocked at a door, and a gigantic native in uniform appeared, bowing and scraping.

"All quiet in there?"

"Only Babo is making trouble. He just tried to kill me."

"What did he do?"

"He put his arm through the hatch when I brought him his food, and managed to grab me around the neck."

"Come with me," said the doctor to Mittel.

A little courtyard, surrounded by buildings resembling a stable

293

block, with identical barred apertures in every door. And behind seven or eight of these barred apertures could be seen mute, haggard faces.

"The lunatics," announced the doctor. "Wait till you see them."

The attendant opened a door to reveal, crouching in the dark cell, a native youth of about seventeen. He was stark naked, and had torn his blanket to shreds. A narrow wooden shelf served as a bed. There was no pillow. No furniture of any kind.

"Whatever they're given, they either smash or tear! They used to be issued clothing, but the next day everything would be torn to shreds."

In the neighboring cell, a woman. She smiled shyly, and her gaze finally rested on Mittel.

"We dare not let this one out into the yard, because the mere sight of a woman gives the men ideas."

They warned him to watch out for the third inmate, Babo, a former native chief from the Marquesas. He believed he was a god; indeed, he looked like a god of classical mythology, with his powerful build and white beard. It was he who had attempted to strangle the attendant, but now he was all smiles and good will, as if anxious to make amends.

"You tried to kill your attendant, I hear!" the doctor shouted sternly. The culprit responded with bows, blessings, and prayers.

Next to him was an Italian, a sculptor, who had arrived in Tahiti three years before and had immediately suffered a sunstroke. No one had been willing to take the responsibility of looking after him. . . .

Mittel could hardly bear to look this white man in the face, this European who, naked like the rest, came eagerly toward them, hoping against hope that they might have some good news for him.

"I've had enough," he sighed.

Mittel felt a profound loathing for the attendant, whose wife he could see sitting on the porch of their house, peeling vegetables.

"Do any of them ever recover?"

"Very few."

It was a long walk back, across sun-drenched courtyards and along corridors with dazzling-white walls. Mittel had a headache, but he was careful not to show it, walking very upright and never allowing his smile to slip.

"I'll give you something that will make you feel better."

"Thanks."

He was floundering in a nightmare. Then, suddenly, he found himself face to face with Mopps. He must have looked terrified for a second or two, for the captain asked, "What's wrong with you?"

"Me? Nothing."

No, nothing! He was determined that there be nothing wrong with him. He sensed that it was vital for him to keep his head, come what may, and to go about his daily business like any normal man.

Above all, they must not be allowed to suspect that he had uncovered their plot. And a very neat plot it was, too! They had all had a hand in it, Charlotte included. That conversation the previous night had been carefully rehearsed. They had tricked him into visiting the hospital, in particular, the wing where the lunatics were housed—a covert threat, he surmised.

Now they were on their way back to the club, he and Mopps. Mopps looked more than a little ashamed. He was almost certainly on the verge of referring to the subject, if only he had dared and could have found the right words.

"You know, young man, in this climate . . ."

"I'm not afraid of death!"

His throat was so dry that it was torture to get the words out.

"Brugnon warned me in no uncertain terms that if I went on drinking and all the rest of it, I'd be dead in less than three years, but that didn't prevent me from carrying on as usual. Quite the contrary! I intend to go out with a bang! . . . Hello, Tita."

She was sitting on the porch steps of her tiny house, which was built of wood and painted green. She was in the middle of cutting her toenails—outside, practically in the street—and she wore, as usual, her red dress, like a sheath dipped in blood in the blazing sun.

"Hello, Mopps! Hello, Jef!"

She was always laughing. She loved people. Above all, she loved life.

As they resumed walking, Mopps said in an undertone, "There's just one thing. The baby must not be exposed to infection. . . ."

"Yes, we mustn't let anything happen to *our* baby!"

The minute these words were out of his mouth, he regretted them. What was the point? The last thing he wanted to do was to give them a hold over him. He thought of Plumier, of his eccentric behavior. At all costs, he must avoid that trap, for he was not mad, he knew that for certain.

"What makes you say that?"

"No reason. It's of no importance."

"Are you angry with me?"

A man all on his own here, turned in upon himself, with nothing to gain and nothing to lose . . .

The truth was that Charlotte was scared of him, that even Mopps was uneasy about him. And the more composed he appeared, the more he forced himself to keep smiling, the more he terrified them!

Yet they were incapable of changing their course. It was a kind of addiction. And what was the most that was required of them? Nothing but a little tact, a little reticence, a little less openly flaunted familiarity.

Why did they have to spend hour after hour at the bar, drinking and exchanging inanities?

They could not help themselves, Mittel could sense it! This was the life they had grown accustomed to. They had achieved a sort of equilibrium, and they clung to it. It was a means of putting off the evil hour when things would come to a head.

And come to a head things would, of that they were in no doubt. . . . They foresaw it so clearly that they had nudged him gently toward the hospital, not so much because they felt he needed a medical checkup as to bring him face to face with the lunatics in their cells.

A kind of threat! Brugnon was all-powerful in that sphere. Commitment papers signed by him, and . . .

Mittel, forgetting that he had the child on his knee, gazed at his neighbor's house, where a servantgirl in white was setting the table and putting vases of flowers beside each glass.

There, that was it! That was the way he would have liked to live. Then he turned to look at the baby, a bright, observant child, and tried to guess what his future would be.

Would he just amount to very little, like Mittel himself? Or would things be still worse for him? He did not even have a name, other than that foisted upon him in the forged passport! He had been born in the equatorial jungle, not long after his mother was close to death. Nevertheless, he was a happy child, always smiling, and a good deal more robust than most of the other white children Mittel had seen in Papeete.

This, then, was Charlotte's miracle, for it had been a miracle, no less. The baby, according to all the laws of nature, should never have been born alive! Given the circumstances, no reliable doctor would have made an optimistic prognosis at the time Charlotte had gone into labor.

Then the long sea voyage . . . their arrival in Tahiti . . . The child had borne up magnificently. Apart from three days of dysentery, he had never suffered any of the ailments that often afflict newborn babies. He seldom cried. He had been weaned without the slightest trouble.

Mittel hugged him a little closer and resolved to have him X-rayed, to find out whether he, too, was tubercular.

It would be evidence of a sort—evidence that the child really was his son!

He no longer knew what to hope for. He could hear the clinking of glasses in the bar, and Tioti's unpleasant voice talking to someone on the telephone.

"Jef! Where are you?"

Charlotte's voice. How he had come to hate the sound of it! He needed a moment's respite before he could answer.

"Jef, it's time for the baby's bottle!"

"Yes," he said, getting up.

And, as usual, to avoid going through the bar, he went into the bungalow by the back door, and handed the baby over to Maria.

"The truck completely wrecked the car. Alexandre was killed instantly," someone at the bar was saying.

"Come on, Charlotte. . . ."

"I'm coming. . . ."

"For God's sake, let's have a drink! What's this place supposed to be, a nursery?"

"At any rate," said Charlotte, "I'm not the nurse."

And Mittel turned to the native girl and whispered, "Are you sure the milk isn't too hot?"

19

SINCE HE WAS NOT MAD, ALL HE HAD TO DO WAS NEVER BEHAVE AS if he were, and that was all there was to it! It was no problem. He had learned much from Plumier's example. He must watch his step the whole time, so as never to play into their hands!

So careful was he in this regard that he would spend time in front of the mirror, studying his facial expressions, his smile.

"Why should I bear you a grudge? Wasn't it you who got us away from Dieppe, and, more recently, took care of us here, when we arrived penniless?"

"You're not being straight with me. It may seem strange to you, but I'll tell you—and it's the honest truth—I love you like a son! But sometimes I find your attitude intolerable, because you're so ready to think the worst of everyone. Do you understand now?"

"What is there to understand?"

"You really are being obtuse! Yes, there is one thing you must understand. A woman like Charlotte simply isn't worth quarreling over."

"That doesn't alter the fact that you contrived to bring her here."

"I don't deny it."

This was the first time he had admitted to Mittel that it was on Charlotte's account that he had written to them in Buenaventura.

"When you reach my age, you'll understand better."

"I won't live that long."

"All the better for you! What's to prevent you from having a good time, like everyone else? Why do you need to hover over her like that, looking so woebegone that you've become the laughingstock of all the local girls?"

"Oh, is that so?"

"Naturally! Nothing escapes them! Do you know what they call you behind your back? Because everyone here has a local name, flattering or otherwise. You are known as the *man who feeds on his own flesh*, or, as we would say, *the man who is eating his heart out*."

The street was lined on both sides with magnificent trees—flame trees, as Mittel now knew. And there, just a hundred meters away, was the sea, with the bungalow on the left, and on the right the Protestant church, with its crudely painted metal belltower.

"Do you really believe that, if I had had any choice, I would not have behaved differently?"

Mopps sounded so sincere that Mittel was almost moved. He glanced at Mopps covertly, then deliberately hardened his heart, determined not to be won over.

"And the doctor! And the rest of us! Don't you see, the whole bunch of us are without hope of a better future, and . . ."

Mittel dug his nails into the palms of his hands. On the other side of the garden hedge he could hear his son wailing, and Maria's deep voice as she tried to soothe him.

What then? Tioti was there, leaning on the counter, his eyes sparkling. It was the same with every one of them when they were alone with Charlotte. Mopps, obviously taking it more philosophically, pretended not to notice.

Mittel walked across the room without a word, and went to change out of the white shirt and detached collar that he had put on for his visit to the hospital, and into the khaki outfit that he usually wore. He went out into the garden through the back door, to find Maria sitting on the lawn, playing with his son.

"What's wrong with you?" asked Maria, using the familiar *tu*, like all the other local girls.

"Nothing! Off you go!"

He sat the child on his knee and gazed at him disconsolately.

Since his flight from Dieppe, his senses had sharpened, and it seemed to him that he could now read the minds of those around him, however trivial their thoughts.

He knew, for instance, that Maria was prepared to devote herself to him, body and soul, but only because she felt for him in his weakness and misery, and because she was aware of all that was going on in the household and was infuriated by it. Maybe she was also a little bit in love with him, and could not understand why, since they slept in the same room, he never offered to share her bed. Perhaps she found this humiliating?

As for the others . . .

If Mittel had not witnessed Plumier's torment—for genuine torment it certainly had been—he might have regarded them differently. But as it was, he could imagine himself in their place. He still recalled his own reactions to the Belgian's eccentric behavior, and the fears this behavior had aroused in him, which he had been at pains to overcome.

His mistake, at the outset, had been to distance himself from the others, and to give way to outbursts of temper. Now, he sometimes remained in the bar and joined in the conversation.

What did such things matter, now that he had made up his mind to act? But how he would act, he hadn't the slightest idea. Or, more precisely, he refused even to think of it. It was so frightful that it would have been stamped on his features for all to see.

Did they not already suspect something of the truth? Charlotte most of all, of course! Women have a special instinct for such things. Recently she had grown afraid of him, and was careful to avoid being alone with him. She was always covertly watching him, and often, when he came in, he found her whispering to little Maria, obviously asking about him: "What did he say to you? Does he sleep well at night? Does he confide in you? Has he ever made love to you?"

He would come indoors humming with assumed cheerfulness,

usually with some remark or other on his lips, it did not matter what. "A yacht has just berthed in the harbor. It's a very small one, a two-master."

Was she taken in? Mopps certainly seemed to be. His manner toward Mittel was invariably affectionate, a little too much so, if anything.

All this started after his visit to the hospital. What could the doctor possibly have said to them? Since then, at any rate, they had all treated him as an object of pity.

"How are you feeling?" they would persist in asking. "Are you sleeping well?"

They all humored him, as one humors an invalid to cheer him up. Even Maria, obviously distressed, reproached him with not eating enough, and said that he needed to keep up his strength.

He had tuberculosis. Well, what of it? Would things have been any different if he had enjoyed perfect health?

Of course not! He dared not even laugh to himself, in case someone caught him at it, for if ever he allowed them to think that he was out of his mind . . .

He was prey to sudden fits of panic. Sometimes, strolling along the waterfront, he would see someone he knew, and, his mind being on other things, would nod absently in greeting. Then, as he pulled himself together, he would fret: had he behaved in a way other people might consider odd?

One thing puzzled him. During his visit to the lunatics in the hospital, he had spent only a few seconds face to face with the Italian in the last cell, and yet it was the Italian he remembered most vividly, down to the minutest detail, such as a missing front tooth, and a slightly round-shouldered bearing.

He had reckoned that the child would be walking within four months. Already! Then, six months after that, he would be start-ing to talk, or at least babbling a few intelligible sounds. But now all he could manage was to blow bubbles with his little pursed mouth.

Mittel kept cool. It was essential. He willed it with all the strength he could muster. Why had Mopps, the other morning—

a Sunday, as it happened—said to him, as he came into the bunga-low, "Jef, do me a favor, go fetch my pills from Tita's."

For he regularly took pills prescribed for him by Brugnon. On two or three occasions, he had been troubled by what he took to be symptoms of a weak heart, and ever since he had begun taking better care of himself, drinking somewhat less, especially in the evening, and always carrying his pills in his pocket.

Mittel set out, attaching no special importance to the incident, and not considering that Sunday was a special day for him, that every significant event of his life had occurred on a Sunday.

He could hear hymns being sung in the Protestant church, while at the same time he saw the natives streaming out of the Catholic church, all in their Sunday best, the girls in white dresses, the men in starched suits and straw hats, just like pious churchgoers the world over.

Mittel had never set foot inside Tita's house. He crossed the little garden, bright with orange blossom, and knocked timidly at the door.

"Who's there?"

"It's me, Jef! The captain wants something he left behind."

"Come on in."

The most distinctive thing about her was her voice, which had a lilting quality, as if she were always singing a sweet, affection-ate song with faintly mocking overtones.

"Come in, Jef! Leave the door open so that we can have some light."

The room was just a room, in a fearful state of disorder. Mopps's razor and shaving brush were lying on the table. Tita herself was still in bed, but she propped herself up on her elbow and murmured, "I wonder if you'd mind getting me a drink? There's some water on the dressing table."

Mittel did not even notice her supple body, which was barely concealed beneath the sheet. He was not much interested in sex, and it took a lot to arouse him.

"Thanks, Jef. You're very kind."

She spoke not merely for the sake of politeness, but in the

303

tones of one who had been thinking this for a long time, and had only been waiting for an opportunity to say it.

"In fact, you're too kind, if anything. That's why everyone makes fun of you."

He started and turned to look at her, his unhappy expression already returning.

"What do you mean?"

"You know very well. Hand me my dress. I want to get up."

And she snatched the red dress from him, pulled it on over her naked body, and stretched in the sunshine.

"What's wrong with you?" she asked, noticing Mittel's desolate expression for the first time.

"Nothing . . . Listen, Tita, you've got to tell me what you meant just now. . . . Who makes fun of me?"

"All right, then. Only please stop looking at me like that. I'm a good friend. Ask Mopps. . . . I've never willingly hurt anyone in my life. Just imagine, I could have set up house with the chief justice, if I'd wanted to. He was ready to send his wife back to Europe. I refused, on her account, even when he begged me on his knees. . . ."

"Who makes fun of me?"

"I don't know. . . . All I mean is that they're not kind to you. Your wife has a baby. What business does she have allowing every man she sees to make up to her?"

But he could feel that this was not what Tita had in mind. She was wiping her face with a damp cloth, and at the same time groping for the right words. The air was very still. There was not a sound to be heard, except the distant lapping of the waves against the coral reef.

"If you were not jealous it wouldn't matter, so they would be right. But they know that you *are* jealous, and yet they carry on regardless. They can see how much suffering it causes you, that it's making you ill. . . ."

"Who says it's making me ill?"

"Everyone! You even had to have an appointment with Brugnon at the hospital."

304

As she spoke, Mittel's mood grew ever more somber. Now, it seemed to him, he could no longer show himself out of doors without people saying to themselves, "Ah, that's the man who's so ill, and whose wife is deceiving him."

He was slumped in a chair beside the table. Tita put on her stockings.

"Take no notice of them. . . . We all have our own lives to lead, don't we? They say all kinds of things about me, too. And do you think I pay any attention? The difference is that you ought to have someone to be nice to you, you're so nice yourself. More than that, you're a good man, one can feel it. Mopps says so, too."

"Good Lord! Is he really so flattering about me?"

"He's not the one to blame, you know. He's fallen in love with her, and I sometimes wonder whether he isn't even more jealous than you are. She's the one who is ill-natured. It amuses her to have men quarreling over her."

Tita babbled on as she completed her toilet, for the sheer pleasure of talking.

"What else do they say?"

"You're a strange man!" she cried, looking him intently in the face. "At times you seem able to shrug off these things, and at other times, such as now, you're frightening. You mustn't be like that! Let me explain. . . . Why should you care one way or the other what Charlotte is up to? It's too late for that, don't you see? You'd do better to make a life for yourself, make friends of your own, girls. . . ."

It was plain enough that she was only too willing to join the ranks. Generally, she regarded the whites with some awe, but Mittel was different, small of stature, sickly, childlike, and unhappy, all of which aroused her maternal instincts.

"They'd be the first to be shocked. For instance, I happen to know that Charlotte took it badly when you decided to move into Maria's bedroom. I know all about everyone, you know? And there's always something of the sort going on at the club. Two years ago it was over an American girl, and it ended up in a fistfight between the doctor and a lieutenant in the merchant marines."

Mittel appeared to have lost interest and was staring at the dusty floorboards, but she went on: "What does it matter what people say about one another? When a person's dead . . ."

At this, he turned slowly around to look at her. The torrent of words that she had poured out, to which he had not paid much conscious attention, had gradually worked him up into a fever. It was as if he were drunk. Suddenly, rising to his feet to emphasize the solemnity of his words, he asked, speaking slowly and distinctly, "What about you? What do you think of me?"

"I told you. You're good and kind . . . too much so! It would be better for you if, from time to time . . ."

He smiled, and there was a hint of menace in his eyes.

"And you don't think I'd be capable of . . . ?"

"Capable of what?"

"Of losing my temper! Of avenging myself!"

She looked terrified, for in his fury, he had enunciated each word like a hammer blow.

"You don't understand, do you? Well, just listen to me, and I'll tell you exactly what's going on. All I have to do is lose my temper, and say one word out of place, for them to have me committed to the lunatic asylum, on the grounds that I'm mad. . . . Oh, yes . . . I know all about it. . . ."

"Jef!"

"I repeat, I know what I know. So I string them along, the idiots. . . . I run messages for them. . . . I go shopping in the market, like a servant. . . . I laugh at their jokes. . . . But the day will come when my mind will finally be made up. . . ."

"What will you do?"

He was silent for an instant, at a loss for an answer. He had spoken thus because he had felt impelled, just this once, to get things off his chest. He had brooded in silence for too long.

"What will I do? I'll do what . . ."

He wiped his forehead with the back of his hand. It was difficult to put it into words, for it was not clear, even in his own mind. It was just that he longed, with all his might, to say something that would convince him of his own power.

"You wouldn't understand. Suppose you knew that you were going to die. . . ."

"But . . ."

"Well, that's something I do know. Consequently, I have nothing to lose, do I? All I ask is a few months of happiness, and that is denied me."

And he recalled the house next door to the club, its cleanliness and order, and the husband and wife bending over the cot. . . .

"And considering that, on top of everything else, they despise me, that they don't even have the grace to wait until I'm dead . . ."

He was so carried away that he had lost the thread of his argument.

"I have every right to take my revenge, by any means I choose! Haven't you heard that Charlotte is plotting to have me committed?"

"That's an exaggeration," she murmured in alarm.

"No! Only she'd better not forget that, if I so choose, I have it in my power to get her thrown into prison tomorrow. And Mopps would be arrested, too! Do you hear that? It would be a dirty trick, but would it be any worse than what they're doing to me? I could kill all of them, one after another. And, what's more, I could . . . What do you and Mopps talk about? Does he say the child is his?"

"I don't know."

"You're lying! He's told everyone it's his!"

"I swear to you, Jef . . ."

"All right, then, suppose . . . Oh, so you regard me as a good man, a kindhearted youngster. And you really believe me capable of just fading out, and leaving the three of them behind!"

It was the first time in his life that he had ever worked himself up into such a state. He was lashing himself into a frenzy like a drunken man. As people do when they are drunk, he felt that every man's hand was against him, and he was determined to

307

fight back. Filled with revulsion, he was adopting an aggressive stance.

Endeavoring to whip himself up into an even greater frenzy, he looked into Tita's eyes to gauge her response to his outburst, and realized that she was holding his hand.

"Stop it, Jef! If you could just hear yourself!"

"Aha! Now we're getting at the truth! They're spying on me, and you know it, and you know that I have only to slip up once for them to have me locked up. But I'll get them first, Tita! They've robbed me of everything, don't you see? When I arrived here, it was like being born again. I wept when I set foot on this island, I wept for joy, because I believed that here, at last, I was on the threshold of a new life. And I was prepared to go to any lengths, to do the work of ten men, to scrimp and save, anything, to keep the three of us together, a happy little family at last!

"Out there in the jungle, while Charlotte was ill, I thought of nothing else. . . . I'd have given all I had for the child to be born alive. I read the medical textbook from cover to cover, over and over again.

"And then there we were at the club, and there was Mopps looking at the baby, and . . ."

He burst into tears. He had taken as much as he could stand. Tita put her arm around him and absently kissed him on the forehead.

"Come on, now! Calm down. . . ."

"Calm down? What for? To enable them to go on living together in peace, with the child? Soon they'll have forgotten I ever existed. Some time in the future, perhaps, they'll say to him: 'Your father died when you were a baby. . . . He was not strong, you see.' Or they may even say, to get him to eat up his soup, 'Be a good boy and finish it; you don't want to end up like your father.' Unless, of course, they don't even mention the man who might or might not have been his father. . . ."

He did not bother to wipe his eyes. The tears streamed down his cheeks, unchecked. He went on talking, and the more he talked, the more he grieved, and the more he grieved, the more he felt the need to grieve.

It was doing him good.

"Don't cry. . . . A man should never cry. . . ."

"Don't worry, I'll think of something. They've stripped me to the bone. It can't be put into words. It's . . . No! You couldn't possibly understand! And they would do nothing for me, they would spare me nothing, not a single unkind word, hint, or action. . . ."

"Do you love her so very much?"

"Who?"

"Charlotte."

He could not reply at once. He seemed to be groping within himself for the truth.

"Her? . . . I don't know. . . ."

It was not Charlotte who mattered, but the three of them, the little family group that had been formed almost by chance out there in South America, and that had come to mean more to him than life itself. Which of the two was the core, Charlotte or the child?

"Listen to me carefully, Tita. Very soon—I can't say when; it may be tomorrow, or in a month—I shall have reached the end, and then . . ."

"Don't say such things!"

"No, I make no secret of it. . . . When that happens, they'll arrest me, and do whatever they like with me. . . ."

"Have something to drink. Here!"

She poured him a glass of rum, hoping it would calm him. He gulped it down, to show that he was past caring.

"It always makes me spit blood," he declared.

"Then you shouldn't have drunk it."

"Yes, I should! Maybe I could turn myself into an alcoholic, like the rest of them. If you knew how they disgust me, Tita! Everything about them disgusts me!"

Footsteps could be heard on the garden path. Mittel turned his head away, to hide his tears from the caller. He sniffed.

"Is Monsieur Jef here?" asked the voice of Maria.

And then she saw him.

"Madame asked me to find you, because she wants you to go and buy some eggs from the Chinese shop."

"Thanks for telling me."

She could see that he had been crying. She could sense Tita's distress, and could picture the scene that had taken place.

"Have you got the medicine?"

"Here, take it. . . . Tell her that I won't be long with the eggs."

He got to his feet hastily, quite composed all of a sudden, as the girl, her thick black hair hanging down to her shoulders, went down the path in her bare feet.

"She won't say anything," Tita assured him.

"I don't care what she says. It doesn't bother me."

His voice was toneless now. The fever was gone, leaving him drained. It was as if he had taken part in an orgy, the very thought of which now sickened him. And indeed, hadn't his recent impassioned outburst been a kind of orgy of self-pity?

"Try not to upset yourself, Jef. Promise me."

"Do I look upset?"

"Not now, but a little while ago you were raving like a madman. . . ."

At this he stalked out of the house, without so much as a word or a glance, so great was his dread of losing his temper, of hitting her, of giving way to another outburst.

She had said, "Like a madman."

He strode along at great speed. He had a feeling of some danger tracking him, close on his heels. Today was a Sunday, exactly like any other Sunday, anywhere on earth. There were ice-cream vendors in the streets. The shops were closed. The young people, in their best clothes, filled the streets, the boys going in one direction, the girls in the other. Whenever they collided there were peals of laughter, and occasionally a chase, ending in a kiss.

What on earth had come over him? Like a man who had been drinking all night, he endeavored to remember all he had said and was appalled by the whole episode.

And yet he had said nothing that was not true. He had merely put into words all the thoughts that tormented him when he was alone; but, spoken aloud, they seemed harsher and cruder.

To put it in a nutshell, he had been showing off! He had been eager to prove to Tita, and to himself as well, that he was something more than a callow youth, a feeble, maudlin youth.

For instance, in referring to the child, he had uttered what almost amounted to a threat. But that had not been his intention at all. There had been no more than a grain of truth in it.

The incident had occurred the week before. On the day in question, Charlotte had come into the bar, dripping from her shower, to get Mopps to dry her back. The room smelled strongly of Pernod, for the previous evening they had been drinking until midnight.

Mittel had taken refuge at the foot of the garden with the baby. He had sat down on the lawn, the child lying beside him, and watched a fat beetle crawl ponderously across the diaper.

It was about eleven in the morning. At this time of day the air was always buzzing with insect life, and flecks of light glittered on the smooth surface of the lagoon.

It felt like a separate, magical world, in which a man's whole being was absorbed and his emotions dissolved, leaving his spirit lapped in languor and warmth.

The baby had closed his eyes, and every now and then his face creased into a thousand wrinkles because a fly had settled on his nose.

Somewhere in the distance, a car horn sounded . . . then bells . . . then Charlotte's raucous voice from the house.

The house, which would remain exactly as it was now, even when he was no longer there! The only likely change was that Mopps would move in, lock, stock, and barrel, instead of sleeping at Tita's place, as at present. In all other ways, life would go on as usual. But who could say? Now that Mopps had money from the sale of his freighter, it would not be beyond Charlotte to persuade him to marry her, to secure her future.

And what of Mopps himself? Why not? Since they only had forged papers, might he not be willing to recognize the child as his own?

The beetle was no longer crawling. It stood motionless, waving its feelers. Mittel wondered what was making it take so much trouble.

Tioti's car pulled up at the door, with one wheel in the flowerbed, as usual, and he went into the bar, to be met with peals of laughter.

Wouldn't it be the best thing for the two of them to go away? Going away, as far as Mittel was concerned, no longer meant boarding a ship and setting sail for another country. He had had more than his fill of ocean voyages to strange countries.

He would never leave Tahiti, and he knew it. He would never again set eyes on Dieppe, or Paris. He would never again see the Rue Montmarte, or Bébé, who was annoyed with him because he wrote so seldom, or Mrs. White and her apartment on the Avenue Hoche.

He would go once and for all, taking the baby with him, without waiting for the hour appointed by fate.

He had stretched out on the grass. The child's face was very close to his.

Would it not be better for him, too? What did the future hold in store for him? Undoubtedly a life of vain hopes, like his father's, an endless search for the unattainable.

It had taken a tremendous effort of will to escape from this quicksand. He had scrambled to his feet, picked up the baby, and walked up and down for a long time before plucking up the courage to go back into the bungalow, so convinced was he that all his thoughts were still there to be read on his face.

There! That was the notion that he had toyed with for a few seconds, no more than a few seconds! It was his child. . . . He could not endure the thought that *afterward* . . .

But that was not what he had said to Tita. He must have been mad—yes, truly mad—when he had shouted those threats in her presence, like some hectoring braggart.

All she had to do was repeat half of what he had said, and the others would use his words to get him put away.

He came to an abrupt halt in front of the Chinese shop where he always bought their eggs. The shopkeeper looked at him with an amazement that was almost comical.

"Well, Monsieur Jef, what can I do for you?"

"Yes . . . We need eggs. . . ."

He was baffled to discover that, by some miracle, he had landed precisely where he was supposed to be.

"Two dozen?"

"Yes."

"Feeling the heat?"

His shirt was clinging to his body, though he had not noticed.

"This is not the time of day for a brisk walk!"

And there was the little Chinese boy, three or four years old, gazing up at him with those huge eyes.

The first thing he heard on his return was the sound of loud music, and it did not take him long to realize that Tioti had brought his phonograph with him. Céline was there as well, along with the governor's secretary. Everyone turned to look at Mittel, and it seemed to him that he could read astonishment in all their faces.

What was it they found so strange? Could they tell that he had been crying? No, of course not! Behind their assumed expressions of surprise, they were laughing at him.

It was Mopps who made the first move. He slapped him on the back so heartily that it was a wonder the eggs were not broken. Indeed, they would have been, if Mittel had not grabbed hold of the bar.

"What's up?"

He could not understand what they were all laughing at, or why Charlotte was looking at him in that odd fashion.

"So you've done it at last! I must say, you took your time about it. Incidentally, I don't remember your asking my permission."

Someone was changing the record. There were eight or nine half-empty glasses on the table. Maria was in the kitchen, stirring food in the saucepans.

"Feeling good, aren't you?"

"But . . ."

"Come on, don't play the innocent! Everyone here knows all about it. . . . The whole of Papeete is talking. . . . Jef has made up his mind at last to taste the delights of love in Tahiti."

He had been prepared for anything, but not that, and he stood there stunned, looking from one laughing face to another. So that's what they thought? That he and Tita . . . ?

It made him sick. So that was all they came up with? Well, after all, they were incapable of thinking anything else.

"Here are the eggs," he said, putting them down on the counter.

"There's nothing to be ashamed of," said Tioti, changing the phonograph needle.

"I'm not ashamed."

"Won't Tita be coming?" asked Céline.

"I don't know."

Completely shattered, he struggled in vain to regain his self-control. And Charlotte had to pick this moment to announce, "Well, I'm not jealous, anyway!"

It was ludicrous, pathetic! He went to his room, then quickly returned in alarm.

"Where's the baby?"

"Taitou has taken him out for a walk."

This was not unusual. One or another of the neighbors would often take the child out in his carriage. But this time, Mittel had taken fright. He had got it into his head, for no apparent reason, that they had robbed him of the child forever.

"She's keeping him for the whole day, because we're all leaving in a little while for a trip to the peninsula."

"Oh, yes . . ."

He must have sounded odd, because everyone burst out laughing. He felt infinitely remote from all this, and it was a hard struggle to come down to earth. Luckily for him, they had got the phonograph working again at last, playing a record of South American tunes.

"Go see how Maria is coming along."

He went into the kitchen, but not before he had caught Mopps watching him intently. Suddenly he was seized with renewed terror, for it seemed to him that Mopps could read his innermost thoughts. . . .

Tita, presumably, had been briefed in advance. She arrived a few minutes later, heralded by a renewed burst of laughter. But she took their teasing in good part, joining in the laughter and making no attempt to disabuse them.

She appeared to ignore him, until, when he happened to be passing by her, she pressed his toes with her foot, as if to remind him to keep calm.

An hour passed, noisy with clinking glasses and bottles, and pleasantries shouted from table to table, not to mention the music of Tioti's phonograph, which he kept rewinding.

A car pulled up, and four musicians joined them. Maria was sent into town to buy chaplets of *tiarés*. The trunk of Mopps's car contained, instead of luggage, a zinc chest filled with twenty bottles on a bed of ice.

"Let's go!"

Mittel would have given a lot to stay behind, but he dreaded the solitude. From time to time, Tita would wink at him conspiratorially.

"Who's taking the lead?"

There were four cars. The doctor had brought a couple of prostitutes with him, and they all piled in anyhow, being careful, however, to avoid separating Mopps and Charlotte.

Everyone wore a chaplet of flowers. Each car had its own musician, who sat at the back and strummed on his guitar.

Mittel found himself sitting next to Tita—or, rather, crushed against her, since there were three people squashed into one seat.

They drove out of town, following the winding road along the coast, never losing sight of the lagoon, with its fringe of tall coconut palms and derelict canoes on the sands.

Mittel's mind was a blank. The music from the rear was no more than a haunting rhythm, like the beat of the tom-toms in the equatorial jungle, which seemed to control the very rhythm of life, perhaps even the circulation of the blood.

It took him a long time to realize that his hand was being held in a tight grip, and when he did, he turned to Tita, who was smiling at him kindly, if a little timidly.

"Well?" she seemed to be asking.

He forced himself to return her smile, and she whispered, very softly and breathlessly, "Wouldn't we have done better to . . . ?"

She was referring to the general misapprehension, and the banter arising from it.

"Wouldn't we have done better . . . ?"

But, fifty meters farther on, Mittel withdrew his hand: he was feeling the heat.

20

TITA EXERTED HERSELF TO TEACH HIM TO ENJOY LIFE. EXCITEDLY, through moist lips, she pointed out every feature of interest in the countryside.

"Look, Jef," she announced, as they came to the first village, "this is where I was born. There's the school. . . ."

And he gazed, wide-eyed, at the little houses with their steep red roofs. The roofs were not tiled, but made of corrugated iron, with a thin coat of paint, which gave them a richness of color admirably harmonizing with the dark-green vegetation. Native huts of woven palm leaves were few and far between, but some were to be seen strung out beside the lagoon, inhabited, for the most part, by fisherfolk, the poorest of the poor, surrounded by hordes of naked children.

But in the villages, the streets were lined on both sides with wooden houses, like pretty playthings. The wooden walls were painted in pastel colors, pale green, sky-blue, and occasionally pink. Each house had a veranda in front, overlooking a garden, a multicolored riot of flowers. And since it was Sunday, in Tahiti, as in any suburb of Paris, the Tahitians were relaxing on their porches, the men in dazzlingly white shirts, the women running to fat, often with a phonograph playing beside them, while the younger generation skimmed along the roads on their bicycles.

Despite the many diverse elements in the landscape, nothing stuck out as discordant or strange. It seemed perfectly natural that the lagoon should be ringed with coconut palms, while, around a bend in the road, there appeared a pretty, bright church with a pointed spire.

The school to which Tita was pointing was a single-story building, surrounded by spacious lawns. All its windows were open, revealing benches, a blackboard, and a desk for the teacher.

A school like any other. Like the village. Like the Tahitians themselves, scarcely darker than the whites, and dressed in European clothes, with their mild eyes and lilting voices.

In Paris, no one would have given Tita a second glance, and they would have been hard put to it to guess her country of origin.

"Stop!" she called to the driver.

And she turned to Mittel, to explain: "I must say hello to Sonia. She's the chef's daughter, and we were at school together."

Sonia was small and plump. She was strolling alone by the side of the road, in a white dress with blue spots, her raven hair braided in a single, heavy plait. She was carrying a flower and smiling quietly to herself.

"Sonia!"

In Tita's eyes, riding in a car conferred distinction, and she was delighted when her little friend stepped onto the running board and gave her a hug.

"Why don't you come with us?"

"No, it will be time for vespers in a few minutes."

On the left, a Chinese shop, with the whole family out on the veranda, an indispensable feature of all the houses in Tahiti.

Since it was Sunday, there was no work to be done, so all were relaxing in the still air as the hours slipped by.

But not everybody spent his leisure in so peaceful a fashion! They had covered another three kilometers and driven over a bridge across the river when they heard shouting; there, behind a screen of coconut palms, was a soccer field where two teams were competing, in spite of the sun. There were a fair number of spectators, who yelled encouragement every time a player got away with the ball.

Looming in the background, that massive mountain, two thousand meters high, uninhabited, almost unscalable. Tahiti's impregnable defensive wall.

The road wound beneath it. Every kilometer or so, they crossed a river or a stream fed by the mountain springs, and they saw people standing in water up to their waists, casting for fish.

"Is there anything as beautiful as this in France?" asked Tita. "I'm sure there isn't."

Their only other traveling companion was the Englishman who owned one of the big stores, and he spoke no French. He ignored them, and spent most of the journey dozing. Tita once more snuggled up to Mittel, and spoke to him in a tone of affectionate playfulness.

"Those things you said this morning . . . You mustn't ever talk like that again. . . . There's so much to enjoy in life! Just look at those boys fishing in the lagoon. . . ."

She was pointing to a cluster of canoes, each with a youth standing peering down into the clear water, a short spear in his hand. Suddenly one of them would dive, swim under water in pursuit of his prey, and reappear on the surface, holding aloft a silvery fish on the end of his pointed stick.

In the leading car, Charlotte was sitting between Mopps and Tioti, who was stroking her thigh, knowing that the captain, who was driving, could not see what was going on. She let him have his way. She, too, was in high spirits, restless and rowdy at the same time. She longed to roll over and over on the grass. Whenever they came to a river, she wanted to get out and swim. She had only to catch sight of a bungalow prettier than the others to want it for herself.

"Let's buy a house like that one, shall we, Captain?"

"I don't see why not."

After they had passed through a second village, the strip of land between the mountain and the sea narrowed, and the scenery was even more picturesque. And every few kilometers here, imposing houses with well-kept gardens could also be seen.

This was the district where the smart set lived, mainly British and American. There were tennis courts, lawns watered by sprinklers and surrounded by neat gravel paths.

"Please cheer up! Promise me you will," Tita said, snuggling closer to Mittel.

He was finding it more and more difficult to maintain his expression of frowning disapproval. There was something in the atmosphere so beguiling that it moved him deeply, in the same way as an organ voluntary in church.

He could not precisely identify the source of his emotion. It was everything and nothing. It was this tiny island set in a boundless ocean. It was the houses like pretty playthings. The men in white trousers, with rolled-up shirt sleeves and broad-brimmed straw hats. It was the pastel-colored dresses of the girls. It was the leisurely tempo of life, the total silence of the luminous cupola of sky above them, like the dome of a cathedral.

Behind him, on the rumble seat, the musician was still absent-mindedly strumming on his guitar. The others were barely conscious of it, and yet the random chords, following no recognizable rhythmic pattern, seemed to penetrate his whole being.

Mittel suddenly realized that he had his arm around Tita, and that she had snuggled up to him even more closely, murmuring, "You'll see! I'll teach you how to be happy. . . . We'll go for a walk together."

Suddenly a thought struck him, a knife in his heart, changing everything.

Wasn't this probably the last time he would see this countryside? This was the first time he had toured the island. It had come about by mere chance, and when would such a chance occur again? Too late, perhaps. Who could say? Next time this same crowd set out in their cars, would they be saying, "Poor Jef . . .Tita will miss him, now that he's no longer here to make love to her"?

"Isn't it all perfectly beautiful, Jef?" she said again.

"Oh, yes, it is!"

That was the trouble. It was too beautiful. It was not just a landscape like any other. It was at one and the same time a painting, a melody, and a poem, a complex and pervasive whole, a world in itself, which enfolded one and which one dreaded losing, a world in which one longed to embed oneself more deeply, which one longed to absorb into oneself.

Above all it was peace, such as was not to be found anywhere else in the world! Words created no more disturbance in the atmosphere than tiny ripples on a pond, and were quickly absorbed into the surrounding stillness.

Yet everything he saw conspired to remind him of something, to bring to the surface the deep unhappiness within him. For instance, that family strolling along by the side of the road, the woman in a bright-blue dress, and her husband, a powerfully built Tahitian, carrying a tiny infant on his shoulder.

It was impossible to imagine them as having a starting place or a destination. No, they were simply there, on the road, walking in single file as the car drove by, their minds untroubled, far from envying the strangers in the vehicle that traveled at such speed.

"Hello!" shouted Tita, waving to them.

The woman waved back amiably.

"They all think you're my lover!"

With a winning little laugh, she suddenly bent over him and brushed his lips with hers.

"Don't be angry with me! Oh, look. There's the waterfall. We'll be stopping here. Listen! I've had an idea. Let's go for a swim."

They parked the four cars in a row at the roadside, on the very edge of the lagoon. Here the narrow plain at the foot of the mountain was barely a hundred meters across, and the perpendicular rock face towered above it.

Seeing that Mopps was making some adjustment to the engine of his car, Tioti took Charlotte's arm, and the two of them walked on ahead, bubbling with excitement and breaking into loud laughter.

"Did you ever see the film *White Shadows*?" Tita asked. "It was shot on location here. I had a part in it."

Wide-eyed, Mittel walked behind them, as if taking part in a procession. He felt crushed by the grandeur of the scene. It was beyond anything he had ever imagined. The greatest poetry had never celebrated anything more sublime, but it was also a scene often reproduced on garish postcards and in popular films.

The waterfall tumbled down the mountainside in broad streamers, and the flying spray, catching the sun, filled the air with rainbows.

Turning around, they could see the spread of the blue-and-green lagoon, with its coconut palms, its little crests of foam breaking on the corals.

At the foot of the waterfall, hedged with a great variety of dense vegetation, was a fresh-water pool, like a hanging bowl between the mountain and the sea.

"Hello!" yelled the people who were already there.

"Hello!" replied the voice of Tioti.

And Tita explained, "They're Americans. They've been shooting a film here for the past two weeks. Nearly all my friends are in it."

A hubbub of voices, a mass of people, a riot of color, men in white, native girls, half naked or wearing *paréos*. Movie cameras on tripods, vans parked in the bushes, silvered screens to reflect the sun, projectors.

At the edge of the lake—or, more accurately, fountain—some twenty Tahitian girls stood waiting, dressed simply in *paréos*. They must have just come out of the water, since the thin fabric clung to their bodies.

"Hello, Tita!"

"Hello, Céline! . . . Taitou! . . . Suzy!"

A pause between two takes. Charlotte lost no time in persuading the cameraman to let her try on his eyeshade, while Mopps chatted with two pretty starlets.

There was only one white actress, and she was wearing a *paréo* like the rest, her face and shoulders covered with greasepaint.

The director shouted an order. All the native girls hastened toward a rock in the background and climbed up a few meters onto a flat ledge. From there the water flowed down a smooth slope like a playground slide, and, at a given signal, the girls slid down it, one after another, into the deep water, where they swam about among chaplets of *tiarés* strewn on the surface.

The cameras were running. Absolute silence was called for. The white film star had joined the others in the water and was swimming in the foreground. It did not escape Mittel that Tioti never left Charlotte's side, and that the two of them were in boisterous high spirits.

"What about a swim?" whispered Tita.

He hesitated. He felt shy. And yet he was seized with a passionate longing to plunge into this limpid pool, dotted with half-naked girls.

"Come on!"

"No!"

"Can't you swim?"

On the contrary, it was the only sport at which he excelled. When he was about twelve, he had lived near the Pont-Neuf and had gone swimming in the Seine almost every day.

Tioti, who was standing a few meters away, caught the drift of their whispering and looked inquiringly at Mittel, as if to say, "Shall we take the plunge?"

And, there and then, he took off his shirt, revealing a bright-pink torso, prematurely bloated. The movie camera had stopped, but the Tahitian girls were still swimming lazily, just for the fun of it. One of them, as graceful as a dolphin, was plunging and gliding under water, to reappear, after a lapse of several seconds, always in some unexpected spot.

Tioti, wearing only his linen undershorts, dived in. Then, all at once, Tita whisked off her red dress and stood bare-breasted, wearing only a tight-fitting pair of black panties.

She, too, dived into the pool, her hair falling over her face. She came up laughing, water dripping down her cheeks, calling to Mittel to join her.

Charlotte came toward him, apparently to speak to him, probably to warn him not to swim, because of the risk to his lungs; but he had already taken off his jacket and espadrilles and, holding his nose, had plunged in, to remain under water until he could no longer breathe. When he rose triumphantly to the surface, he experienced a strange surge of excitement.

"Over here!" Tita called across to him.

He swam toward her, weaving his way among the other girls, whose *paréos* billowed on the surface of the water like great blue-and-red flowers.

He was very thin, and his movements were stiff and jerky, but he knew that his style as a swimmer was impeccable, and, playing to the gallery, he deployed all the skill at his command.

The water was cold, so cold that Tioti, who had scrambled ashore and spotted a towel belonging to one of the film extras, handed it to Charlotte and got her to rub him down.

Meanwhile Mopps, assisted by one of the film technicians, was getting the bottles out of the car and standing them in rows at the foot of a tree.

"Let's see who can stay under longest!" cried Tita.

"I bet it'll be me!"

It was as if he had thrown off all earthly bonds. There was no room for thought here, only motion, which made him feel a little tipsy, as did the sights around him whenever he came to the surface and saw everything through the drops of water clinging to his eyelashes.

He and Tita rose to the surface simultaneously, and she clung to him, panting.

"You're a marvelous swimmer. . . . Where's Tioti? He's given up already! Tioti! Hey, Tioti, what's the matter? Are you scared?"

She was more ebullient, more like a child than ever.

"Can you do this, Jef?"

She performed a kind of somersault under water, and Mittel immediately followed suit.

"And this?"

This time, she did a back somersault. He did the same, but it left him panting, with his ears buzzing. All the same, he wished it could last forever.

"There, you see! It's good to be alive!"

Why did she have to say that? He knew it well enough! He knew it only too well! And it was just because he was so passionately in love with life that he was unhappy. Once again he asked himself the same agonizing question: Would he ever again be able to swim like this, or was this the last time?

On top of the water floated chaplets of white flowers. The water was so clear that, when he dived, he could see, greatly magnified, the pebbles on the bottom.

"Are you cold, Jef?"

"Of course not!"

"Still, you've been in long enough."

Tita was looking at him anxiously.

"I'll tell you what, if you don't want to stay, I'll come out with you. Come with me. We can dry off behind those bushes over there."

A few steps, and they were screened from the crowd, already gathered around the bottles, drinking. They came upon two friends of Tita's who had taken off their *paréos* and spread them out to dry. Neither girl showed the slightest embarrassment.

"Hand me your trousers."

He felt very uncomfortable, but she sounded so determined that he lacked the courage to say no. Now he was wearing nothing but his undershorts.

"Lie down. . . ."

He stretched out in the long grass beside the three of them, Tita and the two other native girls. Opening his eyes, all he could see was the sky and a single crooked tree overhanging the mountaintop.

"Feeling warmer now?"

And, caressingly: "Wait here for me. Don't move. . . ."

She was gone for several minutes, then returned carrying a full bottle of liquor, white rum, which she had pinched from Mopps's chest.

"Drink this!"

The two of them stayed there, some distance from the rest of the party, whom they could hear laughing and thrashing about. Instead of lying on the grass, Tita squatted down beside Mittel and stroked his hair.

"You could be so happy here! I've never known a white man to worry the way you do . . . except when they're drunk, that is. . . . Here, have another swig."

They drank in turn from the bottle, like old friends. Mittel's head was resting against the hip of one of the women, who was still lying there on her back, dozing in the sun. He could see Tita looking down at him tenderly, a little pityingly, and perhaps also with a tinge of irony.

"All the same, you're the nicest . . ."

His mind was a blank; the cold water had set his pulse racing. The rum had gone to his head, and his cheeks were burning. All his senses were intensified tenfold. He could hear the faintest sound, see the slightest movement of the leaves, as if he were dissolving into the life force of the natural world, a force so powerful that he felt crushed by it.

Why must he be forever fretting? Surely moments such as this outweighed all the rest? And what was the point of worrying about Charlotte, when he had Tita beside him, infinitely fresher and prettier, with her feline grace and her ready, brilliant smile?

"You're a strange boy, Jef! If it wasn't for your wife, I'd cure you myself. . . ."

"Cure me of what?"

"Of everything. And we could have a baby, too."

"Don't say that!"

"Why are you frowning? Here!"

And, laughing, she kissed him on the eyes and mouth. Mittel felt his head slipping; when he turned around, he saw that the two native girls had gone, and that he was alone with Tita, who was now lying beside him, pressing her body close against his.

"Jef!"

She was nibbling his lip. There was a broad stripe of brilliant sunlight across her naked shoulder.

He closed his eyes. He could hear the clamor of the crowd of others who, separated from them by a sparse curtain of greenery, were still drinking. And from the sound of splashing in the pool, it was clear that some of the girls were swimming.

Tita was now sitting up beside him. In a voice full of emotion, she asked, "Are you happy now?"

He simply did not know. His forehead was burning hot. He felt as if he would never be able to get to his feet, that he would have to lie there forever, in a state of torpor that pervaded his whole being. All the same, he held on to Tita's hand, and stammered, "I wish so much . . ."

"What do you wish?"

And, with trembling lips, like a child about to burst into tears, he said, "To be the same as everyone else!"

"In what way are you different?"

He shook his head. He didn't know the answer, but he did know that he was different. Certainly he knew of at least one undesirable difference, which was that within a year, or at most two, he would have ceased to exist!

"That's what men always say, Jef! Come to think of it, even I think I'm different from other people. . . . Don't you believe me?"

He smiled in spite of himself.

"At sixteen, I had to go out to earn a living. So I got a job cleaning at La Fayette."

A fleeting shadow crossed her face, but she quickly brushed it aside and returned to stroking Jef's forehead, which was high, smooth, noble.

"You've got small hands, like a woman, and eyes like deep pools. . . ."

Something about him had touched a deep chord in her, there was no doubt of that. She was gazing at him with almost comical intensity.

"If you wanted to, you could be strong. You swim much better than Tioti. He couldn't stay in the water more than a minute or two. He drinks too much. It interferes with his breathing."

Suddenly she raised her elegantly modeled little head and

stretched her neck, like a doe startled by a noise in the woods. It did not take Mittel long to realize what had disturbed her.

A quarrel seemed to be going on, on the other side of the bushes. At any rate, voices could be heard raised in anger, and someone kept expostulating, "Calm down! Come on now, calm down!"

Then Mopps's voice shouting, "You're nothing but a lowdown guttersnipe, with an ugly mug, and, if you don't watch out you'll feel the weight of my fist. . . ."

Tita was by now standing up. Mittel look around for his trousers.

"Don't talk such rubbish. . . . I didn't know . . . You never said a word about it."

"I didn't say anything because I thought you were my friend. But now I know you're nothing but a guttersnipe."

"Mopps! Tioti! Be quiet, both of you, and have a drink."

For it was Tioti who was the target of Mopps's emphatic indignation.

"Let's see what's going on," whispered Tita.

But by the time they reached the scene, Mopps had already taken off. They saw him get into his car and drive away alone toward Papeete, though not before he had backed dangerously, and then jerked forward, grazing one of the film crew's vans. Tioti looked absolutely shattered. Charlotte, standing apart, merely shrugged.

"What's going on?" Tita asked one of her friends.

"I imagine he caught them in the act."

"Who?"

"We were all having a drink. . . . Mopps was spinning us a yarn when suddenly he broke off and said, 'Where's Charlotte?'

"None of us had any idea. We'd been drinking, too, you see. He walked away, and then suddenly disappeared behind those bushes. When he got back he had Tioti with him, and he was cursing him up and down."

Charlotte, meanwhile, was deep in conversation with the governor's secretary.

"You mean to say that Charlotte and Tioti . . . ?" giggled Tita.

"Yes! Mopps was purple with rage."

Tioti was far from proud of his role in the affair. Everyone, to a greater or lesser extent, was thunderstruck, except for the Americans, who were loading their cameras into the vans, having finished shooting for the day.

Mittel looked around for his jacket, feeling dazed and miserable. The red-and-blue *paréos* were trailing underfoot. The Tahitian girls started getting dressed, lending one another combs and mirrors. Piles of empty bottles stood under the trees.

"He's going too far," Mittel heard someone say.

He turned around. Tioti and Charlotte were standing together. It was he who had spoken.

"It's as much your fault as his. What a mess!"

"How could I be expected to know?"

"I always said he was jealous, only he's usually careful to keep it to himself. But he's been drinking all afternoon. Apparently he got through a whole bottle of Pernod, on his own."

She looked worn out. She had not noticed Mittel, who was keeping quiet.

"Do you want me to take you back?" asked Tioti.

"What? And provoke another scene? No! It wouldn't do at all for us to go back in the same car."

And then, finally, catching sight of Mittel, who had recovered his jacket, she jeered, "And while all this was going on, where were you? Playing the fool, I suppose?"

"What?"

"What a brilliant idea, for a man with diseased lungs to go swimming in icy water! And after that, what were you up to?"

He was too stunned to reply.

"Clever, aren't you? Do you think it's not common knowledge that you were behind those bushes with Tita?"

She sounded furious.

"I'd better go back with you. I bet Mopps will be there, waiting in the house."

And she traipsed off toward the car, in which Tita was already installed. Mittel sat between the two of them. He did not venture to open his mouth. His trousers were still damp, and clinging to his stomach and thighs. They had forgotten all about the musician.

Every now and then, Tita, keeping a straight face and not looking at him, put out her hand and pinched Mittel. The nearer they got to town, the more uneasy Charlotte became. She was blind to everything around her, the scenery, the crowds streaming away from the soccer field, the young people on bicycles jamming the road. The sun, on the side of the Moréa, was turning mauve. They passed a number of British residents, driving home from Papeete.

Jef shivered once, twice, a third time. Tita looked alarmed, though Charlotte did not even notice.

"I warned you!" whispered Tita.

And Charlotte grumbled, "I wish you two would stop fidgeting."

Apprehension was making her look almost ugly. The tension in her face, tightening the skin, revealed all its imperfections, including two quite prominent bumps on her forehead.

It felt less like a return journey than a retreat, a getaway. A car behind them tooted its horn, and as it hurtled past them, they caught a glimpse of Tioti, in company with five Tahitian girls.

"Very clever," sneered Charlotte. And to Mittel: "Can't you move over a bit? You're all wet. It makes me shiver."

The vans followed, so full that there were even people on the canvas roofs. Coming home from a day out in Papeete were buses and trucks, crammed with natives in their smartest Sunday outfits. Not one vehicle was without its two or three musicians, strumming on their guitars, and almost all the passengers were singing at the top of their voices.

The red-roofed houses and their tiny gardens were gradually melting into the gathering dusk, and their colors took on a darker hue.

On the edge of the lagoon, the fishermen were preparing to go out in their canoes and were testing the acetylene lamps which they used to lure the fish.

It was still all very peaceful, but now the landscape was tinged with greenish light, and after the excitements of the day, everyone felt a little weary and disconsolate, some even rather disenchanted.

The occupants of the trucks, admittedly, were still singing, but not with the same zest as when they had set out that morning. The day and its pleasures were over.

But *they*, no doubt, would recover their high spirits the following day.

Mittel felt sick at heart, unable to forget the cruel question mark that hung over his future.

To put it out of his mind, and also to dispel the constraint that had developed between them, Mittel, perhaps injudiciously, asked Charlotte, "Whatever made you do it?"

"And what about you?" she retorted.

Suddenly he was overcome with shame at his situation, cornered as he was between the two of them. He shifted away from Tita. He shrank back from Charlotte. As they approached the outskirts of the town, and the houses became more and more tightly packed, all Mittel's haunting anxieties flooded back.

"I hope the baby is all right."

Charlotte had not given the matter a thought. She seemed tempted to shrug her shoulders in reply.

And the doctor? What had become of him? Mittel could not remember seeing him since the commotion at the waterfall. Was this a sign that he was siding with Mopps?

There was one possible solution to all their problems: to take advantage of the present situation, leave Papeete, and settle in one of the villages. Any little village shack would do, however primitive, provided he could get work of some kind, it didn't matter what.

But he was nervous about raising the subject and hesitated, embarrassed by the presence of Tita.

At last he plucked up the courage to murmur, "There are

some charming little houses. . . . I might get a job as a private tutor, or something like that. . . ."

"Don't talk such nonsense!"

It was Tita, once again, who squeezed his hand sympathetically.

"If Mopps is still angry . . ."

"Leave me alone, will you? Save your thoughts for Tita. That's what she's there for, after all."

And Charlotte, her nerves stretched to breaking point, once more withdrew into herself. It was not until they reached the waterfront that she was able to breathe freely again. The electric lights, which were strung out like a necklace above the streets, had just been switched on. She was the first to see that there was light streaming from the windows of the bungalow—not only those of the bedroom and kitchen, where Maria might be, but also of the bar.

Mopps must be there!

And so he was, perched on a bar stool, a glass in front of him. He watched the three of them come in through the door. He was dead drunk, so drunk that when he mumbled, "Get me to bed," the words were barely intelligible.

Between his teeth, he added, "You filthy scum!"

So saying, he almost fell off his stool, and managed to drag himself as far as Mittel's bed only by clinging to the wall.

21

EVERYTHING WAS SUCH A MESS! YES, THAT WAS THE TROUBLE. HE
had been surrounded by disorder all his life, and now it was
worse than ever, it was utterly sickening. He had been born in
the midst of disorder, just like his son, who had been brought into
the world by a drunken doctor.

He could no longer even be sure whether he was awake or
asleep. Mopps was snoring, and the bedroom door was open.
Mittel had insisted on this, because Maria and the child slept in
that room, and the air stank of liquor.

And then there was all that business of the beds! No sooner
was the captain out of the way than Charlotte turned to Tita:

"You don't happen to have a bed I could borrow?"

"There's my own."

"I daresay they'd put you up at the Pacifique!"

Without further ado, Maria and Tita went off to fetch the bed
from the next street, and returned carrying it like a couple of rag-
and-bone merchants. They had put it together and made it up for
Mittel, out in the hall.

Before leaving, Tita had given Mittel a furtive parting kiss,
while Charlotte was undressing in her bedroom.

Jef felt hot. He was sweating much more freely than usual, and
had a scalding pain in his right side, as if a hot poultice had been
applied to it. He spent most of the night drifting between sleep
and wakefulness. The whole time he felt as if he were floating—
in the air during his wakeful periods, and on the lake in his sleep.

Dimly, he heard Mopps getting up and stumbling around in
the dark, searching for the water faucet for a drink.

Next morning he woke late, for he always fell into a deep sleep some time around dawn. Doors and windows were open, and the hissing of the gas indicated that the baby's milk was being heated in a double boiler.

He got out of bed, but was distressed to discover that he could scarcely stand, and that his whole body felt drained of energy. In his pajamas and bare feet, he went into the bar, saw Mopps with his back to him, doing something or other in the kitchen, and suddenly found he must cling to the bar to prevent himself from collapsing on the floor.

Charlotte was in the shower. Mopps shifted position a little, so that Mittel could see what he was doing. He was giving the baby its bottle!

The piercing rays of the sun were everywhere, especially inside Jef's head. He fled back to his bed—yes, fled, mustering every ounce of his strength to reach it.

His pulse was racing, his heart pounding violently. He was terrified, and yet he dared not call for help. Lying with his eyes closed, he remembered that it was Tita's bed he was in, and, exerting himself once more, he stumbled as far as his own bed, which was still unmade.

Charlotte, having heard someone moving around, came to investigate. She was in her dressing gown, with tousled hair, and she looked exhausted.

"Aren't you feeling well?"

"Not too good . . . but it'll pass."

"That's what comes of fooling around the way you did yesterday. It wouldn't surprise me if you'd caught pneumonia. That's all we need."

"No, I'm sure I haven't."

"Feel like anything to eat or drink?"

"Maybe a little hot milk."

He could hear her talking to Mopps in the kitchen.

"Now he's ill, on top of everything else. God! This really looks like it's going to be one of those days. Heat up some milk, Maria."

"There's some already heated."

"Take a cup to Monsieur, then."

Poor Maria! She alone went about her work cheerfully in the midst of all this chaos. Mopps was also unwell, and he slouched around the house with dark shadows under his eyes and a foul taste in his mouth.

"Not feeling too good?" he asked Mittel.

"It's nothing to worry about."

The next to appear was Tita, who had spent the night at the Pacifique. She told him that their party had gone on drinking until two in the morning.

"Are you ill, Jef?"

He was surely getting worse. In the morning he had felt little more than discomfort. By midday, he had developed a high fever, but lacked the courage to ask for the thermometer. Four or five times he was shaken by a fit of hiccups, accompanied by intense pain in his chest.

"Tita!"

"She's just left," shouted someone from the bar.

The others were drinking. The governor's secretary was there, to learn whether there had been any new developments following the incident. For a quarrel such as had broken out the day before was quite an event in Tahiti. It was the talk of the Pacifique and of all the local clubs. Some said that Mopps had challenged Tioti to a duel, others that he had walked out on Charlotte.

As for the captain, wandering around with drooping eyelids, he just kept mumbling, "He's nothing but a little guttersnipe. . . ."

Interceding for Tioti, someone protested, "He was drunk. You shouldn't take it so seriously. You know what he's like!"

"Be that as it may, either he resigns from the club or I do."

Mittel tossed restlessly in bed. As evening approached, his temperature was still rising and he was in mental as well as physical torment, convinced that if he became delirious, they would take the opportunity to put him in the hospital!

And that would be the end of it, he had no doubt at all. If he were ever again to pass through that archway into the spacious courtyard surrounded by white buildings, he would never come out alive.

"Shut the door!" he said to Tita, who had come back to see how he was getting along.

"Are you sure that's wise?"

"Yes, let them think what they like. . . . Listen! Come over here."

And he took her hand between his, which were already burning hot. His voice was harsh, his eyes blazing.

"Listen. I think I'm seriously ill. It may get much worse. If it does, I'm counting on you to protect me. They'll want to send me to the hospital. You mustn't let that happen, Tita!"

"Don't you want to go to the hospital? Why not?"

"Because that would be the end. It's no good trying to explain. . . . Just swear to me . . ."

"Yes, of course, Jef!"

She was puzzled, that was all. She herself had been ill, and had fully recovered after a stay in the hospital.

"What are they doing now?"

"They're having dinner. Mopps is still in a filthy mood. He's been traipsing around in a dressing gown all day, and I'm certain he intends to spend the night here again."

Maria came in to put the baby to bed, and greeted Tita cheerfully.

"Promise!"

"I promise, Jef."

At long last his mind was at rest, and he fell into a deep sleep.

There they were, the two of them, like a couple of shopkeepers after closing time. Charlotte, having checked the cash receipts, locked the till and started clearing away the glasses, bottles, and ashtrays littered all over the bar counter. Meanwhile

Mopps, scratching his head, muttered, not for the first time, "If I see him I'll smash his face in."

"If you do any such thing, I'll never speak to you again."

He shrugged, indicating either that it was a matter of indifference to him, or that Charlotte was incapable of carrying out her threat.

"There's one thing you don't realize. . . ."

"Really?"

"Tioti knows the whole story. He told me so yesterday."

"What story?"

"He knows my real name, and all about what happened in France. . . ."

"So what?"

"He's quite capable of turning me in, just to spite me."

"Go to bed," growled Mopps, heading for Tita's bed, which was still out in the corridor.

"Don't you realize how serious the situation is? I could be sent to prison. If it hadn't been for that, I'd never have given in to him."

"Don't lie to me!"

"I swear it's true!"

"You can swear as much as you like, it's just one more lie to add to all the rest."

He turned his back on her and stared gloomily out to sea. At the Pacifique, drinks were still being served. Tioti was there with a party of friends, and Tita had just come in.

"Where's Mopps?"

"He's still there at the club, like a caged lion. I'm afraid Jef is very ill."

"You don't say? His days are numbered anyway. The very first time I set eyes on him, I said he'd never make it to old age."

"You really think that?"

Suddenly Tita was overcome with sadness. She was fond of Jef, though she could not explain why.

"And Charlotte?" asked Tioti, his elbows resting on the table.

"Same as usual."

"In other words, she doesn't give a damn! She's so cold-blooded, she wouldn't think twice about committing a murder. And what's more, it wouldn't be the first time."

Maybe he was just drunk, but at this everyone turned to look at him.

"You mean she's already killed someone?"

"That's all I have to say on the subject. But I know what I know. Will you come home with me, Tita?"

"No."

Not tonight. Tonight she preferred to be alone. She was thinking that there was no one in the bungalow to take care of Jef, and she wished she were there to look after him herself.

In the morning Tita saw Maria hurrying past her window. Tita called out to her.

"I'm on my way to fetch the doctor," explained the girl. "He's taken a turn for the worse."

"He's worse today," repeated Marius at the bar. "There's a man who won't have lived long among us."

As far as they were concerned, Mittel was as good as dead. Tita felt chilled to the heart. She ran all the way to the club, to find Charlotte wiping tears from her eyes and cheeks. In the bedroom, Mopps was sitting beside the bed, where Mittel lay, his face crimson with fever.

"Not feeling too good, Jef?"

His teeth were clenched, as if to hold back a sob.

Maria must have given an alarming account of Mittel's condition, for Brugnon drove up in his car within a matter of minutes. The three men were left alone together. In the bar, Tita went up to Charlotte, who was distractedly chewing on her handkerchief.

"He won't even let me near him," she said. "He hates me. I can see it in his eyes. Is it my fault that he was born sickly? What could I do about it?"

"Do you think he's dying?"

The door opened, and Brugnon asked for boiling water and

338

towels. No clean ones could be found, so Maria had to go borrow some from the Pacifique.

The doctor's visit lasted over an hour. Twice Mittel was heard to cry out in agony. At long last the doctor reappeared, accompanied by Mopps, who looked very grim.

"Well?"

"The plain fact is, he's had a severe attack of pleurisy."

"Is it serious?"

Mopps shrugged as the doctor washed his hands. Mechanically, the captain began pouring drinks.

"Can he be looked after here?"

"He doesn't want to go to the hospital. I told him that he would be wise to do so, that we had much better facilities there. However . . . we'll see how he is tonight. Cheers! As for you, Mopps, you'd do well to stay off the booze for a few days. I'm certain your blood pressure is too high."

Tita did not dare to speak. She was overawed, sensing something ominous behind these everyday events. When she went back to see Mittel, she found him sobbing, his face buried in his pillow.

"Jef, don't cry! What's wrong with you?"

But the tears kept flowing. He was panting, struggling to draw breath, until suddenly he hiccuped violently and doubled up with pain. Then, looking up at Tita through his tears, he twitched his lips in a pitiful attempt to smile.

"My poor Tita!"

"Why do you say that?"

"I'm a coward. . . . I'm frightened. . . . Tell me honestly, Tita, could you find the courage to stay with me?"

"Of course, Jef!"

"They want to put me in the hospital, don't they? As far as they're concerned, it's all over. They don't have the patience to let me go in my own way—in my own time. What did she have to say?"

"Who?"

"Charlotte."

"I found her in tears."

"Naturally!"

And she would walk behind his hearse weeping. Come to think of it, did they have hearses in Papeete? He asked Tita. She told him that they always used the van from the ice factory for funerals, covering it not with a black cloth, but with the leaves of coconut palms.

"And the child?"

"He's in the kitchen with Maria."

Half an hour after they had this talk about ice, a block was delivered, ordered by Brugnon, with instructions that an icepack be placed on Jef's chest. It was Mopps who undertook this task, Mopps, who had been roaming around the house looking more and more ill-humored, withdrawing into himself, as if he had it in for the whole world.

"You can go now, Tita."

"No! Jef asked me to stay. I'll be the one to look after him."

Mopps looked inquiringly at Mittel, who nodded.

"As you wish . . . Take off your pajamas. I'll be cupping your chest later."

But it was in the evening, when Brugnon came to give him an injection of colloidal silver, that the sickbed truly became the focal point of the house, the stench of illness and drugs pervading even the remotest corners.

Mittel all at once found himself reliving his experiences in the sanatorium; he smiled wryly to realize that there, for a few months at least, he had escaped the chronic disorder of his usual surroundings.

He recalled the huge bay windows overlooking the valley, the nurses in their spotless uniforms, the medication cart covered with a cloth. He heard again the bell that signaled the doctor's rounds and mealtimes.

"Lie still. I won't hurt you."

He knew what to expect. He was prepared for the injection, and screwed up his face as the needle went in.

"Aren't they going to operate?" he whispered, dreading the reply in advance.

For he knew a good deal about lung diseases, and was aware that for some cases of pleurisy, an operation was unavoidable—and almost always successful.

"I don't think so," mumbled Brugnon.

"Ah!"

That could mean only one thing. His condition was beyond help, because of his previous history of tuberculosis.

The window was open. A palm tree, rocked by the breeze, nodded in and out of the window frame, and some small creature outside, probably a Moluccan blackbird, was pecking among the pebbles.

"You would still prefer not to go to the hospital?"

"Yes."

"It'd be the only sensible thing to do. Primarily for your own sake: you'd be better looked after. And then there are the others to consider, having to live for weeks in a sickroom atmosphere. You don't even seem to have considered the baby. . . ."

"Oh, yes, I have!"

"Then you agree?"

"The answer is no!"

Instinctively, his eyes sought Tita's, and he saw that she understood.

"You can't expect them to close down the club on your account. . . . Do you think you'll be able to stand all the comings and goings, and the noise?"

"It won't bother me."

"Let him alone," Mopps said to the doctor.

And the two men went into the dining room, to discuss the situation in undertones.

Mittel whispered to Tita, "Go see if you can hear what they're saying."

He waited, his eyes open. When she returned, he watched her avidly as she approached him.

"They're discussing Tioti. It's the same old story. Tioti has resigned, but five other members have also resigned, in sympathy, which means that there will be big changes around here. . . . And on top of that, Tioti is going around telling all and sundry that, if he chose, he could have you all clapped in jail. . . ."

"That's true," said Mittel, almost with relish.

"Did Charlotte really commit a murder?"

"Oh, yes. The victim was Monsieur Martin of the Boulevard Beaumarchais, and when she fired the shot, someone was giving a violin lesson in the apartment next door. Will you stay with me, Tita?"

"Didn't I give you my word?"

"I'm sorry about what happened yesterday. I honestly don't know what came over me. I didn't want . . ."

"But I did!" she admitted, with a big, open smile.

"Now . . ."

He did not go on. That "now" meant so much more than he could put into words. For one thing, it meant that he was no longer a man. He was flat on his back, an icepack on his chest, his face streaming with sweat.

"Tita, bring me the baby."

She was gone for a long time, so long that he began to grow uneasy, his eyes fixed on the door. When she came back, she had the baby with her, but she was also accompanied by Mopps.

Mittel's expression hardened. Things were reaching a crisis.

"Listen to me, young man," said Mopps. "The kid shouldn't get too close to you. You know what I mean?"

The risk of contagion, of course. He waved them out of the room. He would not even look at his son! He turned over on his side, with his back to the door.

"Take care of yourself, young man. Things aren't all that bad. . . ."

Mittel indicated that he wanted them all out of the room. All of them, even Tita. He wanted to be left alone. After all, when, in the whole of his life, had he been anything but alone?

He needed to think, but he did not think. His mind was filled with images, smells, sounds, memories of long ago, all jumbled together.

Such as the roaring of the coal in the boilers, then the sudden hissing of steam when the thermometer had burst . . . the figure of Napo . . .

And Plumier! The makeshift grave that they had dug for him beneath the trees, and the cross that he had made out of two planks from an old crate.

"Tita!"

Impatiently he called her back, hurt by her defection.

"Stay with me. I can't . . ."

He was trembling. He was afraid.

"Shut the window."

Ever since he had learned about the van from the ice factory covered in palm leaves, he could no longer bear the sight of the palm outside his window.

The little red-roofed houses all along the road.

"Who's in the bar?"

He could hear the murmur of voices.

"Three or four people. Tioti is still in a rage, apparently. He's shooting off his mouth to everyone. Mopps is threatening to go after him and shut him up, but the others are trying to restrain him. . . . What's on your mind?"

"Nothing."

But it wasn't true. He was thinking that Charlotte might be sent to prison, and trying to imagine what the prison in Papeete would be like inside. He had only seen it from the outside. How were the women prisoners treated? He saw gangs of men every day, under the supervision of a native warden, going out to work on the roads. But what about the women?

"You see, Jef, you're much less restless tonight. I bet you your temperature has gone down."

"That's because of the injection."

"Do you think so?"

He was sure of it. He was familiar with the treatment. They

343

would pump quantities of caffeine into him, and this produced a pleasant feeling of unreality for an hour or two. It relaxed the muscles, and the mind, so that one's thoughts became more and more incoherent, like children's dreams.

"Where will Maria be sleeping?"

"They're fixing something up for her at the end of the dining room. Shh! Listen!"

Someone had flung open the door, then slammed it violently. Tita went out and ran toward the bar, and Mittel heard the receding footsteps of three or four men.

When Tita reappeared, she was accompanied by Charlotte, who looked washed out.

"Well, that's that," she announced, collapsing into a chair. "Mopps has gone out. There's nothing anyone can do about it."

"Has he gone looking for Tioti?"

"He won't have far to look. Tioti has more or less taken root at the Pacifique, and he's drunk from morning till night. . . ."

"Do you think they'll come to blows?"

She sighed. "God knows how it will all end!"

He was not to learn the outcome that evening, for he drifted off to sleep before he knew it. When he woke, it was the middle of the night, and his first conscious sensation was one of fear. A faint glow of moonlight filtered through the curtains. He looked around, stretched out his hand, and touched a body. It stirred.

"Is that you, Tita?"

It was indeed Tita, lying on a mat on the floor covered with a blanket. But she was so fast asleep that she did not hear him.

Possibly they were both equally drunk, but the difference was that the more Mopps drank, the calmer he seemed. The three men who had followed him out of the club were trying to hold him back, though secretly hoping to see some excitement. They walked along the waterfront toward the Pacifique, where they could see a few late diners through the lighted windows. Mopps, his heavy footsteps sounding abnormally loud, opened the door, then halted in the middle of the lobby.

"Where is he?"

Voices could be heard from a room at the back that was a favorite meeting place for the regulars. Marius appeared in the doorway and hurried up to the captain.

"Listen, Mopps . . ."

"Where is he?"

Tioti got to his feet, overturning his chair as he did so, and took a step forward. Not uttering a word, Mopps advanced toward him. When they were little more than a step apart, Mopps stopped. It was impossible to tell what his next move would be.

Tioti had turned very pale. He tried to smile, but his lips were trembling.

Then, in a flash, Mopps drove his fist into the other man's face, a hard, accurate blow. They could hear the sound of bone striking bone. Tioti swayed and groped behind him for a table. He leaned his back against it, to keep himself from falling to the floor. And there he stood motionless, his chin cupped in his hand, his eyes glazed.

"Unless you keep your mouth shut from now on, you won't be let off so lightly next time. Understood?" said the captain, turning to leave.

A scream . . . people jostling one another. Someone had spotted Tioti groping furtively in his revolver pocket, but five or six men, springing on him, had already disarmed him.

"Understood?" repeated Mopps from the doorway.

And he stalked out, followed by his companions, and, returning to the club, went to bed in the corridor, not wishing to say anything to Charlotte that night.

By morning the town was buzzing with the story. It was on everyone's lips in the market place, and the taxi drivers talked of nothing else. Groups of people loitered outside the club, discussing the affair, going away, coming back. Tioti was still asleep, and it was said that he had had to bathe his jaw in cold water for two hours straight.

Mopps, feeling quite proud of himself, if the truth were

known, deliberately went out onto the porch in his pajamas and stood there for a while, puffing at his pipe. Charlotte was whining: "He's sure to want revenge. And who will be the one on the receiving end? You? Not likely! It'll be me."

He could not be bothered to reply. By ten o'clock that morning, the bar was beginning to fill up. Some had come as soon as they heard the news, and they went on discussing it while sipping their apéritifs.

"It seems that the governor has heard the news. Tioti's threats were repeated to him, word for word, but he refuses to believe it."

Those most closely concerned were by now split into two factions, the Pacifique versus the club, or so the story went. At the Pacifique, Tioti—who seemed very well informed, though no one could say how—was uttering threats against Mopps, whose past history he knew in all its details, and telling everyone that the freighter had been given cosmetic treatment to prevent it from being seized by the customs people for arms smuggling.

"He'll have to make good on it!" he growled.

All this was repeated to Mopps within minutes. The captain, refusing anything to drink, did not seem annoyed, but merely smiled ironically.

"Let him say what he likes."

"Is it true?"

"What if it is? What difference does it make?"

Tita was running back and forth between Mittel's bedroom and the kitchen, because the ice had to be changed at regular intervals, and drugs administered. At the same time, she kept Mittel up to date on the news, to which he listened avidly.

"And how's the baby?"

"Maria is taking good care of him. She loves him as if he were her own son. Here in Tahiti, we are all crazy about children."

And what about him? The baby was always in the forefront of his mind. Perhaps it was the fever that was filling his head with extravagant notions. But certainly if he had still been in Europe such thoughts would never have crossed his mind.

346

For instance, it occurred to him that, if only he had a little money, he could simply provide Tita with a small income, which would enable her to buy a house with a red roof, not far from a school, such as he had seen in the villages. And they would let her keep the child forever!

He would grow up like a native-born Tahitian. He would scamper barefoot through the streets. On Sundays, they would dress him in his best clothes. Tita and he would spend their evenings sitting on the veranda, serenely enjoying the sunset.

"What did the doctor say?"

"Nothing."

It was the truth. Brugnon had done what had to be done, but in a spirit of skepticism, for he was convinced that it was all to no avail. He called regularly, twice a day. Every time he repeated, "You'd be far better off in the hospital!"

At this Mittel and Tita would exchange glances. He was keeping his end up. As long as he did not fall into a delirium, all would be well, but there were times when he came very near to it.

In the intense midday heat, in particular, when the shutters were closed to keep out all but the thin lines of sunlight between the slats, he sometimes felt completely bemused. The intermingled sounds around him grew meaningless, totally divorced from reality—the reality of his present plight, at least. Memories of Buenaventura became confused with his life in Papeete, and on one occasion he woke up with a start, exclaiming, "Where's Bauer?"

"Who is Bauer?" Tita asked in bewilderment.

"Go and get Bauer."

What did Bauer mean by leaving the bookshop on the Rue Montmartre unattended, so that his son was free to crawl around among the books and tear them?

He struggled to fend off the delirium, pressing both hands against his temples. He closed his eyes. When he opened them again he moaned, "Tita!"

It was more exhausting than walking, or even swimming for hours on end.

347

"What did I say just now?"

"You were asking for Bauer."

"You mustn't let the others hear me, do you understand? You must shut the door, and stop them from coming in."

"I understand, Jef."

"Later I may not have the strength. . . . Has the baby had his milk?"

"Of course."

"I know what I'm saying. Sometimes he doesn't get fed on time. That's all wrong for a child. He needs a regular routine."

He talked and talked, his voice growing steadily weaker, and a few minutes later Tita saw that he had fallen asleep. He was getting so feeble that she had to hold his cup of milk up to his lips. His neck no longer looked like a man's, but more like a young boy's, and his shoulder blades stood out prominently.

"He must be persuaded to go to the hospital," Charlotte was saying to Mopps. "I'm at the end of my tether! And besides, the whole house smells of the sickroom. It makes my gorge rise! I can't even bear the taste of food any longer. You can't call this living!"

She shuffled around in a pair of old slippers, wandering from room to room. The whole place was falling apart, for Maria couldn't possibly see to everything all by herself. They ate only cold food, at the kitchen table. Dirty glasses were left unwashed for two or three days at a time.

22

EACH DAY WAS PUNCTUATED BY WHAT MITTEL THOUGHT OF AS landmarks, which enabled him to get his bearings. The regular twice-daily visits by the doctor, for instance. They were so much a part of Brugnon's routine by now that he no longer even looked at Mittel. Often he would pass through the bar without seeing a soul. Tita never failed to have the syringe sterilized and ready for him. When he took it out of the boiling water, it was Tita who now sawed off the tip of the phial. Then there was the wad of cotton soaked in ether. . . .

These two visits were landmarks for Mittel because they helped him to disentangle the confused network of nightmare and reality.

Almost every morning, he was awake before the doctor arrived. He would wait, lying still, feeling so weak that he could scarcely say a word to Tita. But nothing escaped his notice. He could hear the rustle of the breeze in the garden. It was hot, even at this early hour, and it sometimes seemed to him that he could actually see the waves of heat, little waves, like those that appeared when the breeze ruffled the calm surface of the lagoon.

He seldom wasted the little energy he had in thought. It was too exhausting, and besides, he knew that very soon the pains would begin, reaching their climax at eight o'clock, to coincide with Brugnon's morning visit.

The doctor would feel his pulse from force of habit, pull back the sheet, give him his morphine injection, and go, giving the impression that he had long since lost all interest in the patient's condition.

Or was it perhaps that he, too, realized that the illness was following its predetermined course?

Before the doctor had reached the end of the street, Mittel would begin to feel the benefit, and would pass the next few hours in a pleasant torpor, dozing and dreaming. Then, as time went on, Mittel began to experience discomfort, to toss and turn in bed, and finally to call out Tita's name uneasily, as if he suspected her of having deserted him. Within a few hours his temperature would rise from 100° to 104°.

Six o'clock was the second landmark, the time of Brugnon's evening visit, and a repetition of the morning ritual: the syringe in the saucepan of boiling water, the wad of cotton soaked in ether.

Only this time the room would smell of fever, and the patient's hiccups were as regular as the ticking of a clock. Accustomed to this though she was by now, Tita would always turn to the doctor with an anxious look.

"No change!" he would say, reassuringly.

Mittel's eyes would be open, but in the evening he was past recognizing Brugnon, being by then in the grip of delirium.

During the night, he would gasp for breath, cry out for help, and cling to Tita. Toward daybreak, when the effect of the injection had worn off, he would scream in agony.

Later, when it was over, he could remember nothing about it. He was living two separate lives, or, rather, only one real life, for in the other he played no conscious part.

When his temperature dropped, he was always much calmer than at the beginning, and seemed even to have attained a strange sort of serenity. Could this be merely the effect of ebbing strength? He would lie for minutes at a time watching a ray of sunshine, listening to a blackbird hopping around on the gravel, or straining his ears to catch the sound of distant voices, two women chattering across a garden fence.

Tita's presence had become absolutely necessary to him. She had only to leave the room for a few minutes for him to be overwhelmed with anxiety, mistrust, even a kind of jealousy.

"Where have you been?"

"Nowhere, Jef . . . just to warm up your milk."

So, in the midst of chaos, he had attained a kind of order through the immutable routine of his daily life.

For instance, there was Mopps's daily visit. Every morning, shortly after the doctor's visit, he would come in, pat Tita on the head, and smoke his first pipe of the day.

"Not feeling too tired, I hope?"

Then he would sit down astride a chair and gaze at Mittel for a long time, looking as if he had a great many things on his mind.

"Keeping your spirits up, young man?"

He would stay a quarter of an hour, or twenty minutes, during which both men would pursue their thoughts in silence. They could hear Charlotte in the shower, then Maria coming back from the market. Often Mittel's thoughts would return to incidents on board the freighter, such as the first fine day of the voyage, when everyone had gone out on deck. He could see Napo lying on his back, looking straight into the sun, and Jolet, propped up on his elbows, reading a mathematics textbook.

It was not then, but a few days later, that Mittel and Jolet had had that conversation about freighters.

"Why does the ship have the name of La Rochelle on the stern? She never puts in there, does she?" he had asked.

"The port where she was commissioned is to a ship what his birthplace is to a man. You don't necessarily return to it. A ship puts into this port or that, to take on cargo. Next stop Spain, you may think, but, as likely as not, you find yourself being rerouted to Germany. You may expect to be back where you started within a week, but as it turns out, you get stuck with a cargo destined for the Baltic. It's not like a shuttle."

"What's a shuttle?"

"A shuttle is a scheduled service, with a regular timetable. The ships ply between two fixed points, whether they are fully loaded or not. They set out from Bordeaux on such-and-such a day, put in at Nantes for forty-eight hours, then on to Le Havre, Dunkerque, and Rotterdam, and then return by the same route. . . .

Oh, if only I had been able to get a berth on a shuttle!"

There were other memories, too, but less sharp, less distinct. They were like pictures seen through a mist, full of poetry and hidden meaning. He, like the freighter, had never returned to his birthplace, which was not Paris, but Versailles. Scarcely half an hour away, and yet he had never set foot there. Instead, like a roving freighter, he had gone first to Dieppe, and from there to Panama, then Colombia, and finally Tahiti.

Through this mist of incoherent memories, a name suddenly came into the forefront of his mind: *Barranquilla*. He frowned, struggling to recall what meaning this name could have for him. The effort was such that he began sweating profusely.

What had made him think of *Barranquilla?* Had he ever lived there? Had he passed through it? These questions tormented him. He *must* find the answer, and he muttered the word repeatedly under his breath.

Barranquilla . . . Barranquilla . . . What on earth could it mean?

He asked Mopps, with as much fervor as if his life depended on it.

"It's a seaport in Colombia, on the Gulf of Mexico."

"Did we put in there?"

"No."

Why, then, should he be haunted by the name? The next day he was still obsessed with it. He was also troubled by innumerable little mysteries which he was determined to solve.

Could he not just as easily have been born to travel back and forth along predetermined lines as to wander hither and thither like the freighter? The very thought filled him with longing for the towns named by Jolet, gray towns engulfed in rain, with black, muddy docks. It was towns like Nantes, Dunkerque, and Rotterdam which now seemed to him full of exotic charm.

Charlotte had grown thinner recently. She, too, would take her turn to sit with him. Seeing the tears in her eyes and her genuine expression of despair, Mittel was almost tempted to try to comfort her. But she never stayed long, for the bar was hardly ever empty.

It was no longer any concern of his. It was as much as he could do to ask Tita, from time to time, what was happening in the house. He had made a little enclave for himself, and there he remained, dug in, so absorbed by his surroundings that all the stains on the wall, the gaps in the floorboards, the shifting patterns of sunlight marking the passing of time, had become like old friends to him.

Some of the patches of sunlight, when Mittel looked at them through half-closed eyes, assumed the shape of human heads, and, depending on the time of day, he fancied he could see them smile or scowl. He never spoke of this to anyone, not even Tita. It was no concern of anyone but himself

He scarcely ever allowed his mind to dwell on the approach of death. All that belonged to an earlier stage, when his body was still putting up a fight. Now he was forever dozing off like a baby, and, in a sense, reliving his infant life, recognizing forgotten sounds, a feeling of languor, of numbness, invading his limbs and his brain.

He had done all he could, and that was that! This was the foremost thought in his mind. At heart he had always been good and docile, like a little boy. What had he ever done to incur reproach?

It had been hard for him at times—in the stokehold, for instance, and later, out there in the jungle, when Charlotte had been at death's door. He had held her tight in his arms, as if by doing so he could keep her alive, and perhaps he had succeeded: she had, in fact, survived!

Tita, in her way, was doing as much for him. However tired she was, she always had a smile for him, whenever he looked her way. And there was something in her tone of voice, when she said his name, that filled him with happiness.

It was tender and grave at one and the same time. "Jef," she would say, just "Jef," and yet it was as if she had spoken volumes.

For instance, she might have been saying, "I'm nothing but a little native girl with white blood in my veins, fathered by a European who came to spend a few days in Tahiti, and whose name I don't even know. I used to be a dancer at La Fayette. Sooner or later I'll go back there, but I'm very fond of you in spite of everything. I hate to see you unhappy. I know you're frightened, and I'm doing all I can to comfort you. . . . To me, you're like a little child. . . ."

She adored children. She always referred to them as "babies," in English. Sometimes she even addressed Mittel as "Baby."

It made him smile, which raised an answering smile from her. There was an understanding between them, as if they shared secret thoughts inaccessible to anyone else.

Only she knew with what ferocious tenacity he held on to life, during the night, when his fever was at its height. She counted the hours, then eventually fell asleep, for even her stamina had its limits.

Everyone in the house had grown so accustomed to her presence that they scarcely noticed her, but it would have come as a shock to them if she had ever been absent when it was time to sterilize the syringe. Maria, quite a bit younger than Tita, was the only one to marvel at her dedication, and to treat her with respect, precisely because of that mystifying syringe of which she had been appointed guardian, just as if she had been a white woman.

Whenever Tita said, "You're just a baby," he thought of Bébé.

He could picture his mother correcting proofs, in her glass-walled office beside the linotype machines, as he had so often seen her.

A slightly wrinkled baby, her rouged cheeks a little too pink, her eyes a little too heavily blackened with mascara, a child, with all the failings of a little girl, always wanting to possess everything she saw.

Had she ever managed to get the fur coat that she had been longing for? Had she changed much since that time when she had sought refuge in Versailles, in the house of a friend, to give birth to her son? Had she, too, almost died in giving birth?

He scarcely ever mentioned the child. Sometimes they wondered if he had perhaps ceased to think about him.

And then came a time when there was a renewal of the traffic between the bungalow and the Pacifique, though now there were also frequent visits to the law courts. The Pacifique faction had stood firm, and were pursuing their vendetta with great bitterness. In cafés and private houses, Tioti was energetically whipping up feeling against Mopps and his companions, and there were by now no more than two or three loyal friends who had the courage to be seen entering the club.

There was talk of a cable Tioti had sent to France, which had elicited a reply more than thirty lines long, copies of which he always carried on his person, to show to everyone he met.

Late one evening, the governor's secretary arrived in the middle of a power failure, when the bar was lit by candles stuck to the counter. The doctor had just left. Charlotte was not feeling very well, and Mopps was making an infusion of lime blossoms for her. There were times when he enjoyed puttering around in the kitchen.

"Is he in?"

"I'll go get him."

For the first time since her arrival, she was ordered out of the bar, so, for want of anything better to do, she went to sit beside Tita in Jef's room. He was delirious.

"Bad news, I'm afraid," said the secretary to the captain. "They've been considering your case all day, at the courthouse and at the governor's office. I've just left him. He's invited the public prosecutor and the president of the court to dinner, expressly to continue the discussion."

Mopps seemed prepared for what was coming.

"Tioti has gone into so much detail that it was impossible to ignore him. He even has a cable supporting his allegations in full. . . ."

"Will they arrest Charlotte?"

"No, of course not! For one thing, we have received no instructions and officially the authorities here have no information on the subject. Still, they have a legal right to arrest all three of you, and hold you in custody, pending instructions from Paris. But that would be excessive, especially considering the cost of repatriating you, which would be something in the region of ten thousand francs. They're all more or less agreed on that point. The British liner will be putting in here on the seventeenth; that's five days from now. The governor intends to stall until then, to give you the opportunity, should you feel so inclined, to join the ship and sail in her to Australia. No one could possibly object to that. I want to make it quite clear that I am here only as a friend. I have no official standing in the matter. I repeat: should you feel inclined to join the ship and . . ."

"No one could possibly object to that!" Mopps completed the sentence. "Thanks, old boy. Would you care for a drink?"

"No, thanks. I can't spare the time."

Indeed! Mopps had little doubt that from now on no one would be able to spare the time to drink with him!

"What shall I tell them?"

"Tell them nothing. I don't know. . . . What's the name of the ship?

"The *Mooltan*."

"She's a good ship. I know the captain. What to do . . . ?"

"Is it yes?"

"It's neither yes nor no. We'll have to see."

All of a sudden the lights came on again, and the secretary, as if frightened off by the glare, beat a hasty retreat.

"What did he want?" asked Charlotte, who had lost no time in coming back silently.

"For us to leave on the ship for Australia on the seventeenth . . ."

"Why?"

"Because otherwise we'll be arrested, you on a charge of murder, Mittel and I as accessories. And on top of that, there are the forged papers, the smuggling, and all the rest of it."

356

He was composed enough, but his expression was fierce. His eyelids drooped more than ever, and at first he seized the bottle of whisky. But he put it back on the bar without drinking from it, perhaps because, as had happened more than once recently, he experienced a slight heart spasm.

"Do you have any money?"

"A little, yes."

"Well, then? The climate in Australia is a lot healthier than here."

"Yes . . . only . . ."

It just wouldn't be the same! He would be a fish out of water among the British, with their bars all shut for part of the day and after six o'clock in the evening, and their passion for the outdoor life, and their innumerable regulations.

"Couldn't we go somewhere else?"

"Where?"

Things were pretty much the same in the Dutch East Indies. He had been everywhere in his time, and now, at last, he had found the ideal place to live, a corner of France, where he could drift from day to day without effort, in an atmosphere of voluptuous indolence.

"Go to bed," he said.

"But . . ."

"Go to bed."

"Haven't you given a thought to . . ."

"Of course I have!"

"To what?"

"To poor Jef."

Five days. And then what? How could they take Jef with them in his present state? And let him die on board, so that his body would have to be thrown over the side into the depths of the Pacific?

"How many more times do I have to tell you to go to bed!"

His tone was vicious. Next day, it was Charlotte who took the doctor aside, after sending Maria and the child out of the kitchen.

"What do you think?"

"About what?"

"About Jef. How long has he got to live?"

"I don't know. It could be anywhere from three days to three weeks. He could choke to death in a fit of hiccups at any time."

"Thank you."

She was thinking her own thoughts, and Mopps was preoccupied with his, but both kept their thoughts to themselves. Maria, who could feel that there was something in the wind, was uneasy and on edge. And Tita lived in that other world, Mittel's world, and scarcely ever left it. When she did she looked dazed, as one does when coming from the dark into the light.

Twice Mopps went to the bank. He did not tell anyone at the bungalow what his business was there.

On the second day, ironically enough, Jef's condition seemed to improve. His temperature was lower that evening, his hiccups less frequent.

"Have you booked the tickets?"

He nodded. He felt ashamed, but he had booked them all the same. What else could he do? It was whispered in town that he had secretly been to see the governor, but to no avail. He disciplined himself to walk past the Pacifique without so much as nodding at anyone, which caused offense to a great many people, for he had always been renowned for his cordial and generous disposition.

"What if he's still alive when we have to leave?"

This was what it had come to! If Mittel were still alive, what was to be done with him? There was no chance that the maritime health authorities would allow him to embark. Besides, the ship's doctor would hardly welcome such a troublesome passenger.

Mopps still went every morning to sit with the "young man," as he called him, and gazed at him with swollen eyes, quick to turn away if Mittel asked any questions. As for Charlotte, she was busy packing; they could hear her endlessly bustling from room to room.

"It sounds as if they're getting ready to move out," Jef remarked to Tita one morning.

358

"What nonsense!" she protested, laughing. "They're just straightening up."

Gently, a little ironically, he asked, "What's the point of straightening up?"

Yes, why this sudden concern with tidiness, when they had always lived in such a mess? These days, he could smile at it. As he grew weaker, he became ever more sweet-natured, until, at last, his former bitterness was transmuted into a strange sort of numbness.

On two or three further occasions, he murmured the name "*Barranquilla* . . ."

He wished he could understand why this name came into his mind more often than any other, and sometimes he told himself, wryly, that he might well be dead before he could resolve this small mystery.

This brought a smile to his lips. Yes, it really was funny that he should still trouble himself over such a trivial matter, he who had had so many troubles in his time.

"I must have seen the name on the map when we were crossing the Gulf of Mexico. . . ."

But there was another name that might well have haunted him, the name of the river in Colombia beside which he had lived for many months; yet it had gone completely out of his mind.

There are just some things that remain in the mind, while others leave no impression. The same is true of the affections.

Despite everything Charlotte had done to him, he had lost all sense of grievance. On the contrary, when she came in to see him, he looked at her with some amusement.

On the other hand, Jolet was seldom far from his thoughts— Jolet, who had a house and three children on a cliff near Fécamp, and was forever cramming for his engineer's exams. If he had had the strength, Mittel would have written to him. At heart, Jolet was a shuttle-service man. What a splendid thing that was to be!

"Tita!"

She bent over him. She was always nearby.

"When it's all over, I want you to have a word in private with

Mopps. Tell him that I'd be enormously grateful if he could send my mother enough money to buy herself a fur coat. It doesn't have to be an expensive one . . . something quite ordinary, rabbit perhaps. . . . As long as she can show it off, she'll be perfectly happy. . . ."

He lacked the courage to make the request himself. And he couldn't bring himself to speak of the child. That was a subject reserved for the worst time of the day, when his temperature began to rise. Then he would shut his eyes and think of nothing else.

But there was no certainty that he, and not Mopps, was the child's father, so maybe things had turned out for the best. Mopps still had more than three hundred thousand francs. He would probably not spend the whole amount in his lifetime, which meant that the boy would not be thrust penniless into the world.

"Tita!"

"Yes."

"Where have you been?"

He needed to hear her. When dusk fell, he was always filled with panic, and his hearing grew painfully acute, so much so that he could distinguish all the voices in the bar, and even hear every word spoken.

Which was why, early one morning, he murmured, "I dreamed that we were going away, Tita."

But he was not altogether sure that it had been a dream. He frowned, trying to remember, as with the name *Barranquilla*.

"It's true, we're leaving. Where are we going?"

"You must have been dreaming, Jef."

She had reckoned without Charlotte, who now came into the room.

"Why are we going away, Charlotte?"

"Who told you we were?"

She looked at Tita, who put her finger to her lips, urging silence, but it was too late.

"Where are we going? Why are we leaving?"

Now he really wanted to know.

"We're going to Australia. They've found out who we really are. The authorities are letting us go, to avoid trouble and expense."

"When are we leaving?"

"In a few days."

Exhausted, sick with worry, she went to look for Mopps.

"He knows everything," she wailed. "It's horrible. I let him understand that he would be coming with us."

But of course he was not deceived, as was plain to see when, taking Tita's hand and stroking it, he smiled mischievously and said, "The wandering freighter is off on its travels again!"

"The what?"

"You wouldn't understand. . . . It's just that I must be an awful embarrassment to them."

Suddenly, surprisingly, he burst into tears, sobbing dreadfully, breaking down completely. But it was over almost as soon as it had begun, and was followed by a period of restless, feverish sleep.

There were only three days left, then only two. The following day, the *Mooltan* was due to berth at the quay, and would be leaving again next morning.

Mopps was aging visibly. He said not a word to anyone, and drank nothing all day but mineral water. Nor did he go into town, but paced the waterfront alone, back and forth, back and forth, past the Pacifique.

"What would he have done, Tita, if I hadn't been dying?"

It was terrifying to hear him talk of himself and his imminent death so calmly. Tita, try as she might, could not prevent herself from sniffling, and finally bursting into tears, as she did all she could to make him comfortable.

"I think they would have stayed here."

"Well, I don't. All the same, you know, I have a feeling I'll die in time."

He pulled the sheet over his face and remained that way for

quite a long time, until he was shaken by a spasm of hiccups and pushed the bag of ice off his chest, for he felt crushed beneath its weight.

"There's something I want to tell you, in confidence. . . . The boy . . . I don't think I'm his father. . . . I remember now. . . ."

He did not remember, but that was how he wanted it to be. He asked to see the child. When she brought him, Maria, too, was sniffling, and she kept the baby well away from Mittel, as she had been told to do.

"Take him away. . . . Hurry!"

He would never see him walk. . . .

"Tita, isn't it time yet for my injection?"

The whole town knew. It was the topic on everyone's lips, in the market, in the bars.

"We could always have him transferred to the hospital, with a little money for his keep," Charlotte said to the captain.

She was counting the hours, peering at the horizon for a sight of the little puff of smoke that would signal the approach of the liner. Only when she was safely aboard, on foreign territory, beyond the reach of those with the power to arrest her, would she feel at peace.

She had sent most of their luggage on ahead, where it was piled up on the quayside outside the customs office. She had even bought a new dress from the Chinese shop for the voyage, for she had nothing decent left to wear.

The atmosphere was stifling. But by some miracle, Mittel's temperature was lower, the infection less severe!

"Is there a chance he might recover?" Charlotte asked the doctor, who replied by shaking his head.

"But he could linger on indefinitely, couldn't he?"

Her panic was a hundred times worse than in the Chaco. Now it was her freedom that was at stake, perhaps even her life. The very thought of going back to France, of passing through the doors of the police station, and then being sent to Saint-Lazare prison . . .

There was no longer anything left for her to do. She wandered

362

aimlessly around the house, looking in on Mittel at least ten times a day.

The ship put into the harbor. Jef was, perhaps, the first to hear its siren, for all that night he was very restless and his temperature was high, while Charlotte and Mopps, who had not gone to bed, paced back and forth between the harbor and the bungalow.

He was not dead, they had to face it! There was no way Mopps and Charlotte could stay with him. The scheduled time of departure was eight o'clock in the morning, at the precise moment when Jef's injection was due. Brugnon had refused to take the money offered him, but had promised to admit Jef to the hospital and continue treating him there.

Tita, huddled in a corner of the bedroom, cried all night long, and in the morning she went from room to room in the already empty house, wide-eyed at the realization that its inhabitants would never return.

But she was mistaken. Charlotte and Mopps did come back, in a cab, for they had very little time left.

"Is he asleep?"

No. He had just opened his eyes, and he looked at them without emotion: Mopps wearing a stiff collar and tie, and Charlotte in her new dress.

"Forgive me!" she wailed, kneeling at the foot of the bed. "It's not my fault, Jef. There was no other way!"

Mopps did not speak; his eyes were averted, his face puffy, and his lips so inflamed that they seemed about to burst.

"Speak to me, Jef. Tell me you forgive me. You know I never meant to hurt you. . . ."

"The child . . ." he croaked, struggling for breath.

They had not brought him with them. He was already out there on the deck of the liner, surrounded by English officers who were all trying to get him to laugh! They had bought him a cot especially for the journey, and had left him in Maria's care until it was time to leave.

The child? He, too, was setting out on his wanderings, like the freighter! They wouldn't stop at Australia. From now on there would be no stopping for them. Somewhere or other, Mopps in his turn would desert the land of the living. And then what?

"Tita!" Mittel called.

One hand would not be enough. He needed to hold both. He turned his face to the window and gazed at the sunlight.

"Tita!"

He called her because she had moved away from him, because . . .

It was all for the best. It would soon be over.

"Please go," he gasped. "Go! I beg you, go!"

The first blast of the siren had already sounded. In a quarter of an hour, it would be time to weigh anchor. Fortunately, they had had enough foresight to keep the taxi!

"Go!"

At all costs, they must not be present.

"Mopps, I implore you . . ."

And Mopps had ceased even trying to hide his red eyes and wet cheeks. He pulled Charlotte to her feet.

"Come on!"

He made a move toward Mittel, but Mittel, gathering all his strength, gasped, "Go! . . . Tita!"

He drew her closer, as if meaning to embrace her. But it was only because he could no longer see her clearly, because he could no longer feel her.

"Have they gone? Tita!"

His eyes widened as he heard the car drive away.

"Tita! Listen!"

He was dribbling. A violent fit of hiccups lacerated his chest.

And suddenly, as though he were confiding a great secret to her, he mumbled twice, "*Barranquilla . . . Barranquilla . . .*"

He seemed to smile, because she was the only one to whom he had confided the secret of his destination.

"Barran . . ."

He did not know where it was. . . . He was the freighter. . . . He . . .

———

The whole town was there to stare at Tita as she sped toward the docks, shrieking like a madwoman. She reached the quayside just as the ship was swinging around on its anchor. She, too, ignorant though she was of its significance, repeated the name:

"*Barranquilla.*"

Catching sight of the doctor, she seized him by the lapels and cried, "Tell me! What did he mean?"

Jef lay alone, growing cold, inside the bungalow, with the front door wide open.